MIDNIGHT AT MARBLE ARCH

Anne Perry

MIDNIGHT AT MARBLE ARCH

headline

First published in 2012 by
HEADLINE PUBLISHING GROUP

1

Cataloguing in Publication Data is available from the British Library

ISBN 978 0 7553 9711 2

Typeset in Plantin by Palimpsest Book Production Limited,
Falkirk, Stirlingshire

Printed and bound in Great Britain by
CPI Group (UK) Ltd, Croydon, CR0 4YY

HEADLINE PUBLISHING GROUP
An Hachette UK Company
338 Euston Road
London NW1 3BH

www.headline.co.uk
www.hachette.co.uk

To Susanna Porter

Chapter One

PITT STOOD at the top of the stairs and looked across the glittering ballroom of the Spanish Embassy in the heart of London. The light from the chandeliers sparkled on necklaces, bracelets and earrings. Between the sombre black and white of the men, the women's gowns blossomed in every colour of the early summer: delicate pastels for the young, burning pinks and golds for those in the height of their beauty, and wines, mulberries and lavenders for the more advanced.

Beside him, resting her hand lightly on his arm, Charlotte had no diamonds to wear, but he knew that she had long ago ceased to mind that. It was 1896 and she was now forty years old. The flush of youth had gone, but the richness of maturity became her even better. The happiness that glowed in her face was lovelier than flawless skin or sculpted features, which were mere gifts of chance.

Her hand tightened on his arm for a moment as they started down the stairs. Then they moved into the throng of people, smiling, acknowledging this one and that, trying to remember names. Pitt had recently been promoted to head of Britain's Special Branch and it was a heavier weight of responsibility than he had ever carried before. There was no one senior to him in whom he could confide, or to whom he could defer a difficult decision.

He spoke now to ministers, ambassadors, people of influence far greater than their casual laughter in this room might suggest. Pitt had been born in the most modest of circumstances, and gatherings like this were still not easy for him. As a policeman he had entered through the kitchen door, like any other servant, whereas now he was socially acceptable because of the power his position gave him, and because he was privy to a range of secrets about almost everyone in the room.

Beside him Charlotte moved easily, and he watched her grace with pleasure. She had been born into Society, and knew its foibles and its weaknesses, even if she was too disastrously candid to steer her way through them, unless it was absolutely necessary, as it was now.

She murmured some polite comment to the woman next to her, trying to look interested in the reply. Then she allowed herself to be introduced to Isaura Castelbranco, the wife of the Portuguese Ambassador to Britain.

'How do you do, Mrs Pitt?' Isaura replied with warmth. She was a shorter woman than Charlotte, barely of average height, but the dignity of her bearing made her stand apart from the ordinary. Her features were gentle, almost vulnerable, and her eyes were so dark as to seem black against her pale skin.

'I hope you are finding our summer weather agreeable?' Charlotte remarked, for the sake of something to say. No one cared about the subject: it was the tone of voice, the smile in the eyes, the fact of speech, that mattered.

'It is very pleasant not to be too hot,' Isaura answered immediately. 'I am looking forward to the Regatta. It is at Henley, I believe?'

'Indeed it is,' Charlotte agreed. 'I admit, I haven't been for years, but I would love to do so again.'

Pitt knew that was not really true. She found the chatter and the pretentiousness of lavish Society events a little tedious, but he could see in her face that she liked this woman with her quiet manner.

They spoke for several minutes more before courtesy required that they offer their attention to the others that swirled around under the lights, or drifted to the various side rooms to left and right, or down the stairs to the hallway below.

They separated with a smile as Pitt was drawn into conversation with a junior minister from the Foreign Office. Charlotte managed to catch the attention of her great-aunt, Lady Vespasia Cumming-Gould. Actually she was great-aunt by marriage to Charlotte's sister Emily, but over the years that distinction had ceased even to be remembered, let alone to matter.

'You seem to be enjoying yourself,' Vespasia said softly, amusement lighting her remarkable silver-grey eyes. In her prime she had been reputedly the most beautiful woman in Europe, certainly the wittiest. Did they but know it, she was also one who had fought at the barricades in Rome, during the turbulent revolution that had swept Europe in '48.

'I haven't forgotten all my manners,' Charlotte replied with her more usual frankness. 'I fear I am reaching an age when I cannot afford to wear an expression of boredom. It is terribly unflattering.'

Vespasia was quite openly amused, her smile warm. 'It never does to look as if you are waiting for something,' she agreed. 'It makes people sorry for you. Women who are waiting are so tiresome. Who have you met?'

'The wife of the Portuguese Ambassador,' Charlotte replied. 'I liked her immediately. There is something unusual in her face. I'm sorry I shall probably never see her again.'

'Isaura Castelbranco,' Vespasia said thoughtfully. 'I know little of her, thank heaven. I know too much about so many other people. A little mystery lends such charm, like the softness of the late afternoon, or the silence between the notes of music.'

Charlotte was turning the thought over in her mind before replying when there was a sudden commotion a dozen yards away from them. Like those around her, she turned towards it. A very elegant young man with a sweep of fair hair took a step backwards, raising his hands defensively, a look of disbelief in his face.

In front of him a girl in a gown of white lace stood alone, the skin of her bosom, neck and cheeks flushed red. She was very young, perhaps no more than sixteen, but of a Mediterranean darkness, and already the woman she would become was clear in the curves of her body.

Everyone around the two fell silent, either in embarrassment or possibly confusion, as if they had little idea what had happened.

'Really, you are quite unreasonable,' the young man said defensively, his voice light, trying to brush off the incident. 'You misunderstood me.'

The girl was not soothed at all. She looked angry, even a little frightened.

'No, sir,' she said in slightly accented English. 'I did not misunderstand. Some things are the same in all languages.'

He still did not seem to be perturbed, only elaborately patient, as with someone who was being unintentionally obtuse. 'I assure you, I meant it merely as a compliment. You must be used to such things?'

She drew in her breath to answer, then could not find the words she wished.

He smiled, now openly amused at her, perhaps just a little mocking. He was good-looking in an unusual way. He had a strong and prominent nose and thin lips, but fine dark eyes.

'You'll have to get used to admiration.' His look swept up and down her with just a fraction too much candour. 'You'll receive a great deal of it, I can promise you.'

The girl was shaking now. Even from where she stood, Charlotte could see that she had no idea how to deal with such inappropriate appreciation of her beauty. She was too young to have learned the necessary composure. It seemed her mother was not close enough to have overheard the exchange, and young Neville Forsbrook was very confident. His father was one of London's foremost bankers and the family had wealth and status, with all the privilege that brought. He was not used to being denied anything, most especially by a girl who was not even British.

Charlotte took a step forward, and felt Pitt's hand on her arm, restraining her.

Angeles Castelbranco looked terrified. The colour had drained out of her face leaving her ashen. 'Leave me alone!' Her voice was shrill and a little too loud. 'Don't touch me!'

Neville Forsbrook laughed quite openly now. 'My dear young lady, you are being ridiculous, and making something of a spectacle of yourself. I'm sure that is not what you wish.' He was smiling, and he took a step towards her, one hand out in front of him as if he would soothe her.

She swung her hand wildly in an arc, catching his arm with hers and knocking it aside roughly. She swivelled around to escape, lost her balance and almost fell against another young woman, who promptly screamed and flung herself into the arms of a startled young man close to her.

Angeles fled, sobbing now. Neville Forsbrook stood with a half-smile on his face, which quickly changed to a look of bewilderment. He shrugged and spread his hands, elegant and strong, the shadow of the smile still there. Was it embarrassment, or the faintest of mockery?

Someone stepped forward and began a polite conversation about nothing in particular. Others joined in gratefully. After a few moments the hum of voices resumed, the rustle of skirts, distant music, the slight sound of feet moving on the polished floor. It was as if nothing had happened.

'That was very ugly,' Charlotte said to Vespasia as soon as she was certain they were not overheard. 'What an insensitive young man.'

'He must feel foolish,' Vespasia replied with a touch of sympathy.

'What on earth was that all about?' a dark-haired woman near them asked confusedly.

The elderly man with her shook his head. 'These Latins tend to be rather excitable, my dear. I wouldn't worry about it. It's just some misunderstanding, no doubt.'

'Who is she, anyway?' the woman asked him, glancing at Charlotte also, in case she could shed light on it.

'Pretty young thing,' the elderly man remarked, not really to anyone. 'Going to be a beautiful woman.'

'That's hardly relevant, James!' his wife snapped. 'She doesn't know how to behave herself! Imagine her doing that at a dinner party!'

'Quite bad enough here, thank you,' another woman joined in. The brilliance of her diamonds and the sheen on her lush, green silks could not disguise the bitterness of her expression.

Charlotte was stung to the girl's defence. 'I'm sure you are right,' she said, meeting the woman's eyes boldly. 'You must know far more about it than we do. All we saw was what appeared to be a rather self-assured young man quite clearly embarrassing a foreign ambassador's daughter. I have no idea what preceded it, or how it might more kindly have been handled.'

Charlotte felt Vespasia's hand very lightly on her arm, but she ignored it. She kept the fixed, enquiring smile on her face and did not lower her gaze.

The woman in green coloured angrily. 'You give me too much credit, Mrs . . . I'm afraid I do not know your name . . .' She left the denial hanging in the air, not so much a question as a dismissal. 'But of course I am well acquainted with Sir Pelham Forsbrook, and therefore his son, Neville, who has been kind enough to show a very flattering interest in my youngest daughter.'

Pitt rejoined them with a glance at Vespasia, but Charlotte did not introduce either him or herself to the woman. 'Let us hope it is more graciously expressed than his flattering interest in Miss Castelbranco,' she continued in a tone so sweet as to be sickly. 'But of course you will make sure of that. You are not in a foreign country and uncertain how to deal with . . . ambiguous remarks from young men.'

'I do not know young men who make ambiguous remarks!' the woman snapped back, her eyebrows arched high.

'How charitable of you,' Charlotte murmured.

The elderly man coughed, and raised his handkerchief to conceal his mouth, his eyes dancing.

Pitt turned his head away as if he had heard some sudden noise to attract his attention, and accidentally pulled Charlotte with him, although in truth she was perfectly ready to leave. That had been her parting shot. From here on it could only get worse. She gave a dazzling smile to Vespasia, and saw an answering sparkle in her eyes.

'What on earth are you doing?' Pitt demanded softly as soon as they were out of earshot.

'Telling her she's a fool,' Charlotte replied. She had thought her meaning was obvious.

'I know that!' he retorted. 'And so does she. You have just made an enemy.'

'I'm sorry,' she aplogised. 'That may be unfortunate, but being her friend would have been even more so. She's a social climber of the worst sort.'

'How do you know? Who is she?' he asked.

'I know because I've just seen her. And I have no idea who she is, nor do I care.' She knew she might regret saying that, but just at the moment she was too angry to curb her temper. 'I am going to speak to Senhora Castelbranco and make sure her daughter is all right.'

'Charlotte . . .'

She broke free, turned for a moment and gave him the same dazzling smile she had offered Vespasia, then moved into the crowd towards where she had last seen the Portuguese Ambassador's wife.

It took her ten minutes more to find her. Senhora Castelbranco was standing near one of the doorways, her daughter with her. The girl was the same height as her mother, and closer to, even prettier than she had appeared at a distance. Her eyes were dazzling, and her skin softly honey coloured with a faint flush across her cheeks. She watched Charlotte approach them with an alarm that she could not hide, even though she was clearly trying to.

Charlotte smiled at her briefly, then turned to her mother. 'I'm so sorry that wretched young man was rude. It must be impossibly difficult for you to do anything, in your diplomatic position. It was really inexcusable of him.' She turned to the girl, then realised she was uncertain how fluent her English might be. 'I hope you are all right?' she said a little awkwardly. 'I apologise. We should have made sure you were not placed in such an ugly situation.'

Angeles smiled, but her eyes filled with tears. 'Oh, I am quite all right, madame, I assure you. I . . . I am not hurt. I . . .' she gulped. 'I just did not know how to answer him.'

Isaura put a protective arm around her daughter's shoulder. 'She is well, of course. Just a little embarrassed. In our own language she could have . . .' She gave a little shrug. 'In English one is not always sure if one is being amusing, or perhaps insulting. It is better not to speak than risk saying something one cannot later withdraw.'

'Of course,' Charlotte agreed, although she felt uneasy in case the girl had actually been far more distressed than they were admitting. 'The more awkward the situation, the harder it is to find the words in another language,' she agreed. 'That is why he should have known better than to have behaved as he did. I am so sorry.'

Isaura smiled back at her, her dark eyes unreadable. 'You are very kind, but I assure you there is no harm done beyond a few moments' unpleasantness. That is unavoidable in life. It happens to all of us at some time or another. The Season is full of events. I hope we will meet again.'

It was gracious, but it was also a dismissal, as if they wished to be left alone for a while, perhaps even to leave.

'I hope so too,' Charlotte agreed, and excused herself, walking away. Her feeling of unease was, if anything, greater.

As she returned to where she had left Pitt, she passed several groups of people talking. One of half a dozen included the woman in green, of whom she had undoubtedly made an enemy.

'Very excitable temperament,' she was saying. 'Unreliable, I'm afraid. But we have no choice except to deal with them, I suppose.'

'No choice at all, so my husband informs me,' another assured her. 'It seems we have a treaty with Portugal that is over five hundred years old, and for some reason or another, we consider it important.'

'One of the great colonial powers, I'm told,' a third woman said with a lift of her fair eyebrows, as if the fact were scarcely credible. 'I thought it was just a rather agreeable little country off the west side of Spain.' She gave a tinkly laugh.

Charlotte was unreasonably irritated, because she knew very little more of Portuguese colonial history than did the woman who had spoken.

'Frankly, my dear, I think she had possibly taken rather too much wine and was the worse for it,' the woman in green said confidentially. 'When I was that age we never drank more than lemonade.'

The second woman leaned forward conspiratorially. 'And too young to be engaged, don't you think?'

'Is she? Good heavens, yes.' Her voice was emphatic. 'Should wait another year, at the very least. She is far too immature, as she has just most unfortunately demonstrated. To whom is she engaged?'

'That's the thing,' the third woman said, shrugging elegantly. 'Very good marriage, I believe. Tiago de Freitas, excellent family. Enormous amount of money, I think from Brazil. Could it be Brazil?'

'Well there's gold in Brazil, and it is Portuguese,' a fourth woman told them, smoothing the silk of her skirt. 'So it could well be so. And Angola in the south-west of Africa is Portuguese, and so is Mozambique in south-east Africa, and they say there's gold there too.'

'Then how did we come to let the Portuguese have it?' the woman in green asked irritably. 'Somebody wasn't paying attention!'

'Perhaps they've quarrelled?' one of them suggested.

'Who? The Portuguese?' the woman in green demanded. 'Or do you mean the Africans?'

'I meant Angeles Castelbranco and Tiago de Freitas,' came the impatient reply. 'That would account for her being a bit hysterical.'

'That doesn't excuse bad manners,' the woman in green said sharply, lifting her rather pronounced chin, and thereby making more of the diamonds at her throat. 'If one is indisposed, one should say so, and remain at home.'

At that rate, you should never set foot out of the door, Charlotte thought bitterly. And we should all be the happier for that. But she could not say so. She was an eavesdropper, not part of the conversation. She moved on quickly before they became aware that she had been standing in the same spot for several moments, for no apparent reason except to overhear.

She found Pitt speaking with a group of people she did not know. In case it might be important, she did not interrupt. When there was a break in the discussion, he excused himself temporarily and came over to her.

'Did you find the ambassador's wife?' he asked, his brow slightly furrowed with concern.

'Yes,' she said quietly. 'Thomas, I'm afraid she's still very upset. It was a miserable thing to do to a young girl in a foreign country. At the very least, he made public fun of her. She's only sixteen, just two years older than Jemima.' In the moment of saying her own daughter's name she felt a tug of fear, conscious of how terribly vulnerable Jemima was. She was part-way between child and woman, her body seeming to change every week, to leave behind the comfort of girlhood but not yet gain the grace and confidence of an adult.

Pitt looked startled. Clearly he had not even imagined Jemima in a ball gown with her hair coiled up on her head, and young men seeing so much more than the child she was.

Charlotte smiled at him. 'You should look more carefully, Thomas. She's still a little self-conscious, but she has curves, and more than one young man has looked at her a second and third time – including her dance teacher and the rector's son.'

Pitt stiffened.

She put her hand on his arm, gently. 'There's no need to be alarmed. I'm watching. She's still two years younger than Angeles Castelbranco, and at this age two years is a lot. But she's full of moods. One minute she's so happy she can't stop singing, an hour later she's in tears, or lost her temper. She quarrels with poor Daniel, who doesn't know what's the matter with her, and then she's so shy she doesn't want to come out of her bedroom.'

'I had noticed,' Pitt said drily. 'Are you sure it's normal?'

'Think yourself lucky,' she replied with a slight grimace. 'My father had three daughters. As soon as Sarah was all right, I started, then when I was more or less sane again, it was Emily's turn.'

'I suppose I should be grateful Daniel's a boy,' he said ruefully.

She gave a little laugh. 'He'll have his own set of problems,' she replied. 'It's just that you'll understand them better – and I won't.'

He looked at her with sudden, intense gentleness. 'She'll be all right, won't she?'

'Jemima? Of course.' She refused to think otherwise.

He put his hand over hers and held it. 'And Angeles Castelbranco?'

'I expect so, although she looked terribly fragile to me just now. But I expect it's all the same thing. Sixteen is so very young. I shudder when I remember myself at that age. I thought I knew so much, which shows how desperately little I really did know.'

'I wouldn't tell Jemima that, if I were you,' he advised.

She gave him a wry look. 'I had thought of that, Thomas.'

Two hours later the idea had crossed Pitt's mind a few times that possibly he and Charlotte could excuse themselves and go home, satisfied that duty had been fulfilled. He caught sight of her at the far side of the room, talking to Vespasia. Watching them, he could not help smiling. Charlotte's dark chestnut-coloured hair was almost untouched by grey; Vespasia's was totally silver. To him, Charlotte was increasingly lovely, and he never tired of looking at her. He knew she did not have the staggering beauty that was still there in Vespasia's face – the grace of her bones, the delicacy – but he could see so much of each in the other's poise and vitality, and standing together now they spoke as if they were oblivious of the rest of the room.

He became aware of someone near him, and turned to see Victor Narraway a few feet distant, looking in the same direction. His face was unreadable, his eyes so dark they seemed black, his thick hair heavily streaked with silver. Less than a year ago he had been Pitt's superior in Special Branch, a man with the power of a host of secrets and the iron will to use them as need and conscience dictated. He also had a steadiness of nerve Pitt thought he himself might never achieve.

Betrayal from within the department had cost Narraway his position and Pitt had been set in his place, his enemies sure he would not have the steel in his soul to succeed. They had been wrong, at least so far. But Victor Narraway had remained out of office, removed to the House of Lords where his abilities were wasted. There were always committees, and political intrigues of one sort or another, but nothing that offered the immense power he had once wielded. That in itself might not matter to him, but not to use his extraordinary talents was a loss he found hard to bear.

'Looking for the cue to go home?' Narraway asked with a slight smile, reading Pitt as easily as he always had.

'It's not far off midnight. I don't think we really need to stay much longer,' Pitt agreed, returning the slightly rueful smile. 'It'll probably take half an hour to make all the appropriate goodbyes.'

'And Charlotte – another half-hour after that,' Narraway added, glancing across the room towards Charlotte and Vespasia.

Pitt shrugged, not needing to answer. The remark was made with affection – or probably more than that, as he well knew.

Before his train of thought could go any further, they were joined by a slender man well into his forties. His dark hair was threaded with grey at the temples but there was an energy of youth in his unusual face. He was not exactly handsome – his nose was not straight and his mouth was a little generous – but the vitality in him commanded not only attention but an instinctive liking.

'Good evening, m'lord,' he said to Narraway. Then without hesitation,

he turned to Pitt, holding out his hand. 'Rawdon Quixwood,' he introduced himself.

'Thomas Pitt,' Pitt responded.

'Yes, I know.' Quixwood's smile widened. 'Perhaps I am not supposed
to, but seeing you standing here talking so comfortably with Lord
Narraway, the conclusion is obvious.'

'Either that, or he has no idea who I am,' Narraway said drily. 'Or
who I was.' There was no bitterness in his voice, or even in his eyes,
but Pitt knew how the dismissal had hurt, and guessed how heavily
his new idleness weighed on him. A joke passed off lightly, a touch
of self-mockery, did not hide the wound. But perhaps if Pitt had been
so easily deceived he would not belong in the leadership of Special
Branch now. All his adult life in the police had made understanding
people as second nature as dressing a certain way, or exercising courtesy or discretion. Seeing through the masks of privacy worn by friends
was a different matter. He would have preferred not to.

'If he did not know who you were, my lord, he would be a total
outsider,' Quixwood responded pleasantly. 'And I saw him speaking
with Lady Vespasia half an hour ago, which excludes that as a possibility.'

'She speaks to outsiders,' Narraway pointed out. 'In fact, I have
come to the conclusion that at times she prefers them.'

'With excellent judgement,' Quixwood agreed. 'But they do not
speak to her. She is somewhat intimidating.'

Narraway laughed, and there was genuine enjoyment in the sound.

Pitt was going to add his own opinion when a movement beyond
Narraway caught his eye. He saw a young man approaching them, his
face pale and tense with anxiety. His gaze was fixed on Pitt with a
kind of desperation.

'Excuse me,' Pitt said briefly, and moved past Narraway to go
towards the man.

'Sir . . .' the man began awkwardly. 'Is . . . is that Mr Quixwood
you were speaking to? Mr Rawdon Quixwood?'

'Yes, it is.' Pitt wondered what on earth was the matter with him.
'Is there something wrong?' he asked, only to prompt the man. His
distress was palpable.

'Yes, sir. My name's Jenner, sir. Police. Are you a friend of Mr Quixwood's?'

'No, I'm afraid not. I've only just met him. I'm Commander Pitt, of Special branch. What is it you want?' He was aware that by now at least one of the other two would have noticed the awkward conversation, and Jenner's obvious unhappiness. They might be refraining from interruption on the assumption it was Special Branch business. But if that were so, why did Jenner not know Narraway, at the very least by repute?

Jenner took a deep breath. 'I'm sorry, sir, but Mr Quixwood's wife has been found dead at her home. It's worse than just that, sir . . .' He gulped and swallowed with difficulty. 'It looks pretty plain that she's been murdered. I need to tell Mr Quixwood, and take him there. If he has any friends that could . . . be there to help him . . .' He tailed off, not knowing what else to say.

After all his experience with violent and unexpected death, Pitt should have been used to hearing of it and been familiar with the grief it would cause. But, if anything, it seemed to grow more difficult.

'Wait here, Jenner. I'll tell him. I dare say, if he wishes, Lord Narraway will go with him.'

'Yes, sir. Thank you, sir.' Jenner was clearly relieved.

Pitt turned back to Narraway and Quixwood, who had been talking together, deliberately not paying him attention.

'Never off duty, eh?' Quixwood said with much sympathy.

Pitt felt the knot of pity tighten inside him. 'It isn't actually me he was looking for,' he said quickly. He put his hand on Narraway's arm in a kind of warning. 'I'm afraid there has been a tragedy.' He looked directly at Quixwood, who stared back at him with nothing more than polite bemusement in his eyes.

Narraway stiffened, hearing the catch in Pitt's voice. He glanced at Pitt, then back at Quixwood.

'I'm sorry,' Pitt said gently. 'He's from the police. They have found your wife's body in your home. He has come to take you there, and anyone you may wish to accompany you at this time.'

Quixwood stared at him as if the words made no sense. He seemed to sway a little before making a deliberate effort to compose himself.

'Catherine . . .?' He turned slowly to Narraway, then back to Pitt. 'Why the police, for God's sake? She wasn't even ill . . . What's happened?'

Pitt wanted to reach out and take the man's arm to steady him. However, on so brief an acquaintance, such a gesture would have been intrusive, unless he was actually on the brink of falling. 'I'm very sorry, it looks as if there was some kind of violence.'

Quixwood looked at Narraway. 'Violence? Will . . . will you come with me?' He passed his hand across his brow. 'This is absurd! Who would hurt Catherine?'

'Of course I'll come,' Narraway said immediately. 'Make my excuses, Pitt, and Quixwood's. Don't give the reason. Just an emergency.' He took Quixwood's arm and led him towards where Jenner was waiting, and together the three of them left.

The ride by hansom cab was one of the most distressing Narraway could recall. He sat next to Quixwood, with the young policeman, Jenner, on the far side. Half a dozen times Quixwood drew in his breath to speak, but in the end there was nothing to say.

Narraway was only half aware of the brightly lit streets and the warm, summer night. They passed other carriages, one so closely that he glimpsed the faces of the man and woman inside, the brief fire of the diamonds at her neck.

They turned a corner and were obliged to slow down. Light spilled out of open doors and there was a sound of laughter and distant music from inside. People were starting to leave, too busy talking to each other, calling goodbyes, to pay attention to the traffic. The world continued as if death did not exist and murder was impossible.

Could it really have been murder, or was Jenner misinformed? He looked young and very upset.

Narraway did not know Quixwood well. Theirs was a social acquaintance, a matter of being pleasant on a number of occasions where both were required to attend, and now and then a drink at a gentlemen's club or dinner at some government function. Narraway had been head of Special Branch; Quixwood was involved in one of the major merchant banks, handling enormous amounts of money. Their paths had never crossed professionally. Narraway could not even remember meeting Quixwood's wife. Perhaps he had, and had simply forgotten it.

They were coming from the Spanish Embassy in Queen's Gate, Kensington, travelling east towards Belgravia. Quixwood lived on Lyall Street, just off Eaton Square. They had less than two hundred yards to go. Quixwood was sitting forward, staring at the familiar façades as they slowed down, then came to a stop just short of the house where police were blocking the way.

Narraway alighted immediately and paid the driver, telling him not to wait. Jenner came out from the same side with Quixwood beside him. Narraway followed them across the pavement and up the steps through the classically pillared front door into the vestibule. Every room was lit and there were servants standing around, white-faced. He saw a butler and a footman, and another man who was probably a valet. There were no women in sight.

A man came out of the inner hallway and stopped. He was probably in his forties, hair mostly grey, his face weary and crumpled with distress. He glanced at Jenner, then looked at Narraway and Quixwood.

'Which of you is Mr Quixwood?' he said quietly, his voice cracked a little as though his throat were tight.

'I am,' Quixwood answered. 'Rawdon Quixwood . . .'

'Inspector Knox, sir,' the man answered. 'I'm very sorry indeed.'

Quixwood started to say something, then lost the words.

Knox looked at Narraway, clearly trying to work out who he was and why he had come.

'Victor Narraway. I happened to be with Mr Quixwood when the police found him. I'll be of any help I can.'

'Thank you, Mr Narraway. Good of you, sir.' Knox turned back to Quixwood again. 'I'm sorry to distress you, sir, but I need you to take a very quick look at the lady, and confirm that it is your wife. The butler said that it is, but we'd prefer it if you . . . you were to . . .'

'Of course,' Quixwood replied. 'Is she . . .?'

'In the inner hall, sir. We've covered her with a sheet. Just her face, if you don't mind.'

Quixwood nodded and walked a little unsteadily through the double doors. He glanced to his left and stopped, swaying a little, putting out his hand as if to reach for something, and failing to find it.

Narraway went after him in half a dozen strides, ready to brace him if he were to stagger.

The body of Catherine Quixwood was lying sprawled, face down on the wooden parquet floor, all of her concealed by the bed sheet thrown over her, except her face. Her long, dark hair was loose, some of it fallen over her brow, but it did not hide the bloody bruises on her cheek and jaw, or the split lip stained scarlet by the blood oozing from her mouth. In spite of that it was possible to see that she had been a beautiful woman in a subtle and highly individual way.

Narraway felt a knot of shock and sorrow that he had not expected. He had not known her when she was alive, and she was far from the first person he had seen who had been killed violently. Without thinking, he reached out and grasped Quixwood's arm, holding him hard. The other man was totally unresisting, as if he were paralysed.

Narraway pushed him very gently. 'You don't need to stay here. Just tell Knox if it is her, and then come into the withdrawing room, or your study.'

Quixwood turned to face him. His skin was ashen. 'Yes, yes, of course you're right. Thank you.' He looked beyond him to Knox. 'That is my wife. Can I . . . I mean . . . do you have to leave her there like that? On the floor? For God's sake . . .' He took a deep breath. 'I'm sorry. I suppose . . .'

Knox's face was pinched with grief for him. 'Mr Narraway, sir, perhaps if you would take Mr Quixwood into the study . . .' He indicated the direction, by using his hand. 'I'll ask the butler to bring brandy for both of you.'

'Of course.' Narraway did not bother to correct him as to his title. Nothing could be less important just now. He guided Quixwood to the door Knox had indicated.

The room would at any other time have been pleasant and comfortable. The season being early summer, there was no fire lit in the large hearth, and the curtains were open onto the garden. The lamps were already lit. Possibly Knox and his men had searched the house.

Quixwood sank into one of the large leather-covered armchairs, burying his face in his hands.

Almost immediately a footman appeared with a decanter of brandy and two balloon glasses on a silver tray. Narraway thanked him. He poured one and gave it to Quixwood, who took it and swallowed a mouthful with a wince, as if it had burned his throat.

He did not take one himself. He looked at Quixwood almost collapsed in the chair.

'Would you like me to ask this man Knox what happened, as far as they can tell?' he offered.

'Would you?' Quixwood asked with a flash of gratitude. 'I . . . I don't think I can bear it. I mean . . . to look at her . . . like that.'

'Of course.' Narraway went to the door. 'I'll be back as soon as I can. Is there anyone you would like me to call? Family? A friend?'

'No,' Quixwood answered numbly. 'Not yet. I have no immediate family, and Catherine . . .' He took a shaky breath. 'Catherine's sister lives in India. I'll have to write to her.'

Narraway nodded and went out into the hallway, closing the door softly behind him.

Knox was standing beyond the body on the floor, closer to the outside doors. He turned as Narraway's movement caught his eye. He walked past the body towards him.

'Sir?' he said politely. 'I think, if you don't mind, it would be better if you could keep Mr Quixwood in there, with the door closed, for the next half-hour or so. The police surgeon is on his way.' He glanced at the body, which was now entirely covered by the sheet. 'Mr Quixwood shouldn't have to see that, you understand?'

'Do you have any idea what happened yet?' Narraway asked.

'Not really,' Knox replied, his politeness distancing Narraway as a friend of the victim's husband, but not someone who could be of any use, apart from comfort to the widower.

'I might be able to help,' Narraway said simply. 'It's Lord Narraway, by the way. Until very recently I was head of Special Branch. I am not unacquainted with violence, or regrettably, with murder.'

Knox blinked. 'I'm sorry, my lord. I didn't mean to—'

Narraway brushed it aside. He was still not used to the title himself.

'I might be of some assistance. Did she disturb a burglar? Who was it that found her? Where were the rest of the servants that they heard nothing? Isn't it rather early in the night for someone to break in? Taking a big risk?'

'I'm afraid it isn't that simple, my lord,' Knox said unhappily. 'I'm waiting on Dr Brinsley. Taking a while because I had to send someone for him. Didn't want just anyone for this.'

Narraway felt a twinge of anxiety, like a cold hand on his flesh.

'Because of Quixwood's position?' he asked, knowing as he said it that it was not so.

'No, sir,' Knox replied, taking a step back towards the body. After placing himself to block any possible view from the study doorway, he lifted the sheet right off.

Catherine Quixwood lay on her front, but half curled over, one arm flung wide, the other underneath her. She was wearing a light summer skirt of flowered silk and a muslin blouse, or what remained of it. It had been ripped open at the front, exposing her bosom. There were deep gouges in her flesh, as if someone had dragged their fingernails across the skin, bruising and tearing it. Blood seeped out of the scratch marks. Her skirt was so badly torn and raised up around her hips that its original shape was impossible to tell. Her naked thighs were bruised and from the blood and other fluids it was painfully obvious that she had been raped and beaten.

'God Almighty!' Narraway breathed. He looked up at Knox and saw the pity in his face, perhaps more undisguised than it should have been.

'I need Dr Brinsley to tell me what actually killed her, sir. I've got to handle this one exactly right, but as discreetly as possible, for the poor lady's sake.' He looked again towards the study door. 'And for his too, of course.'

'Cover her up again,' Narraway requested quietly, feeling a little sick. 'Yes . . . as discreetly as possible . . . please.'

Chapter Two

'SPECIAL BRANCH, sir?' Knox asked, reassuring himself.

'Not now,' Narraway replied. 'I have no standing any more, but that means no obligations either. If I can help, and at the same time keep this as quiet as possible, I would like to. Have you any idea at all how this happened?'

'Not yet, sir,' Knox said unhappily. 'We haven't found any signs of where he broke in, but we're still looking. Funny thing is, none o' the servants say they opened the door to anyone. Least, not the butler or the footman. Haven't spoken to all the maids yet, but can't see a maid opening the door at that time o' night.'

'If a maid had let this man in, surely she would have been attacked also?' Narraway observed. 'Or at least aware of something going on? Could she have . . .' He stopped, realising the idea was ugly and unwarranted.

Knox was looking at him curiously. 'You mean was he expected?' He said what Narraway had been thinking. 'Someone Mrs Quixwood knew?'

Narraway stared at him. 'Who does this sort of thing to a woman they know? It's bestial!'

Knox's face tightened, the lines of misery deepening around his mouth. 'Rape isn't always by strangers, sir. God knows what happened here. But I swear in His name, I mean to find out. If you can help, then I'll accept it gladly, long as you keep quiet about it. Can't do with every amateur that fancies himself thinking he can move in on police business. But you're hardly that.' He sighed. 'We'll have to tell

Mr Quixwood what happened, but he doesn't have to see her. Better not to, if he'll be advised. Don't want that to be the way he remembers her.' He passed his hand over his brow, pushing his hair back. 'If it were my wife, or one o' my daughters, I don't know how I'd stay sane.'

Narraway nodded. He wasn't going to get it out of his mind easily, even though he had never met Catherine Quixwood.

They were interrupted by the arrival of Brinsley, the police surgeon. He was at first glance an ordinary-looking man with drooping shoulders and a tired face, which was not surprising after midnight on what had probably become a long day for him even before this.

'Sorry,' he apologised to Knox. 'Out on another call. Man dead in an alley. Appears to be natural causes, but you can't tell till you look.' He turned towards the sheet on the floor. 'What've we got here?' Without waiting for an answer, he bent down and with surprising gentleness, pulled the covering away. He winced and his face filled with sadness. He said something, but it was under his breath and Narraway did not catch it.

In case Quixwood should come out into the hall, possibly wondering what was happening, or to look for him, Narraway excused himself and went back into the study, closing the door behind him.

Quixwood was sitting in the big armchair exactly as he had been before. Aware of movement and perhaps hearing the door close, he looked up. He started to speak, and then stopped.

Narraway sat down opposite him. 'Knox seems like a decent and competent man,' he said.

'Won't you help then . . .?' Quixwood left the half-spoken request hanging in the air, as if he did not know how to finish it.

'Yes, of course I will,' Narraway answered, surprising himself by his vehemence. The face of the woman lying on the floor only a few yards from them had moved him more than he expected. There was something desperately vulnerable about her, as if she had been robbed of far more than her life.

'Thank you,' Quixwood said quietly.

Narraway wanted to talk to him, distract his attention from what was going on out in the hallway, above all to make absolutely certain that Quixwood did not go there while the surgeon was working. His examination of her would be intimate and intrusive; it would have to be. The violation would be so terribly obvious that seeing it would be almost as bad as witnessing the rape itself. But what was there to say that was not facile and rather absurd in the circumstances? No conversation could seem natural.

It was Quixwood who broke the silence. 'Did they find where he broke in? I don't know how that happened. The doors and windows all lock. We've never been robbed.' He was speaking too quickly, as if saying it aloud could make it true. 'The house must have been full of servants, this early. Who found her? Did she cry out?' He swallowed hard. 'Did she have time to . . . I mean, did she know?'

That was a question Narraway had been dreading. Quixwood would have to hear it some time. If Narraway lied to him now he would not be believed in the future. Yet if he told him anything even close to the truth, Quixwood would want to go out and look. Such a need would be instinctive, hoping that it was not as bad as his imagination painted.

'No,' he said aloud. 'They haven't found any broken locks or forced windows so far. But they haven't finished looking yet. There might be a pane of glass cut somewhere. It wouldn't be easy to see in the dark, and there's little wind to cause a draught.' He went on to describe the burglar's skill of pasting paper over the glass of a window, cutting it soundlessly and then being able to pull out a circular piece large enough to let a hand pass through to undo the latch. 'Star-glazing, they call it,' he finished. It was all irrelevant; he said it merely to fill up the time and hold Quixwood's attention.

'Do you know that in Special Branch?' Quixwood asked curiously, as if it puzzled him.

'No, I learned it from a friend of mine who used to be in the regular police.' Narraway went on reciting other tricks Pitt had mentioned at one time or another: small details about forgers of many different sorts, about pickpockets, card sharps, fencers of all the different qualities of stolen goods. Neither of them cared about it but Quixwood listened politely. It was better than thinking about what was going on in the hall only feet away.

Narraway was just about out of explanations of the criminal

underworld in which Pitt had educated him, when at last there was a knock on the door. At Quixwood's answer, Knox came in, closing it behind him.

'Excuse me, my lord,' he said to Narraway, then turned to Quixwood. 'The surgeon's left, sir, and taken Mrs Quixwood's body with him. Would you mind if I ask you one or two questions, just to get things straight? Then I don't know if you wish to stay here, or perhaps you'd rather find somewhere else for the night? Do you have any friends you'd like to be with?'

'What? Oh . . . I'll . . . just stay here, I think.' Quixwood looked bemused, as if he had not even considered what he was going to do.

'Wouldn't you rather go to your club?' Narraway suggested. 'It would be more comfortable for you. The servants here are bound to be upset.'

Quixwood stared at him. 'Yes, yes, I suppose so. In a little while.' He turned to Knox. 'What happened to her? Surely you must know now?' His face was white, his eyes hollow.

Knox sat down in the chair between Quixwood and Narraway. He leaned forward a little.

Narraway could not help wondering how often he had done this, and if anything ever prepared him for it, or made it any easier. He thought probably not.

'I'd rather not have to tell you this, sir,' Knox began. 'But you're going to know it one way or another; I'm sorry. Mrs Quixwood was raped, and then killed. We're not quite sure how she died, but the surgeon will tell us that when he's had time to make an examination in his own offices.'

Quixwood stared at him, eyes wide, his hands shaking. 'Did . . . did you say "raped"?'

'Yes, sir. I'm sorry,' Knox said unhappily. 'I'd have kept that from you if it was possible, but you've a right to know.'

'Did she suffer?' Quixwood's voice was hardly audible.

'Probably not for very long.' Knox would not lie. Sooner or later Quixwood would have realised it.

Quixwood rubbed his hand over his face, pushing his hair hard back, as though the slight pain of it somehow distracted him from what Knox had said. His skin was ashen. There was no blood in it, and the darkness of his hair and brows looked almost blue. 'How did it happen, Inspector? How did anyone get in here to do that? Where were the servants, for God's sake?'

'We're looking into that, sir,' Knox answered.

'Who found her?' Quixwood persisted.

Knox was patient, knowing the answers were needed, no matter what they were.

'The butler, Mr Luckett. It seems he frequently goes for a short walk along the street and over the square before retiring. He found her when he checked the front door last thing before going to bed himself, sir.'

'Oh . . .' Quixwood looked at the floor. 'Poor Catherine,' he murmured.

'I presume he left for his walk through the back door and up the area steps?' Narraway asked Knox.

'Yes, sir. And returned the same way, bolting it after him for the night.'

'And saw no one?' Narraway asked.

'No, sir, so he says.'

'It'll be the truth,' Quixwood interjected. 'Been with us for years. He's a good man.' His eyes widened. 'For God's sake, you can't think he had anything to do with this?'

'No, sir,' Knox said calmly. 'It's just practice to check everything we can, from every angle.'

'Does Luckett know what time he came back to the house?' Narraway asked Knox.

'Yes, sir, just after half-past ten. He sent the footman for the police immediately.'

'No telephone?' Narraway looked surprised.

'Yes, of course,' Quixwood cut in. 'Probably too flustered to think of it. Wouldn't know the police station number anyway, or think to ask the exchange for it.'

'I understand,' Knox agreed. 'Fall back on habit when we're shaken up badly. Find the first policeman on the beat. Turned out to be a good idea, as it happens. He ran into Constable Tibenham a couple of hundred yards away, other side of Eaton Square. He came here at once, and used the telephone to call me. I got here just after quarter-past eleven. Sent for you at the Spanish Embassy. You got back here, I made it half-past midnight. It's now about twenty minutes past one.'

He shook his head. 'I'm sorry, Mr Quixwood, but I need to speak to everyone in the house before I let them all go to bed. Got to have it when it's fresh in their minds. Could forget something if I wait until morning.'

Quixwood looked down at the carpet again. 'I understand. Do you . . . do you need me?'

'No, sir. Not necessary you should know anything as you'd rather not. Not much I need to ask you.'

Quixwood seemed confused. 'What?'

'This was a party at the Spanish Embassy you were attending, sir?' Knox asked.

'Yes. What of it?'

'It was a social sort of thing? Ladies there as well as gentlemen?'

Quixwood blinked.

'Oh! Oh, I see what you mean. Yes. Catherine didn't go because she wasn't feeling very well. Bad headache. She has . . . she had them sometimes.'

'But she was invited?'

'Of course. She said she preferred to go to bed early. Those parties can drag on a long time.'

'I see.'

Quixwood frowned. 'What are you saying, Inspector? There was nothing so remarkable in that. My wife didn't go to lots of the social parties I have to attend. Great deal of noise and chatter, most of it with very little meaning. I wouldn't go myself it it weren't part of my profession to make new acquaintances, contacts and so on.'

'What time did you leave the house to go to the Spanish Embassy, sir?'

'About half-past eight or so, arrived a little before nine. I didn't need to be early.'

'Take a hansom, sir?'

'No, I have my own carriage.' He looked momentarily stunned.

'Dear heaven, I forgot all about them! They'll still be at the embassy, waiting for me.' He half rose out of his chair.

'No,' Narraway answered him. 'I gave your apologies and asked that your driver be informed.'

Quixwood shot him a quick glance of gratitude, then turned back to Knox. 'So when did it happen?'

'Probably about ten o'clock, sir, or thereabouts. After quarter to, when the maid was in the hallway and spoke to Mrs Quixwood, and before half-past, when Mr Luckett came back and found her.'

Quixwood frowned. 'Doesn't that help?'

'Yes, sir, it probably does,' Knox agreed, nodding slightly. 'It's very early yet. We'll know more when we've spoken to the servants and had a proper look around in the daylight. There may even be other people out walking who saw something. Now, if you'll excuse me, sir, I need to go and speak to the servants, so at least some of them can get to bed. Also, we don't want anyone clearing everything up, not realising that it could be evidence.'

'No, no, of course not,' Quixwood said hastily. 'Please do what you must. Forgive me. I shall just sit here a little while.' He looked across at Narraway. 'I quite understand if you want to leave. It must have been a damned awful night for you, but I would be more grateful than I can say if you'd just . . . just keep an eye on things . . . do what you can . . .' His voice trailed off as if he were conscious that he was asking a great favour and it embarrassed him.

'Anything that Inspector Knox will allow me,' Narraway said in response. He had no hesitation in agreeing, not only for Quixwood's sake, but for that of the dead woman whose face had made such an impression on him.

'Thank you,' Quixwood said quietly.

'Come with me, by all means, my lord,' Knox said. 'If you wish, that is? I'm going to speak to the rest of the servants, back in their own quarters. They're a bit shaken up. Best to have them in the housekeeper's room, with her there. Cup of tea. Familiar surroundings.'

Narraway saw the wisdom of it. 'Good idea. Yes, I'd like to come,' he accepted. 'Thank you.'

Narraway followed Knox back through the hall, which was now

occupied solely by a woman on her hands and knees with a bucket of water and a brush in her hand, scrubbing to clear the blood off the parquet floor where Catherine Quixwood had lain.

There were no other visible signs of disturbance. Presumably whatever else had been knocked or broken was already attended to. Narraway was grateful. At least when Quixwood himself emerged there would be no violent reminders of what had happened here.

In the housekeeper's room, very comfortable and surprisingly spacious, he found the housekeeper herself. She was a plump, middle-aged woman in a black stuff dress, her hair pinned back up again hastily. With her was a young maid, red-eyed and dabbing a wet handkerchief to her nose. There was a tray of tea with several clean cups, a jug of milk and a bowl of sugar. Knox looked at it longingly, but it seemed he did not think it suitable to indulge himself.

Narraway felt the same need, and exercised the same discipline. To do less would seem a little childish; also it would put a distance between them and mark him as something of an amateur.

The maid was the one who had last seen Catherine Quixwood alive. Knox spoke to her quietly, but there was nothing she could add beyond being quite certain of the time. The long-cased clock in the hallway had just chimed, and it was always right, so Mr Luckett assured her.

Knox thanked her and let her go. Then he sent someone to fetch Luckett himself from wherever he might be.

'Trying to keep the staff calm, sir,' the footman told him. 'And see that everything's tidied up and all the windows and doors fast. I expect they are, but the women'll rest better if they know he's checked, personal, like.'

Knox nodded his head. 'Then ask him to come as soon as he's done. In the meantime I'll speak with Mrs Millbridge here.' He indicated the housekeeper.

'Yes, sir; thank you, sir,' the footman said gratefully, and went out, closing the door behind him.

Knox turned to the housekeeper. 'Mrs Quixwood stayed at home alone this evening. Why was that, do you know? And please give me the truth, ma'am. Being polite and discreet may not actually be the best loyalty you can give, right now. I'm not going to tell other people anything I don't have to. I have a wife and three daughters myself. I love them dearly, but they have their funny ways, like all of us.' He shook his head. 'Daughters, especially. I think I know them, then I swear they do something as has me completely lost.'

Mrs Millbridge smiled very slightly, perhaps as much as she dared in the circumstances.

'Mrs Quixwood wasn't all that fond of parties,' she said quietly. 'She liked music and the theatre well enough. Loved some of the more serious plays, or the witty ones, like Mr Wilde's used to be.' She blinked, aware that since Oscar Wilde's disgrace, perhaps one shouldn't admit to enjoying his work.

Knox was momentarily at a loss.

'So do I,' Narraway put in quickly. 'His wit stays in the mind to be enjoyed over and over again.'

Mrs Millbridge shot him a glance of gratitude, then turned her attention back to Knox.

'So did Mr Quixwood quite often go to certain parties by himself?' Knox asked her.

'I suppose so, yes.' She looked anxious again, afraid that she might unintentionally have said the wrong thing.

Knox smiled at her encouragingly, the lines of weariness on his face momentarily disappearing. 'So anyone watching the house, maybe with a mind to burgling it, might have noticed that she would be alone, after the servants had retired for the night?'

She nodded, her face pale, perhaps picturing someone waiting in the dark outside, watching for that moment. She gave a very slight shiver and her body remained rigid.

'She wouldn't have visitors?' Knox went on. 'Not have a lady friend come over, for example?'

'No,' Mrs Millbridge answered. 'Nobody that I know of.'

'And would you know, ma'am?'

'Well . . . if she had someone visit her, she would want tea, at the very least, and perhaps a light supper,' she pointed out. 'There would be someone to fetch that, and then wait to let the visitor out and lock up. So that'd be at least one maid, and one footman.'

'Indeed,' Knox said calmly. 'And if she were to leave the house herself, then I suppose there would have to be a footman up to let her back in again. Not to mention, perhaps, a coachman to take her wherever she was going?'

'Of course.' Mrs Millbridge nodded her head.

Narraway thought of the other alternative, that a man had visited her, she had let him in and out herself. Any refreshment he had taken would be a glass of whisky or brandy from the decanter in the study. However, he did not say so. The inspector would surely have thought of it also.

Knox left the subject of visitors. 'What did Mrs Quixwood like to do with her time?'

Mrs Millbridge looked puzzled, and the anxiety was back again. She did not answer. Narraway wondered immediately what it was she feared. He watched Knox's face, but he had no idea what lay behind the furrowed brow and the sad down-turn of his mouth.

'Did she enjoy the garden, perhaps?' Knox suggested. 'Maybe even direct the gardener what to plant, and where?'

'Oh, I see,' Mrs Millbridge said with relief. 'Yes, she was interested in flowers and things. Arranged them often herself, she did. In the house, I mean.' For a moment there was life in her face again, as if she had allowed herself to forget why they were here. 'Went to lectures at the Royal Horticultural Society now and then,' she added. 'Geographical Society, too. Liked to read about other places, even far-off ones such as Africa, and Egypt. She read about the people who used to live there thousands of years ago.' She shook her head in wonderment at such a fancy. 'And the Greeks and Romans too.'

'She sounds like a very interesting lady,' Knox observed.

Mrs Millbridge gulped and the tears spilled down her cheeks. Suddenly her grief was painfully apparent. She looked old and crumpled and very vulnerable.

'I'm sorry,' Knox apologised gently. 'Maybe you could leave anything else for another time. You must be tired.' He glanced at the clock on the mantelpiece. 'It's after two.'

'It's all right,' she insisted, lifting her chin and looking at him with a degree of defiance, her dignity returned. Perhaps it was what he had intended.

'I'm sure,' he agreed. 'But you'll have your hands full in the morning.

The maids are all going to look to you. You'll have to be like a mother for them.' He was telling her what she knew, but the reminder of her importance was steadying. 'They won't have known anything like this before,' he went on. 'We're going to have to see Mrs Quixwood's lady's maid tomorrow anyway. I know she's too upset to speak to us tonight. But when we do, she's going to be still in considerable distress. It's only to be expected.'

'Yes,' Mrs Millbridge stood up. 'Yes, of course. Flaxley was devoted to her.' She smoothed her skirt down. 'You're right, sir.' She glanced at Narraway, but she had no idea who he was. For her, Knox was in charge. 'Thank you, sir. Good night.'

'Good night, Mrs Millbridge,' Knox answered.

When she had gone Knox at last drank his tea, which was now cold. He said nothing, but it was clear in his face the strain this questioning placed on him. Narraway was overwhelmingly grateful that his professional years had not put him again and again in this position. Not seeing the confusion and the grief so closely, but dealing instead with the greater issues of danger to the country, having to distance himself from the individual human loss, had insulated him from the hard and intimate reality of it. The responsibility he had carried was heavy, sometimes almost unbearably so, but it still did not have this immediacy. It called for courage, strength of nerve and accuracy of judgement; it did not need this endurance of other people's pain. He looked at Knox with a new regard, even an admiration.

The butler, Luckett, knocked on the door and came in. He looked exhausted, his face deeply lined, his eyes red-rimmed. Still he stood to attention in front of Knox.

'Please sit down, Mr Luckett,' Knox waved at the chair where the maid and then Mrs Millbridge had been. 'I'm sorry, the tea's cold.'

'Would you like some fresh tea, sir?' Luckett asked, without making a move towards the chair.

'What? Oh, no, thank you,' Knox replied. 'I meant for you.'

'I'm quite well, thank you, sir,' Luckett said. He followed Knox's gesture and sat down. 'The house is in order, sir, and all the doors and windows are locked. We're safe for the night.'

'Did you find where anyone had broken in? Or windows where

someone could have pushed them wider and climbed through?' Knox asked.

'No, sir. I don't know how he got in.'

'Then it looks for now as if he must have been let in.' Knox said the only thing he could, and what he must have known they were all thinking.

'Yes, sir,' Luckett agreed obediently, but his face was tight with unhappiness.

'Have you known Mrs Quixwood to have visitors late in the evening, and see them in and out herself on any other occasion?' Knox asked.

Luckett was acutely uncomfortable at the question and all the implications that had to follow from it. 'No, sir, I haven't,' he said a little stiffly.

'But it is possible?' Knox pressed.

'I suppose it is.' Luckett could not argue. There was no other conclusion possible than that that was what had happened tonight, and no one had been aware of it.

'Was the front door locked when you found Mrs Quixwood's body tonight?' Knox asked.

Luckett stiffened, and for seconds he did not answer.

Narraway waited.

Knox did not ask again but sat staring at Luckett with tired, sad eyes.

Luckett cleared his throat. 'It was closed, sir. The bolts were not sent home.' He looked back at Knox levelly.

'I see. And the other doors, from the side, or the scullery?'

'Locked, sir, and bolted,' Luckett said without hesitation.

'So whoever it was, he came in the front, and left the same way,' Knox concluded. 'Interesting. At least we have learned something. When you went for your walk in Eaton Square, how did you go out, Mr Luckett?'

Luckett froze, understanding flooding into his eyes, his face.

'I went out through the side door to the area,' Luckett said very quickly. 'I had a key. I locked it, but of course I could not fasten the inside bolts. I came back through the same way. It was after that, when

I came through to check the front door a last time – that was when I saw Mrs Quixwood.'

'Do you normally do it that way?' Knox asked. 'Walk, then come through and check the front door?'

'Yes, sir.'

'So the side door bolts would be undone while you were out?'

'Yes, sir, but the door itself was locked,' Luckett said with certainty. 'I had to use my key to open it. There was no doubt, sir. No doubt at all. I heard the latch pull back, I felt it!'

Knox inclined his head in agreement. 'Thank you, Mr Luckett. Perhaps we'll speak again tomorrow. I think it would be a good idea if you went to your bed now. This isn't going to be easy for you for quite some time. You'll be needed.'

Luckett rose to his feet with something of an effort. Suddenly he seemed stiff, his joints painful. He was an old man whose world had imploded in one short evening and the only guard he had against it was his dignity. 'Yes, sir,' he said gratefully. 'Good night, sir.'

When he had gone Narraway wondered who was going to lock up the house after he and Knox had left. He turned to Knox to ask, just as there was a loud ringing on the bell board outside the house-keeper's door.

Knox looked up. 'Front door?' he asked of no one in particular. 'Who the devil can that be at . . . three o'clock in the morning?' He hauled himself up out of his chair and led the way from the servants' quarters to the hallway and the front door. As he stood there, Narraway almost on his heels, the bell rang again. In the hall it was only a dim chime, from the board just the other side of the baize door, and the one outside Mrs Millbridge's room.

There was a constable standing to attention on the outside step. Narraway could see his shadow through the hall window, and another person a little further away.

Knox opened the door and the constable turned to face him.

'Gentleman of the press, sir,' the constable said in a voice so devoid of expression as to be an expression in itself.

Knox stepped out and faced the other man. 'When there's something to say, we'll tell you.' His voice was cold and had an edge of suppressed anger in it. 'It's three o'clock in the morning, man. What the devil are you doing knocking on people's doors at this time of night? Have you no decency at all? I've half a mind to find out where you live and wait until you've had a tragedy in your family, and then send a constable around to bang on your front door in the middle of the night!'

The man looked momentarily taken aback. 'I heard—' he began.

'I told you,' Knox grated the words between his teeth, 'we'll tell you when there's anything to say! You damn carrion birds smell death in the air and come circling around to see what profit there is in it for you.'

Narraway saw a fury in him that took him aback, and then the instant after he realised how deeply Knox was offended for those inside the house, who were shocked and frightened by events they could not even have imagined only hours ago. There was a raw edge of pity in the man as if he could feel the wound himself. Narraway was about to go out and add his own weight to the condemnation when he heard a step on the polished floor behind him and turned to see Quixwood standing there. He looked appalling. His face was creased and almost bloodless, his eyes red-rimmed, his hair dishevelled. His shoulders drooped as if he were exhausted from carrying some huge, invisible weight.

'It's all right,' he said hoarsely. 'We will have to speak to the press some time. I would as soon do it now, and then not face them again. But I thank you for your protection, Inspector . . . I'm sorry, I forget your name.' He ran his fingers through his hair as if it might somehow clear his mind.

'Are you sure, sir?' Knox said gently. 'You don't have to, you know?'

Quixwood nodded very slightly and walked past him to the open front door. He went out onto the step, acknowledged the constable, then looked at the man from the press.

'Perhaps I should say "good morning" at this hour,' he began bleakly. 'You have no doubt come because you heard we are in the middle of tragedy so overwhelming we hardly know how to act. I was summoned here before midnight because my wife was found assaulted and beaten to death in the hallway of her own home. At the moment we have no idea who did this hellish thing, or why.'

He took a deep shuddering breath. 'We don't seem to have been robbed, but on further search we may find we have. The servants were at the back of the house and heard nothing, except for the butler, who was out for a brief walk before going to bed. He discovered my wife's body on his return. I have really nothing more to say at the moment. I am sure the inspector will inform you when there is anything more that is of public interest rather than private grief. Good night.'

'Sir!' the man called out.

Quixwood turned back very slowly, his face like a mask in the light from the lamp above the door. He said nothing.

The man lost his nerve. 'Thank you,' he acknowledged.

Quixwood did not reply, but walked back inside and allowed Knox to close the door, leaving the constable outside.

Quixwood faced Narraway. 'Thank you, Narraway. I am enormously grateful for your support.' His eyes searched Narraway's face. 'I would appreciate it if you would do what you can to help the inspector keep speculation as . . . as low as possible. The circumstances are –' he swallowed – 'are open to more than one interpretation. But I loved Catherine and I will not allow her memory to be soiled by the vulgar and prurient, who value nothing and know no honour. Please . . .' His voice cracked.

'Of course,' Narraway said quickly. 'Anything Knox will allow me to do, I will. There may be avenues I can explore that he can't. I still have influences in some places.'

Quixwood gave the ghost of a smile. 'Thank you.'

Narraway took one of the cabs that the police had kept and went home to get a few hours' sleep before facing the next day, and trying to see the case with clearer vision. He had a hot bath to wash away some of the weariness and the tension that gripped him, then went to bed.

He slept deeply, out of exhaustion, but woke before eight, haunted by dreams of the dead woman and the terror and the searing pain she must have felt as the most intimate parts of her body were torn. His head was pounding and his mouth was dry. The emptiness in his own life since losing his position as head of Special Branch seemed ridiculously trivial now, something he was ashamed to own, compared with what had happened to Catherine Quixwood.

He washed, shaved and dressed, then went down to have a quick breakfast of scrambled eggs, toast and tea before going out into the warm early summer day and finding a hansom to take him to find Dr Brinsley.

The morgue was a place Narraway loathed. It was too much a bitter reminder of mortality. The smell of it turned his stomach. He could always taste it for hours afterwards.

Today the heat and dust, the smell of horse manure in the street outside, was suddenly sweet compared with what he knew he would face as soon as the doors closed behind him.

He found Brinsley almost immediately. The man's long-nosed, wry-humoured face told him that the news was ugly, and probably complicated.

''Morning, my lord,' Brinsley said with a grimace. 'Not seen Inspector Knox, I take it?'

'No, not yet,' Narraway replied tersely. 'Are you able to tell me anything?'

'Come into the office,' Brinsley invited him. 'Smells a little better, at least.' Without waiting, he walked along the corridor, turned right and led the way into a small room piled high with books and papers on every available surface. He closed the door.

Narraway waited. He did not want to sit; it implied remaining here for longer than he wished to.

Brinsley noticed and understood. The recognition of it flickered in his eyes.

'She was raped and pretty badly beaten. The damn animal even bit her breast,' he said with anger harsh in his voice. 'But I don't think that was what killed her, at least not directly.'

Narraway was startled, momentarily disbelieving.

Brinsley sighed. 'She died of opium poisoning.'

Narraway felt a bitter chill run right through him. The smell of the place seemed to have crept into his nose and mouth. 'Before she was raped, or after?' His voice sounded hoarse. 'Do you know?'

'After,' Brinsley said. 'Knox found the glass from which she'd taken laudanum, and there was blood on it.'

'He forced her to drink it?' Narraway knew the question was foolish even as he said it.

Brinsley's face was filled with pity, not only for Catherine, but possibly for Narraway as well. 'Far more likely she was stunned, close to despair,' he answered. 'Either didn't realise how much she'd taken, or more probably, meant to. It was very brutal. God knows what she must have felt. Many women never get over rape. Can't bear the shame and the horror of it.'

'Shame?' Narraway snapped.

Brinsley sighed. 'It's a crime of violence, of humiliation. They feel as if they have been soiled beyond anything they can live with. Too many times the men they think love them don't want them after that.' He swallowed with difficulty. 'Husbands find they can't take it . . . can't live with it. They can't get rid of the thought that somehow the woman must have allowed it.'

'She was beaten to—' Narraway started, his voice rising to a shout.

'I know!' Brinsley cut him off sharply. 'I know. I'm telling you what happens. I'm not justifying it, or explaining it. It does strange things to some men: makes them feel impotent that they couldn't defend their own women. I'm sorry. It was the laudanum that killed her, and it looks as if she drank it herself. God help her.' He swallowed, his face pinched with pain. 'Find this one, will you? You can't hang him for murder, but get rid of him somehow.'

'I will.' Narraway felt his throat tighten and a helpless anger scald through him. 'I will.'

Chapter Three

PITT WAS distracted at the breakfast table. He ate absent-mindedly, his attention absorbed by whatever he was reading in the newspaper. He looked up briefly to bid goodbye to Jemima and Daniel, then returned to his article. He even allowed his tea to go cold in the cup.

Charlotte stood up and took the teapot to the stove, pushed the kettle over onto the hob and waited a few moments until it reached the boil again. With the teapot refreshed, and carrying a clean cup, she returned and sat down.

'More tea?' she asked.

Pitt looked up, then glanced at his cup beside him, puzzled.

'It's cold,' she said helpfully.

'Oh.' He gave a brief smile, half apologetic. 'I'm sorry . . .'

'From your expression, it's not good news,' she observed.

'Speculation on the Jameson trial,' he replied, folding the paper and putting it down. 'Most people seem to be missing the point.'

She had read enough about it to know to what he was referring. Leander Starr Jameson had returned to Britain from Africa, accused of having led an extraordinarily ill-conceived invasion from British-held Bechuanaland across the border into the independent Transvaal in an attempt to incite rebellion there, and overthrow the Boer government, essentially of Dutch origin.

'He's guilty, isn't he?' she asked, uncertain now if perhaps she had misunderstood what she had read. 'Won't we have to find him so?'

'Yes,' Pitt agreed, sipping his new hot tea. 'It'll be a question of what sentence is passed, and how much the public lionise him.

Apparently he's a remarkably attractive man, not in the ordinary sense of being handsome or charming, but he has a certain magnetism that captivates people. They see him as the ideal hero.'

She looked at Pitt's face, the sombre expression in his eyes that belied the ease of his voice.

'There's more than that,' she said gravely. 'It matters, doesn't it?'

'Yes,' he answered softly. 'Mr Kipling believes him a hero for our time: brave, loyal, resourceful, seizing opportunity by the throat, a born leader, in fact.'

Charlotte swallowed. 'But he isn't?'

'Mr Churchill says he is a dangerous fool who will, in the near future, cause war between Britain and the Boers in South Africa,' he replied.

She was horrified. 'War! Could it?' She put her cup down with a slightly trembling hand. 'Really? Isn't Mr Churchhill being . . . I mean, just drawing attention to himself? Emily says he does that a bit.'

Pitt did not answer immediately.

'Thomas?' she demanded.

'I don't know. I have a fear that Churchill could be right.' His gaze did not waver from hers. 'Not just because of the Jameson Raid – there are other things as well. The gold and the diamonds are going to attract a lot of adventurers and profiteers.'

'Will it affect us?' she asked him. 'Special Branch? You?'

He smiled. 'I can't absolutely ignore it.'

She nodded, started to say something else, then decided it would be wiser not to go on asking him questions no one could yet answer. She stood up.

'Charlotte,' he said gently.

She turned, waiting.

'One thing at a time.' He smiled.

She put out a hand and touched his. It was not necessary to say anything.

She had been looking forward to the garden party that afternoon, largely because she was going with Vespasia, who would call to pick her up. It was only lately, since Pitt's promotion, that Charlotte had been able to afford new gowns suitable for such occasions, rather than borrowing something either from Vespasia, which would fit her very well, but be a little different from her own taste; or from her sister Emily, who was slimmer and a couple of inches shorter. Not to mention the fact that Charlotte's colouring was more vivid than Vespasia's exquisite silver or Emily's delicately fair hair and alabaster skin.

Charlotte always enjoyed Vespasia's company. She never spoke trivially, and yet she was informed about all manner of things, from the most important to the merely amusing. Charlotte was ready, and filling the time reading a book in the parlour when Vespasia arrived and the maid, Minnie Maude, showed her in. Although Minnie Maude had been with Charlotte over a year now, she was still overawed in announcing, 'Lady Vespasia Cumming-Gould, ma'am.'

Charlotte rose to her feet immediately, without even marking her place in the book.

'You are early. How very nice,' she said warmly. 'Would you like a cup of tea before we leave?'

'Thank you,' Vespasia accepted. She sat gracefully in the other large chair and arranged her sweeping skirts as if she were immediately at home in this modest room with its comfortable, well-used furniture, bookshelves and family photographs.

Charlotte nodded to Minnie Maude. 'The Earl Grey, please, and cucumber sandwiches,' she requested. She knew without having to ask what it was that Vespasia would like.

As soon as the door was closed Charlotte regarded Vespasia more closely and noticed a certain tension in her.

'What is it?' she asked quietly. 'Has something happened?'

'I believe so,' Vespasia replied. 'At least, beyond question, something has happened, but I believe it is more serious than it is pretending to be.' She smiled very briefly, as if in apology for the darkness she was about to introduce. 'I heard from a friend of mine that Angeles Castelbranco has broken off her engagement to Tiago de Freitas.'

Charlotte was puzzled. 'Is that so serious? She is very young. Perhaps that is why she was so highly strung the other evening? She is not yet ready to think of marriage. She's only two years older than Jemima. She's still a child!'

'My dear, there is a lot of difference between fourteen and sixteen,' Vespasia responded.

'Two years!' Charlotte could not possibly imagine Jemima thinking of marriage in two years. Any thought of her leaving home was years away.

Now Vespasia's smile was gentle but bright with amusement. 'You will be surprised what a change those two years will bring. The first time she will fall in love with a real man, not a dream, is not nearly as far away as you think.'

'Well, perhaps Angeles is in love, but not yet ready to think of marrying,' Charlotte suggested. 'It is fun to be in love without the thought of settling down in a new home, with new responsibilities, and before you know it, children of your own. She has barely begun to taste life. It would be very natural to wish for another year or two at least before that.'

'Indeed. But one may remain engaged for several years,' Vespasia pointed out.

Charlotte frowned. 'Then what is it you think may have happened? A quarrel? Or she imagines herself in love with someone else?' A more painful thought occurred to her. 'Or she has heard something distressing about her fiancé?'

'I doubt that,' Vespasia answered.

Minnie Maude knocked on the door and came in with a tray of tea and very thin cucumber sandwiches, which Charlotte had recently taught her to cut.

Minnie Maude glanced at Charlotte to see if she approved.

'Thank you,' Charlotte accepted with a little nod of her head. Minnie Maude had replaced Gracie, the maid the Pitts had had since their marriage. Gracie herself had at last married Sergeant Tellman and set up her own house, of which she was immensely proud. Her place would be impossible to fill, but Minnie Maude was gradually making the role her own. Now a wide smile split her face for a moment, then she recalled her decorum again, dropped a curtsy and withdrew, closing the door behind her.

Charlotte looked at Vespasia.

Vespasia regarded the sandwiches. 'Excellent,' she murmured.

'Minnie Maude is coming on very well.' She took one and put it on her plate while Charlotte poured the tea.

'What do you fear has happened to Angeles Castelbranco?' Charlotte asked a few moments later.

'The marriage was an arranged one, naturally,' Vespasia replied. 'The de Freitas family is wealthy and highly respected. For Angeles it is a good match. He is six or seven years older than she and, as far as I hear, nothing ill is known of him.'

'How much is that worth?' Charlotte asked sceptically, surprised how protective she felt of a girl she had seen only once. Was she preparing to be overprotective of Jemima, already? She could remember her own mother doing the same, and she had hated it.

Vespasia was watching her with wry amusement, and perhaps also with recollections of her own daughters growing up. 'A good deal,' she replied. 'I am sure Isaura Castelbranco was young once, and has not forgotten what she dreamed of for herself. As, no doubt, you will be telling Jemima soon.'

'Then why are you worried?' Charlotte asked, suddenly grave again. 'What is it you fear?'

Vespasia was silent for several moments. She sipped her tea and ate another of Minnie Maude's cucumber sandwiches.

Charlotte waited, remembering the party at the Spanish Embassy and the look in Angeles' face, trying to recall it exactly, and knowing she was now putting her own feelings into it.

'What is it you think has happened?' she asked more urgently.

'I don't know,' Vespasia admitted. 'But I think the girls was very distressed. She wasn't just angry or embarrassed. It is a big thing indeed to break an engagement in a family like that. If she does not give a powerful reason, then other reasons will be suggested, largely unflattering. It has been said, so far, that it is she who broke it off, but sometimes a young man will allow that, as a gallantry, when in fact it is he who has done so.'

Charlotte was startled. 'What are you saying? That she has . . . has lost her virginity? She's sixteen, not a thirty-year-old courtesan. How could you even think such a thing?'

'I didn't,' Vespasia pointed out gently. 'You did. Which perfectly makes my point. People will look for reasons, and if they are not given them they will create their own. Breaking a betrothal is not something one does lightly.'

Charlotte looked down at the carpet. 'I suppose I know that. I just didn't want to acknowledge it. She's so young. And she looked so vulnerable at that party. The room was crowded with people, and yet she was alone.'

Vespasia finished her tea and set the cup down. 'I hope I am mistaken. Too many hours to fill with things that do not matter, I imagine.' She rose to her feet. 'Shall we leave?'

For some time at the party Charlotte accompanied Vespasia as they met friends or acquaintances and exchanged the usual polite remarks. She had wanted to come, to be in the swirl of conversation, gossip, the exhilaration of meeting new people, but after half an hour or so she realised how much they were really not new at all. Like clothes, their manners and their speech both revealed the person beneath, and yet covered up far more of the truth.

Looking at a woman in a bright dress, she wondered was it exuberance that prompted her to wear it, or bravado to hide uncertainty, even fear or grief? And the woman in the plain-cut, subdued shades of blue – was that modesty, the supreme confidence that needed no display; or simply the only gown she had not already worn in this same company? So much could be interpreted half a dozen different ways.

It was about ten minutes later that Charlotte encountered Isaura Castelbranco and with pleasure found an opportunity to engage her in conversation. It seemed very easy to ask what region of Portugal she grew up in and to hear a description of the beautiful valley that had been her home until her marriage.

'Port wine?' Charlotte said with an interest she did not have to feign. 'I often wondered how they made it, because it is quite different from anything else, even sherry.'

'It is wine from the grapes in the Douro Valley,' Isaura replied, enthusiasm lighting her eyes. 'But that is not really what makes it special. It is fortified with a brandy spirit, and aged in barrels of a particular wood. It takes a great deal of skill, and some of it is kept . secret.'

She smiled and there was pride in it. 'We have made it for centuries, and the arts are passed down the generations within a family. Not that mine is one of them,' she added hastily. 'We just lived in the region. My husband's family grew the grapes with which it began. His father and brothers were disappointed when he studied politics and chose the diplomatic service, but I think he has never regretted it. Although, of course, we still feel that tug of memory when we go back to the vineyards, the sun on the vines, the labour of picking, the excitement of the first taste of the vintage.

'As a girl I used to daydream of it maturing in the wood, and then one day imagining the gentlemen whose tables it would be passed around. I pictured who they would be, what great events of state might be discussed with a glass of port in one hand.' She laughed a little self-consciously. 'I would think of daring adventures planned, explorations, discoveries recounted, theories put forward on a hundred new ideas, reforms to change the laws of nations. Silly, maybe, but . . .'

'Not silly at all!' Charlotte said quietly. 'Much better than half the daydreams I had, I promise you. It is something to be proud of.'

Isaura laughed. 'Some of it was in the glasses of great Portuguese explorers, navigators around the world, traders in exotic silks and spices, but a great many were on English dining tables after the ladies had withdrawn. In my mind every great Englishman drank port, while he planned to settle America or Australia, find the Northwest Passage to the Pacific, or discover the circulation of the blood, laws of gravity, or write about the origin of species.' She flushed slightly at her own audacity.

'I think it is a marvellous idea,' Charlotte agreed warmly. 'I shall never look at a good bottle of port again without my imagination on fire. Thank you for enriching me so happily.'

Before Isaura could respond they were joined by three other ladies in highly fashionable gowns and hats that drew the attention, and certainly the envy, of every woman who caught even a glimpse of them. With regret, Charlotte reverted to the conversation of gossip and trivia.

'Marvellous,' one woman enthused. 'You can't imagine how it looked, my dear. I'll never forget it.'

'Do you suppose she'll marry him?' another asked with intense curiosity. 'What a match that would be!'

'I shudder to think.' A third gave the slightest indication with a twitch of one elegant shoulder. 'Anyway, I'm quite sure she has her eye on Sir Pelham Forsbrook.'

Charlotte's attention was caught by that last name. He was the father of Neville Forsbrook, who had so cruelly taunted Angeles Castelbranco. She glanced sideways at Isaura and saw the distress in her face before she could conceal it with a feigned smile of interest.

'Is Sir Pelham thinking of marrying again?' Charlotte asked, with no idea of the circumstances, except that, with a son he owned to, he had to have been married once.

'*She* is thinking of it, my dear,' the first woman said with a smile very slightly condescending. 'Pelham is worth a fortune. All kinds of things invested in Africa, I believe. Probably gold, I should think. Didn't they find masses of it in Johannesburg last year? And he's a very charming man, sort of dark and interesting, a powerful face.'

One of the others giggled slightly. 'I do believe you are attracted to him yourself, Marguerite.'

'Nonsense!' Marguerite said a trifle too quickly. 'Eleanor was a friend of mine. I wouldn't dream of it. Such a tragedy. I haven't got it out of my mind yet.'

Charlotte made a mental note to ask Vespasia what had happened to Eleanor, who was presumably Forsbrook's wife. For the moment she turned to Isaura and said how delighted she had been to meet her again, and excused herself from the conversation.

She was still wondering about the Forsbrook family when she noticed a group of young women, perhaps seventeen or eighteen years old, laughing and talking together. They were all pretty, with the unlined features and blemishless complexions of the young, but one of the girls in particular caught Charlotte's attention because her looks were striking. She had an air of intensity that instantly made her stand out from the easy exchange of the others. She seemed far more serious, with an air of being occupied in some concern of her own. Also, her hair and her eyes were both startlingly dark and quite beautiful against the peach tones of her high-necked gown.

Charlotte watched her for several moments as one of the other girls spoke to her and she had to ask for the words to be repeated before she replied. Even then her answer was vague, drawing a taunt, and then giggles from two of the others.

There was something familiar in her unease, and then Charlotte realised that she was Angeles Castelbranco. Her dress was utterly different from the ball gown she had worn at the embassy, but the resemblance to her mother should have been sufficient for Charlotte to recognise her again, even at a slight distance and from an angle.

There was more laughter. A young man passed close to them and smiled. Discreetly he regarded all of them but clearly it was Angeles who took his eye. Beside her the others looked pallid, even ordinary, though today her dress was extremely modest and she made no attempt to hold his glance.

The young man smiled at her.

She gave a very slight half-smile back at him, then lowered her eyes.

He hesitated, uncertain whether he dared speak to her when they were strangers and she had given him no encouragement.

One of the other girls smiled at him. He inclined his head in a small bow, then walked on. Two of the girls giggled.

Angeles looked unhappy, even uncomfortable. She excused herself and moved away towards where Isaura was still involved in conversation.

Charlotte found Vespasia again. Together they strolled over towards a magnificent bed of mixed flowers, bright with pink and blue spires of lupin and dozens of gaudy oriental poppies in a profusion of scarlets, crimsons and peaches.

Charlotte described to Vespasia what she had seen with Angeles Castelbranco, the other girls and the young man.

'And it troubles you?' Vespasia asked quietly.

'I'm not sure why,' Charlotte admitted. 'She looked so ill at ease, as if she had a deep unhappiness she was trying to overcome, and could not. I suppose I have forgotten what it is like to be sixteen. It is an alarmingly long time ago. But I think I was awkward rather than unhappy.'

'You were not engaged to be married,' Vespasia pointed out.

'No, but I would like to have been!' Charlotte said ruefully. 'I thought about it nearly all the time. I looked at every young man, wondering if he could be the one, and how it would happen, and whether I could learn to love him or not.' She recalled with embarrassment some of the wilder thoughts that had passed through her mind then.

'Of course,' Vespasia agreed. 'We all did. The grand romances of the imagination were . . .' she smiled at her own memories, '. . . like reflections in the water – bright, a little distorted, and gone with the next ripple of wind.' Then the slight banter vanished. 'Did you sense something more seriously wrong?'

'Perhaps not. It is an arranged marriage, you said? Sixteen is very young to feel that your fate is already decided, and by someone other than yourself.'

'It is a common practice,' Vespasia pointed out. 'And I dare say our parents' choice for us was no more reckless than our own would have been. I remember falling in love at least half a dozen times with men it would have been disastrous for me to have married.'

Charlotte drew in her breath to ask if the choice that she had made in the end had been so much better. Then she realised how appallingly intrusive that would be. From the little she knew of Vespasia's life, her marriage had been tolerable, but not a great deal more than that. The great love she had known had been elsewhere, brief and ending in all but memory when she returned from Italy to England. What Vespasia had felt she did not know, and did not wish to. There were many things that should remain private.

Charlotte smiled, watching a bumblebee meander lazily through the blossoms.

'I thought I would die of it when Dominic Corde married my elder sister, Sarah,' she said candidly, turning the conversation away from the intrusive. 'I cherished an impossible infatuation with him for years. Thank heaven, I don't think he ever knew.'

'Perhaps Angeles Castelbranco knows someone rather better than she knows her fiancé, and finds it difficult to reconcile herself to keeping her promise,' Vespasia said, smiling a little in the sun and watching the same bee as it settled in the heart of a scarlet poppy. 'Life can tend to lurch from one wild emotion to another at that age. Of course, with a lot of laughter, excitement and soaring hopes in between. I don't think I could bear all that anguish again.'

Charlotte looked at her quickly. Vespasia was still beautiful, but – in spite of her poise, her wit and all her accomplishments – perhaps she was also still vulnerable. Certainly she was still very much alone. Charlotte had never thought of it before, but it struck her now with the force of a blow. Had Vespasia ever known the safety of heart that Charlotte took so much for granted?

She changed the subject quickly, before her face betrayed her thoughts.

'I think I am being fanciful about Angeles,' she remarked. 'I expect there is no grand passion for someone else, and no betrayal by her fiancé with another woman. I am more bored with Society than I had remembered, and I can see that the devil has made more work for idle minds than he ever does for idle hands. Sometimes I wish Thomas were back in the regular police instead of in Special Branch where all his cases are secret. I can't help any more, because he can't even tell me what they are about.'

'Be careful what you wish for,' Vespasia warned gently. 'It may not be so pleasant if you are granted it.'

Charlotte glanced at her and, seeing the gravity in her eyes, changed her mind about answering. Instead she said, 'By the way, I was listening to a piece of gossip just now and they mentioned Pelham Forsbrook possibly marrying again. They hinted at some tragedy regarding his first wife. I had no idea what they were referring to.'

Vespasia's face filled with a sudden sadness. 'Eleanor,' she said quickly. 'I knew her only slightly, but she was charming and funny, and very kind. I'm afraid she was killed in a traffic accident. Something startled the horse and it bolted. One of the wheels caught against something and the whole carriage was overturned. Poor Eleanor was crushed. I think she died instantly, but it was an appalling thing to happen.'

Charlotte was taken aback. 'I'm sorry. Was it long ago?'

'About three or four years. I don't think Pelham ever considered marrying again, but of course I could be mistaken. I never knew him well.' She smiled, dismissing the subject. 'I should like you to meet Lady Buell. She is ninety if she is a day, and has been everywhere and met everyone. You will find her most entertaining.'

An hour later Charlotte was looking for somewhere to set down her empty cup. She went into the big marquee, which had been set up for the unlikely event of rain, or for those who wished to shelter from the sun more adequately than even the most excellent parasol could offer.

She set her cup down and was moving towards the way out again when she saw Angeles Castelbranco four or five yards away, on the other side of a table set with samovars for tea, partially concealing her from view.

Angeles was holding her cup and saucer and was also facing the door when a young man came in. He was tall and fair-haired, and when he smiled at Angeles he was good-looking enough to be considered handsome.

'Good afternoon,' he said warmly. 'Geoffrey Andersley. May I pour more tea for you, Miss . . .?' He hesitated, waiting for Angeles to introduce herself.

She took a step backwards, holding onto her cup and saucer.

He reached for it and his fingers brushed her hand.

She dropped the cup instantly and it fell to the grass.

'I'm sorry,' he apologised, as if it had been his fault. He bent to pick it up, moving closer to her to reach it.

Angeles jerked backwards as though he had in some way threatened her.

He looked embarrassed as he rose to his feet again and straightened up.

'I say, I'm sorry. I didn't mean to startle you.'

She shook her head, her face flushed with colour, her breathing heavy, as if she had been running. She began to speak and then stopped.

'Are you all right?' he asked anxiously. 'Would you like to sit down?' He held out a hand as if to steady her.

She flinched and backed further away, knocking against another table set with glasses and clean cups and saucers. They clattered against each other and half a dozen tall champagne flutes fell over.

Angeles swung around, distressed by her own clumsiness. Now her face was scarlet.

'I'm perfectly all right, Mr . . . Mr Andersley. If you will allow me to pass, I would like to go outside and get a little air.'

'Of course,' he agreed, but he did not move.

'Let me pass!' she repeated, her voice rising, wobbling a little, out of control.

He took a small step closer to her, his face creased with concern. 'Are you sure you are all right?'

Charlotte decided to intervene, even though it was possibly tactless and certainly none of her concern.

'Excuse me.' She came out from behind the samovars and moved towards Angeles.

Angeles saw her and her face filled with relief.

'Perhaps you don't remember me, Miss Castelbranco,' Charlotte said smoothly. 'We met the other evening. I am Mrs Pitt. I should so like you to meet my great-aunt, Lady Vespasia Cumming–Gould. Would you care to come with me?'

'Oh, yes!' Angeles said immediately. 'Yes. I would be delighted.' She stepped closer to Charlotte, even though it was actually further from the way out.

Charlotte looked at Andersley and smiled. 'Thank you for your courtesy. I hope you have a pleasant afternoon.'

'Mrs Pitt.' He bowed and stepped back to allow them both to pass, giving them room for their wide skirts. Even so, Angeles was obliged to pass within a yard of him. Her face was pale as she did so, and she moved hastily and without looking at him.

Outside in the sun Charlotte kept up the pretence while they walked side by side the hundred yards or so to where Vespasia had just left another conversation. She was standing in the sun, her face lifted a little to its light, looking more like the Italians with whom she had stood at the barracks in '48, than the English aristocrat she was now. Charlotte wondered what memories were in her mind, or her heart.

She and Angeles approached her. They went through with the charade, the polite smiles, the affected interest, the trivial exchange of words until convention was satisfied. Angeles excused herself and Vespasia looked at Charlotte.

'I think perhaps you had better explain,' she invited her.

Charlotte told her briefly what she had observed, adding no comment, watching Vespasia's face for her reaction.

'Oh dear.' Vespasia's eyes were sad, her face in an expression of profound gravity.

Charlotte waited, fear beginning to grow inside her. She had been clinging to a hope that she was being unnecessarily alarmed, and now it was melting away.

'What is it you think?' she said at last.

Still Vespasia hesitated. 'I think that Angeles Castelbranco has had a terrible experience,' she said at last.

It was exactly what Charlotte had thought also, and hoped she was being melodramatic. 'How terrible?' she asked. 'More than just . . . a forced kiss, perhaps a torn gown?'

Vespasia's mouth pulled tight in deep unhappiness. 'She appears a healthy young woman. I'm sure she could slap someone hard enough to make her refusal known very plainly. And from what you say, she was not acquainted with this young man, Andersley.'

'No. He introduced himself. It seemed they had not even met until that point.'

'But she was so frightened that she backed away from him even though he did not actually touch her?'

'Yes. She didn't look just unwilling, or even as if it were distasteful, she looked terrified.' Charlotte pictured Angeles' face again. Her expression had been unmistakable. 'She was far more seriously assaulted, wasn't she?'

'I think that is probably so,' Vespasia agreed, her voice low and strained with pity.

'What are we going to do?' Charlotte's mind raced over the possibilities, beginning with talking to Pitt.

'Nothing,' Vespasia replied.

'Nothing! But if she was actually raped that's one of the worst possible crimes.' Charlotte was outraged. It was totally out of character for Vespasia, of all people, to be so callous. 'She must be helped,' she said hotly. 'And above all, whoever did it must be punished, put in prison.' The thought of the man getting away with such a thing was intolerable.

Vespasia put her hand very gently on Charlotte's arm. 'And if Angeles names a young man and says that he raped her, what do you suppose will happen?'

Charlotte tried to imagine it. The anguish would be profound. Isaura Castelbranco would be distraught for her daughter. Charlotte felt cold throughout her body at the thought of such a thing happening to Jemima. It was almost impossible to hold in the mind, it was so appalling. But if it had happened, then she would injure somebody in the most terrible revenge she could imagine. She would destroy him! And it would change nothing. After all the pain she could inflict it would do nothing to help Jemima.

'Exactly,' Vespasia agreed gently, as if she had followed Charlotte's thoughts in every detail. 'It is an injury no punishment is ever going to heal. To blame anyone else, even if you could prove her total innocence—'

'Of course she's innocent!' Charlotte interrupted her. 'She's sixteen! She's a child!'

'For goodness' sake, my dear, were you innocent at sixteen?'

'Of course I was! I was innocent until—'

'I'm not questioning your chastity,' Vespasia said a little more tartly. 'I took that for granted. I am speaking of innocence in the sense of offering no temptation to a man with more appetite than decency, and no belief that he needs to exercise self-control.'

Charlotte remembered her passion for Dominic Corde, and how far she might have gone, quite willingly, had he given her the chance. She felt the blood surge up her face. She did not know whether to be furious or humiliated.

'It is not so simple, is it?' Vespasia observed. 'And if this wretched young man should accuse her of being just as willing as he was, how does she convince people that she was not? I saw no cuts or bruises to prove her reluctance, did you?'

Charlotte was amazed. She stared at Vespasia with complete disbelief. For once she was lost for words.

'People can be very cruel,' Vespasia continued, her voice very quiet. 'Which, if you think about it, my dear, you know as well as I do. Perhaps I have a few years' advantage of you, but it makes little difference. Think what she will face: the whispers, the disapproval, the sniggers from young men, the alarm from other young women, the prurient interest. There will be questions from those who imagine it might secretly have been rather fun, because they have no idea that it has nothing to do with romance or passion, except the desire to humiliate and conquer – if that can be said to be a passion, however crude.'

Charlotte looked at Vespasia's face and saw that the pain in it was even greater than the anger.

'You knew someone, didn't you?' The words were spoken before she gave them thought. Immediately she regretted them.

Vespasia's mouth pulled tight in remembered grief and she blinked several times.

'I have done, long ago. More than one. Some things are bearable only if no one else knows of them. Then at least you do not imagine that every remark you don't quite hear is about you, every joke you don't understand is an oblique reference to your shame.' She winced. 'You do not believe that every party to which you are not invited is because you are no longer considered eligible. Above all, you do not face the knowledge that you are soiled for ever and no man will want to touch you, except for his own amusement, and you will never marry, and never have children.'

'But that's—' Charlotte stopped as the full impact of what Vespasia had said overwhelmed her. 'But it's not her fault,' she said quietly, her own voice choking now. 'Do we really have to just . . . just pretend it didn't happen, and let him walk away, untouched? For heaven's sake, won't he do it again?' She was so angry, so horrified she could hardly get her breath. The act itself almost paled compared with the misery that must follow, the life-long guilt and loneliness.

'Almost certainly,' Vespasia agreed. 'But it is not our decision to make. If you were her mother, would you want any stranger, or even a friend, to make the choice and use your daughter in order to prosecute this man, on the chance that you might win – if proving to the whole world that your daughter had been raped would be regarded as winning? Would you do that to Jemima?'

Vespasia knew the answer as she asked. Charlotte saw it in her eyes.

'No. I . . . I would find some way of taking revenge myself,' she admitted.

The ghost of a smile touched Vespasia's mouth. 'And would you tell Thomas?'

'Of course.'

'Are you sure? What do you think he would do?'

'I don't know, but he'd certainly do something!'

'Of course he would, in fury and pain, without thinking of his own safety or comfort,' Vespasia said.

'Naturally! He'd be thinking of Jemima!' Charlotte protested.

Vespasia shook her head very gently. 'Charlotte, my dear, you would have to protect Thomas just as much as you would Jemima. If he accused some young man from a good family –' she lifted her head slightly and indicated an elegant, wealthy young man moving easily from one group to another, laughing, flirting very slightly – 'what do you imagine would happen to him?'

Charlotte started at the young man, and then at Vespasia. She felt suffocated, even though they were standing in the open air and there was a very slight breeze tugging at parasols and ruffling the flower heads. She tried to remember her own days before her marriage when she had moved in Society, the rules she had known implicitly, the fun, the laughter, and the cruelty.

Vespasia supplied the answer for her. 'The oldest defence has always been to blame the victim. They would tell him his daughter was a whore in the making, and while they pitied him, if he made any more trouble he would find himself without a job. He, and you, would no longer be welcome in Society. And Jemima would feel even more quilty because she was inadvertently the cause of your ruin.'

'That's monstrous.' Charlotte's voice trembled.

'Of course it is.' Vespasia put her hand on Charlotte's arm. Her touch was warm and very gentle. 'It is one of the very worst of the private tragedies we have to bear in silence, and with as much dignity and grace as we can. Kindness is perhaps the only gift we can offer, and of course silence. And perhaps we will then have a little more gratitude for the griefs we do not personally have to bear.'

Charlotte nodded, too full of emotion at that moment to answer.

But when she was home that evening and Pitt was sitting downstairs in the parlour, absorbed in reading papers he had brought with him from his office, she went upstairs alone and soundlessly opened Jemima's bedroom door.

Jemima was asleep, lying on her back, arms spread wide, smiling a little. She looked very young, and desperately vulnerable. She had not even imagined the kind of pain that Charlotte and Vespasia had been talking about, and which had already begun for Angeles Castelbranco – if, of course, their assumptions were correct.

Perhaps two years ago Isaura had stood in the bedroom doorway and watched her daughter sleep. Had she been full of dreams for future happiness, or had fear touched her as it did Charlotte now?

She stayed there only a few moments longer. She did not want Jemima to waken and see her. She would feel spied on, perhaps even that Charlotte had intruded into the privacy she had a right to expect. Charlotte would not like to think someone watched her asleep, whoever they were.

Quietly she closed the door, then walked along the passage a few steps to Daniel's room. The man who had raped Angeles was somebody's son. Had they any idea what he had become?

She opened that door also, very softly, and looked in on Daniel. He was curled over, facing the window where the curtains were wide open and the last of the summer evening light still glowed. His dark eyelashes shadowed across his smooth, unblemished cheek. It was an impossible thought, but in another eight years he would be a man.

Suddenly she felt frightened, aware of how precious everything was, of the happiness, the safety, the hope she took for granted; even the little things like daily certainty of kindness, someone to touch, to love, to talk to, people who mattered to her.

Just a short while ago Isaura Castelbranco had had those things too.

She felt tears slip down her cheeks and the tightness in her chest for the enormity of life, the joy and the pain, the caring so deeply it was almost too much.

She closed the door in case she disturbed him, and walked very slowly along the passage. She hesitated at the top of the stairs. She was not ready to go down yet. Pitt would wonder what on earth was the matter with her, and she was not ready to try to explain.

Chapter Four

NARRAWAY HAD dreaded this encounter with Quixwood, imagining how the man might feel, yet he felt compelled to come here to the club where he had, very understandably, taken up residence. The servants would have cleared away all possible evidence, but it had been only days since Catherine's death. The sight of her sprawled across the floor, so obviously violated, would remain printed on Quixwood's memory, perhaps for the rest of his life. The very pattern of the furniture, the way the light fell across the wooden parquet, everything would remind him of it.

Perhaps in time he would have the hall changed entirely, move all the furniture, hang the pictures in another room. Or would it make no difference?

The club steward conducted Narraway through the outer lounge with its comfortable, leather-covered chairs and walls decorated with portraits of famous past members. They approached the silent library where Quixwood was sitting. There was a leather-bound volume open in his lap, but his eyes were unfocused and he seemed to be looking far beyond its pages.

'Lord Narraway to see you, sir,' the steward said gently.

Quixwood looked up, a sudden light of pleasure in his face.

'Ah, good of you to come.' He rose to his feet, closing the book and holding out his hand. 'Everyone else is avoiding me. I suppose they think I want to be alone, which is not true. Or – more than likely – they have no idea what to say to me.' He smiled bleakly. 'For which I can hardly blame them.' He gestured towards the other chair a few feet from him.

The steward withdrew, closing the door behind him. There was a bell to summon him should either of them wish for anything.

Narraway grasped Quixwood's hand for a moment, then sat down. 'Sympathy hardly seems enough,' he agreed. 'Whatever one says, it still sounds as if you have no idea what the person is suffering and all you want to do is discharge your duty, and then leave.'

'Aren't you going to tell me that this is the worst, and time will heal the pain?' Quixwood said wryly.

Narraway raised his eyebrows. 'It would seem a little redundant. I'm sure several people here have already said so.'

'Yes. And it's a lie anyway, isn't it?'

'I don't know,' Narraway admitted. 'I hope not. But I can't imagine you want to hear that now. It sounds . . . vaguely belittling, as if the fact that the pain might eventually become less somehow makes it better now. I'm afraid you probably aren't going to like what I have to say either, nevertheless I am going to say it.'

Quixwood looked surprised. 'What, for heaven's sake?'

'Have you heard anything further from Inspector Knox?'

Quixwood shrugged. 'No, not beyond a polite message to say that he is pursuing every piece of evidence he can find. But I had assumed as much.' He leaned forward earnestly. 'Tell me, Narraway, what was your impression of him? Please be honest. I need truth, something I can rely on and not lie awake wondering what is being kept from me, albeit with the best motives. Can you understand that?'

'Yes,' Narraway replied without hesitation. 'Left to imagination we suffer not one ill but all of them.'

Quixwood searched Narraway's face feature by feature. 'Do you do that too? About what? Have you ever lost anyone to something so . . . so vile, so bestial?' he asked finally.

Narraway made a tiny gesture of denial. 'This is nothing to do with my situation, Quixwood, it's about you and your loss. You know, at least by title, what my job has been. Do you think I have never experienced loss, disillusion, horror, and then a sense of total helplessness?'

Quixwood lowered his eyes. 'I'm sorry. That was a stupid remark. I didn't mean to be offensive. I feel so inadequate. Everything is slipping out of control and I can't stop it.'

Narraway felt an overwhelming pity for the man. Until a day or two ago he had barely known him – what kind of friendship could he offer that would help anything? Quixwood deserved at the very least a degree of honesty.

'I think Knox is a good man, I mean at his job. He'll find whatever there is that anyone can know.' He said it with certainty.

'Will you help him?' Quixwood asked quickly.

'If you still wish me to. But I think there may be things you would prefer not to learn. All facts are open to different interpretation, and your wife is not here to explain them as they were to her.' Was he being so delicate as to be incomprehensible?

Quixwood frowned and gave a slight, self-mocking smile. 'You don't need to tiptoe around it. You are trying to warn me that I may discover things about Catherine I would prefer not to have known? Of course. I'm not entirely stupid, or blind. I loved Catherine very much, but she was a complicated woman, far more so than she appeared to be on a brief acquaintance. She made friends of people I never would have. She saw good in them, or at least interest, that I didn't.' He looked away. 'She was always seeking something. I never knew what.'

Narraway drew in his breath to interrupt, then changed his mind.

'I want justice for her,' Quixwood said with sudden vehemence. 'She deserves that, even if I learn a few things that perhaps are not comfortable for me. I didn't save her from this. I wasn't there. Allow me at least to do what I can now. I am not so squeamish or self-regarding that I need to hide from the truth.'

'I'm sorry,' Narraway apologised sincerely. 'I meant that when they have sufficient to charge the man, whoever he is, don't look beyond that. Leave the details of the evidence to Knox. Don't press him to tell you more than will be made public at the trial, anyway.'

'The trial . . .' Quixwood's face tightened and his hands, resting easily on his lap to this point, now clenched. 'I admit I hadn't thought of that. Will they need to say any more than that she was killed?'

'I don't know. I imagine the man will put up a defence.'

'Surely they won't allow—'

'If they find him guilty he may be hanged,' Narraway pointed out. 'He must be allowed to fight for his life.'

Quixwood looked down at the floor. 'Of course. Catherine fought for her life – didn't she?'

Narraway said nothing. Quixwood would know his wife's courage better than he.

'Help me, please!' Quixwood begged. 'He can't be allowed to walk away from that!'

'I'll do everything I can,' Narraway promised. 'To hang a man is a sickening thing, but this is one I would have few qualms over.'

'Thank you.' Quixwood took a deep breath. 'Thank you,' he said again.

Narraway went first to the local police station to find Knox, and was informed that he was at Lyall Street, so he followed him there. He approached Quixwood's house with an odd mixture of familiarity and complete strangeness. The only time he had been here before was at night, in Quixwood's company, and with the terrible knowledge of Catherine's death. Her body was still lying on the floor where she had been found and the shock of it sharpened his senses so he could remember every detail of the corpse with awful clarity, and yet he could recall only foggy impressions of anything else.

Now, in the daylight, it looked as ordinary as any other wealthy and elegant street in the better parts of London. An open carriage passed by, then another in the opposite direction, coming towards him. The second was a landau, bodywork dark, brass gleaming in the sun. The liveried coachman sat bolt upright, the reins held tightly in his gloved hands.

In the back two women sat talking to each other, pink and yellow embroidered muslins fluttering in the breeze. One of them laughed. It was jarring, a waking nightmare, to think of Catherine lying obscenely flung like a broken doll on the floor of one of these quiet, sedate houses with their exquisite façades, and life went on outside, as if it were of no importance.

Narraway's hansom came to a halt. He alighted, paid the driver, and walked towards the front door. Flickering in his mind was the memory of Pitt telling him how, in his early days, he used to be sent to the servants' entrance. No one wished to have the police in the front part of the house, as though they were equals. Now Narraway was doing what had been essentially Pitt's job, and he intended to use every privilege and artifice he could to obtain information, whether it was intended to be shared with him or not.

The door was opened by a footman whose face was appropriately polite and blank, just as if everything in the household were as normal.

'Yes, sir? May I help you?' He clearly did not recognise Narraway from the night of the murder. Narraway recalled him, but it was his profession to remember faces.

'Good morning.' He produced a card out of the silver case in his pocket. 'If you would be so good as to ask Inspector Knox if he can spare me a few moments?'

The footman was about to refuse him when training took over from instinct and he looked at the card. The name was unfamiliar but the title impressed him.

'Certainly, my lord. If you would care to follow me to the morning room, I shall inform the inspector.'

It was a full ten minutes before Knox appeared, walking straight in without knocking, and closing the door behind him. He looked tired; his shoulders drooped and his tie was slightly askew. There were lines of anxiety etched deep in his face.

''Morning, sir,' he said with a sigh. 'Sorry, but I really don't have any news that'll help Mr Quixwood. Nothing for certain, only bits and pieces.'

Narraway remained standing rather stiffly by the mantelshelf.

'What have you found?' he asked. 'Regardless of its apparent lack of meaning? You must know how the assailant got in by now, and have an excellent idea of what, if anything, is missing. Have you found any witnesses, if not nearby, then within a block of here? Has any missing jewellery or artefacts, or whatever, turned up at a pawn shop, or with a receiver of such things? Have there been any similar crimes reported? Any break-ins at all? Any other attacks on women of this brutality, even if not fatal?'

Knox looked down at the ground, his lips pursed in sadness rather than thought.

'There's no sign of a break-in anywhere, Lord Narraway,' he

answered. 'We've searched every door and window. We've looked at the downpipes, ledges, everywhere a man could climb, and a few where he couldn't. We even have a lad up in the chimney to look.' He saw Narraway's expression of irritation. 'Some of these houses in this part have big chimneys. You'd be surprised how a skinny little lad can come down one o' these an' open a door.'

Narraway acknowledged his error. 'Yes, of course. I didn't think of that. Then how did he get in? I assume you are not saying he was here all the time? One of the servants? Please God, you are not saying that! We'll have every household in London in a panic.'

'No, sir.' Knox gave a twisted little smile. 'The servants are all very well accounted for.'

Narraway felt a chill. 'Then you are saying she let him in herself? That seems the only alternative left.'

Knox looked even more crumpled.

'Yes, sir, I am. Nothing was damaged, nothing torn or broken except what you already saw in the room where we found her. Which leaves us with the conclusion that he was someone with whom she was comfortable enough that she let him in herself.'

Narraway started at him. 'Are you suggesting he tricked her somehow? Pretended he was a friend, a messenger from her husband, or the husband of a friend, gave a false name?'

Knox did all he could to keep his face expressionless, and failed. 'No, my lord, I'm saying he was someone she knew, and she felt no apprehension about allowing him into the house without having a servant present. Someone she opened the door to herself rather than waiting until one of the servants heard the bell. She already knew him, maybe even expected him.'

Narraway breathed in and out deeply, slowly. He had done all he could to avoid facing this, even in his mind. His muscles clenched, chest and stomach tight. 'You mean a lover?'

Knox chewed his lip, profoundly unhappy. 'I'm sorry, sir, but that does seem probable. I'll be most obliged if you can think up a more agreeable alternative.'

Narraway forced himself to picture again the inner hallway where they had found Catherine. She had fought hard for her life, but only there, not closer to the front door. She had allowed her attacker inside the house, beyond the vestibule.

'How did none of the servants hear her?' he demanded. 'She must have cried out. A woman doesn't submit to rape without a sound. Didn't she scream, at the very least?'

'The servants had been excused for the night,' Knox replied. 'The baize door through to their quarters is pretty heavy. Sound proof, if you take my meaning? If she'd wanted anything she'd have rung one of the bells and someone would have come, but a shout, especially from the front of the house, no one would have heard.'

Narraway imagined it. The baize door gave such privacy, locked you off from intrusion – or help. Perhaps one stifled cry, then a hand over your mouth and only a muffled choking after that. If a servant heard anything at all, they would take it for a quarrel, and the last thing they would want to do would be intrude on such a scene.

What were they used to, the well-trained servants in this outwardly respectable house, exactly like all the others on this street? Did they recognise a mistress's dismissal for the evening as a tacit command not to return?

He looked at Knox.

'Sorry, sir,' Knox said quietly. 'This man may have stolen things, but the servants don't recognise anything gone, and there's very definitely been no break-in. The bolts across the front doors were undone. The butler and the footman have both sworn, without any hesitation, that where she was found, the doors were closed only with the latch that shuts itself.'

'But the butler was alone when he found her,' Narraway pointed out. It was a foolish difference. He knew it as he said the words, just as he knew what Knox would say in reply.

'Yes, sir,' Knox answered wearily. 'He called the footman. Couldn't really call any of the women. I'm sorry, there's no way around it, my lord. She let him in. We can only conclude that she knew him.'

'Then we'd better find out who he was,' Narraway said grimly. 'Any ideas?'

'Not yet. The servants are either very loyal, or else they don't know.

I've spoken to Mr Quixwood.' His face pinched with distaste at the memory. 'He says he has no idea either.'

'And you believe him?' Narraway pressed.

'No, sir, not entirely.' Again unhappiness filled Knox's tired face. Narraway wondered if he was thinking of his own family. He had said he had a wife and daughters. His voice had altered when he spoke of them: there was a gentleness, even a pride in it. Narraway had liked him for that.

'Have you looked at Mrs Quixwood's diary?' Narraway asked. 'Or spoken to her maid?'

'Yes, but it doesn't tell me anything,' Knox replied. 'She was busy, lots of engagements, but very few names mentioned, none of them outside of what you'd expect.' He frowned. 'Do you want to see it? Maybe . . .' He left the idea hanging in the air, on the edge of asking Narraway something, and not quite certain if he wanted to, or how to word it.

'Yes,' Narraway answered. 'I'd like to look. I may know some of the names, at least.'

Knox frowned. 'Do you think . . . I mean . . .' His expression was bleak. 'A secret acquaintance? It's going to be very hard to prove. That kind of thing . . .'

'Rape?' Narraway said the word with distaste. 'I'll settle for proving the murder.'

Knox smiled at him, as if they had reached some kind of under-standing. 'I suppose you'd like to speak to the lady's maid as well. Read the diary first. It won't take you long. Then I'll send for her.'

Narraway thanked him and went into the garden room to wait while a constable fetched Catherine's diary.

The room was sunny and warm in the morning light, a curious sense of peace in it, in such a troubled house. It was surprisingly feminine, greens and whites, white woodwork around the windows. The curtains were patterned, but only with leaves, echoing the potted plants, none of them with flowers. It was at the same time both bright and restful.

He was almost at ease in one of the rattan chairs when the constable brought the diary. He thanked him and sat down to read it.

He started in January. At first it was not very interesting, just the usual brief comments on the weather as it affected her daily life. 'Very cold, steets slippery with ice.' 'Ground quite hard, all very clear and glittering. Very beautiful.' 'So wet today I really would rather not go out – I'll get drenched no matter how careful I am.'

Then as the days lengthened and the weather became milder she commented on the first buds in the trees, the snowdrops, the birds. She saw a starling with twigs in its beak and wrote a short paragraph on the faith of building a nest when the days were still so dark. 'How can such a small creature, who knows nothing, be so sure of a good future? Or is it only a blind and exquisite courage?'

The comments on the weather continued, with notes as to the flowers that had pleased her. Her botanical interest was written with acute observation, but mostly it was their beauty that moved her.

Narraway put the book down and wondered what Catherine Quixwood had thought as she had written those words. Was the loneliness he felt in there, the sense of confusion hers, or his own? Unwillingly he pictured her again, but lying on the floor. The only time he had seen her was after her death; the only reality for him was the way she had died. There had been such possibility of passion in her face, such turbulence, even in death. Or did he imagine that too?

He picked up the diary again and resumed reading it, paying more attention to where she had been and, when she had noted it, with whom.

As the weather grew more clement she had attended lectures at the Royal Geographical Society. After one on Egypt she had made a note of its excellence. Reading on, he saw that she had gone to an exhibition of paintings of the Nile by various watercolourists, and then to the library to find books on Egyptian history.

In May she had gone to a lecture on astronomy. This time it was not the night sky that drew her most enthusiastic comments, but the sublime order of the stars in their courses, from the most random comet or meteor to the most immense galaxies. There was too little room on the page for all she wanted to say to remind herself of her emotions, and her writing eventually became so small he could not read it.

Then she went back to the library and searched for other books on astronomy, and more lectures she might attend. In the following weeks she travelled further away, even going by train to both Birmingham and Manchester to learn more.

But, as Knox had said, there were very few names in the diary. They all seemed exactly the acquaintances one might have expected: other married women in Society of her own age and station, a couple of distant cousins, one unmarried and apparently of considerable means. She had travelled and Catherine seemed to enjoy her company when it was available. There were also two aunts mentioned, the vicar and his wife, and business associates of Quixwood's and their wives.

He reached the day before she was killed, and closed the book. He asked Knox if he might now speak to the lady's maid, although he did not hold much hope of learning anything from her that would be of value.

Flaxley was a tall, spare woman with brown hair, which was now liberally threaded with grey. The marks of grief were too evident in her face for any disguise or apology. She came in and sat down opposite Narraway as he invited her, then folded her hands in her lap and waited for him to speak. Her back was ramrod straight, probably from a lifetime of self-discipline, but everything emotional within her seemed to have been drained away. There was no expression in her tired face.

Narraway was deeply moved by her loyalty. He wondered for a fleeting moment how many people had inspired such sense of loss, even from among their own families.

'I'm sorry to disturb you, Miss Flaxley,' he said quietly. He decided to be completely honest with her. 'But the more I learn of Mrs Quixwood, the more I am determined to do what I can to see that the man who killed her is punished.' He chose very deliberately not to use the word 'rape'. There was no need to distress Flaxley with a new and even deeper grief.

He saw the flicker of surprise in her eyes.

'I am certain that if you had any idea how to achieve this,' he went on, 'with as little unpleasant speculation as possible, you would already have told Inspector Knox. I have been reading Mrs Quixwood's appointment diary, and I feel I know her better than I did before.'

'Appointment diary?' she repeated with puzzlement. She did not ask if he believed that Catherine could possibly have had any idea what would happen to her, but it was implicit in the lift of her voice and the contempt in her eyes.

'Do you believe Mrs Quixwood would have opened the front door to a man she did not both know and trust?' he asked her.

'No, of course . . .' She stopped. Clearly she had not even considered the matter. 'Was he not a thief?'

'I don't know what he was, Miss Flaxley, but he did not break into the house, which leaves only one other possibility, which is that she let him in. Indeed, that initially she had no fear of him. Therefore he was someone she already knew quite well enough not to call a servant to attend her.'

She started at him, her eyes filling with horror. She straightened very slightly and her hands knotted in her lap so the knuckles shone white. He noticed with surprise how delicately boned they were. In their own way, they were quite beautiful.

'What can I do to help? I will not smear her reputation.' There was anger in her voice, and warning.

He admired her for it. He hoped that she would be able to keep that resolve and it pained him that she would probably not.

'Please go through the diary with me and tell me which of her friends she kept company with, and something about each of them. I will call on them in due course, but your insight will be more acute than mine. You knew Mrs Quixwood, and possibly her true feelings about them rather than the socially polite face she showed. Also, I have learned to my cost that women can judge each other far more observantly than men can.' He allowed himself a very slight smile.

He saw it echoed in a momentary easing in her expression also.

'Yes, my lord, of course,' she agreed.

It took Narraway the next three days to meet with eight of the people mentioned in Catherine's diaries. He found it difficult, which surprised him. They were all women very like those he had known and mixed with all his adult life, and yet when speaking of Catherine the artificiality of polite conversation between strangers irritated him.

He began with a cousin of Catherine's, a dark, rather elegant woman with beautiful hair and a very ordinary face. Her name was Mary Abercrombie.

'Of course we are deeply grieved,' she said earnestly, but without any signs of pain that Narraway could see. 'I don't know what I can tell you, Lord Narraway. I was very fond of Catherine, of course. We grew up together.' She fidgeted slightly with her skirts. 'But as so often happens when we both married, we drifted apart. Our tastes were . . . different.'

'But you still went to the British Museum together,' he pointed out. 'Or was the entry in her diary incorrect?'

Mrs Abercrombie smiled and looked down at her hands. Narraway had a fleeting and irrelevant thought how much uglier they were than those of Flaxley, the lady's maid.

'It was incorrect?' he prompted.

'Yes . . . and no,' she equivocated. 'We did meet there, and visited a few of the exhibits. I met a friend and left to take tea. It was about that time in the afternoon. Catherine stayed on, I presumed by herself, but I don't know. When I spoke to Rawdon a few days later at a reception, he implied that Catherine had been very late home. I'm afraid I rather let her down by saying to him that I had left the museum before four o'clock.'

'And Catherine was not at the reception?' he asked.

'No.' She shook her head, a shadow of disapproval crossing her face. 'I'm afraid she found such light social exchanges rather tedious. So do many of us, but one must make the effort.' It was a statement, as if it were a fact agreed to by all.

Narraway wondered if she had made the remark to Quixwood on purpose. Catherine had been beautiful. Even in violent death the remnants of it were there in her face. Mary Abercrombie was agreeable enough and without obvious blemish, but she had no beauty, at least not for Narraway.

'Was that the last time you saw her?' he said aloud.

'Yes. Except briefly at a concert about two weeks ago.'

'Who was she with at the concert?'

'I'm not sure she was with anyone.' She raised her eyebrows slightly. 'When we spoke she was alone.'

'Did that surprise you?'

'Frankly, no. Catherine was inclined to go to events alone. If it was something she wished to do, she would prefer to be alone to indulge in it, rather than go with company who might require conversation from her.' Her disapproval of such behaviour was clear, if still unspoken.

Narraway had a sudden vision of Catherine bent forward listening to great, sweeping symphonies of music while the fashionable women around her were talking to each other, gossiping, flirting or merely pretending to listen while they waited for the opportunity to recommence speaking. He imagined in her an inner loneliness he found disturbing, and frighteningly easy to understand.

Or was he simply projecting his own emotions onto her, because he had never known her alive and there was no one to refute his picture?

'Was there anyone to whom she was particularly close?' he asked.

'You mean someone who might know if she were . . . having an unsuitable friendship?' Mrs Abercrombie asked, delicate eyebrows raised. 'Possibly. But I cannot imagine that they would be indiscreet enough to speak of it, even had she been foolish, and totally disloyal. Poor Rawdon is suffering enough, don't you think? And Catherine has certainly paid for it.'

Narraway smiled coldly, feeling the temper like an ice storm inside him. 'Actually, Mrs Abercrombie, I was thinking of someone who might know if she were being troubled by unwanted attentions,' he corrected her. 'Men sometimes look at a beautiful woman and imagine she has given them some encouragement, when in truth she was no more than civil, or at best kind. Denials do not always persuade them of their error.'

She opened her pale eyes very wide. 'Really? I have never known anyone so . . . disturbed.'

'No,' he agreed without a flicker in his expression. 'I imagine not.'

The anger burned up her face. She understood the insult well enough, even if she chose to pretend she did not.

'But most perceptive of you to have realised Catherine may have,' she retorted. 'Remarkable, since apparently you did not know her. But then perhaps you know women like her.'

'Unfortunately not,' he said, keeping his eyes on hers. 'From all I hear, she seems to have been unique. A tragedy to lose her when there are already so many people who are so similar as to seem interchangeable. Please accept my condolences on your loss, Mrs Abercrombie.' He rose to his feet and gave a very slight inclination of his head.

She remained seated, her eyes like ice. 'You are too kind,' she said sarcastically.

Still annoyed and somewhat confused in trying to make sense of Catherine's seemingly innocent life, Narraway called on the police surgeon, Brinsley, to see if he had anything further to report, any medical history he might have learned, or marks of self-defence that would tell them more of the attacker. Because it would be painful, he preferred to get it over with as soon as possible. It was not as if he could dismiss from his memory the image of Catherine's body lying bleeding on the floor.

Brinsley was busy with another autopsy, but he did not keep Narraway waiting more than fifteen minutes. He came into the sparse waiting room rolling down his shirtsleeves, his hair a little tousled.

''Afternoon, my lord,' he said briskly. He did not hold out his hand. Perhaps he had experienced too many people's revulsion, imagination picturing where it had just been.

'Good afternoon, Doctor,' Narraway replied. 'Am I too soon to learn if you have anything further to say about Mrs Quixwood's death?'

'No, no. Did it this morning,' Brinsley's face was pinched. 'I've really nothing to add, unless you want the details of the rape? Can't think it'll help you. Very violent.' His voice sunk even lower, grating with anger. 'Very ugly.'

'Can you tell if she fought, or at least tried to?' Narraway asked.

Brinsley winced. 'She tried. A good few bruises came out now. They do, after death, if they were inflicted just before. Wrists, arms, shoulders. He was unnecessarily brutal. Thighs, but you'd expect that. And the bite, of course, on her breast.' His mouth was tight, as if his jaw were clenched. 'Only thing that might make a difference to you is that I'm now quite certain that she actually died of opium poisoning.'

Narraway said nothing. He had hoped it was some accident or misreading.

'Overdose of laudanum,' Brinsley explained. 'Dissolved in a glassful of Madeira wine. Pretty heavily laced, I must say. Far more than enough to kill her.'

Narraway stood paralysed, grief washing over him with a pain he could not have foreseen. He had hoped it was an error. Now he tried to grasp the despair she must have felt, as if everything she was had been torn violently from her: her body, her dignity, the very core of herself damaged beyond hope.

'I'm sorry,' Brinsley said hoarsely. 'I keep thinking that one day I'll get used to it, but I never do. I can't say for certain that it was suicide, since we don't know if the man stayed long enough to force her to drink it, but that seems extremely unlikely. If he'd wanted her dead he could simply have broken her neck. I'm afraid everything suggests she crawled to the cabinet and poured herself enough to deaden the pain, and either accidentally, or intentionally, overdid the dose.' His face was bleak. 'I'm sorry.'

Narraway struggled to picture it. 'Could she have dragged herself that far? And why on earth would she keep laudanum in the cabinet in the hallway? Wouldn't she keep it upstairs? Probably in the bedroom.'

'I've no idea,' Brinsley said patiently. 'But there was no one else in that part of the house, and obviously she did crawl over to the cabinet. She must have got at least onto her hands and knees and opened it up, then poured and drank the Madeira. The dregs were full of laudanum, both in the glass and in the bottle.' He shook himself. 'For God's sake! The poor woman can't have had the least idea of what she was doing. She just tipped the laudanum into the bottle and drank the whole damn thing. Can you blame her?'

Narraway did not answer. Any reply was redundant anyway. He was numb with the horror of it.

'I'm sorry,' Brinsley said again. 'Those are the facts. I don't know what else you can make of them. But I hope to hell you find whoever did it, and if you can't hang him literally for murder, then find a way to hang him for rape.'

'I'll try,' Narraway swore. 'Believe me.'

★   ★   ★

He visited and spoke with all the other people on Miss Flaxley's list. He gained a wider view of Catherine Quixwood, but it did not alter radically from that already given him by Mary Abercrombie. Catherine had been interested in all manner of art and science, in the artefacts of other times and places, in human thought and above all in the passions of the mind.

She seemed to have skirted more carefully around the edges regarding passions of the heart. He wondered if they had frightened her, perhaps come too close to breaching the walls of her own safety, or her loneliness.

Or was that his overfanciful imagination seeking in her a likeness to himself? He could understand being drawn to the music of Beethoven, and yet at the same time frightened of it. It challenged all the flimsy arguments of safety and dared beyond the known into something far bigger, both more beautiful and more dangerous. At times he wanted to stay with what his mind could conquer and hold. To be enchanted by the brilliance of the mind was exciting without injury. To be shown the gateway to happiness but not allowed through was to be left forever starved. Far more comfortable not to have looked, not to have seen how much more there was.

Look at vases of flowers, not the wild paintings of Turner in which all the light was caught and imagined on canvas. Look at the artefacts of ancient Troy, but do not think of the passion and the loss. Always keep the mind busy. Do not think of Helen's beauty, which for the Greeks had to be of the soul even more than of the face or form.

Was that what Catherine had been doing?

At the end of three days Narraway had a plethora of facts, statements and stories, but no fixed frame into which to place them. If she had made secret assignations with anyone she had been sufficiently clever in concealing them that he had found no trace. She was charming to everyone and intimate with none. Again, perhaps that was a little like himself. Or did he imagine that too?

About the only thing she did not appear to have had any interest in was the last few years of extraordinary events in Africa. There was one brief note on the discovery of gold in Johannesburg, which led to wealth beyond imagination, but no mention of the massacres carried out by Lobengula, or the extraordinary career of Cecil Rhodes, or even of the catastrophic Jameson Raid only months ago. For a woman interested in so many things it was a curious omission.

Narraway was driven to going back again to speak to Quixwood himself, little as he wished to. He owed the man a report of his discoveries so far, fruitless as they were.

He found him in the library of the club, as before, but this time he was busy writing letters. He looked up as Narraway came in. He was clearly tired, the lines in his face more deeply scored. It was marred as well by anxiety, and he did not rise from his seat.

'Have you found anything further?' he asked as Narraway sat down in the smooth, comfortable leather.

'I'm not certain,' Narraway replied honestly. 'I have been asking questions of her friends, mostly the people with whom she attended lectures and concerts, visited museums and theatres, and that sort of thing.'

Quixwood frowned. 'Why? How could that have anything to do with her death?' His voice held a note of disappointment.

'She knew whoever killed her.' Narraway found no difficulty in keeping his patience. He could think of little more painful than the possibility Quixwood now faced. If he balked at it, or blamed the man who told him, it was a very human reaction. He needed someone to be angry with for his pain.

Quixwood blinked as if caught in a sudden, bright light. 'And you think one of her friends might know who it is?'

'Without being aware of the connection, of course, yes I do,' Narraway told him. 'If you consider it, do you not?'

Quixwood stared at him for several long seconds, then he lowered his gaze. 'Yes, you are quite right, of course. I suppose it is what I have been trying hard to deny to myself. Such things do not happen in isolation. And I can't wilfully refuse to accept that she let him in. I appreciate your patience in letting me come to it a trifle more slowly.'

'I'm sorry,' Narraway said with intense regret. 'I cannot see any other answer that fits the facts we have.'

'And . . . do you know who it was?' Quixwood framed the words with difficulty, staring down at his half-written paper.

'No, not yet. But I have further questions I intend to ask Flaxley. She seems a sensible woman, and loyal, but I believe she wishes to see this man punished, as far as is consistent with protecting Mrs Quixwood's reputation.'

Quixwood looked bleak, his eyes still avoiding Narraway's.

'Can I ask you to keep me aware of all you learn?' He glanced up quickly. 'This is the darkest moment of my life. I couldn't have thought in my most dreadful nightmare of the pain it is. I don't care what Catherine did, or why. Allow me to protect her in death the little I can. I loved her, you know? Let me not lose the memory of her as well as the reality.'

'I'll do all I can,' Narraway promised. He never gave his word lightly and that had not changed through all the secrecy and the deceit of Special Branch.

'Thank you.' Quixwood forced a rather shaky smile. 'I'm sure Flaxley will give you all the help she can. She's a loyal creature and she was devoted to Catherine. I've no idea what she'll do now, because there is nothing for her in what is left of my household. I suppose I can offer her an excellent reference, but that's not much to do for a woman who's given so many years of her life and seen it end in such hideous crime.' He took a deep breath. 'And a pension, of course. Fortunately I'm in a position to do that.'

'That would be good of you, and quite appropriate,' Narraway agreed. 'But I would be obliged if you kept her on until we have solved this case.'

'Of course! I'll do all I can in every way. Good God, man, no one could care about it more than I do!' Quixwood reasserted control of himself with something of an effort. 'Someone else who might be able to help is Alban Hythe, a young man with a good position in the Treasury. I know he shared many of Catherine's tastes, because she told me so herself.' He made a slight gesture with his strong, slender hands. 'Apparently he is a most intelligent and civil young man, who travelled widely earlier in his career, and is a lover of music and art. At least, that is what she said. I imagine if there is someone who became . . . who became obsessed with Catherine and imagined there was something between them, then Mr Hythe might have noticed it. Narraway, I would be extraordinarily grateful if you did not speak of the . . .' he swallowed, '. . . of the details of her death to others. To hear the word is ugly enough, without being able to picture her in the mind.'

'Of course,' Narraway agreed. 'I will tell him nothing except that she was attacked in her own home by someone she had assumed to be a friend, and therefore she was not initially afraid of him. That will cover all the truth he needs to know.'

'Thank you.' Quixwood gave the ghost of a smile. 'I'm sure he will help you if he can. She spoke so well of him. He must also have been fond of her.'

Narraway felt a chill of surprise and familiarity. Was it really as simple as this? Without realising it, had Quixwood himself known the answer all the time and simply looked beyond it because it was too painful, a double betrayal?

Narraway himself did not wish to believe it either. In fact, he thought now, perhaps so close to the answer, he did not want Catherine to have been having an affair at all. He could understand her loneliness. Everything he had learned about her indicated a woman unfulfilled in her life, desperately seeking something more. He had thought it was purpose she was looking for to exercise her intelligence and her hunger to reach out to the passion and creation of the great minds of the past. But maybe it was simply a love more immediate to her nature than that offered to her by her husband.

He rose to his feet. 'Thank you. I had better go and visit this man Hythe, and see what I can learn. I shall be as discreet as possible.'

He arrived at Hythe's address in a very nice part of Holborn just before seven. It was not really a courteous hour to call – people would be preparing for dinner, or to go out for the evening – but he was not willing to wait another day. Added to which, if he were honest, he was sufficiently angry for the part he suspected Hythe of playing in Catherine's death that he had no concern whatever for his convenience.

He was admitted by a parlourmaid and had only moments to wait before Hythe himself appeared, looking startled but not worried. He was a handsome man, probably in his late thirties, tall and slender with brownish hair streaked fair where already the summer sun had bleached it.

'Lord Narraway?' he said questioningly, closing the door of the parlour behind him. The house was charming but modest and had no separate morning room for visitors.

'I am sorry to disturb you so late,' Narraway apologised. 'In fact for calling upon you at all, unannounced. If the matter were not so serious I would have made an appointment in the usual way.'

Hythe frowned, indicating a chair for Narraway to be seated. 'Is it something at the Treasury?'

Narraway sat, and Hythe lowered himself into the chair opposite.

'No,' Narraway replied. 'As far as I am aware there is nothing amiss at the Treasury. This concerns the recent death of Mrs Catherine Quixwood.'

He saw the anxiety in Hythe's face change to deep grief, a look so genuine it was hard to disbelieve it. But he had known people before whose loyalties had been so violently torn apart that they could kill and weep for the victim at the same time.

'How can I possibly help?' Hythe seemed genuinely confused. 'For heaven's sake, if I knew anything at all, I would already have contacted the police.' He frowned. 'Who are you? My maid said "Lord Narraway", so clearly you are not a policeman.'

'Until recently I was head of Special Branch,' Narraway replied, caught slightly off guard by the question. He had not expected to have to explain himself except casually, and in his own way. 'Mr Quixwood asked me to help him as much as I am able to, both to close the matter as quickly as possible, but also to keep it as discreet as circumstances allow.'

'And the police?' Hythe said with some anxiety. 'Is there need to be concerned as to their . . . clumsiness?'

Narraway smiled bleakly. He found Hythe agreeable, and disliked the thought of having to suspect him. It was easy to see how Catherine Quixwood could have liked him also, even though he was perhaps a decade younger than she.

'Actually, I think Inspector Knox is both capable and discreet, but the situation is not easy to deal with,' he answered.

'How can I help?' Hythe appeared still to have no idea how he was involved. 'Both my wife and I were very fond of Mrs Quixwood, but I have no idea what I could do to be of use.'

'She was killed by someone she knew well enough to let into the house, quite late in the evening, and to be comfortable without sending for one of the servants to be present,' Narraway answered. He saw the surprise in Hythe's face, and a degree of apprehension, perhaps even alarm. Had he not expected anyone to deduce so much?

'I see from Mrs Quixwood's diary that she went to many interesting events,' Narraway went on. 'Lectures, displays at the British Museum, concerts and the theatre, which Mr Quixwood was unable to attend. He tells me that they were subjects that also interested you, and you might be able to tell me a little of others she would have become acquainted with.' Narraway shrugged slightly. 'It is unpleasant to have to question her friends in such a way, but she was not the kind of woman who would have allowed into the house a man whom she did not know, at least reasonably well. He must have been someone of her own social standing, and possibly similar interests.'

'I see.' Hythe rose to his feet and went to the door. He excused himself and disappeared for several minutes, returning accompanied by a young woman who at first glance seemed quite ordinary apart from the steadiness of her gaze. Her hair was the colour of honey and had a deep, natural wave.

Narraway rose to his feet immediately.

Hythe introduced her as his wife.

'How do you do, Lord Narraway?' Maris Hythe said with interest. Her voice was soft and surprisingly deep, giving her a gravity that her smooth, candid face belied.

'How do you do, Mrs Hythe?' he replied. 'I am sorry to intrude on your evening with such an unhappy subject.'

She sat down gracefully and the men followed her lead.

'That is hardly of any importance, if we can help.' She dismissed it with a slight gesture of one hand. 'I liked Catherine very much. She was funny and wise and brave. I have no idea who could have wanted to kill her, but if I can help you find them, then all my time is yours.' She looked at him gravely, waiting for his answer.

He told her of his conversation with Flaxley, and then later with Quixwood, explaining why he needed to know Catherine's friends, but always skirting around the subject of rape. However, he was not subtle enough to deceive her.

'Was his intention robbery?' she said very quietly, almost under her breath. 'Or did he attack her . . . personally?'

There was nothing to be gained by evasion, and he needed her help. 'I am afraid he did. The details of that would be better not spoken of.'

'I see.' She did not argue with him, nor make any response to her husband's quick look of surprise and distress.

'Perhaps if I give you a list of her most recent engagements,' Narraway suggested, 'then you can tell me who you remember as also being present, and who might have become close to her recently. I realise it is distasteful, but—'

'We understand,' Hythe interrupted him. He glanced at Maris and then back at Narraway, holding out his hand for the list.

Narraway passed it to him, and watched as he read it, offering it to Maris simultaneously.

For half an hour they mentioned names back and forth, and Narraway learned something of each of the events Flaxley had described. Hythe appeared to have enjoyed those he had also attended, and there was pleasure in his voice as he told of the interest, excitement or beauty of each. If the grief as he remembered Catherine was artificial, he was a superb actor.

But Narraway had know people every bit as convincing who would kill without hesitation if their own needs were thwarted or their safety in jeopardy. Quixwood was right: Hythe and Catherine had clearly been good friends, and Maris also, especially where music was concerned. If there had been an affair between Catherine and Hythe then it was well concealed. But he had to grant that it was easily possible. Everything Hythe said seemed to be true, and yet looking at the tenseness in his shoulders, the awkward way he sat, without moving, Narraway grew increasingly certain that he was concealing something that he knew mattered, something that frightened him.

Maris explained that she was close to one of her sisters who was recently widowed, and she spent much of her time helping her, offering comfort, simply being there so her sister was not alone. Alban Hythe could not account for his time on most of these occasions, including the night of Catherine's murder.

At the end of over two hours, Narraway thanked them both and left, walking out into the soft dusk of the summer evening, the last light fading pink in the west. He was saddened by the growing possibility that Alban Hythe had begun an affair with Catherine because of her loneliness and his temporary solitude, and perhaps a weakness in both of them, played on by the depth of intellectual understanding, mutual love of the interesting, beautiful and creative.

What terrible change had led it from guilt to such furious violence? Had he wanted more and she had refused him? Or had she wanted more, possibly even a commitment, and he had refused her? Had she threatened his safety in some way and he had responded from a fearful darkness in his character she had not for a moment imagined?

Narraway walked along the pavement towards the lights of the main thoroughfare and felt sadness overwhelm him. His rage turned against Hythe, and he hurt for the life and passion that, he was beginning to suspect, Hythe had destroyed.

Chapter Five

'MAMA, I can't possibly wear that!' Jemima said indignantly. 'I shall look terrible. People will think I am ill. They'll be offering me chairs to sit on, in case I fall over.' Her face was flushed with temper and frustration. She appeared the picture of health, as if it would take a runaway carriage to knock her off balance, not a fainting fit.

Pitt looked up from the newspaper he was reading. They were all in the parlour, the summer evening air drifting in from the open french windows. Daniel was absorbed in a *Boy's Own Paper* and Charlotte had been looking at the *London Illustrated News*.

Pitt regarded the dress Jemima was holding up. 'You wanted that last year,' he pointed out. 'It suited you excellently.'

'Papa, that was last year!' she said with exasperation at his lack of understanding.

'You haven't changed all that much.' He looked her up and down quite carefully. 'An inch taller, perhaps,' he conceded.

'Two inches taller,' she corrected him. 'At the very least. And anyway, I'm completely different.' It distressed her that he had not noticed.

'You don't look completely different to me,' he answered.

'Yes, she does,' Daniel argued. 'She's a girl. She's getting all . . .' Suddenly he realised what he was saying and was lost for the appropriate words.

Jemima blushed. 'You're trying to make me look like a child,' she accused her father. 'Genevieve's father does the same thing. He doesn't want her ever to become a woman.'

'You're fourteen,' Pitt said flatly. 'You *are* a child.'

'I'm not! That's a terrible thing to say!' Unaccountably Jemima was on the edge of tears.

Daniel bent his head back to his *Boys' Own Paper*, lifting it a little higher to hide his face.

Pitt looked at Charlotte. He had no idea how he had offended, or what to do about it. It was totally unreasonable.

Charlotte had grown up with two sisters and there was no mystery in it for her.

'You are not having a purple dress, and that's all there is to it,' she told her daughter. 'If you feel that that one is too young for you, then wear the blue one.'

'Blue's ordinary,' Jemima responded. 'Everyone has blue. It's dull. It's safe!' That was the worst condemnation she could think of.

'You don't need anything special,' Pitt told her gently. 'You're very pretty whatever you wear.'

'You just say that because you're my father!' Her voice choked as if she could not control her tears any longer. 'You have to like the way I look.'

'I don't!' He was surprised and a little defensive himself. 'If you wore something I didn't like, I would say so.'

'You'd have my hair in braids down my back as if I were ten!' she said furiously. She turned to Charlotte. 'Mama, everyone wears blue, it's boring. And pink looks like you're a child!'

'Yellow?' Daniel suggested helpfully.

'Then I shall look as if I have jaundice!' she responded. 'Why can't I wear purple?'

Daniel was not to be put off. 'Green?'

'Then I'll look sick! Just be quiet!'

'Aunt Emily wears green,' he pointed out.

'She's got fair hair, stupid!' she shouted at him.

'Jemima!' Charlotte said sharply. 'That was quite uncalled for. He was being perfectly sensible, and pale green would look very nice—'

'I don't want to be "nice"!' Jemima said furiously. 'I want to be interesting, different, grown up.' The tears spilled from her eyes onto her cheeks. 'I want to look lovely. Why can't you understand?' Without waiting for an answer she swung round and stormed out. They heard her feet banging on the treads up the stairs and then a door on the landing slam.

'What did I do?' Daniel asked incredulously.

'Nothing,' Charlotte assured him.

'Then why is she like that?'

'Because she's fourteen,' Charlotte replied. 'She wants to look nice at the supper party she's going to.'

'She always looks nice,' Pitt was reasonable, and confused. 'She's very pretty. In fact she looks more like you every day.'

Charlotte smiled ruefully. 'I'm not sure she'd appreciate your saying so, my dear.'

'She did the other day,' he argued.

'That was then, this is now,' she answered. There was no use trying to explain it to him. He had grown up without sisters. Girls of that age were as incomprehensible to him as mermaids or unicorns.

Daniel shrugged and turned the next page of his *Boys' Own* to the story of a pirate adventure off the coast of India. 'Why couldn't she have been a boy?' he said resignedly. 'That would have been better for all of us.'

'It would have been easier,' Charlotte corrected him. 'Not better.'

Pitt and Daniel exchanged glances, but both were wise enough not to take issue with her.

An hour later Charlotte went upstairs to Jemima's room and knocked on the door. When there was no answer she rapped sharply, then went in anyway. Jemima was sitting on the bed, her hair loose and tangled, her cheeks tear-stained. She glared defiantly at her mother.

'I suppose you've come to tell me off,' she said belligerently. 'And that I have to wear blue, and be glad of it. If I smile I'll look charming anyway, and about as interesting as a jug of milk!'

Charlotte did not ask whose interest Jemima was working to awaken; she already knew. His name was Robert Durbridge and he was eighteen. He was far too old for Jemima at the moment, but otherwise a pleasant-seeming young man, the son of the local rector and bent on every kind of rebellion against the path in the Church that his parents had planned for him.

'Wear a green sash around your waist and you will be quite different from other girls,' she suggested helpfully.

'What?' Jemima's eyes flew wide open. 'Mama, you can't wear blue and green together! Nobody does that!'

Charlotte smiled at her. 'Then you will be the first. I thought you wanted to be different. Have you changed your mind?'

'Blue and green?'

'Why not? Blue sky and green trees. You see it all the time.'

'I don't want to look like a field,' Jemima said in disgust.

'A willow tree against the sky,' Charlotte corrected her. 'Stop being so obstructive. There is nothing less attractive than bad temper, I promise you. Now wash your face and pull yourself together. It is not your father's fault, or your brother's, that you are full of emotion and indecision. It's part of growing up and we all experience it. You are behaving as if you are the centre of the world, and you aren't.'

'You don't understand!' Jemima wailed, her face crumpling.

'Of course not,' Charlotte agreed with a smile. 'I was never fourteen, I went straight from being twelve to being twenty. So did both of my sisters.'

'Twenty!' Jemima was horrified. 'You mean I'm going to feel like this for another six years?'

'Please heaven, I hope not!' Charlotte said with feeling.

In spite of herself, Jemima smiled, and then started to giggle. 'Can I really wear a green sash on my dress?'

'Of course. So you had better walk with your head up, and smile to everyone, because they will all be looking at you, including young Robert Durbridge.'

'Do you think so? But then . . .' Jemima blushed.

'Jemima!'

'Yes, Mama.'

'The subject is closed,' Charlotte said sternly.

Charlotte and Pitt attended yet another reception that duty obliged them to, but Charlotte admitted to herself that there were elements of it she thoroughly enjoyed, not the least being that she was nobody's guest. She was here because Pitt was invited.

In the swirl of greetings, polite conversations and the swapping of suitably trivial enquiries and answers, they began to move among the throng of people. Charlotte noticed Vespasia, strikingly elegant as usual. Pitt looked for those he needed to speak with.

Charlotte met various women she had encountered before and was polite, but found her attention wandering. They were discussing family matters: who was engaged to marry whom; love affairs and misfortunes she was thankful did not concern her. She realised that all too soon she would have to consider Jemima finding a suitable husband, but she had three or four years' grace yet before that needed to be a preoccupation. When she was young and single she had loathed being presented to various people in the hope that some young man might please her, and she him. Now she felt an embarrassing wave of sympathy for her own mother. She knew perfectly well that she had been extraordinarily difficult, and in the end decided to marry a policeman, and virtually disappear from Society.

By that time her mother had been relieved to accept any settled life for her middle daughter and had put up barely any resistance.

She was still smiling at the memory when she saw Isaura Castelbranco looking to be struggling in a conversation with a group of women Charlotte herself would hate to be trapped among. She determined to rescue her, as much for the pleasure of talking to her as anything else. She found the Portuguese Ambassador's wife both interesting and attractive. There was an abundance of things they could discuss with genuine pleasure.

An hour later Charlotte was alone again, with no idea where Pitt was, when she saw Angeles Castelbranco with some other young women. They were all laughing with two young men who were all quite openly admiring Angeles. Charlotte could not blame them or find it surprising. She was a beautiful young woman, and at the moment her face was flushed and her eyes brilliant.

Then Neville Forsbrook, whose father, Pelham Forsbrook, Pitt had mentioned as a prominent banker, approached the group. Neville moved towards her now, smiling.

Seeing him, Angeles' face fell and she backed away sharply. It was an awkward movement, completely without grace.

One of the other young men laughed.

Angeles did not even look at him. Her eyes were fixed on Forsbrook. No one else in the room seemed to notice.

Forsbrook said something to Angeles and gave a slight bow. He was still smiling.

Angeles blushed hotly. She started to speak, but seemed unable to find the words she needed. She ended apparently saying something angry in Portuguese, and the other young women moved away uncomfortably.

The young men looked at each other and laughed again, although it was more a snigger than outright amusement.

Forsbrook took another step towards Angeles, this time with one hand forward as if he would touch her arm.

She snatched it away, and in stepping backwards lost her balance a little. Forsbrook lunged forward and grasped her, preventing her from falling. She gasped, and then cried out.

Forsbrook held her more firmly. It could have been because he feared she might fall.

Both other young men were highly amused. They looked at each other and guffawed with laughter.

Angeles tried to wrench her arm away from Forsbrook and he held on to her. She swung her other arm and slapped him across the face as hard as she could. One of the young men let out a cry of surprise and anger.

Forsbrook let go of her with a very slight push, so little that even Charlotte was not certain if it was hard enough to cause her fall. She staggered backwards, tripping on her skirt and collapsing into a couple of girls, who were giggling and oblivious of everyone else. The three of them clung together to avoid ending up on the floor, angry and now embarrassed.

'For God's sake, what's the matter with you?' Forsbrook shouted at Angeles, as she struggled to find her balance. His voice was sufficiently loud that at least a dozen people heard him and swung around to stare.

Angeles' face was scarlet. She looked desperate, turning from left to right to find some way of escape.

Charlotte stepped forward to intervene. At the same moment she saw Vespasia several yards away, her face filled with deep anxiety. She also was trying to make her way towards the open space where Angeles and Forsbrook now stood facing each other.

'Stop it!' Forsbrook was still raising his voice and he took another step closer to her, again reaching for her arm.

She staggered backwards, her face twisted as if in terror.

'Stop it!' he repeated. 'You're making yourself ridiculous!' He lunged forward to take her hand as a waiter with a tray of glasses passed within a yard of her.

She gasped and cried out. He jerked sideways and tried again. This time she crashed straight into the waiter and sent the glasses flying in all directions, splintering on the floor. The poor man tripped in his effort to regain his feet, and only made it worse. He ended up splayed across the floor, arms and legs wide, champagne and slivers of glass everywhere.

'What's the matter with you?' Forsbrook demanded furiously of Angeles. 'You're hysterical! Are you drunk?'

Angeles picked up a dish of cakes from the table nearest her and hurled it at him. It struck him in the chest, covering his dinner suit with jam and cream.

He swore, in language he surely could not have intended anyone to hear in a public place.

One of the other young men was laughing, high-pitched and out of control.

Forsbrook lunged forward and grasped Angeles by the arm, holding her hand. She screamed again and lashed out, kicking with all her strength, even turning her head and biting him on the hand so hard he cried out and slapped her. When she let go there was blood dripping scarlet from the flesh between his finger and thumb.

Now most of the room was standing staring, confused and alarmed. No one knew what to do.

Vespasia was helping the waiter to his feet.

Charlotte moved towards Angeles, calling her name.

Angeles seemed aware only of Forsbrook. She was swearing at him in Portuguese, her face twisted with something close to terror.

Charlotte turned her attention to Forsbrook, at least to try to stop him from moving any closer to Angeles, but he was too angry to see anyone else.

'You stupid girl!' he said, waving his hand around as if the pain were almost unbearable. 'You bite like a mad dog! What the hell's wrong with you?' He kept on moving towards her.

Charlotte caught his arm but all she held on to was cloth. He tore it out of her hand, perhaps unintentionally bumping her so she steadied herself and remained on her feet only with difficulty.

Angeles turned and ran, plunging through the knots of people, banging into tables and upsetting dishes, breaking things left and right. Twice she reached for plates of cakes or sweetmeats and threw them at Forsbrook. One sailed past him and struck one of the other young men, who was also shouting at her. The other caught Forsbrook on the side of the face and left a gash along his cheekbone. He lost the last remnants of his temper.

Angeles, terrified, ran straight towards the great window that over-looked the paved terrace two storeys below.

Forsbrook took a couple of strides, his face contorted with emotion, hands stretched out and grasping.

Angeles screamed, her words unintelligible, her body turning one way, then the other until, arms flailing, she crashed into the high, multi-paned window. It shattered, sending glass everywhere. One moment she was in front of it, all white silk and dark hair, the next there was only a jagged hole and wooden splinters on the floor.

For a terrible second everyone was silent. Then Isaura Castelbranco screamed: a high, thin sound of utter despair. Extraordinarily, she did not faint but remained standing stock-still, as if frozen.

Rafael Castelbranco appeared from nowhere and staggered towards the remains of the window, staring into the darkness beyond.

Forsbrook too was appalled. However, far from remaining still, he turned to those beside him, first one way then another, as if to find someone to say it had not been his fault.

In the next room someone was shouting. Footsteps sounded, running.

Charlotte moved towards Isaura, then realised there was nothing whatever she could do, and even to try would merely be intrusive. They barely knew each other.

Other people started to speak, to move aimlessly and then stop, then start again. There were shouts from outside on the terrace. Several women were gasping, one or two weeping openly. The hostess went towards Isaura, then also stopped, not knowing what to say or do.

Castelbranco turned slowly from the window and faced the room. His grief was palpable in the air, washing outward to touch everyone.

Isaura took a step, then another, floundering as if she were wading through deep water. She called something to him in Portuguese. If anyone else understood they did nothing.

Castelbranco replied abruptly, his voice hoarse. It was filled with anguish.

Charlotte remained rooted to the spot. Something terrible had happened and the two people shouting at each other were racked with pain beyond bearing, as if they had been naked, and there was nothing any one of the horrified onlookers could do to help. They were trapped as intruders, ashamed of it as though it had been indecent.

It was Vespasia who broke into the horror. Charlotte knew that she did not speak Portuguese, but the meaning of the words was irrelevant. The grief was showing itself as rage, a storm against life and against God. It was completely universal.

She walked over to Isaura and took her arm.

'Come with me,' she said firmly. 'There is nothing for you to do here.'

Isaura fought against her for only a moment; then, as if acknowledging some overwhelming defeat, she allowed herself to be led away.

No one went to Castelbranco. He stood physically as separated from them as he must have felt, the cool wind blowing in through the remnants of the window ruffling his hair, chilling him until he shook with it. The sound of men's voices drifted up from the terrace below, very quiet, edged with shock. It must be servants deciding what to do, whom to call. Perhaps their host was with them.

Charlotte was undecided. Would it be intrusive, even socially inappropriate for her to go over to Castelbranco? It seemed inhuman simply to stand here staring at him, even worse to look away as if distancing yourself from the tragedy, as if your own comfort could possibly matter at such a time.

Where on earth was Pitt? Surely word of what had happened would have reached everyone in the house? The noise of the window smashing, the cries . . .

Then she looked at the tall clock against the wall and realised it had been only minutes. In another room with the doors closed, away from the back of the house and the window, no one would have heard anything.

She should find Pitt immediately. She turned away from the crowd now huddled into little groups trying to gain comfort from each other, and walked towards the main doors. She was just outside on the gallery at the top of the stairs when Pitt reached it, coming up the steps two at a time. He looked pale, his eyes shadowed with horror. He crossed the few yards between them and stood in front of her. One look at her face was enough to make any questions unnecessary.

'How did it happen?' he asked quietly, so as not to be heard by the people standing below them, or going down the far stair, clinging onto the banister as though afraid of slipping.

'Ugly teasing,' she answered. 'A mixture of humour, as far as they were concerned, and cruelty. It all got out of hand, but they didn't stop.'

She found her voice choked and thick in her throat. She was losing control. 'It all happened so quickly.' She took a deep breath. 'I should have done something!' She was to blame. She had stood there watching. She was furious with herself for her stupidity.

He put his hand on her arm, holding on to her surprisingly hard. 'Charlotte, stop it. You couldn't know she was going to go through the window. That was what happened, wasn't it?'

'Yes, but I didn't even try,' she gasped. 'And I knew something was wrong.'

'And did you know what to do about it? In fact, do you know now?'

'No! But something . . .'

He slipped his arm around her and she relaxed a little against him. A wave of gratitude engulfed her that he was there, that in all the years his strength had never failed her.

'Thomas . . .' She did not know if she was going to sound foolish, or even if it mattered now that Angeles was dead. After that fall she had to be. Charlotte refused to picture it.

'What?' he asked. 'I can't just leave. I have to—'

'I know,' she cut across him. 'That wasn't what I was going to say.' She pulled away from him so she could met his eyes. He waited, frowning a little. Even as she said it she was uncertain. 'She wasn't just angry, Thomas, she was terrified. We saw her a day or two ago, Vespasia and I. She was frightened then.'

He frowned. 'Of what? Are you certain?'

'Yes, I am. Vespasia thinks – we both thought – that she had been assaulted.'

'Assaulted? Do you mean raped?' He was trying to keep the incredulity out of his voice but it was there in his eyes.

'Yes, I do. Why not? You don't have to be covered in blood and bruises.' She pictured in her mind Angeles' face in the marquee when the young man had spoken to her. It was not distaste that had made her back away in such an extreme manner, it had been fear, a reaction to something else. 'Yes, I do,' she repeated. 'I don't know – of course I don't – but something terrible happened to her before this.'

'I'm sorry,' he said very quietly. 'I wish it were not so. But does it matter now? Would it not be better for everyone, especially her parents, if we did not raise that question?'

'But if somebody did that to her, it's appalling!' she protested. 'It's one of the worst crimes you can commit against anyone!'

'Do you know it?'

'No! Of course I don't. But what does anyone know about a crime before you investigate?' Even as she said it she knew her words were hollow. It was a nightmare dancing at the edge of her mind. She did not know the shape, or even the reality of it. 'I . . .' she started, and then stopped again.

'I know.' He touched her cheek. 'You feel as if there ought to have been something you could do. We all feel that after a tragedy, especially one we saw happen.'

'Can we do anything to help now?' Charlotte asked.

'I doubt it, but I'll try. Perhaps you should find Aunt Vespasia? I won't be any longer than I have to. No doubt the police will come. A fatal accident has to be properly investigated.'

'I suppose so. Should I say anything, if they ask me?'

'Only exactly what you saw. And be careful! Only what you saw, not what you think it meant.' It was a warning, softly spoken but grave.

'I know!' She calmed herself deliberately. 'I know.'

All around her people were huddled together, many in silence. The police had been called and were speaking to them, making notes of what everyone said. Footmen moved among them almost silently, offering whatever refreshment might help, including quite a few stiff shots of brandy.

As Charlotte had expected, the police spoke to her, merely as being one of the many present in the room where it had happened. She was very careful in her answers, adding nothing to the facts.

'Is that all you saw?' a gaunt-faced older policeman asked her doubtfully. 'You seem much more . . .' he searched for the word, '. . . composed than the other ladies I've spoken to. Do you know something more about what happened?'

She met his eyes. 'No.' Was that a lie? 'My husband is head of Special Branch,' she explained. 'Perhaps I am just a little more careful of what I say. I want to tell you what I saw, not what I felt or might have imagined, knowing what happened after.'

'Special Branch?' His eyes opened wider. 'Is this—'

'We came socially,' she answered him. 'This happened without any warning. One moment it was a little banter, then within seconds it became ugly.'

He frowned. 'Ugly? What do you mean, Mrs Pitt? Were there threats? An assault of some kind? Or something which Miss Castelbranco might have interpreted as an assault?' He looked puzzled now.

'No, just hectoring, a little cruel. Miss Castelbranco was clearly upset, and Mr Forsbrook didn't let it go. Everyone else could see that it was no longer funny, but he seemed to . . .' She stopped, aware that finishing her train of thought was more than she wished to say.

'Yes?' he prompted her.

'I don't know.'

'Were you acquainted with Miss Castelbranco, Mrs Pitt?'

'Only sightly. If you are asking me if she confided anything to me, then she did not. I can tell you only what I saw.'

But when she met Vespasia later, just before they were permitted to leave, she was much more honest.

Vespasia was as immaculate as always, but she looked tired and pale, and she was clearly distressed.

'What should we say?' Charlotte asked her when they had a few moments alone in a small anteroom off the main hallway.

'I have been turning over all possibilities in my mind,' Vespasia answered slowly. 'I can think of no answer that satisfies me. We do not know the reason for what happened, we can only guess. The poor girl is not here to answer for herself. I think the bare truth, without interpretation, is all we can afford to say.'

Charlotte stared at her. 'She was terrified. If we say nothing then aren't we lying, by omission?'

'Terrified of what, or of whom?' Vespasia said very quietly.

'Of . . . of Neville Forsbrook,' Charlotte replied. 'Or of one of the other young men.'

'Or of something she believed she saw, or understood,' Vespasia went on. 'Or of something that had already happened, and she was afraid it might happen again.'

Charlotte felt helpless. She did not need Vespasia to point out the damage such an answer could do. Speculation would run wild. Neville Forsbrook was alive to defend himself, and his friends. He could say that Angeles was hysterical, that she had misunderstood a remark, perhaps her English was not so fluent as to grasp a joke, or a colloquialism. Or even that she had had rather too much champagne, or had quarrelled with someone else and was hysterical. All of those answers were reasonable, and could even be true. Charlotte did not believe any of them, but it was no more than instinct, fear, even the thought of her own daughter, not so much younger, lying asleep at home. Others would point that out, and perhaps they were right.

'Is there nothing we can do?' she asked aloud.

Vespasia's eyes were full of pain. 'Nothing that I know of,' she replied. 'If it were your child, what would you want strangers to do, apart from grieve with you, and make no speculation, no gossip whatever?'

'Nothing,' Charlotte agreed.

And even riding home silently with Pitt, she could not add anything to that.

When they alighted and went inside, even before going to her own room, she went up the stairs. As gently as she could, she opened Jemima's bedroom door and stared at her sleeping in the faint light that came through the imperfectly drawn curtains. Her face was completely untroubled. Her hair, so like Charlotte's own, was spread across the pillow, unravelled out of its braids. She could have been still a child, not on the verge of womanhood at all.

Charlotte found herself smiling, and the tears running down her cheeks.

Chapter Six

VESPASIA WAS deeply troubled by the terrible death of Angeles Castelbranco. She went over and over it in her mind, waking in the night and turning up the light in her elegant bedroom. She needed to see her familiar belongings around her and become rooted again in her own life with the beauty and the pleasures she was accustomed to. With it necessarily came also the deep, almost suppressed loneliness that underlay it all. At least she was physically safe from everything except illness and age. As the events at Dorchester Terrace a short while ago had reminded her so painfully, no one was free from those. Death need not be gentle, even in one's own home. There was no answer except courage, and faith in an ultimate goodness beyond the limited sight of the flesh.

That was little use now to Isaura Castelbranco; and Angeles, poor child, was beyond the reach of any of them.

But whoever had brought about her death, even indirectly – and Vespasia was certain that someone had – they need not be beyond the reach of justice, and maybe even more importantly, of being prevented from ever doing such a thing again.

She had heard of the death of Catherine Quixwood, and the speculation as to how she had brought it on herself, which in a sense was just as distressing. She knew that Victor Narraway had involved himself in the case and wondered if he really had any perception of the horror behind such a desperate act. She realised she was afraid to approach him concerning it because it would hurt her if he could not – or would not – grasp the pain.

That made the decision for her. If she feared it then it must be faced. Fear that you ran away from pursued you with a mounting darkness that eventually consumed you. Fear that you faced might injure all hope, but did not rob you of courage or your own identity.

She sent him a note arranging to meet him for luncheon in one of her favourite restaurants, and found him already waiting for her when she arrived. There were some tables in the open air, set well apart under the dappled shade of trees. They were set with white linen, and the ever-moving light caught the edges of cut-crystal glasses. The air smelled of earth and flowers, and the murmur of the river nearby made private conversation easy.

He greeted her with evident pleasure. For the first few minutes they considered the menu and made choices, as if nothing ugly or sordid ever thrust itself into the beauty of their world.

When they were served and the waiter had excused himself, Vespasia finally approached the subject that had caused her to arrange the meeting.

'How is the case going regarding the death of Catherine Quixwood?' She tried to make it sound as if her interest were out of concern rather than anxiety.

He did not answer immediately but studied her face, searching for the depth behind her words.

She felt foolish. She should have known that even with her years of experience in Society at saying one thing and meaning another, she could not delude him. He was not so very much younger than she, and he had been in Special Branch much of his life.

'I have a reason for asking,' she said, then realised she was offering an explanation that had not been asked for. She smiled. 'Am I transparent?'

His answering smile was quick. 'Yes, my dear, today you are. But have we ever spoken idly to each other, looking for something to say?'

She felt a faint warmth creep up her cheeks, but it was from pleasure, not discomfort. 'Perhaps I had better be frank from the beginning. It seemed a little clumsy at the luncheon table.'

His eyes were so dark as to be black with his back to the light. Now they widened slightly in surprise. 'Disturbing, perhaps, forthright always, but never clumsy. Is it my involvement you fear may be inappropriate? Or is it something to do with Catherine Quixwood herself? Did you know her?'

'No. So far as I am aware, I never met her,' she said with a strange touch of regret. 'And it had not occurred to me that you would behave other than as always. It is the subject of . . .' she found herself reluctant to use the word, and yet to circle around it was somehow an insult to the victims, as if making less of it. 'The subject of rape,' she said distinctly. They were not close enough to anyone else to be overheard. 'I am afraid that there may have been another incident, ending equally tragically, and I am uncertain what to do for the best.'

The concern in his face became profound. 'Tell me,' he said simply.

Quietly and without elaboration she recounted what had happened at the party during which Angeles Castelbranco had met her death. She was startled and even a little embarrassed that her throat ached with the effort to keep control of herself. She had not intended him to be aware of the depth of her feelings. It made her more vulnerable than she wished.

'There was nothing you could have done,' he said gently when she had finished.

The pity in his eyes, almost a tenderness, caught her with a raw edge, awakening other more complex emotions.

'I didn't try,' she said sharply.

'To do what?' he asked. 'From what you say it was all over in a few terrible moments. What could you have done?'

She took a deep breath and stared down at the tablecloth and the silver and crystal set out on it, still winking in the dappled light as a breath of wind stirred the leaves above them. 'I knew there was something wrong several days ago,' she answered. 'I should have done something then. I failed to see how grave it was. I dithered, as if there were time to spare.'

'Do you mean that you knew, or that you thought there might be?' he said.

'Stop making excuses, Victor. It doesn't help.'

'What is it you want me to say?' he asked reasonably.

She felt a completely uncharacteristic flare of temper. She wanted to lash out at him for being patronising and completely missing the point, and she knew that was unfair. She sipped her wine and set the glass down again.

'I think that Angeles might have been assaulted, possibly raped, and that is why she reacted to young Forsbrook so violently. She was terrified, of that I am quite certain. What I do not know is what to do about it now.'

'Is Pitt aware of it?' he enquired.

'I imagine so; most certainly Charlotte is. But it is not a police matter, let alone one for Special Branch. I very much doubt that the Castelbrancos will report it to anyone. They are foreigners here, in many senses alone in a strange country that has most appallingly betrayed their trust.'

'Vespasia—' he began.

'I know,' she said quickly. 'It is not my right to interfere, and if I do so I will assuredly make it worse. But regardless of what the law may think, it is a monstrous wrong, and if there is something I can do, then I must. I am not involved with the police, or law, or government. There are avenues I can explore that they cannot. And I have no other demands on my time.'

'It could be dangerous,' he began urgently, his face creased with anxiety. 'Pelham Forsbrook is a very powerful man, and you have no proof whatever that it was anything other than a simple tragedy. You . . .'

She fixed him with a withering look.

He stopped speaking and smiled, but he did not lower his gaze.

She realised with surprise that the look with which she could freeze almost anyone else was having no effect upon him, but she did not avert her gaze either.

'What is it you wish of me?' he asked. 'Other than discretion, which you have.'

'I want to know what the law does about rape, where they are tragically certain of it. What this policeman is doing to find out who raped Catherine Quixwood,' she replied.

She saw the shadow in his face immediately, as if the reminder of it had touched a wound already painful.

'It seems that whoever attacked her was someone she knew, and she let him in without fear,' he said simply. 'The rape was violent and brutal, but in itself it didn't kill her. She managed to drag herself to the cabinet and pour herself a glass of Madeira, which was heavily laced with laudanum. It seems a strange place to have laudanum, but apparently she did. She liked it with the wine perhaps because it masked the taste, or possibly even the idea that she was drinking alcohol. I don't know.'

She was stunned. It was an answer she had not expected at all. Then the ugly aftermath crowded in on her and she felt crushed by its inevitability. Catherine herself would be blamed for it. Drinking the laudanum would be interpreted as an act of shame, an admission of some kind of guilt. The fact that she had opened the door to her attacker would be read as an invitation to intimacy, not her innocent trust in the man.

Narraway was watching her. She saw the pain and confusion in his eyes and wondered how much he understood of what people would say, and what the additional burden would be for Quixwood: all the searing confusion and anger, the awareness of his own life violated also.

'I see,' she said in little more than a whisper.

'I don't,' he answered. 'Not really. I can't shake it from my mind. To realise that another human being has experienced such horror and pain stays with me, as if a part of myself had been touched unforgettably.'

She looked at him with surprise and then an unexpected warmth for a sensitivity in him she had never perceived before. She wanted to reach out and touch his hand, but it was too intimate a gesture and she did not make it.

'Tell me about her,' she asked instead. 'Have you learned anything that might be of use in discovering who her assailant was? In whatever way she knew him, it still cannot be excused.'

The waiter came and removed their dishes, replacing them with another course.

At the table next to them a couple were talking, heads bent close together. He laughed and moved his hand across the white cloth to touch hers. It was a possessive gesture. She pulled away from him, her face colouring.

Vespasia noticed it but looked away. She could remember being so young, so uncertain. It seemed very long ago.

Narraway began slowly, feeling his way. 'Knox seems to be a competent man and I think he understands the crime better than many. He moves very carefully. To begin with I wished he had been quicker. Now I begin to appreciate how very complicated it is.'

'And Quixwood?' she said gently. 'He must be torn apart.'

'Yes. And I fear that if we find who did it, it will be even harder for him when it comes to trial. It will be as if it all happened again, this time in public. Strangers will be discussing the intimacy and the horror of it, pulling apart the details and speculating as to what happened. Even if it is done with compassion that will hardly make it any easier.'

'No, it won't,' she said simply. 'Perhaps that is why the people who do such things are not afraid. They know that most of us will do nothing about it. We would rather suffer in silence, even lie to protect them, before living it all over again in front of everyone else. Except that she is dead, and can do nothing for herself now.' She saw him flinch. 'I'm sorry.'

'You are right.' He shook his head fractionally. 'I have looked at least to a deeper side of her life. She seems to have been intelligent, sensitive, full of imagination and interested in every kind of beauty, discovery or invention that one can explore. And lonely. She had nothing to do that mattered—' He stopped abruptly, a shadow of self-knowledge in his face. Then he went on quickly. 'There's a young man called Alban Hythe whom Mrs Quixwood seems to have met much more frequently than would be accidental.'

'An affair?' she asked.

'I don't know. It seems a strong possibility.'

'How very sad.' For several moments Vespasia said nothing, picturing in her mind the arrival of a lover, the expected excitement, the emotion, the vulnerability, and then the sudden shock of violence. Had there even been a quarrel? What could possibly have happened that made the mood change from love to uncontrollable fury in a matter of minutes? How well do any of us really know the people we think we do?

Narraway waited, watching her. She could not read his expression. 'Do you think it was this man?' she asked him.

'Reason says it is likely,' he replied. 'Instinct says not. But that may be only what I want to think. I want to think she didn't mean to take her own life, she just . . . misjudged the dose. But the police surgeon said it was many times the appropriate amount.'

'She might have meant to, Victor,' Vespasia said gently. Surely to be less than honest would be patronising? 'I have no idea how I would feel were such a thing to happen to me. I don't think it is something I have power to imagine. People can be very cruel when they are frightened. It brings out the worst in many of us – cruelty we would not have been capable of ordinarily.'

He frowned. 'Women? Surely—'

'Of course women,' she said quickly. 'We have more excuse to be frightened than anyone. We have everything to lose.' Her voice wavered, harsh with emotion. 'We can find that we are blamed for being victims, not only by the men we love and who no longer find us desirable, and because they cannot look at us without remembering what happened, but even by other women also.'

She saw the confusion in his face, the disbelief. 'It isn't so very difficult to understand,' she said urgently, leaning forward over the elegant table. 'If somehow rape is the victim's own fault – they said or did something, wore indiscreet clothes, behaved in a certain way – then if we do not do whatever it is, it will never happen to us. It's not compassionate, it's not realistic, but it is understandable.'

Anger burned up in Narraway's eyes. 'It sounds monstrous to me, callous and brutal. It is almost like consenting to it, by omission of defence. It is contemptible, the final betrayal.'

'It is because admitting that it can happen to decent and completely innocent women is to accept that it could happen to themselves,' she pointed out. 'That is unbearable. It tears away the last defence. And of course some even hate the woman for creating an uncontrollable passion they have never woken themselves. They don't understand that it is a crime of hatred, or of power, not of passion.' She had a sudden afterthought. 'Or perhaps they do, and it is wakening that animal inside the man which they hate her for. They want to pretend it does not exist any more.'

'Are we so fragile?' he said unhappily.

'Some of us, yes.' She thought for a moment. 'And of course they might also be afraid for the men who love them – the rage in them, the need for revenge – even if only to prove themselves in control after all,' she added. 'It might lead them not to comfort the victim, hold her in their arms and assure her that she is still the same, still loved, but instead to go out and beat, or even kill, the man who has taken from her so much. And in their blindness of pain they might not even choose the right man.'

'I begin to see why Angeles Castelbranco told no one, if you are right and she was raped,' he said very quietly. 'And why Catherine Quixwood, in the despair of that moment, chose to take her own life rather than go through the ordeal of what would inevitably follow.'

'What are the chances of a successful prosecution anyway?' Vespasia searched his face now, looking for an answer. 'Even if Knox finds the right man, will the verdict be worth the price it will cost?'

'I don't know,' Narraway admitted. 'But what happens to the law itself if we don't try?'

'What does Quixwood want?' she asked instead of answering.

Narraway spoke slowly. 'At the moment he wants to know the truth, but he may well find that he would rather not, if it turns out that Catherine was having an affair with Alban Hythe. I don't know. Justice, perhaps, or revenge. Or to do whatever is possible to clear Catherine's name and show that she was innocent. Perhaps all he really wants is to be doing something rather than nothing. To feel that he is fighting the reality and not simply submitting to it. I can understand that . . . I think.'

'That is very honest,' she observed.

'Are we not past pretending?' he asked. 'I can return to it, if you wish, but I would rather not. I would like to have someone with whom I do not have to. I have lived with secrets for as long as I can remember. Some were worth keeping, probably most were not. Being too careful has become a habit.'

'Not a bad one,' she responded, smiling again. 'Most of us tell others far too much, and then are embarrassed next time we meet them, trying to remember exactly how much we said and then replaying it over and over to convince ourselves it was less indiscreet, less revealing than it seemed.'

'I cannot imagine you being indiscreet,' he remarked.

'Don't be polite,' she said a little tartly. 'You don't know me as well as you might think. Certainly, at times, I have been at the very least duplicitous.'

'I'm greatly relieved,' he said fervently. 'A few imperfections and the occasional vulnerability are very attractive in a woman. It allows a man to imagine he is, now and again, just a fraction superior. In your case, of course, he is not, but it is a necessary illusion, if we are to be comfortable.'

'I should like you to be comfortable,' she said, hiding a smile and turning to the waiter, who was enquiring as to their choice for the final course. She was not even certain if she saw a faint colour in his cheeks, or not.

Vespasia had made up her mind what she would do regarding Angeles Castelbranco. To begin with she must acquire as much information as possible. The longer any secret was kept the less likely was any recollection to be accurate. If Angeles had indeed been raped, then it must have been very recently. It should not be difficult to find out which functions she had attended in the last month. There were a considerable number of them, but they involved largely the same people. Diplomatic circles were not large, and occasions suitable for a girl of sixteen were limited.

A little invention, a great deal of tact, and half a dozen enquiries of friends produced a list of such parties over the previous four or five weeks.

It required all of the following day, and more evasion than was comfortable, before Vespasia had a rough draft of the guest lists. It would have been simpler to have asked Isaura Castelbranco which ones Angeles had attended. However, for that she would have had to give a reason, and there was none that would not be painful, or for which she could in any way account as her concern. She could not even imagine how the woman felt. Vespasia's own family had caused her many emotions over the years, some of them pleasant, many one kind of anxiety or distress, or another. To love was to be vulnerable, especially regarding children. One feared for their safety, their happiness, their good health. One felt guilty for their unhappiness or their failures. One was mithered by their dependence, and terrified by their courage. One forgot one's own mistakes, risks, high and absurd dreams and wanted only to protect them from hurt.

Then they grew up, married and too often became almost strangers. They could not imagine that you were also afraid, fallible, could dream and still fall in love.

Perhaps that was as well. One needed privacy, above all from one's own family.

So she wrote and rewrote guest lists, and asked questions in round-about ways. Two days after lunching with Victor Narraway, she had found what she believed was the event at which Angeles had been raped. Obtaining details was more difficult. She pondered for some time whom she could ask to give her an account of the evening, who was willing and observant enough. More than that, what reason could she offer for making such a request?

And who would be discreet enough afterwards to keep their own counsel and not mention it to anyone at all? How could she even suggest to whoever it was that the matter must remain confidential? To most people, the very secrecy of it would be a spur to gossip, at least to one's closest friends, and then of course to their closest, and so on. Each retelling would grow and mutate in the exercise.

She studied more closely the list of those who had been present at that event. There seemed to have been a considerable number of young people. It was in observing how many that the answer came to her.

It was far easier making such enquiries face to face than on a telephone. Accordingly she arranged to have luncheon with Lady Tattersall. The following day they sat pleasantly gossiping over a dessert apple flan, and far more cream than was good for either of them. Vespasia introduced the name of a fictitious sociable friend.

'She heard it was a great success, and would have to make her own party equally delightful,' Vespasia approached the subject at last. 'She does not know anyone who was there and whom she might approach, so I promised her I would ask you.'

'Of course,' Lady Tattersall said agreeably. 'What would she like to know?'

Vespasia smiled. 'I think a simple account of how it went would be excellent, perhaps, with a little detail, particularly as to how the younger guests responded to the evening. That would serve very well, and be most kind of you.'

Lady Tattersall was delighted to recount everything she could remember. Vespasia had been careful enough to make her fictitious friend live quite out of the way, in Northumberland, so the absence of such a party ever taking place would not be noticed. She learned a great deal: a vivid first-hand account of a large but outwardly successful event. The only person less than happy had been Angeles Castelbranco, but her distress had been put down to her youth, and her foreign blood.

Vespasia left, certain in her own mind that Neville Forsbrook had raped Angeles there, exactly as she and Charlotte had feared. Now the question was what to do with that knowledge, beside informing Thomas Pitt.

In the late morning of the day after her luncheon with Lady Tattersall Vespasia was taken very much by surprise when her maid announced that Mr Rawdon Quixwood had called and asked if he might take a few moments of her time. He had a matter of some importance he wished to discuss with her.

She gave the maid permission to ask him in. A moment later he was standing in her quiet sitting room with its view onto the garden. It was in full summer bloom, hot colours of roses and, in the background, the cool blue spires of delphinium.

Quixwood was a stark contrast to the gaudy profusion of the background beyond the windows. He was smartly dressed, but in black, relieved only by the white of his shirt. His thick hair was combed and his shave immaculate, yet his face was that of a man haunted by grief. His skin was pale and the lines around his mouth furrowed deep.

Vespasia struggled to think of anything to say that would not be banal. What could one say to a man who had suffered so appallingly?

'Good morning, Mr Quixwood,' she began. 'May I offer you tea, or – if you would prefer it – something more?'

'That is kind of you, Lady Vespasia, but I shall return to my club for luncheon. I am presently living there. I . . . I cannot yet face returning to my home.'

'I can imagine not,' she agreed quickly. 'I would not find it hard to understand if you never did. I am sure there are other properties that would be equally agreeable, and convenient for you.'

He smiled very slightly. 'You are quite right. Forgive me for intruding on you without warning. If the matter were not of some urgency and moral importance, I would not do so.'

She indicated the chair opposite her and, as he sat down, she resumed her own seat. 'What can I do for you, Mr Quixwood?' she invited.

He looked down, smiling very slightly in a wry expression of amusement and pain.

'I have heard from a friend of mine that you have been making certain enquiries about Pelham Forsbrook's son, Neville, after the tragedy where young Angles Castelbranco met her death.' He winced. 'It is . . . it is a painful reminder of my own wife's death.' His voice was husky and he clearly found mastery of his emotions almost impossible.

Vespasia tried to think of something to ease his awkwardness, but she had no idea what he meant to say, so nothing appropriate came to her mind.

He looked up at her. 'I don't know how to say this graciously.' He bit his lip. 'I know that young Neville behaved in a manner that can only be described as crass when he teased the poor girl. If something . . . terrible had happened to her earlier that made her so desperately vulnerable, he did not know of it. If he were my son, I hope I would have raised him to be more sensitive, more aware of the feelings of others, no matter how much wine he might have taken. His behaviour was disgusting. There can be no argument on that. I imagine he will regret his cruelty for the rest of his life.'

His eyes searched her face. 'But I know that he did not assault her, seriously or even trivially, at Mrs Westerley's party. I was there myself, when young Angeles appeared looking a trifle dishevelled, and her face tear-stained. I assumed at the time that she had had some youthful quarrel, perhaps even an unexpected rejection. I'm afraid I thought no more of it than that, and possibly I was horribly wrong.' Now his face was filled with distress. 'Since I . . . since . . .' He faltered to a stop.

Vespasia was overwhelmed with pity for him. He must feel doubly guilty, for not being able to protect his wife, and now for having failed to see Angeles' terrible distress, masked by her own need to hide it, and his assumption that youthful tears came and went easily.

She leaned forward a fraction. 'Mr Quixwood,' she said very gently, 'no sane person would have assumed otherwise in the circumstances. Of course girls her age both laugh and cry over things they barely remember the day after. There was nothing you could, or should, have done.' She hesitated, and then continued, 'It is natural when there has been a tragedy that we relive the time before, wondering how we could have averted it. In most cases there was nothing at all to have been done, but we torture ourselves anyway. We want to have helped. Above all we want to undo the past and relive it with greater wisdom, more kindness, but as the pain settles, we know we cannot. Only the future can be changed.' She wanted to comfort him regarding Catherine, but there was no comfort to give. To try would simply make it clear that she had no grasp of the reality, and perhaps not even the courage to acknowledge it.

His smile was now rueful. 'I am beginning to realise that, Lady Vespasia, but slowly, and I am some distance from acceptance. What I came to say, which matters, and why I took the liberty of disturbing you, was that whatever happened to Angeles Castelbranco, I know it was not Neville Forsbrook who caused it. I was with him when she left the company and went to look at the paintings in the gallery. It was not Neville she went with, although I admit I don't know who it was. Perhaps our names are still difficult for her. I admit some Portuguese names escape me.'

Vespasia drew in her breath to ask him if he was certain, then realised it would be pointless, and a trifle insulting. Of course he was certain. He had come out of his grief and his cocoon of protection to say so.

'Thank you, Mr Quixwood,' she said gravely. 'It would be monstrous to blame the wrong person, even for a day. Whispers are not easily silenced. You have told me this before I had the chance to speak to anyone, and perhaps have saved me from a profound error. I am grateful to you.'

He rose to his feet, moving with stiffness, as if he hurt inwardly.

'Thank you for seeing me, Lady Vespasia. Thank you for your wisdom. In time it will be of comfort.' He bowed, just a gesture of the head, and went to the door.

She sat for several minutes afterwards without moving, thinking, in the silent, sunlit room, how desperately fragile the illusion of safety could be.

Chapter Seven

PITT FOUND it extremely difficult to forget the tragedy of Angeles Castelbranco's death. Every time he heard the clink of glass or the sound of someone's laughter, it took him back to the party where the tragedy had happened. In his mind he saw the ambassador's face, all expression wiped from it, as if he were dead.

Worse was the raging grief of his wife, who made him think of Charlotte, although she looked nothing like Charlotte at all. Yet both were mothers, and that gave them a similarity that was greater than all differences of appearance could be.

He sat in his office in Lisson Grove, which used to be Narraway's. He was trying to concentrate on the papers in front of him to the exclusion of every other thought, and he was not succeeding. He was relieved when there was a knock on the door. The moment after, Stoker looked in.

'Yes?' Pitt said hopefully.

There was no pleasure in Stoker's bony face. 'The Portuguese Ambassador would like to see you, sir. I told him you were busy, but he said he'd wait, however long it took. Sorry, sir.'

Pitt pushed his papers into a rough pile, turning the top one face down. 'Putting it off won't make it any better. Ask him to come in,' he requested.

'Do you want me to interrupt in fifteen or twenty minutes?' Stoker asked.

Pitt gave him a bleak smile. 'Not unless it's genuine, and please heaven it isn't. The regular threats of violence and sedition are enough for the moment, we don't need more.'

Stoker nodded and withdrew. Two minutes later the door opened again and Rafael Castelbranco came in. He looked ill, and ten years older than he had a few days ago. His cheeks were sunken; there was no colour in his skin, as if the flesh beneath it were lifeless. His clothes were neat, even elegant, but now they seemed a mockery of other times, like a joke at a funeral.

Pitt rose to his feet and came around the desk to offer his hand.

Castelbranco gripped it as if that in itself were some promise of help.

At Pitt's invitation they sat in the two armchairs between the fireplace and the window. Castelbranco declined any refreshment with a small gesture of his hand. He had fine hands, brown-skinned, and slender.

'What can I do for you, sir?' Pitt asked. There was no point in enquiring after his health, or that of his wife. The man was shattered by grief, and she could only be the same.

Castelbranco cleared his throat. 'I know you have children,' he began. 'Mrs Pitt has been most kind to my wife, both before my daughter's death, and since. You may, perhaps, imagine how we feel, but no one could know . . . could even think of . . .' He stopped himself, took several deep breaths, and continued in a more controlled tone. 'I wish you to help me find out as much as I can about what happened to my daughter, and why.' He saw Pitt's expression. 'I am not looking for justice, Mr Pitt. I realise it may be beyond anyone's reach.' He closed his eyes a moment; whether to regain control of his voice or to hide his thoughts it was impossible to tell.

Pitt did not interrupt. He could think of nothing to say that would not imply a certain impatience, at the very least a lack of understanding.

Castelbranco opened his eyes again. 'I wish to silence the rumours, not only for my own sake, and in justice to my daughter, but for my wife. Until we know what happened we cannot refute even the ugliest whispers. We are helpless. It is a . . .' Again he stopped. None of his diplomatic skills or experience came to his aid. He could have been a clerk or a tradesman; his grief was universal.

This matter was not within the area of Special Branch's duties, except that Castelbranco was the ambassador of a foreign country with whom Britain had a long and valued relationship, and that the death had taken place in Britain. Certainly it was outside the purview of the local British police, or indeed anybody else of authority.

But apart from that, simply as a human being with a daughter of a similar age, Pitt felt a sharp, very personal understanding of his grief.

'I'll do what I can,' he promised, wondering as he said the words if he was being rash and would regret it. 'But I must be discreet, or I may risk making the rumour worse rather than better.' Did that sound like an excuse? It was not. Enquiring into a rumour, or even denying it too vehemently, could result in spreading it further. In order to deny it one had to repeat it, therein keeping it alive and spreading it further.

'I understand the risks,' Castelbranco said grimly, 'but this is intolerable. What have I left to lose?' His voice trembled in spite of himself. 'Angeles was betrothed to marry Tiago de Freitas, a young man of excellent family, with a bright future ahead of him, and an unspotted reputation. It was in all ways an excellent match.' His hands tightened, even though they were resting in his lap. 'Now people are suggesting that he discovered something about Angeles that was so shameful he could not live with it, and he broke the engagement.'

Pitt felt a wave of fury break over him, then of terrible pity for the man in front of him. His body was so tense every muscle in him must ache, and yet how could he possibly rest? Did he sleep at all? Or perhaps in nightmare he saw his daughter crash through the glass into the night, again and again, and he watched, helpless to save her?

Or was it even worse than that? Did he see her laughing, young and excited at all that lay ahead of her? Did he feel her hand in his, small and soft like a child's, and then waken and remember that she was dead, broken outside by glass and stone, inside by terror and humiliation? Then he would get up and face the day, trying to live, to put one foot in front of the other, do his job, comfort his wife and find some kind of meaning.

'Exactly what has this young man said?' Pitt asked.

'That it was Angeles who ended the betrothal,' Castelbranco replied.

'But he has not denied the rumour. He smiles sadly, and says nothing.' His voice shook with anger and the colour washed up his face. The knuckles were white on his hands. 'Sometimes a silence can speak more than words.'

Pitt searched for something to say that would draw the poison of what was being whispered, and failed to find anything. He could understand Castelbranco's anger and his helplessness. In his place, Pitt had no doubt he would want to strike out at de Freitas, verbally, physically, anything to let loose some of the agony inside himself.

'I'll speak to him,' he promised. 'See if he knows anything of fact, and if he does I'll follow it up. If not, I'll warn him of the dangers of careless speculation at the expense of someone else's reputation. I don't know what result that will have. Is his business in Britain?'

For a moment Castelbranco's eyes softened. 'At least some of it. Your words may have an effect on him. Thank you. There is no one else to defend my daughter. It makes me wonder if de Freitas was as good a choice to marry Angeles as we thought. How do you know the measure of a person, before the event that betrays them, and then it is too late?'

'Half my job would be unnecessary if I knew that,' Pitt replied. 'If we had that ability then no man, no country would ever trust unwisely.'

Catelbranco rose to his feet. 'Perhaps it was a foolish question. I thought I knew him. I concentrate on the lesser pain of disillusion, to take my mind off the greater one of loss, imagining it will ease my grief. I apologise.'

'I would do the same,' Pitt acknowledged, rising also and holding out his hand. 'I will inform you as soon as I have anything to say.'

Tiago de Freitas received Pitt reluctantly. Pitt was sure he did it at all only because he could not refuse, considering Pitt's office and the power it gave him. They met in a side office in de Freitas' father's highly prosperous wine import and export offices just off Regent Street. The rooms were sombre, but in their own way luxurious. There was a lot of exquisite wood, much of it carved. There was embossed leather in the furniture and beneath the feet rich carpets that silenced movement.

De Freitas was a handsome enough young man with fine dark eyes and a magnificent head of black hair. He would have been more striking still had he been a few inches taller. Now he regarded Pitt somewhat cautiously.

'What can I do for you, sir?' He did not invite Pitt to be seated, as if the conversation might last any time.

Pitt was pleased. There was a certain informality to sitting, and he wanted the interview to be courteous, but not easy.

'First of all, Mr de Freitas, I am extremely sorry for the tragic death of your fiancée, and I regret having to disturb you at such a time. I will try to be as brief as I can,' he replied.

De Freitas stiffened almost imperceptibly, with just a movement of the muscles in his neck.

'Thank you,' he acknowledged it. 'But I am sure you did not come here to express your condolences. Your card says that you are commander of Special Branch, which I am aware is a part of the Intelligence Service of this country. I will do all I can to assist you, as a guest here, but I am Portuguese, and I'm sure you understand the interests of my own country must come first.'

Pitt was about to deny that his business was anything to do with national interest, then he realised that would rob him of the power he needed.

'I would not ask it of you, sir,' he replied smoothly. 'You spoke just now of Miss Castelbranco as if she were still betrothed to you. I was informed that the engagement had been broken. Was that incorrect?'

De Freitas' black eyebrows rose. His voice was not openly defensive, but it was guarded. 'How can that concern you, Mr Pitt?'

Pitt answered with a slight smile. 'It has to do with another matter I cannot discuss. Is it in some way a secret? If it is so, then I am obliged to suppose that rumours I heard may be correct. I am hoping they are not, and that for the sake of the pleasant relations that have existed between Britain and Portugal for half a millennium, I can lay them at rest.' He let the invitation hang in the air for de Freitas to pick up, or make himself conspicuous by avoiding.

De Freitas hesitated, caught in uncertainty. A very slight flush of annoyance coloured his cheeks.

'I had preferred not to speak of it, for the sake of her family, but you force my hand.' He gave a very slight shrug, not perhaps as discreetly as he had intended. 'The engagement was ended.'

'How long before her death did that happen, Mr de Freitas?'

He looked startled. 'I really don't see how this can be of concern to the British Secret Service.' There was a touch of anger in his voice now. 'It is a very personal matter.'

'The announcement of a betrothal to marry is a very public event,' Pitt pointed out. 'It is not possible to end the betrothal secretly, however personal the cause of it may be.'

De Freitas hovered between anger and capitulation. Seconds passed as he fought with a decision.

'I am trying to quell rumours that can only hurt the Portuguese Ambassador to Britain, Mr de Freitas,' Pitt pressed. 'It is a small courtesy we can accord him at the time of a very dreadful loss. Miss Castelbranco was his only child, as I am sure you are already aware.'

De Freitas nodded. 'Yes, yes, of course.' He let out a very slight sigh. 'We broke our engagement a couple of days before she died. I'm sorry about it, of course I am.'

Pitt noticed how gracefully de Freitas had evaded the issue of who had made the initial move to end the relationship. He had made it sound like an inevitable mutual agreement.

'Was Miss Castelbranco extremely upset?' he asked, determined to force the young man into an answer.

De Freitas looked up sharply, his face reflecting a sudden anger. 'If you are suggesting that her death was . . . was a result of my breaking off an engagement, then you are completely mistaken.' He lifted his chin a little. 'It was she who ended it.'

'Indeed? What reason did she give? One does not do such a thing lightly. Her parents would have been most distressed. As I imagine yours were also.'

De Freitas did not answer for several moments, then he gave a brief, tight smile. 'You have me at something of a disadvantage, Mr Pitt. I had hoped to give you a vague answer, and that you would have been gentleman enough to accept it. I'm afraid I cannot say anything further without dishonouring a young woman I had thought to make my wife.

Of course I understand you wish to protect her reputation, and give her family whatever comfort is possible, and I respect you for it. Indeed, I admire it. However, to assist you in that I must decline to say anything further. I'm sorry.'

'It was you who broke the engagement,' Pitt concluded.

De Freitas shrugged. 'I've told you, sir. I can say nothing further. Let her rest in peace . . . for everyone's sake.'

Pitt knew he would get no more from him, and he thanked him for his time. Excusing himself, he walked back through the hushed, wood-lined corridors as if he were leaving some kind of church.

'You mean he implied it was he who broke it off, and that he was lying to protect her?' Charlotte said incredulously that evening when Pitt was at home and dinner was finished and cleared away. They were in the parlour, with the windows ajar. The slight breeze carried on the rustle of leaves and the smell of earth and cut grass. The door to the passageway was closed. Daniel and Jemima were in their respective bedrooms reading or doing homework.

'More or less,' Pitt conceded. He was not sitting. He felt too restless to settle to such comfort, perhaps because Charlotte was so angry she also could not sit.

Charlotte looked stricken. 'So whatever it is they are saying he either believes it, or else he doesn't care, he wanted to be rid of her anyway?' she accused.

'The engagement was broken off before she died,' Pitt pointed out, shaking his head.

'Exactly!' she retorted. 'He listened and believed it, and so he abandoned her!' Her face was flushed and her eyes brilliant. She was so quick to defend the vulnerable. He loved her for it and he would not have changed her, even if it would have been far wiser to weigh the matter first. She had been wrong before, dangerously so, but that did not stop her now.

'I know what you're thinking,' she accused him. 'Of course I might be wrong. Would you weigh it this carefully if it were Jemima?'

'It isn't Jemima,' he said reasonably.

'It isn't this time! What about when it is?' she demanded.

He took a deep breath and turned to face her. 'I shall probably be just as furious as you are, just as hurt and just as impetuous,' he admitted. 'And it would also probably do no good at all. Loving someone makes you care passionately. It makes you a decent person, warm, vulnerable, generous and brave. It doesn't make you right, and it certainly doesn't make you effective in finding the truth.'

'I think she was raped,' she said quietly, tears suddenly bright in her eyes. 'The truth isn't going to help.'

'No one can blame her for that,' he responded reasonably.

'Oh, Thomas! Don't be so . . . blind!' she said desperately. 'It doesn't have anything to do with reason. Of course they can blame her. They have to! If they say it can happen to innocent people, then it can happen to anyone, to them or their daughters. It's like a disease. You don't go anywhere near it, in case it's contagious and the next thing you know, you have it too.'

She shook her head, the muscles in her neck and shoulders tight. 'Or else you're the kind of person who has to stand and stare at it, probe to see where it hurts the most, and make yourself important by knowing something other people don't.' Her voice was brittle with contempt. 'Then you can be the centre of attention while you tell everyone else, making up any details you might not happen to know.'

He took a step towards her, touching her lightly. Her arms were rigid under his fingers. The wind outside rattled harder in the trees and blew in through the door with the first patter of rain and the sweet, rich smell of damp earth.

'Aren't you being a little hard on them?' he asked.

'You mean I'm exaggerating?' Her eyes widened. 'Being a bit hysterical, perhaps? Because I'm afraid that one day it could be Jemima? If she was really innocent, then it could be, couldn't it?'

'No,' he said firmly. 'Rape is very rare, thank God, and Jemima will not be allowed to keep the company of any young man we don't know, or whose family we don't know.'

'For the love of heaven, Thomas!' Charlotte said between her teeth. 'How on earth would you know how many rapes there are? Who is going to talk about it? Who's going to report it to the police? Do you think it happens only to girls no one cares about? Or to loose women who invite it by behaving like tarts? Or for that matter, that it's never young men we know who could do such things?'

Pill felt a sudden icy twinge of fear, and then helplessness. His imagination raced.

She saw it in his eyes, and bent her head forwards to rest her brow against his neck. The wind through the open door ruffled her skirt and then it swung wider, banging against the wall.

'No I haven't!' she said emphatically. 'And so far as I know, neither has Emily. But it's a hidden crime, and I haven't the faintest idea what we can do about it. Except bite the heads off anyone who speaks lightly or viciously about Angeles Castelbranco. And don't tell me I shouldn't do that. I don't care if it's appropriate or suitable, or even if it's true. I care about protecting her mother, and in time, my own daughter.'

He slid his arms around her and held her very tightly. He was trying to think of something to say that would comfort, and still be true, and he could not think of anything at all.

Pitt could not devote his own time to making discreet enquiries into the character and reputation of Angeles Castelbranco, and to send anyone else might raise more speculation than it would answer. Why would any man unrelated to her be asking such things unless there were cause to suspect her virtue? It would inevitably appear that it was done not to protect Angeles, but to shield whoever might be accused by her distraught parents, who were unable to face the truth of their daughter's moral collapse and sought to find someone else to blame.

He was still weighing the various possibilities open to him, and discarding them one by one, when two days later Castelbranco came into his office again, his face even more haggard than before. He seemed barely able to stand and he gripped his hands together when he sat in the chair Pitt offered him, as though to keep them from trembling. Twice he began to speak and then stopped.

'I visited de Freitas,' Pitt told him quietly. 'He equivocated. First he said that it was Angeles who broke off the engagement, then he admitted that it was he. I have been considering how to prove it without raising even further malicious speculation.'

'It is too late,' Castelbranco said, shaking his head. 'I don't know what happened or who is behind it. I cannot think who would say such things, or why they would. I fear it is some enemy I have made who is taking the cruellest possible revenge on me.'

'If that is so, there may be something we can do,' Pitt began, then realised he might be offering a false hope. 'What makes you think this?'

'Someone has said that her death was not a terrible accident but a deliberate act of suicide,' Castelbranco had difficulty keeping his voice from choking. 'And suicide is a mortal sin,' he whispered. 'The Church will not bury her with Christian rites . . . my . . . my child is . . .' The tears slid down his cheeks and he lowered his head.

Pitt leaned forward and put his hand on Castelbranco's wrist, gripping him hard. 'Don't give up,' he said firmly. 'That decision is hasty and may be born of serious misinformation.' He tried to keep the contempt out of his voice for men who would make such a cruel decision – childless men without pity or understanding – and he knew he failed. He had not wanted to add that grief to Castelbranco's all but unbearable burden. Now, above all things, he needed his faith. It was all that was left him.

'Perhaps this should be the subject of a proper enquiry after all,' he said more gently. 'If such a thing is being said, then the discretion I have tried to exercise may be pointless.'

'It is,' Castelbranco said hoarsely. The tears were now running down his cheeks. He was too harrowed to be self-conscious. 'It has been suggested that she was with child, and the disgrace of it drove her to take both their lives. That is a double crime, self-murder, and murder of her innocent babe. I don't know how my wife can live with it. She is dying inside too.'

His eyes searched Pitt's face as if to find some hope he could not even imagine. He was teetering on the edge of an abyss of despair. 'I need the truth,' he whispered. 'Whatever it is, it cannot be worse than this. I loved my daughter, Mr Pitt. She was my only child, more than I ever cared about myself. I would have done anything to make her safe and happy . . . and I could not even keep her alive. Now I cannot save her reputation from the mouths of the filthy, and I cannot save her soul to heaven. She was a child! I remember . . .' He lost command of his voice and faltered to a stop.

Pitt tightened his grip. 'I know. I have a daughter myself. She's wilful, erratic, hot-tempered one moment, tender the next.' He could see Jemima in his mind. He remembered holding her as a baby, her tiny, perfect hands clinging to his thumb. He remembered her discovering the world, its marvels and its pain, her innocence, her trust that he could make everything better, and her laughter. He had not known Charlotte as a child, but at times it was as if he could see her in his own daughter.

'She can seem so wise I marvel at her,' he went on. 'Then the instant after she's a child again, with no knowledge of the world. She's a baby and a woman at the same time. She looks so like my wife, and yet when I look into her eyes, it is my own I see looking back at me. I can imagine what you are suffering well enough to know that I know nothing of it at all.'

Castelbranco bent his head and covered his face with his hands.

Pitt let go of his wrist and sat back in his own chair, silent for several seconds.

'I have a certain degree of discretion as to what I can investigate,' he said at last. 'Since you are the ambassador of a country with whom we have a powerful and long-standing treaty, it could be in the national interest that we do not allow you to be victimised in this way while you and your family are in London. I promise you I will learn all I can about what actually happened, and who is behind the whispers of malice. I will not act against them without informing you first. That I can do, as a courtesy to you as the representative of your country.'

Castelbranco rose to his feet awkwardly, swaying a little until he regained his balance.

'Thank you, sir. You could not have offered more. I appreciate your understanding.' He bowed and turned round slowly before walking upright and a little unsteadily to the door. Once outside he closed it softly behind him.

Pitt sat where he was without moving. He had meant what he said: he could not grasp the enormity of the man's pain, his helplessness that his child had been destroyed both on earth and, in his belief, in heaven also; and he had been unable to do anything to prevent it.

Pitt was not sure what he believed of heaven. He had never given it deep thought. Now he was certain he did not worship a God who would condemn a child – and Angeles was little more than that – for any sin, let alone one unproven, and for which she had already paid such a hideous price.

Had Jemima slipped in such a way, he would have been furious, possibly shouted at her, told her bitterly of his disappointment, but he would never have stopped loving her. Could God be less than Thomas Pitt was? And surely the measure of a man's worth was the courage and the compassion he had, his ability to love unselfishly, to reach out to those in need, to help – always to help?

Castelbranco must be wrong about God's nature. Such a judgement was a law of men, who flexed their muscles to dominate, to keep the disobedient under control, to frighten the wilful into submission. God must be better than that, or what was the mercy of Christ supposed to be for? What was anything for: humanity, beauty, the very meaning of life and love?

But that was an argument for another time. Nothing would bring Angeles back. The truth might restore at least her good name, and perhaps find some way around the bitter damnation of the Church. It was the retaliation of men who, by their very calling, had no children of their own, no understanding of the endless tenderness that a parent feels, no matter how tired, how frustrated or how temporarily angry.

Did any woman ever put her child beyond forgiveness? He could not imagine Charlotte doing so, for all her impetuosity, her high hopes and at times instant judgements, hot tempers, impatience, ungoverned tongue. She would defend those she loved to the last breath of her own life, instinctively, passionately. To do less would be inconceivable to her.

He smiled as he thought of her. She was exasperating, sometimes even a professional liability with her crusading ideas, and in the past her incessant meddling in his cases. But she was never, ever a coward. She might have been a lot less trouble if she had been, and a lot safer. And, he admitted, a lot less help. But without question, he would never have loved her as he did.

Heaven help him, was Jemima going to be the same? At three years younger, Daniel was already more level-headed. But it was Jemima who would leap to his defence, right or wrong.

One day she would be a mother like Charlotte: protect first, and chastise afterwards. Punish, but forgive. And having forgiven, she never mentioned the offence again. She had sent Daniel to his room without supper for carrying a grudge after a matter had been resolved.

Pitt knew now at least where he would begin. He rose to his feet and sent for Stoker. When he came, Pitt assigned certain business of the day to him. Then he went alone to see Isaura Castelbranco. He was dreading it and half hoped he would be turned away at the door. There was no way to deal with such grief: no words could ease it, but clumsiness might make it worse. So would ignoring it, when he knew that there was a remote chance he could at least find some of the answers as to what had precipitated the tragedy.

He caught a hansom with ease, and all too rapidly made his way through the busy, jostling streets to the ambassador's residence. Perhaps Castelbranco had prepared her, because Isaura received him without any excuses or prevarication. He was asked to wait in the private study where mirrors were turned to the wall, pictures draped with black and the curtains on the windows pulled all but closed.

Isaura came in quietly. The only sound he heard was the click of the latch as the door closed. She stood straight, but she seemed smaller than he remembered, and her face was bleached of all colour except the faint olive of her complexion. There was no pink of blood beneath the surface.

'It is kind of you to come, Mr Pitt,' she said with a slight huskiness, as if she had not used her voice after so much silence and weeping.

In the face of her dignity it would be faintly insulting to be anything but direct.

'The ambassador asked me to look into the events leading up to Miss Castelbranco's death and find out whatever facts I can,' he explained. 'I expect you can tell me at least some things that I do not know, and I would prefer not to have to ask others. I feel very strongly that we should be as discreet as possible.'

A slight movement touched her mouth, almost a smile.

'My husband is deeply grieved. He loved his daughter very much, as did I. I think perhaps I am a little more realistic as to what may be done.' She looked down for a moment, then up again, meeting his eyes. 'Of course part of me wishes for revenge. It is natural. But it is also futile. Anger is a quite understandable reaction to loss. And he has lost his only child. You did not know her, Mr Pitt, but she was lovely, full of life and dreams, warm-hearted . . .' She stopped, unable for a moment to keep up her brave demeanour. She turned half away from him, concealing her face.

'I have a daughter myself, Senhora Castelbranco,' he said. 'She is fourteen, and already half a woman. One minute she is very grown up, knowing things I barely grasp myself and so like her mother. The next she is still a child, completely innocent. I can imagine at least something of what you feel. I suppose that is why the case matters so much to me. I could easily be in your place.'

'Please God, you will not be.' She turned back to him slowly. Something in his words had returned to her at least a semblance of self-mastery. 'If you were, you might feel the fury my husband does, and the desire to clear our daughter's name from the slander that is being spread. But your wife would tell you, as I tell the ambassador, we are helpless to bring any charges. It will only prolong the speculation and the gossip. It will cure nothing.'

Pitt was taken aback. She was as much ravaged by grief as her husband, and yet she seemed quite calm in her refusal to take the issue further. It was not defeat. Meeting her eyes he knew she was not emotionally frozen by shock. She spoke from determination, not emptiness.

'Don't you want to know what happened?' he asked. 'Even for your peace of mind, for the future, perhaps?'

Her lips tightened for a moment, not a smile so much as a grimace. 'I do know, Mr Pitt. Perhaps I should have told my husband, but I did not. I knew it would . . .' she drew in a deep breath, '. . . it would hurt him to no purpose. There is nothing we can do.'

Pitt was surprised and confused. He knew from Vespasia not only what had happened, but where and when, and almost certainly by whom. This did not seem like the response of a mother who has lost her only child so terribly.

'I can't act without your permission, Senhora, but for the sake of the valued relationship between England and Portugal, I must find out what happened,' he said gently.

She blinked her dark eyes. 'What happened? A young man who has a twisted soul raped my daughter, and then made light of it, as if it were of no importance. He sought out opportunities in public to mock her with pretended courtesies, and when she retreated from him, he taunted her the more, until in hysteria she backed away as far as she could, and beyond, crashing through a window to her death. I saw it, and was helpless to do anything to save her. That is what happened.' She stared at him, almost challengingly.

'Forsbrook?' He breathed the name rather than speaking it. He had known from Vespasia and Charlotte, who had witnessed Angeles' final moments, and yet there was still a monstrousness about it.

'Yes,' Isaura said simply.

'Neville Forsbrook?' He repeated, to be certain. 'You knew? When did it happen, and where?'

'Yes, Neville Forsbrook, the son of your famous banker who is responsible for so much investment for your countrymen,' she answered. 'I knew because my daughter told me. It happened at a party she attended. Forsbrook was there, among many other young people. He found Angeles alone in one of the apartments for the family. He raped her and left her there, terrified and bleeding. Here at home one of our maids found her weeping in her room and sent for me.'

'She said she had been raped, and who it was?' He hated pressing her. It seemed pointlessly cruel, and yet if he did not he would only have to come back later to ask.

'She was bleeding,' Isaura replied. 'Her clothes were torn and she was bruised. I am a married woman, Mr Pitt. I am perfectly aware of what happens between a man and a woman. If it is anything like love, or even heat-of-the-moment weakness, hunger, it does not leave bruises such as Angeles had.' She lifted her chin. 'Do I know it was Neville Forsbrook? Yes, but I cannot prove it. Even if I could, what good would it do?'

She gave a tiny, hopeless shrug. 'Angeles is dead. He would only say she was willing, a whore at heart, even if she looked respectable. And his father would turn the goodwill of the people he knows against us. They would close ranks, and we would find ourselves outcast because we have made a fuss and exposed to public ridicule what should have remained a private sin.'

Pitt did not argue. His mind raced to find a rebuttal, and there was none. Politically, socially and diplomatically it would be a disaster. The most that would happen to Neville Forsbrook would be that he might marry less fortunately than otherwise. Even that was not certain. He might continue to make people believe that it was all the imagination of a hysterical young foreign girl who had got herself into disgrace, possibly even pregnant, and blamed him for it. There would be no way to prove him a liar.

Even the testimony of the maid would hardly be viewed as impartial. Angeles' humiliation would be painted in detail for everyone, and branded on the memory even more deeply than it was now. Isaura was right: they were helpless. Anything they did would only make it worse.

Forsbrook would never allow his son to be blamed, and he had the strength to protect him. He would use it. Perhaps it was Pitt's job to see that it did not come to such a thing.

What would he tell Castelbranco? That England was powerless to protect his daughter, or bring to any kind of justice the young man who had raped her and driven her to her death? Not only that, but they felt it better not to try to seek any kind of justice, because it would be uncomfortable, raise fears and questions they preferred to avoid?

And if Castelbranco then thought them barbarous, was he wrong?

'What about his mother?' Pitt said aloud, casting around for any other avenue at all. 'Do you think . . .?'

She shook her head. 'Forsbrook? Eleanor Forsbrook died a few years ago, I'm told. There was a terrible carriage accident in Bryanston Mews, just off the square where they live. People speak very well of her. She was generous and beautiful. Perhaps if she had still been alive this would not have happened.'

'Probably not,' he conceded. 'But the loss of a mother does not

excuse this. Most of us lose people we love at some time or other.'
He thought of his own father, taken from him when he was a child,
unjustly accused of theft and deported to Australia. It was a long time
ago now. Nobody was deported any more. He had been one of the
last. Pitt had no idea if he had even survived the voyage, or what had
happened to him if he had. He might still be alive, but he would be
old, close to eighty. He was not sure if he even wanted to know if his
father still lived. He had never returned, or made any contact. It was
an old loss better left alone.

'Most of us have wounds of some sort,' he said quietly.

'Of course,' Isaura agreed. 'But there is nothing you can do. I am
grateful for your kindness in coming to me in person rather than
sending a letter.'

Pitt was too angry to accept her dismissal. It was intolerable.

'I would still like to speak to your maid, Senhora,' he said grimly.
'I will be discreet, I give you my word, but I want to know for myself
all that I can. Special Branch has a long memory.'

Her eyes flickered for a moment. Was it hope? All that was left for
them was some kind of justice. Would it really help?

'Of course,' she agreed with a slight inclination of her head. 'I shall
ask her to come.' She turned and left, going out of the door with her
head high, her shoulders still awkwardly stiff.

Pitt wondered how rash his promise was, and when Isaura
Castelbranco would tell her husband the truth. Probably when she
was sure he would not take his own revenge. She had more than
enough grief already.

Chapter Eight

NARRAWAY WENT to Lisson Grove reluctantly. It had been his office, his domain, for so many years, that going back as a visitor heightened his sense of being superfluous. He did not belong any more. He looked much the same as he had, not even noticeably any greyer, certainly not heavier or stiffer. He walked swiftly, with a certain grace. His mind felt just as sharp, in fact in some ways more so. It was emotionally that he felt different. Surely gentleness, an awareness of others, a greater humanity was part of wisdom?

He had time in which to do anything he wished, to travel, if he wished. Surely he had not forgotten how to enjoy himself? He could go to the beautiful cities of Europe he had only visited in haste before. He could admire the architecture, steep himself in the history of the cultures, the music, the great art created down the centuries. He could stop and talk to people purely for the pleasure of it. He could ignore or forget anything that bored him. There were no boundaries, no responsibilities.

Was that what troubled him? He needed boundaries? What for – an excuse? Responsibilities, or he felt unimportant? Did that mean there was little to him, except the job? He had started in the army at eighteen, straight from Eton, where he had excelled academically. The military had been his father's idea, much against his own intention.

He had arrived in India almost coincidentally with the beginning of the Mutiny, and seen at first-hand the horrors of war. It had been brutal and desperate, women and children slaughtered as well as soldiers. It was there that he had first become aware of the unnecessary human errors – stupidity would not be too strong a word in some cases – that caused such tragedy. It had sparked his appreciation for military intelligence and, even above that, the understanding of people and events, of political will, the perception of social movement that had eventually matched him with his true gifts, Special Branch. He had given the rest of his life to it.

Was it the loss of purpose that hurt now, or the loss of power? Who was he without it? That was the question he had avoided asking himself, but now that it was in his mind in so many words, he could not sidestep it any more. He had never been a coward before. He could not begin now. There was still something left to play for.

He had brought Pitt into Special Branch, originally as a favour to Cornwallis when Pitt got himself thrown out of the Metropolitan Police because he knew too much about a particular area of corruption. Now Pitt was head of Special Branch and Narraway was retired to kick his heels in the House of Lords, very much against his will. After the miserable Irish business he had had no chance of remaining in office.

He walked up the steps and in the door self-consciously, aware of the surprise and then discomfort of the men who used to snap to attention, and call him 'sir'. Now they were uncertain how to greet him. He could see in their faces the indecision as to what to say to make it plain to him that he had no place here, no position. He should have the grace to relieve them of that.

'Good morning,' he said, giving a very slight smile, which was not familiarity, just good manners. 'Would you please inform Commander Pitt that I am here, and would like to speak with him regarding a matter in which my advice has been requested. He is already aware of it.'

'Yes, sir . . . my lord,' the man replied, relief filling his face that Narraway seemingly knew his place. 'If . . . if you'll take a seat, sir, I'll deliver that message.'

'Thank you.' Narraway moved back from the desk and obeyed, feeling ridiculous, slightly humbled in what had been his own territory, asking favours of men he used to command. Would Pitt feel obliged to see him, however inconvenient it was? Might he even feel a slight pity for him, a man with no purpose?

He was too tense to sit down. Perhaps he should not have come? He was not old; he was still more than capable of doing the job. He had been dismissed because of a scandal deliberately and artificially created by one of the most dangerous plots of the decade, perhaps of the century.

But he had made enemies. The very nature of Special Branch made it impossible for Narraway to justify himself without also telling the truth as to what had happened. And that he could never do. He acknowledged with a bitter irony that the very act of talking to the public would have made him unfit for the position.

And Pitt was a worthy successor. He would grow into the job. He had both the intelligence and the courage. With luck he would last long enough to gain the experience. The only quality in doubt was the steel in his soul to take the decisions where there was no morally clear answer, where other men's lives were at stake and there was no time to weigh or measure possibilities. That required a particular type of strength, not only to act, but afterwards to live with the consequences. Narraway could not count the number of times he had lain awake half the night, second-guessing himself, regretting. There was no other loneliness quite like it.

The man returned. Narraway remained where he stood, waiting for the response without moving.

'If you'll come with me, my lord, Commander Pitt has a little time free and would be happy to see you,' the man said.

Narraway thanked him, wondering whether the 'little time free' was Pitt's wording or the messenger's. It was very faintly patronising and did not sound like Pitt.

''Morning.' Pitt rose to his feet as if Narraway were still the superior. 'The Quixwood case?' he asked as Narraway closed the door.

Narraway was a little surprised. 'Yes,' he replied, accepting the seat offered him. 'What made you suppose that? Do you know something?'

Pitt resumed his own seat, smiling ruefully. 'Experience. I'm beginning to realise just what a complicated, misunderstood and horrible crime rape is. It stirs up emotions nothing else does, not even murder.'

For a moment Narraway was caught by surprise. 'You're not interested in the Quixwood case, are you? I mean officially?'

'No. As far as I know, it's an ordinary tragedy, no political implications. I'm thinking of Angeles Castelbranco.'

Narraway blinked. 'The Portuguese Ambassador's daughter who died in that appalling accident? Or did she kill herself, as is being suggested?'

'I think it probably was to some degree an accident,' Pitt answered. 'At least on her part. Or his, I don't know.'

'His?' Narraway raised his eyebrows. 'What are we talking about? I thought it happened very much in public?'

'It did.' Pitt's face creased with distaste. 'It was a public taunting – baiting, if you like – largely orchestrated by Neville Forsbrook. I don't think she had any intention of going out through the window.'

Narraway began to see a different picture. 'Are you saying she was raped too? Presumably by Forsbrook?'

'I think so. But I have no way whatever of proving it. And worse than that, if I could it would probably do her more harm than good. All Forsbrook has to say is that she was thoroughly willing, and no virgin anyway, and she's doubly ruined. But what can I do to help you with Catherine Quixwood?'

There was a horrible irony in Pitt's sudden switch from Angeles to Catherine, a mirror of helplessness. Narraway tried to marshal his thoughts. To be honest required more self-examination than he found easy.

'Knox is a good man,' he began. 'But he doesn't seem to have got anywhere beyond the fact – which now seems inescapable – that she let the rapist in herself.' He watched Pitt's face closely, trying to see if his thoughts were critical, or open. He saw no change in Pitt's eyes at all. 'I can see that he hates it, but he is beginning to believe that she had a lover,' he went on.

'What do you think?' Pitt asked, no expression in his voice.

Narraway hesitated. 'I've done a lot of digging into her actions over the last six months or so.' He measured his words carefully. When he had been in Pitt's job he had not allowed emotions to touch his judgement. Well, not often. Now he was thinking of Catherine Quixwood as a woman: charming, interested in all kinds of things, creative, probably with a quick sense of humour, someone he would have liked.

Was it because the whole tragedy had nothing to do with danger to the country, no issues of treason or violence to the state, that he allowed himself to visualise people capable of laughter and pain? People with dreams, vulnerabilities like his own? He could not have afforded to before. What had that robbed him of, and that he was discovering only now?

'Was her marriage reasonably happy?' Pitt asked.

'Happy?' Narraway thought about it and was puzzled. 'What makes a person happy, Pitt? Are you happy?'

Pitt did not hesitate. 'Yes.'

For an instant Narraway was overtaken by a sense of loss, of something inexpressible that he had missed. Then he banished it. 'No, I don't think she was,' he answered. 'She was making as much happiness for herself as she could, but out of aesthetic or of the intellectual appreciation, not of the heart.' He was aware of how much of his own pleasure lay in exactly these same things. Was that why he cared about her, a sense of identity? He did care. Her crumpled body and the beauty of her face returned to his memory again and again.

'Has Knox given up looking for suspects?' Pitt asked.

'There's a young man named Alban Hythe who seems increasingly likely,' Narraway replied. 'He is intelligent, appreciates the same arts and explorations that she did and attended many of the same functions. He admits to being acquainted with her, although since they were seen together a number of times he could hardly deny it.'

Pitt frowned. 'Then what troubles you? Her reputation, if she was known to have a lover? Or are you concerned for Quixwood's embarrassment? There's nothing you can do.' His face was filled with regret. He gave a very slight shrug. 'I'm finding it hard to face that fact myself.'

Narraway heard Pitt's dilemma and for the moment ignored it.

'I'm not certain I believe it was Alban Hythe,' he argued. 'The rape was violent.' Deliberately he allowed the picture of Catherine back into his mind. 'Whoever did it hated her. It doesn't seem like a lover unexpectedly denied – not a sane one. Alban Hythe is frightened because he can feel the net closing in around him, but that's perfectly natural.'

Pitt shook his head. 'If rapists didn't appear perfectly natural we'd find them a lot easier to catch.'

'I can believe it of an arrogant young pup like Neville Forsbrook a lot more easily,' Narraway retaliated, startled by his own anger.

Pitt looked at him in silence for several moments before replying. 'If Hythe is innocent, then someone else is guilty,' he said at last. 'Whether he was her lover or not, whoever it was raped her violently this time, and he killed her. That can never be excused.'

Narraway took a deep breath. 'That's part of the problem,' he admitted. 'The medical evidence says that he didn't kill her, except perhaps indirectly. She actually died of an overdose of laudanum, which, as you know, is a derivative of opium. It could very easily have been suicide. In fact, there isn't a reasonable way in which it could have been murder. No one could convince a jury that a man raped her violently, left her with physical injuries, torn clothes, blood all over the place, and then stayed with her and forced her to add laudanum to her wine and drink it. I don't believe it myself. Whoever did that to her was in an uncontrolled fury.'

Pitt remained staring at him, his grey eyes steady and full of pain. 'We know far too little about it, this rape or any other,' he said levelly. 'Perhaps we know too little about ourselves as well. But if Alban Hythe isn't the man then you need to prove it, or he may eventually hang for something he didn't do. Not to mention the fact that whoever did do it will escape entirely, and probably do it again. There may be something to be salvaged of Catherine's reputation, or maybe not.' His mouth turned down in a bitter twist. 'People are now suggesting that Angeles Castelbranco was with child, and that was why she killed herself.'

'I don't think she wanted to go out that window,' Narraway said with some heat. 'I doubt she thought of anything except getting away from Neville Forsbrook and the other young men who were taunting her.'

'Neither do I,' Pitt agreed. 'But if I say so, then Pelham Forsbrook will defend his son by saying that Angeles was a whore and his son was only following a long line of other young men.' The misery and the anger were cut deep in his face. 'How does anyone prove him wrong?'

Narraway clenched his fists, hardly aware of it until his nails dug into the flesh of his palms. 'I refuse to be so bloody helpless!'

'Good.' Pitt smiled bleakly. 'When you find the answer, please share it with me.'

Narraway rose to his feet. 'Can't you at least prove Angeles wasn't with child? There would have been signs, surely?'

'That isn't the point,' Pitt answered him wearily. 'If she thought she was, or could have been, then her reputation is equally ruined.'

Narraway did not argue any more. He felt a coldness close around him, in spite of the warmth of the day and the sunlight streaming through the window. The brightness seemed curiously far away, even empty. He should recall what he had come for and ask Pitt, before the opportunity slipped away.

'I haven't dealt with rape before,' he said. 'What kind of proof do the police look for if the victim is dead and can't say anything herself? He didn't kill Catherine Quixwood. It does seem she took her own life with the overdose of laudanum.'

Pitt thought for several moments. 'I'm not sure that they would try to prove rape,' he said at last. 'If she was badly beaten that might be enough. That is a crime, and the jury would read more into it, in the circumstances. The sentence could be as heavy as if it had been rape. Obviously she could not have done that to herself. If you can prove the accused was there, and no one else could have been, it should be sufficient.'

'I see. I imagine that won't be too difficult.' Narraway rose to his feet. 'Thank you.'

Pitt relaxed a fraction. 'It was good to see you,' he replied.

Narraway was still turning the matter over in his mind early that evening. He sat with the windows open onto the deepening colours as the sun lowered towards the horizon. He was startled when his manservant knocked discreetly and stood in the doorway to say that Mrs Hythe had called and wished to speak with him.

'Shall I bring tea, my lord?' he added with elaborate innocence. 'Or a glass of sherry, perhaps? I don't know the lady sufficiently well to guess.'

'But you know her sufficiently well to assume that I will see her?' Narraway said a trifle waspishly. He was tired, more by frustration than action, and would have been happy to forget the whole issue of the Quixwood case for a few hours.

'No, sir,' the manservant replied, his eyes momentarily downcast. 'But I know you, my lord, well enough to be certain you would not refuse someone in considerable distress, and who is counting on you to be of help.'

Narraway stared at him and did not see even a flicker of irony in the man's face. 'You should have been a diplomat,' he said drily. 'You are far better at it than most of those I know.'

'Thank you, my lord.' A light glinted for a moment in the man's eyes. 'Shall I bring tea or sherry?'

'Sherry,' Narraway answered. 'I would like it, whether she would or not.'

'Yes, my lord.' He withdrew silently and a moment later Maris Hythe came in. Her face was as charming as before, with the same blunt gentleness, but she could not hide the fact that she was both tired and frightened. Instantly Narraway regretted his own self-absorption with what was no more than a slight inconvenience.

He rose to his feet and invited her to sit down in the chair facing the window and the deepening sunset.

'I apologise for coming uninvited, my lord,' she said a little awkwardly. 'Normally I would have had better manners, but I am frightened, and I don't know of anyone else who might help.'

Narraway sat down opposite her, leaning forward a little as if he too were tense. 'I assume the situation has worsened with regard to Mr Knox's investigation? I haven't spoken to him for a day or two. What has happened?'

Her answer was forestalled by the return of the manservant with a silver tray bearing sherry and two long-stemmed crystal glasses.

Maris hesitated.

The manservant poured a little of the rich dark golden liquid into one of the glasses and placed it on the table beside her. He poured a second and gave it to Narraway.

After he had gone Narraway picked his up, so she might do the same, and waited attentively for her to speak.

'Nothing Mr Knox finds could prove my husband's guilt, because he is not guilty,' she said, forcing herself to meet his eyes. 'But every new fact does make it look worse for him.'

'He has never denied that he and Mrs Quixwood were friends,' Narraway pointed out. 'What new has been added to that?'

She kept her composure with difficulty, taking a sip of the sherry, probably more to hide her eyes for a moment than because she wished for its taste.

He waited.

'Small gifts he gave her,' Maris replied very quietly. 'I didn't know about them. I think he was sorry for her. She . . . she was very lonely. Mr Quixwood has been both honest, and contrite about it, as if he blamed himself for putting so much effort into his work that he did not accompany her to the places she wished to go.'

'It is natural to feel guilty when it is too late to go back and make a better task of it,' he said with a twinge of guilt for his own sins of omission.

She smiled very slightly. 'I think he is a kind man who did not see how she really felt. And perhaps she did not tell him. One doesn't. It sounds so like complaining, and when you have comfort, position, no need to worry for any of most people's needs . . . and respect as well, from a man who is honourable, to ask for more is . . . greedy, don't you think?' She looked at him as if she genuinely wished for an answer.

'I have no idea,' he admitted. He tried to think of the women he knew. Charlotte would certainly want more. She would sacrifice financial security or social position for love, she had already proved that. Perhaps within the definition of love she would include a sharing of purpose, and a commonality of interest. Above all she might require to be needed, not an ornament but a part of the fabric of life.

Her sister Emily had considerable wealth and social position, and yet she envied Charlotte her purpose, her excitement, the danger and variety. Narraway had seen it in her eyes, heard it in the sharp edge of her voice in a rare unguarded moment.

And what of Vespasia? That was a question perhaps he preferred not to consider. Because of her title and extraordinary beauty she had lived in the public eye all her adult life, but she was still an acutely private person in her emotions. He had never thought of her as vulnerable, capable of such frailties as doubt or loneliness.

'My lord . . .' Maris interrupted a little anxiously.

He returned his attention to her, slightly embarrassed to have been discourteous. 'I'm sorry. I was considering what you had said about Catherine Quixwood.' That was true, in a way. 'It is perceptive of you to have seen the possibility of her loneliness.'

A look that he could not read flickered across her face. The only thing he recognised for certain was fear.

He leaned forward a little to assure her that she had his attention, in spite of his earlier lapse. 'What is it you would like me to do, Mrs Hythe?'

'Mr Knox is still working on the case,' she replied. 'I really don't think he will give up until his superiors tell him that he must. He seems to me to be a good man, gentle, in spite of the terrible things he has to deal with every day.' The ghost of a smile was in her eyes for an instant. 'He speaks of his family once in a while, when he is in my house. He admired a teapot I have, and said his wife would like it. It seems she collects teapots. I wondered why. Surely two or three are sufficient? But he said she likes to arrange flowers in them, so I tried it myself – daisies. It worked extraordinarily well. Now every time I look at the thing it makes me think of him, and then of Catherine.'

Narraway did not know how to answer her. How did Pitt deal with the reality of people, the details of their lives that stayed in your mind? He thought of Catherine lying on the floor, and the ornaments in the room. Had she chosen them, put them there because they pleased her, or reminded her of someone she cared for?

'You have not told me what it is you wish of me, Mrs Hythe?' Deliberately he brought the conversation back to the practical.

'Every detail he finds makes it clearer that Catherine was fond of my husband,' she answered. 'And that they both liked and trusted each other, and met . . . often.' She swallowed with a tightening of her throat that looked painful. 'He believes that she let her attacker in herself, and that could only be because she knew him—'

'I know,' he cut across her. 'There was no break-in, and she dismissed the servants, which she would hardly do if it were someone she did not know very well.'

She lowered her eyes. 'I know that too. Everything he finds makes it more obvious. I just know that my husband is a good man – not perfect, of course, but decent and kind. He was sorry for her and he liked her, no more than that.' She looked up at Narraway earnestly. 'And if they were having an affair, perhaps I would have hated her for it, and – if I were crazy enough – have wished her harm. But I could not have raped her.'

She gave a little shiver. 'Her husband could have, but I believe he was at a party at the time she was attacked, so it could not have been he who did it. Mr Knox cares very much that he catch someone. So do I. I think any woman would. It is a terrible way to die.' She took a deep breath and continued, 'But in spite of his kindness to her, the small gifts she gave him, the times they met at one exhibition or another, my husband was not her lover. But even if he had been, he would not have killed her.'

Narraway was brutal, to get it over with. It would lie unsaid, if he left it. 'And if he found her fascinating, flattering to his vanity, a beautiful older woman with sophistication and intelligence, and she suddenly rebuffed him?' he asked. 'How would he react to that? Are you certain that it would not be with anger?'

The colour burned up her face, but she did not look away from his gaze. 'You don't know Alban, or you wouldn't ask. I know you think I am being idealistic and naïve. I'm not. I know Alban very well. He has his faults, as do I, but losing his temper is not one of them. Sometimes I wish he would do so more. For some time, I am ashamed to say, I thought him something of a coward because he was so gentle.' She winced. 'Now I risk seeing him hanged for a crime he would never even imagine. He was sorry for her, Lord Narraway, and he liked her. I think perhaps he helped her in something she was troubled with, although I don't know what. He never mentioned it to me. Don't let him be destroyed for that.'

Narraway stared at her, trying to assess if she truly believed what she said, or if, even more than to convince him, she was trying to convince herself.

'Have you no idea what it was?' he urged. This was a new thought and perhaps worth pursuing.

She looked down at her hands for a moment, weighing her answer before she spoke.

'Alban is a banker. I know he is young yet, but he knows a great deal about business, especially investment. Please don't press me, because I have no reasons to give you, but I think it may have something to do with Africa, the Boers, and Leander Jameson. I know Alban read a lot about the raid, and the difference it might make to people if Dr Jameson is found guilty. He listened to Mr Churchill, and his talk of the possibility of war.'

Narraway drew in his breath to interrupt her. Surely she was being fanciful, desperate to say or do anything to defend her husband, and this was ridiculous? But Quixwood was a man involved in major finances also. He might have made an investment that his wife feared was risky, even potentially ruinous. Was it conceivable that she had sought advice behind his back, from an independent source?

He would see that as a betrayal, a complete failure of loyalty to trust his judgement.

But Catherine's future depended upon it too!

It sounded desperately unlikely that a woman like Catherine – beautiful, dependent, without any knowledge of international affairs, let alone of finances – would have undertaken to learn such things, and from a young man like Alban Hythe.

Narraway wanted her to be innocent, as did Maris Hythe, for different reasons. Were they not both reaching too far, grasping for impossible answers and refusing to see the inevitable?

She looked at him, breathing in as if to ask again. Then changed her mind and something of the light faded from her eyes.

He answered rashly, knowing he would regret the words even as he said them. 'I'll do all I can, Mrs Hythe. I shall see Knox straight away.'

She blinked hard and smiled. 'Thank you, Lord Narraway. You are very kind.'

He did not feel kind as he waited for Knox in the police station the following day; in fact he felt particularly foolish. When Knox finally came in, hot and tired, his boots covered in dust, his face tightened when he saw Narraway.

'I don't know anything more, my lord.' There were smudges of weariness under his eyes and when he took his hat off his hair stuck up in spikes. 'I can tell you half a dozen places where she met with this Alban Hythe, but I can't tell you for certain whether it was accident or arranged.' He put his hat on the hat rack. 'They turned up at an awful lot of the same events. Hard to see it as always accidental, like. Things she was interested in, but far as I can tell, he hadn't been until he met her.' He sat down heavily in the chair opposite Narraway, but he was not sufficiently at ease to cross his legs.

'Do you really think he was having an affair passionate enough to rape her and beat her like that, if suddenly she cooled off?' Narraway asked, allowing his doubt to reflect in his expression.

'No,' Knox said frankly. 'But somebody raped her. The evidence is not capable of any other interpretation that I can see. And she's dead, poor woman, so we can't ask her. It looks like Alban Hythe, and there's nothing to show it wasn't him, except my own feeling that he's a decent young man. Haven't you ever been wrong?'

'Yes,' Narraway admitted. 'Sometimes seriously. I suppose you've looked into his background? How on earth did he have time to spare to wander around art galleries and National Geographic luncheons and exhibitions of crafts from God knows where? I haven't!'

'Nor I,' Knox said ruefully. 'But I'm not a venture banker with fancy clients to please. And from what I can find out, he's very good at it indeed.'

Narraway was startled. 'Is that what he says he was doing?'

Knox gave a bitter smile. 'As far as I can determine, but he quite willingly offered me the names of some of the clients concerned, and I contacted them. Of course they didn't discuss their business, but they affirmed that they had dealings with him, and that they were quite often made in social surroundings – usually over a damn good lunch or dinner. It seems that introductions are made in such places. He mentioned an exhibition of French art, in particular, where certain British investors met with French wine growers, all very casually. Pleasantries were exchanged, and then agreements about very large sums of money were made.'

'That would hardly involve Catherine Quixwood,' Narraway pointed out. 'It could be an explanation for one or two meetings, not more.'

'Three or four maybe,' Knox corrected. 'Quixwood himself is one of the investors. He appears to know Hythe professionally, just not much on a personal level.'

Narraway was puzzled. He could not see how it excused what appeared to be a very personal friendship with Catherine. Unless, of course, Maris Hythe's extraordinary idea had some truth in it?

He pursued it with Knox because he very much wanted an answer that exonerated Catherine. He acknowledged to himself that he also was angry enough, wounded enough, that he wanted someone to be provably in the wrong. He needed someone to be punished for the pain and the humiliation she had suffered. He could only guess blindly at Quixwood's grief.

'What does Quixwood say of him?' he asked aloud.

'Nice young man, and good at his job, in fact gifted at it,' Knox replied unhappily. 'He seemed very distressed at the thought that Hythe could be guilty.' He sighed. 'It would be a very personal kind of betrayal, both for Quixwood, and for Mrs Hythe. But then rape is, when the people know each other. I sometimes wonder which is worse, to be attacked so intimately by a complete stranger, or by someone you had trusted.'

'Do you think Hythe is guilty?' Narraway said bluntly.

Knox looked up again, meeting Narraway's eyes. 'Did you ever get really surprised by who was a traitor, or an anarchist, Lord Narraway? Did you have that kind of sense for judging people, regardless of evidence, or what anyone else said?'

Narraway thought for a moment. 'Occasionally,' he replied. 'Certainly not most of the time. But rape is . . .'

'Bestial?' Knox said for him. There was a bleak humour in his eyes that could have meant anything.

Narraway was going to answer, then as he looked at Knox longer he saw the intelligence in the man, the perception and experience of things Narraway had passed by without seeing, never considering them.

'Depends on who you believe, doesn't it, sir?' Knox answered his own question. 'I dare say if I were to ask a few ladies you'd loved and left, if they bore some kind of resentment, they would tell a tale you wouldn't recognise as the truth – my lord.' He sat motionless, as if half waiting for Narraway to be angry at his impertinence, but there was no shame in his face.

Narraway did not answer immediately. Memories raced through his mind: women who had attracted him intensely and on occasions women he had used because they were attracted to him. Certainly he was not proud of it and he would have found it difficult to explain to someone else had any one of them accused him of rape. Nothing like that had ever been suggested – although in Ireland he had earned the undying hatred of one man by seducing his wife. Recollection of that burned with hot shame up his face, even now. It had been years ago, and they were all dead. It did not lessen what he had done.

Were it recent, and someone had charged him, how could he account for it with any honour? What words would he find to tell a courtroom why he had acted as he did, all the little details, the lies, the carefully fabricated deceptions, why he had felt it was the only thing to do . . . at that time? The thought of Vespasia's ever hearing about it scalded him. Would it be the end for ever of their friendship, her trust, her respect? No wonder people lied!

And of course there had been other women over his long life. Some he had loved, briefly, knowing it would end. He had never seduced an unmarried woman, or made a promise he had not kept. He would like to think he had never intentionally lied.

What a piece of spurious self-excusing! Would anyone else see it like that? Even the simplest act could be viewed in so many ways. The mind could create a dozen different interpretations of a word, a gesture, a meeting, a gift. People believed what they wanted to, or what they feared to; saw what they expected to see.

'Could you defend yourself, if you had to, my lord?' Knox said softly. 'I've had times when I couldn't have.'

No one had accused Narraway of anything, and yet he felt the fear as closely as if it had touched his skin. Of course he had incidents in his life he would prefer other people knew nothing about. He cared surprisingly much what his friends thought of him – Charlotte, Pitt, other people he had known and worked with, above all, Vespasia.

He faced Knox again. 'There was no misunderstanding in what

happened to Catherine Quixwood,' he said grimly. 'Whether it was a lover or not, whether she lied to him, betrayed him, seduced him or whatever else, he beat and raped her and now she is dead, not of natural causes. He did that to her, either directly or indirectly, and he is responsible.'

'Indirectly,' Knox said, the pain back again in his eyes, all the lightness gone. 'The actual cause of her death was opiate poisoning. But I agree, he was responsible, and if I can, believe me, I will see that he pays.'

Narraway said nothing, but felt his face relax into a kind of smile. It was not pleasure so much as an ease in Knox's company, a respect for this man he had not felt for anyone else except Thomas Pitt.

In keeping with his promise to Maris Hythe, Narraway sought out Rawdon Quixwood, who was still spending much of the time at his club. He waited impatiently for him in the lounge, well into the late afternoon. Most of the time he tried to concentrate on the newspapers and their comments on the forthcoming trial of Leander Starr Jameson for the armed raid he had led in Africa, patriotically inspired, but disastrously misguided.

Occasionally he was too restless to remain seated, and paced up and down the largely deserted room. Then an elderly man, almost hidden by the wings of the huge armchair he was sitting in, coughed repeatedly and glared at him over the top of his spectacles. Narraway realised that he was being inconsiderate and returned to his seat.

He picked up the newspaper again and found his place in the varied accounts and letters to the editor.

He was still reading when the steward informed him that Mr Quixwood had returned, and enquired if he would like tea, or perhaps whisky.

'Ask Mr Quixwood if he will join me,' Narraway answered. 'And then serve whatever he chooses.'

The steward inclined his head in acknowledgement and withdrew.

Fifteen minutes later Narraway was sitting opposite Quixwood in the quietest part of the lounge. He looked across and studied the man for several moments while they both sipped their whiskies in silence. Narraway would rather have had tea, but he was not here for his pleasure.

Quixwood looked exhausted. His skin was pale except for the dark circles under his eyes, but the hand holding his glass was perfectly steady. Narraway admired his self-discipline. He must be feeling both the ordinary grief of losing a wife suddenly and violently, and the loneliness, but he had the additional torture of imagining her last moments, and the speculation in the press, which was no doubt read by almost everyone he met. It was not only a question of who had raped her, but whether he had been her lover. Now it was written about in daily newspapers for everyone in the street to think about, talk about, even make jokes over.

Until it was solved, there would be no end to it.

'Do you know something new?' Quixwood asked. His voice was so low that Narraway had to concentrate to hear.

'I imagine Knox has told you that he suspects Alban Hythe?' Narraway answered. 'Or at least that the evidence suggests that he and Mrs Quixwood knew each other unusually well.'

Quixwood shook his head fractionally. 'Yes, but I find it very difficult to believe.' He smiled faintly, and with an effort. 'But then I imagine a man always finds it difficult to believe that his wife was having an affair with someone else.'

A day ago Narraway would have agreed with him. After his experience with Knox he responded differently. 'It is very disturbing to realise how easily we go through life assuming,' he said, watching Quixwood's face. 'People change slowly, so infinitesimally that day by day we don't see it. Like glaciers: so many feet in a year – or maybe it's inches.'

Quixwood looked down at his glass and the light reflecting in its amber depths. 'I thought I knew her. I'm slowly facing the fact that perhaps I didn't.' He looked up abruptly. 'You know the worst thing? I'm not even as certain as I was that I really want to know exactly what happened. I . . . I don't want all my illusions shattered. I trusted my wife and believed she loved me, and even at our most cool or difficult moments, she would never have betrayed me.'

A smile flickered a moment and vanished. 'I thought Hythe was my friend, and now that I know his wife a little better, I know that she also trusted him. She still cannot accept even the possibility that he could be guilty of this. I suppose it is part of my own grief that I want to comfort her as well.'

Narraway did not answer, not because he did not care, but because there was nothing he could say that added to what was already spoken.

Quixwood sipped his whisky again. 'Am I a coward not to want to know?'

Narraway considered it for a moment before replying; the man deserved an honest answer, not an automatic one.

'I think you may be unwise,' he said at last. 'I can imagine how you would prefer to leave your wife's last days, and especially her last moments, unknown. In your best times you will not think of it at all. In your worst you will visualise it brutally, in all the ways that hurt you most. Sometimes you may even find an answer that is bearable.'

Quixwood was watching him, waiting for him to finish.

'But it isn't only you,' Narraway continued. 'Maris Hythe may find she cannot live with the uncertainty. If Hythe is innocent, he surely deserves to have that proved. How could he live with that, hinted at but unproven, for the rest of his life?'

'And if he's guilty?' Quixwood asked.

'Then he deserves punishment,' Narraway said without hesitation. 'And even more than justice towards him, what about the rest of society?'

Quixwood blinked.

'Do you want to live in a country where such appalling crimes go unpunished?' Narraway asked. 'Where we are sufficiently indifferent to the horror of it that we prefer not to enquire too closely in case the answer is one we don't like? What about other men's wives, or daughters? What about the next woman raped?'

Quixwood closed his eyes. His hands clenched around his glass so tightly that had it not been heavy cut crystal it would have broken. There was no answer, and Narraway did not press him.

They spoke of other things, briefly, and after a little while Narraway left, wishing there were more he could do and knowing there was not.

Chapter Nine

IT WAS early evening but the sun was still high. Charlotte was at the stove, her back to the kitchen table, but she could hear Pitt's fingers drumming irritably on the wood. She could have asked him to stop, but she knew it was pointless. He was not even aware of doing it. His sense of helplessness was eating away at him. The death of Angeles Castelbranco was unexplained; in his mind it was a wound still bleeding.

She knew that it was not only a matter of solving a crime. It was not even the taking of some small step to absolve England's reputation as a gentle and civilised country where women, children, the vulnerable were treated with respect. They must show that brutality was punished swiftly, and no one pleaded for justice in vain.

Beyond that, it was the deep, visceral nature of the crime that ate at him: the knowledge that those he loved could as easily have been the victims, could yet be, and he had found nothing he could do to prevent that.

He loved his family fiercely, and she had never doubted it. Sometimes he was too strict, expected too much of them, other times she thought he was too lax, but whatever the disappointments, the love was as certain as the ground beneath her feet or the warmth of the sun.

All over the country there were other men the same, in every town and village – people who loved, who worried, who protected their loved ones the best they could, who lay awake at night thinking the unthinkable, praying that they would never have to face it.

But Pitt had had to face it, to see it in Rafael Castelbranco and be unable to do anything, unable even to try, because there was nothing to grasp, no evidence. Witnesses abounded, and yet they had seen nothing that did not lose substance, like mist, when it was examined.

Castelbranco had said his daughter's violator was Neville Forsbrook. Charlotte herself had seen him taunt Angeles and felt her terror as if it were palpable in the room. Rawdon Quixwood, himself stricken and bereaved by rape, had sworn to Vespasia that he had been at the event where it seemed the rape of Angeles must have taken place, and he knew young Forsbrook could not be guilty. It was not a reference to his character but to his whereabouts.

Who was lying? Who was mistaken? Who was terrified, revolted, ashamed, so prejudiced as to be unable to see or tell the truth?

To Pitt it was more than that. He felt uniquely responsible because he had been there. He was a guardian of the law, supposed to protect people, or at the very least to find justice for those who were wronged. Charlotte knew that was in his mind far more than the angry words, the long silences, the over-protectiveness that was infuriating Jemima, or the lectures begun and broken off that confused Daniel.

She wanted to say something to help, at least to let Pitt know that she understood and did not expect him, or any man, to slay all the dragons of the mind or keep safe all the dark corners of life, whether they were far away or in the familiar rooms of one's own house.

Pitt was still drumming his fingers on the table top.

Charlotte lifted the lid of the pan with potatoes and pushed a skewer into one, then another, to see if it was time to put on the cabbage. She hated it overcooked. The potatoes could do with a few more minutes. The table was already set and the cold meat carved. There were three separate dishes of chutney out: apple and onion, orange and onion, and spiced apricot. She was rather pleased with herself for that.

'Only three places,' Pitt said suddenly. 'Who's not here?'

'Jemima,' she replied. 'She's spending the evening with a friend.'

Pitt's voice sharpened. 'Who is it? Do you know them? What is she like, this friend? How old is she?'

Charlotte put the lid down on the potato pan and turned around to face him. She saw again how tired he was. His hair was as untidy as usual, even though it had been cut recently. The light caught on the grey at his temples. His skin was pale and there were fine lines around his eyes she had not noticed before, although they must have come slowly.

'A very pleasant girl called Julia,' she replied as lightly as she could, as if she had not seen the tension in him. 'She is rather studious and she likes Jemima because Jemima makes her laugh and forget to be self-conscious. I know her mother – not well, but enough to be certain Jemima is quite safe there. And before you ask me, no, Julia is fourteen as well, and she has no older brothers.'

Pitt lowered his head wearily. 'Am I being ridiculous?' he asked.

Charlotte sat down on the chair opposite him. 'Yes, my dear, completely. But I might think less of you if you weren't.' She reached out her hand and put it lightly over his on the table, stopping his fingers in their nervous movement. 'How could we look at people living our worst nightmares, and feel nothing? Then I would really think Special Branch had changed you from the man I love into an efficient person I could only respect, and mourn over.'

He was quite still for several moments, and she had no idea what he was thinking. She wanted to ask, but knew it would be intrusive.

'I don't know what I would do if it were Jemima,' he said suddenly, avoiding her eyes. 'I looked at Isaura Castelbranco a couple of days ago. She has courage, and immense dignity; in a way, more composure than her husband. But she's broken inside. Whoever did this has destroyed far more than just one person. The pain he's inflicted is beyond measure, and it will go on all their lives. Would any kind of justice help?'

'I don't know,' she said honestly. 'Maybe, at times. But don't we all need there to be justice? What safety is there for anyone if people can do what this man did, and then walk away free? If there's no price, why shouldn't they do it again, whenever they wish to and have the chance? And surely if there's no public justice, won't there be people who'll look for it privately? What are the chances they'll take it from the wrong person? Or the right person, but who was guilty only of being intimate with the wrong person, but not of rape?'

Pitt pushed his hair back hard as he straightened up and leaned again against the hard frame of the chair. 'Isaura knows who it is, and she's right, prosecution would only make it worse.'

Charlotte was stunned, as if she had blindly walked into something that had physically hurt her. 'But you told me Vespasia had said it couldn't be! Quixwood was there! You must make absolutely certain that the ambassador doesn't take—'

'Isaura didn't tell him,' he cut across her. 'She won't. She knows as well as you do that the temptation would one day be more than he could resist. She didn't even tell him that Angeles was raped, although I imagine he guesses.'

She frowned, tense now.

'You are sure?'

'Yes.' There was no uncertainty, no equivocation in his voice. 'I spoke to the maid as well. Angeles was raped.' He winced as he spoke and his voice was raw with pain. Charlotte knew he was imagining Jemima. 'She was bleeding and badly bruised. Whoever it was, he must have used considerable force. But she's dead. We can't prove it now, and even if we could, we cannot prove who it was. He has only to deny it, and we have made it worse rather than better. Isaura knows that. She's right, there's nothing we can do.'

Charlotte thought about it for several moments, her mind racing. The pain inside her was not only for Isaura Castelbranco, but for every other woman who lived with fear or grief, or who would do in the future, everyone else who felt humiliated and helpless. But deep beneath it all was the knowledge that it could happen to her own daughter.

'But she did say it was Forsbrook?' she said aloud.

'Apparently Angeles said so to her mother. But if Quixwood was right, she must have been mistaken. Perhaps someone even pretended to be Forsbrook. That's not impossible. I've asked a few questions . . .' He smiled bleakly. 'Don't look like that. I was discreet. I asked people about functions in the last month or two, who attended and any incidents concerning the Portuguese. This damned Jameson Raid is an excellent cover for all kinds of questions.'

Charlotte had forgotten about the Jameson trial. It was on everybody's lips, and yet she had heard them and it had held no meaning for her, because of the other things she had heard also. There was pity for Isaura Castelbranco. However, in too many instances it was tempered by cruel remarks about foreigners, different standards, as if the girl were to blame for her own death. Since the Church's decision that she could not be buried with Catholic rites, the conclusion was that she must have committed suicide. The kindest speculation was that she was in love with someone who did not return her feelings. The cruellest that she was with child, that her fiancé had very understandably called off the betrothal, and in despair she had killed herself and her unborn baby.

Charlotte had seethed with anger, but all she could do was accuse the speaker of malice. That would gain nothing, except enemies she knew she could ill afford, for Pitt's sake, as well as her own. If she was helpless, how much more so was Isaura Castelbranco?

'Did you learn anything?' she asked Pitt.

'Nothing that could be proof,' he replied.

'Did anyone see anything at this party?' she asked. 'What else did Mr Quixwood say?'

'Only that Forsbrook was charming, flattered her in the way most young women enjoy, but that she seemed to be upset by it. They implied that either she thought herself too good for him, or her English was not sufficiently fluent for her to have understood him properly. The prevailing opinion was that she was really too young, and too unsophisticated to be in Society yet, even when her mother was present at the same function, as she usually was. They suggested that perhaps Portuguese girls were more sheltered and less prepared to conduct themselves with appropriate grace.' He stopped, looking at Charlotte with a frown of puzzlement.

'You're right,' she said miserably. She wanted to say something to help, and she knew she was only making it worse.

She had tried several times to speak to him about the subject, knowing that it troubled him and wanting to share her own fears with him also. Part of her was sensitive enough to know that he was evading it, and yet she needed his comfort on it.

'It doesn't prove anything.' She tried again. 'Everyone is saying whatever makes them feel most comfortable. It's disgusting! How desperately alone she was . . . and her family is now.' She wanted to encourage him, but what was there to say? 'There must be something you can do,' she tried. 'Even indirectly, perhaps? Isn't there any diplomatic issue involved, even national pride? Anything?'

Pitt raised his head and his fingers stopped their drumming.

'I haven't given up.' His voice had an edge to it he failed to hide. 'I just don't know what to do that won't simply make it worse.'

'I'm sorry,' she said quickly. 'I'm asking for miracles, aren't I?'

'Yes. And your potatoes are boiling over.'

She leaped to her feet. 'Oh blitheration! I forgot them. Now it's too late to put the cabbage on.' She pulled the pan off the stove and lifted the lid cautiously. She jabbed the skewer into one of them. They were very definitely cooked, a little too much so. She would have to mash them.

Pitt was smiling. 'We'll just have more pickle,' he said with amusement. She was always teasing him that he used too much.

The following morning in his office Pitt studied the newspapers as usual, mostly looking for matters that he needed to know about professionally. Often they were selected for him by Stoker, to save him the time.

'Lot about the Jameson trial coming up,' Stoker observed drily, putting more down on Pitt's desk.

'Anything there I need to know right now?' Pitt asked, hoping he could avoid reading them altogether.

'Not much.' Stoker's face creased in distaste. 'Still haven't solved the murder of Rawdon Quixwood's wife. Sometimes I think I'd understand it if somebody murdered a few of these journalists, or the damn people who write letters expressing their arrogant opinions.'

Pitt looked up at Stoker curiously. It was an unusual expression of emotion for him. More often he showed only disinterest, or occasionally a dry humour, especially at political contortions to evade the truth, or the blame for anything.

Rather than ask him, Pitt turned over the pages of the first newspaper until he came to the letters to the editor. He saw with anger what Stoker meant. A good deal of space was devoted to the subject of rape.

One writer expressed the heated opinion that morality in general, and sexual morality in particular, was in serious decline. Women of a certain type behaved in a way that excited the baser appetites in men, leading to the destruction of both, and to the general degradation of humanity. Rapists, if caught and the matter proved beyond any doubt, should be hanged, for the good of all. No names were mentioned, but Pitt noted that the visitor lived not more than two streets away from Catherine Quixwood.

'Why the devil does the editor print this sort of thing?' he demanded angrily. 'It's vicious, ignorant and will only stir up ill feeling.'

'And produce more letters in answer,' Stoker replied. 'Dozens of them, of all opinions. And loads of people will buy the paper, to see if their answer has been printed, or just for the fun of watching a scrap. Same thing as the idle who gather to watch a street fight, and then demand we clean up the mess afterwards, all the time shaking their heads and saying how terrible it is. But heaven help you if you get between them and the view.'

Pitt looked up at Stoker with surprise. There had been more heat in his voice than he had heard in a while. It flickered through his mind to wonder if Stoker had known and cared for someone who had been violated: a sister, even a lover at some time. He knew little of Stoker's personal life, or that of most people in Special Branch, for that matter. And this subject was the sort of thing a man did not talk about, even to those he knew best.

'Of course,' Pitt looked down at the newspaper again. 'It was a stupid question. People attack what they're afraid of. Like poking a hornets' nest with a stick. Makes you feel brave, as if you're doing something. Don't care who the damn things sting afterwards. Looks as if they're no closer to solving it. Poor Quixwood must feel like hell.'

'Yes, sir,' Stoker agreed. 'But Knox is a good man. If anyone can find the truth, it's him.'

Pitt looked up at him again. 'I notice you didn't say "catch who did it". Do you think it wasn't murder then? Suicide, because she allowed herself to be raped?' He heard the anger in his own voice and could not control it.

Stoker looked slightly embarrassed. 'Whoever it was, sir, she let him in herself, with no servants around. That doesn't make attacking her right, but it does make it a lot more complicated.'

'Sometimes, Stoker, I look back to my time in Bow Street when murders seemed simpler. Greed, revenge, fear of blackmail I can understand. I quite often felt a degree of pity for even the worst people, but I knew that I still had no acceptable choice but to arrest them. If the jury decided they were innocent then I could accept that and it was a comfort to know they might catch my mistakes, if that's what they were. But who catches ours?'

Stoker chewed his lip. 'Sometimes we do,' he said with a raised eyebrow. 'Otherwise, probably no one. You'd like me to say different?' He was polite, just, but there was a challenge in his voice, one he would not have dared give Narraway.

'No, not if you can't do it believably,' Pitt retorted. 'At least we're not in the diplomatic service, or the Foreign Office. Thank God Leander Starr Jameson and his damn raid is not on our desks.'

'No, sir. And neither is poor Angeles Castelbranco.'

'Yes, she is,' Pitt replied grimly. 'Someone raped her here in London, and brought about her death.'

'Not a diplomatic incident, sir,' Stoker said firmly.

'Are you sure?' Pitt stared at him, holding his gaze.

Stoker blinked, for the first time uncertainty in his face as he considered other possibilities. 'Rape, as a tool of fear, civil disruption? I don't think so, sir. It's just a regular crime of selfishness, violence and uncontrolled appetite. She was a very pretty girl, and some vicious bastard saw his chance and took it. I don't see it makes any difference that she was Portuguese, except maybe it made her easier to get at.' He swallowed. 'And maybe he reckoned her parents would be in less of a position to go after him, although honestly I don't believe he'd even have thought of that. Rape's a kind of hot-blooded crime, isn't it?'

'Not necessarily. It's violence, hate rather than lust. But does that make any difference?' Pitt asked, still holding Stoker's gaze. 'If an anarchist throws a bomb on impulse, or shoots a political figure, is it less dangerous than if he'd planned it ahead?'

This time Stoker's answer was immediate. 'No, sir. For that matter, I suppose her being Portuguese doesn't matter, whether it's chance or deliberate. D'you think it'll become an international incident? That might put it on our plate. Castelbranco didn't seem the sort of man to use his daughter's death like that. Although I suppose he could change, if we don't charge anyone.'

'And if he doesn't, others could,' Pitt pointed out. 'I'm pretty sure I'd want to see someone pay, if it were my daughter. In fact, it wasn't my daughter and I do anyway. I think most fathers would.'

Stoker looked bleak. 'Except the father of whoever did it, sir. He sure as hell wouldn't. Maybe some of that is what's behind it?'

'You open up some ugly possibilities, Stoker,' Pitt admitted. 'We need to look further into the thought of people taking advantage of the event for political manipulation, repulsive as that is. Bring me what we know about Pelham Forsbrook and any interests he might have that connect in any way to Portugal, or Castelbranco personally.' He rose to his feet. 'I think I need to know a lot more about this. With the Quixwood case we will – it's on everyone's minds – but not this, poor girl. I don't know where else to look for suspects.'

'Maybe we'd better try, sir, just in case? We don't want to be caught looking as if we didn't care. Someone could dig a real deep hole for us with that.' There was no light in his face at all, only anxiety without a shred of his usual humour.

That was when Pitt realised he was utterly serious. 'Yes,' he agreed with a shiver. 'You'd better see if you can find out who else was at that party I told you Lady Vespasia mentioned. See if you can find a servant who noticed people, things. Some of them do. You'd better cover it up as a robbery. Be careful what you say.'

'Right, sir. Thank heaven the Quixwood case is nothing to do with us,' Stoker said with feeling. 'Count it up how you want, it looks as if it had to be a lover. I'm sorry for Quixwood. Not only lost his wife pretty horribly, but the whole world knows she was betraying him. There's another man you couldn't blame if he lost his control and killed the bastard . . . if they find him.'

'If they find him they'll hang him,' Pitt replied, taking his hat and jacket from the coat stand. 'It shouldn't be different, but it is.'

'Even if she took her own life, which is what some people are saying?' Stoker questioned.

'She was a respectable married woman,' Pitt answered, jamming the hat on his head. 'Important husband with influence. And she was British.'

Stoker pulled a sour face, but he did not reply.

Pitt went to Lincoln's Inn to find the man he had been advised was the best and most experienced prosecuting lawyer in cases of rape. He had telephoned in advance to make an appointment, using his position as leverage to force himself into the man's already busy schedule.

Aubrey Delacourt was tall and lean, with a shock of dark brown hair. He had a long face with heavy-lidded eyes, which were surprisingly blue.

'I can spare you about twenty minutes, Commander,' he said, shaking Pitt's hand briefly, then indicating a chair opposite his desk. His manner was impatient, making it clear he resented being obliged to disrupt his day. 'You might be best served by omitting any preamble. I already assume this is important to you, or you would not waste your own time, never mind mine.'

'You are quite right,' Pitt agreed, sitting down and crossing his legs comfortably, as if he refused to be hurried. 'I wouldn't. What I say to you is in absolute confidence. If you require me to retain your services then give me a bill for your time.'

'Not necessary,' Delacourt replied. 'You have told me you are the head of Special Branch, and I took the precaution of confirming that for myself. What is the advice you wish for?'

Very briefly indeed Pitt summarised his account of the rape and death of Angeles Castelbranco. Before he had finished Delacourt interrupted him.

'You have no case to bring,' he said bluntly. 'I would have expected you to know that.' There was brisk condescension in his tone. 'Even if you find the man who raped her, from what you have said, you cannot prove it. All you will do is damage the poor girl's name even more.'

'I know that.' Pitt did not hide his own irritation. 'I have advised her father to that effect, but quite naturally he cannot bring himself to accept it. I myself have a daughter only two years younger, and when I look at her I know perfectly well I would not accept it either. I would want to tear the man apart with my own hands, even beat him senseless. I dare say that would do no good, except temporarily relieve my own feelings. I would end up in gaol for assault, and it would leave my wife and children in an even worse position. That might stop me, but I can't swear to it.'

Delacourt's eyebrows rose slightly. 'You want me to advise you how to stop Castelbranco? Say to him exactly what you have said to me.'

'I want to know more about rape,' Pitt answered sharply. 'It can't always be as hopeless as this. If it is, then we need to do something about the law. Does everyone just . . . give in? One of the misfortunes of life, like a cold in the head, or measles?'

Delacourt smiled and the anger seeped out of him, his body easing in his chair into a different kind of tension.

'I won't wrap it up for you, Commander. Rape is a crime that is desperately difficult to prosecute. That is partly why I chose to specialise in such cases. I like to delude myself that I can achieve the impossible.'

He steepled his fingers. 'People react to it in different ways. Most often, I believe, it is not even reported. Women are so ashamed and so hopeless of any justice that they tell no one. Strangers tend to think they must have deserved it in some way. That is the most comfortable thing to think, especially for other women. Then it cannot happen to them, because they do not deserve it.'

He moved slightly again. 'Some people believe that if you defend yourself thoroughly then you will not be raped.' He smiled bitterly. 'Only beaten to a pulp, or murdered, which would, of course, show that you were a virtuous woman, albeit a dead one.'

Pitt said nothing, but began to feel enveloped in a crippling helplessness.

'Men whose daughters are raped feel the rage that you just described,' Delacourt went on, his face puckered with his own anger and sense of futility. 'The younger the girl, the deeper the pain and the fury, and usually a sense of personal failure that they did not prevent the atrocity from happening. What use are you as a father if your child is violated in this terrible way, and you were not there to stop it?'

Pitt could imagine it only too easily. He could not get Jemima's face out of his mind. She thought she knew embarrassment, anger, hurt, even disillusion, but actually she had barely tasted any of them. He and Charlotte had protected her. She was still a child – growing up, certainly, but with no concept of real horror. He realised now that he wanted to keep her from it always. What parent didn't?

Delacourt was watching him. 'We don't want our children to grow up, except in the sense of happiness,' he said self-mockingly. 'We want them to find someone who will love them, when they are ready for the idea, not before. Or possibly even when we are! We want them to have children of their own, and if they are sons then to have successful careers – all without the pain and the failures that we have had.'

Pitt shook his head, but he found no words.

'We know it's not possible,' Delacourt agreed. 'We are still not ready for reality. If it is our wives who are raped then we are confused, outraged not only for her, but for ourselves. She has been violated, and something we considered ours has been taken away – not only from her but from us. Life will not ever be the same again. Somebody must be punished very hard indeed. Our civilised minds say it should be long imprisonment. Our more primitive core demands death. Our dreams that we would not admit to would accept mutilation as well.'

Pitt opened his mouth to protest, then merely sighed, and again said nothing.

'And thoughts we don't want to have enter our minds,' Delacourt had not yet finished. 'Was it really rape? Did she in some way invite it? Surely she must have? Why did it happen to her, and not to someone else? She's different now. She doesn't want anyone to touch her, even me! And I'm not certain that I want to touch her, anyway. This man has ruined my life . . . I want to ruin his, slowly and with exquisite pain, as he has done to me.'

Delacourt leaned forward a little. 'And if it is brought to trial she will have to tell the whole court, detail by detail, everything he did to her, and how hard she fought, or not. He will be there, in the dock, watching, listening and reliving it himself. Possibly as you look at him you will see the light in his eyes, his tongue flickering over his lips. His lawyer will say everything he can either to suggest she has the wrong man, is mistaken, hysterical, deliberately lying, or else that she was perfectly willing at the time, but is now saying otherwise to try to protect her reputation. Perhaps she is afraid that she is with child, and her husband knows perfectly well it is not his, but a lover's?'

'I am back to the beginning,' Pitt replied, now paralysed by futility. 'We can do nothing. We rule an empire that stretches around the world, and we cannot protect our own women from the depraved among us?'

Delacourt gave a very slight shrug, rueful, but there was a gentleness in his face. 'It's not impossible, Commander, just extremely difficult, and even when we succeed the cost is high, not to us but to them. You have to be certain that you think it is worth it. Legally you have the right to decide for her, but do you have it morally? Are you sure you are willing not only to live with the result yourself, but to watch her living with it?'

Pitt managed a bleak smile. 'Do you tell this to all your clients?'

'Perhaps not quite as brutally as that,' Delacourt admitted. 'What is it you want to achieve, Mr Pitt? Angeles Castelbranco is dead. Her reputation is ruined. If you could prove she was raped, and that would be extremely difficult without her alive to speak, then you might achieve something. But the young man would no doubt defend himself vigorously, and whatever he says, there is no one to say otherwise. I assume you must have considered that?'

'Yes. But if we do nothing then the Portuguese Ambassador will believe that we don't care,' Pitt argued. 'It might damage relationships between our two countries for some time, not vastly perhaps, but how can you trust a nation who allows such a thing to occur and then go unpunished?'

Delacourt grimaced. 'I can see the ugliness of that. I don't know what help I could suggest, but I will give it thought.'

'And the other part of it is that if the young man gets away with it completely, as seems the case, will he do it again?' Pitt asked. 'Put simply, why shouldn't he?'

Delacourt clenched his teeth and shook his head very slightly. 'There you have the worst of it, Commander. Almost assuredly he will. From the little you've told me, it was hardly a crime of passion,' Delacourt said quietly. 'A crime of hate, the desire to dominate, and to shame. Have you ever been in the slightest tempted to take by violence a woman for whom you had the slightest regard?'

The thought was repulsive. 'Of course not!' Pitt said with more feeling than he had intended to show. 'But I am not . . .' He had been going to say 'a rapist', but the thought answered itself.

'A man subject to desire?' Delacourt asked with quite open amusement.

Pitt felt himself colouring with embarrassment, not that he had felt desire, almost overwhelmingly at times, but that he should have sounded so naïve.

'I'm sorry,' Delacourt apologised. 'I led you into that, partly to show you how easy it is to twist someone's words and feelings on the subject. Even a man as experienced as you are in police work, and in evidence in so sensitive a matter, can be led to awkwardness. Imagine being on the witness stand, vulnerable, trying desperately to be both honest, and to give evidence that will trap a dangerous man and still preserve some dignity and reputation for the woman concerned.'

'And you say he'll do it again?' Pitt repeated.

'Probably,' Delacourt agreed. 'Don't most thieves do it again? Most arsonists? Most embezzlers, vandals, liars, anyone whose crime benefits them in some way either in their appetite for money, power, revenge, or excitement?'

Pitt rose to his feet.

'There is one thing,' Delacourt added, looking up at Pitt. 'All that I have said is true, I know it by bitter experience in the courtroom. But if this young man is as violent as you say, then it is possible that he has shown it in other ways. Look for loss of temper when he is crossed, when he is beaten in some sport or other, or even loses badly at cards, or whatever he does competitively. If he is a risk-taker, look for gambling losses that are heavy or unexpected.'

Pitt was not certain he grasped the importance of things so trivial. 'How will that help the Castelbrancos? Proving Forsbrook is ill-tempered is a far cry from rape.'

'Not so very far, if he is a bully who can't take losing,' Delacourt replied. 'But that isn't my point. I've tried to convince you of the difficulty of proving rape at all, never mind the danger to the victim of trying. Sometimes one can settle for what is admittedly far less, pathetically so, but a prosecution for assault can damage a man's reputation. People don't want to do business with him, invite him to the better social events, have him marry into your family. Several such convictions, or even prosecutions without a serious sentence, can mar his life.'

Pitt said nothing, thinking slowly.

Delacourt was watching his face. 'A small victory,' he admitted, 'when you want to beat the man to pulp, and then tear him apart for what he has done to a woman you care about. But it is better than nothing – and it can be a foundation on which to build if you do ever get him to court on a heavier charge.'

'Thank you, Mr Delacourt,' Pitt replied. 'You have spared me more time than you can probably afford. At least I am wiser, if only moderately encouraged. I understand why people take the law into their own hands. They have looked hard at those of us who are supposed to protect them, or at the very least avenge them, and see that we are powerless. I shall try to prevent the Portuguese Ambassador from taking action, but I can't say that I am entirely averse to it. In his place I would do so, and then leave immediately for Portugal and never return.'

Delacourt shrugged. 'Frankly, Mr Pitt, so would I. And even as an officer of the court, I would find some reason why I was not able to prosecute him, and every reason why I would defend him, were he to allow me that chance.'

Pitt hesitated, wanting to say more, and then did not know what that would be. 'Thank you,' he said again. 'Good day.'

Outside in the street he walked slowly, oblivious of passers-by, of the traffic, even of the open brougham with a beautifully dressed woman riding in it, parasol up to protect her face from the sun, coloured silks fluttering in the slight breeze.

What Delacourt had said to him filled his mind. He believed that it was true, but he was unable to accept that there was no possible way to fight it. There had to be. They must make it so, whatever that demanded of them. To be helpless was unendurable.

Was it fear that held them captive, paralysed their will to act? Fear of shame, of scandal, of other people's beliefs about them, cruel words spoken by those who were also afraid, ignorant, runnning away from the truth because it made them aware of their own vulnerability?

He came to the kerb and waited a moment or two for a brewer's dray to pass, then crossed the road.

Pitt was afraid for Jemima. A man worth anything at all would fear for his daughter. But how many men feared for their sons? What would Pitt do if Daniel, grown to adulthood, should be wrongly accused of such a violent and repulsive crime?

The answer was immediate, and shaming. His instinctive reaction would be to assume that the woman was lying, to protect herself from blame for some relationship she dare not acknowledge. His own assumption would be that Daniel could not be at fault, not seriously.

In two or three years Jemima would be a young woman. That brief time would make no change to him. Six years, seven years, and Daniel would be a young man, with all the hungers and the curiosity, the challenge to his manhood that was there for all young men. His father was probably the last person with whom he would discuss it. How would Pitt know what he thought of women who perhaps teased him, provoked him, with little or no idea of what tigers they were awakening?

The answer was simple. He would defend Daniel as passionately and instinctively as if he were the boy Pitt still saw him as in his mind. Perhaps any father would.

He crossed Drury Lane into Long Acre, only peripherally mindful of the traffic. He was walking without purpose, simply out of the need for action.

How did he prevent Daniel from becoming a young man who treated women as something he had the right to use, to hurt, even to destroy? Where did such beliefs begin? How would he ever make certain he could lose any competition with the same grace as he would win? How would he govern temper, loss, even humiliation? The answer was obvious – at home. Would it be Pitt's fault if Jemima did not act wisely, without being crippled by fear? Would it be Pitt's fault if Daniel grew up arrogant, brutal? Of course it would.

If Neville Forsbrook were guilty of raping Angeles Castelbranco and thereby causing her death, was it his father's fault as well as his own? Probably. Would that same father defend him now, if he were accused? Almost certainly. Any man would, not only to save his child, and out of a refusal to believe he was guilty, but also to defend himself. Pelham Forsbrook would be socially ruined, and perhaps professionally damaged irreparably, if his son were convicted of such a crime.

The defence would be savage, a fight for survival. Was Pitt prepared to involve himself in that? Winning would not bring Angeles back, and the risks were great. He had little chance of winning, and if he lost he could not even estimate the cost.

And if he did not try? What would that cost?

Without being aware of it he increased his pace along the footpath. How would he feel if it were his daughter, his wife who was violated in such an intimate and terrible way? What if it was not so immediate, so visceral? What if it were Charlotte's sister Emily? He had known her as long as he had known Charlotte.

What if it were Vespasia? Age was no protection. No woman was too young, or too old. Vespasia had such courage, such dignity. Even to imagine her violation was like a kind of blasphemy. It would almost be better if her attacker were to kill her.

He visualised Vespasia lying on the floor as Narraway had told him he had seen Catherine Quixwood. It jerked him to a stop on the footpath with a pain that was almost physical. He must not allow Neville Forsbrook, or anyone else, to break his world in pieces like that. Whatever the cost, to stand by and do nothing, paralysed with fear and hopelessness, was even worse. He must think how to attack. It was they who should feel frightened and cornered, not he, not the women he cared for, or any others.

He started along the pavement again, moving as if he had purpose.

Chapter Ten

NARRAWAY CONTINUED to learn what he could about the occasions on which Catherine Quixwood had met with Alban Hythe. He studied her diaries and found notations ahead to remind her: small marks, sometimes initials, quite often figures, as if for a time of day. Others were larger numbers, and he copied them down to see if they might be for telephones, even though there were no names of exchanges in front of them. Perhaps she knew the areas in which people lived sufficiently well that that reminder was not necessary.

He questioned the staff at Quixwood's house. They were still shocked and grieving, and above all filled with uncertainty as to their future.

'No,' Flaxley said unhappily when he showed her the diary. 'I don't know what she meant by that.'

'Telephone numbers?' he asked.

She looked at them again. Most of them were in four digits. 'Perhaps – I don't know.'

They were sitting in the housekeeper's room again, a sudden squall of rain battering against the windows. Flaxley was pale and tired, even though she had little to do, except consider what position she would be able to obtain after it became known she had worked for a victim of rape and murder. People were terrified of scandal and there were plenty of good lady's maids.

Narraway was acutely conscious of that as he sat opposite her, probing her memory, and unavoidably trampling over all the past she had valued.

Having achieved nothing with his questions so far, he changed direction and became more blunt.

'Did she ever speak to you about Mr Hythe?'

'Not often,' she replied. 'Just that he was a very pleasant gentleman. It was only in connection with what dress to wear.' She smiled for a moment. 'She did not care to dress in the same gowns if she was aware she had done so on a previous occasion meeting the same person.' There was affection in her voice, in her eyes, and for a moment she was back in the happier past.

'She knew he would notice?' Narraway said quickly. He hated to break the spell of memory, and yet he had to learn all he could.

For an instant there was a flicker of contempt in her eyes, then she carefully concealed it again. 'No, my lord, most gentlemen don't know more than if they like a thing or if they don't. Another lady, of course, would know exactly, and might even be unkind enough to remark on it, but mostly ladies dress to make the best of their appearance and have the confidence then to forget about themselves and behave with wit and charm.'

Narraway had never considered the subject before, but it made perfect sense. He could see it true, above all, of Vespasia. He could not imagine her dressing to impress anyone else.

But that did not answer the question of whether Catherine had been in love with Alban Hythe or not. Or, for that matter, anyone else!

Was there any point in asking Flaxley? He looked at her rather bony face, still smudged with grief, and now anxiety as well. Her skin was scrubbed clean, her eyelids a little puffed. Her hair was pinned up neatly, but without softness, without care. He felt suddenly profoundly sorry for her. A year ago he would have brushed by the thought of being no longer needed as merely a part of life that had to be accepted. Now it cut with a very real pain, one that he felt in his own flesh and understood.

'Miss Flaxley,' he said, leaning forward slightly and meeting her eyes with more urgency, 'it was clearly important to Mrs Quixwood that she meet with Mr Hythe. She seems to have made arrangements to do so increasingly often, as much as every week or even twice a week, in the month before her death. Other things were set aside to fit with his convenience, and as far as I can find out, she mentioned these meetings to no one else. In fact she barely referred to the acquaintance at all. It was not exactly secret, but it was certainly discreet.'

Flaxley did not reply, but her gaze never left his.

'It was important to her that they met,' he went on. 'She dressed carefully, but not so as to draw undue attention to herself, not as if she were meeting a lover with whom she dared to be seen.' He stopped as he saw the flare of anger in Flaxley's eyes.

'Please describe her manner before she went out on these occasions, and when she returned,' he pressed. 'I know I am asking you to speak of things that normally you would regard as a trust that you did not ever betray, but someone abused her terribly, Miss Flaxley. Someone beat her and caused her death as surely as if they had put their hands around her throat and choked the life out of her.' He saw the tears spill over and run down her cheeks and he ignored them. 'If that was Alban Hythe, then I want to see him hang for it! And if it was not, then I want to save him. Don't you?'

She nodded so minutely it was hardly a movement at all.

'How was she, Miss Flaxley? Excited? Frightened? Anxious? Sad? Tell me! It is too late to protect her now. She has no privacy. All we can get for her at the very best is some kind of justice. And if it is loyalty to Mr Quixwood you are considering, either for his sake, or for your own – and I am aware that you will need his goodwill in securing another position – I will tell him nothing that you say unless I have to, and then I will attribute it to other sources.'

She was surprised, confused, sad to the point of rocking herself back and forth very slightly, as if the movement offered some relief.

'She was anxious,' she said in little more than a whisper. 'But not as if she were going to meet a lover, more as if she were going to hear something that was good news, or . . . or bad news. She liked Mr Hythe, but more than that I think she trusted him.'

She looked down, avoiding Narraway's eyes. 'I have known her, in the past, when she was a little in love with a gentleman. Of course she never did anything . . . wrong. But she wasn't excited like that over Mr Hythe. But she would never miss an appointment, no matter what else had to be set aside. And it seemed to grow more important to her as time went by. I swear, my lord, I don't know why. I'd tell you if I knew, whatever it was. I'd tie a rope myself to hang whoever did that to her.'

Narraway believed her. He said so, thanked her and took his leave. There was nothing more to be gained. He made a note in his mind to speak to Vespasia and see if a position could be found for Flaxley among her friends. Then he smiled as he walked out of the front door, down the steps and turned towards the square. He was becoming soft. What was the fate of one elderly lady's maid in a city of millions? A year ago he held the fates of whole nations in his hands!

How are the mighty fallen! Or was it just a realignment of his focus? Perhaps one a trifle overdue.

He continued to follow Catherine's engagements and learned little details of her tastes, what made her laugh, what angered her.

When he spoke to Quixwood about it a couple of days later, again in the library of the club, they seemed to have achieved little new. Quixwood was tired. It was easy to imagine he had found sleep elusive. He looked thinner than before and the lines in his face deeper. There was a certain hectic light in his eyes.

Narraway felt a gnawing pity for him, and a guilt that he had no real progress to report.

'She saw him often?' Quixwood said, his voice curiously flat, as if he were deliberately trying to keep it unemotional.

'Yes, at least once a week, or more, in the last month of her life,' Narraway agreed. 'But judging from her diary, and what Flaxley says of her dress and her manner, it was not a love affair.'

Quixwood gave a tiny, painful laugh. 'Dear Flaxley. Loyal to the end, even when it has become absurd. She's a good servant. It's a shame I have no possible position for her now. If Catherine was not meeting Hythe for an affair, what could it have been? He is a handsome man, at least ten years younger than she was, maybe more.'

He smiled, blinking hard. 'Catherine was beautiful, you know? And perhaps she was bored. I could not spend all day with her. I loved her.' He stared at some point in the distance, perhaps at a vision or a memory only he could see. 'But I assumed she knew it. Maybe I should have told her so more . . . more believably.'

Narraway searched for something to say that would not sound trite, and nothing came to him. What was there that was not insulting in the face of such tragedy?

'She seemed to have many interests,' Narraway said at last, when the silence was dragging heavily. The footsteps of servants could be heard on the wooden floor outside in the passageway.

Quixwood looked up. 'You mean other than going to museums and galleries?'

'She seemed to find Africa as fascinating as many others do, especially with the present unrest.'

'Unrest?' Quixwood said quickly.

'The Jameson Raid in particular,' Narraway elaborated.

'Oh.' A brief smile crossed Quixwood's face and vanished again. 'Yes, of course. That trial should start soon. The man can't have had the wits he was born with.' He sighed. 'Although I admit that in the beginning I can see how many would have thought it was a grand adventure, with money to be made.' He drew in a deep breath and let it out slowly, his voice thick with unshed tears. 'I . . . I went home the other day. I can't stay away for ever.'

Narraway waited.

Quixwood kept his eyes lowered. 'I collected some of my own clothes, a few personal things. I thought I might be ready to move back again, but I . . . I can't. Not yet.' He looked up at Narraway. 'I was looking at Catherine's jewellery. I thought I should put it in the bank. I don't really know why. I don't know what to do with it, except keep it safe. I suppose there will be something to do with it . . . one day. I . . .' Again he stopped and took a long, jerky breath. 'I found this.' He held out a small, delicate brooch, not expensive but very pretty – three tiny flowers in various stages of opening, like buttercups. It could have been gold, possibly pinchbeck. 'It's new,' he said softly. 'I didn't give it to her. I asked Flaxley where it came from. She didn't know, but she could tell me when she last saw it. It was after Catherine had met with Hythe at an exhibition of some sort.'

Narraway looked more carefully at the piece, without touching it. 'I see,' he said with sharp regret. 'Is there any proof that Hythe gave it to her?'

Quixwood shook his head. 'No. Only Flaxley's word that that was the day she first had it.'

'And Flaxley would know?' Narraway pressed.

'Oh, yes. She is very good at her job, and completely honest.' Quixwood smiled. 'She hated admitting it, but she would not lie . . . to me, or to anyone. Of course it proves nothing, I know that. But I have no idea what would!' He looked very steadily at Narraway. 'Perhaps it will help?'

Narraway took the brooch. 'I'll see if I can find out anything about it. It's very attractive – individual. If I can trace it, it would at least be indicative.'

Quixwood stared at the floor. 'Whatever happens, I'm grateful to you for your time and your patience, and . . . and for your great compassion.'

Narraway said nothing. He was embarrassed because he felt he had done so little.

He took the brooch to a jeweller he had consulted in the past when wanting to know the origin or value of a piece.

'What can you tell me about it?' Narraway asked, offering the old man the delicate little golden flowers.

The old man took it in his gnarled fingers, turned it over and squinted at the back, then looked at the front again.

'Well?' Narraway prompted him.

'Old piece, perhaps fifty or sixty years. Pretty, but not worth a great deal. Perhaps two or three pounds. Individual, though, and women tend to like that. Come to it, I like that.' He looked at Narraway curiously. 'Stolen? Who'd bother? Couldn't sell it on. Come from a crime?' He shook his head. 'Shame. Somebody took care and I'd say a lot of pleasure in making that. Innocent little flowers. Tainted with blood and treason now?'

Narraway evaded the question. 'Where would you buy or sell something like this?'

The old man pursed his lips. 'Sell it to a pawnshop, not get more than a few shillings for it at most. Buy it there again for a bit more.'

'And if I wanted to be discreet?' Narraway pressed.

'Barrow in Petticoat Lane. You don't need me to tell you that.'

'Gold or pinchbeck?'

'Pinchbeck, Mr Narraway. You don't need me for that neither. Pretty thing, nice workmanship. Sentimental, not worth money.' He handed it back. 'You got as much chance of tracing it as you have of winning the Derby.'

'Somebody has to win,' Narraway pointed out.

'You've got to ride in it first,' the old man said with a dry laugh. 'You thought I meant putting money on it? Any fool can do that.'

Narraway thanked him and went back outside into the sun, the little brooch in his pocket again.

Reluctantly he visited Maris Hythe in her home that evening to show her the brooch and see if she had ever seen it before. He loathed doing it, but he would be derelict not to ask.

She took it and turned it over in her hand. She looked puzzled.

'Have you seen anything like it before?' he asked.

'No.' She looked up at him. 'Whose is it? Why do you bring it to me?' There was fear in her eyes.

'It was Catherine Quixwood's,' he replied. 'Her husband says he didn't give it to her.'

'And you think Alban did?' It was a challenge. 'He would hardly have told me.'

'Is it the sort of thing he would like?'

She looked down, avoiding his eyes. 'Yes. It's individual. It's old. I expect it has history. Several people might have owned it, worn it.' She held it delicately, as if she too would have been pleased with it as a gift. 'She might have bought it for herself,' she said at last, passing it back to him.

He took it. Had he achieved anything more than to raise doubts in her mind, more questions as to her husband's involvement with the woman who had owned it? He felt slightly soiled by the act.

'I suppose it will make no difference if my husband tells you that he has not seen it before?'

'It means nothing one way or the other without proof,' Narraway replied. 'Mr Quixwood mentioned it to me as something among her jewellery that he had not seen before.'

'Or not noticed,' she corrected wryly. 'Men frequently do not notice an entire garment that is new, let alone one small item. Ask any woman, she will tell you the same.'

'But a man knows which jewels he has bought his wife,' he pointed out. 'That's rather different.' There was also the matter of Miss Flaxley's not seeing the brooch before.

She looked up at him, meeting his eyes, her face very pale. 'I have told you what I know, Lord Narraway, which is only that my husband was doing Mrs Quixwood a favour in a matter that was of great importance to her. He will not tell me what it was but I trust him.' Her voice wavered a little, but her eyes did not.

He admired her, but he was aware with deep sorrow and a chill inside himself that she might one day have to face a far uglier truth. He certainly would not tell her so now. Let her keep hope as long as possible. He was not yet certain beyond doubt that she was mistaken. If a woman loved him as Maris Hythe loved her husband, Narraway would wish her to keep faith in him, whatever the evidence appeared to be, even whatever a jury might decide. Only irrefutable proof, or his own confession, would be enough to break it.

They were discussing other avenues to explore when Knox came in through the door, walking past the white-faced maid standing with her back rigid.

'What can I do for you?' Maris asked, startled, her voice trembling and now defensive. 'My husband is in his study. He still has work to complete. Do you require to see him at this hour?' There was reproof in her face, as if he were uncivil.

Knox looked tired and deeply unhappy. There was a light summer rain outside and his coat was wet. He seemed bedraggled, like a bird whose plumage was moulting.

'I'm afraid I do, Mrs Hythe. But I'm glad Lord Narraway is here to be with you.'

She looked startled, but said nothing, still sitting on the sofa, as if afraid her legs would not support her.

Although it seemed incredible, Narraway suddenly realised what Knox was here for. He stood up.

'Why?' he demanded. 'Aren't you being precipitate?'

Knox looked at him sadly, biting his lip. 'No, my lord. I regret not. Unfortunately in our search of Mr Hythe's possessions we found what can only be described as a love letter from Mrs Quixwood.'

'When?' Narraway demanded, his mind racing to think of some innocent explanation of such a thing. 'When did you search Mr Hythe's belongings? Just now?'

'No, my lord, earlier today, with Mrs Hythe's permission.'

'But you didn't arrest him then?' There was challenge in Narraway's voice, but it was emotion rather than reason.

'No, my lord. Mr Hythe denied knowing about it. I wanted to give him every opportunity, even on the assumption that the letter was not genuinely in Mrs Quixwood's hand. I have verified that it is unquestionably hers, and the contents of the letter could not be interpreted as anything but between lovers. I'm sorry.'

Maris rose to her feet at last, swaying a little, her chin high.

'That . . .' Narraway swallowed hard. 'That does not prove that he raped her . . . or killed her!' He sounded ridiculous, and he knew it, and yet he seemed unable to help himself.

'If it were innocent, my lord, Mr Hythe would explain it, not deny it,' Knox said with a shake of his head, barely a movement at all. 'Don't make it harder than it needs to be, sir.'

Narraway had no answer. His throat was tight, his mouth dry. He looked across at Maris's ashen face and turned his attention to her, going across to stand beside her, even put his arm around her as she struggled to keep her balance, giddy with horror and grief.

They heard footsteps down the stairs, and then the opening and closing of the front door.

Without speaking, his shoulders bowed, Knox went out also, disappearing into the night and the rain.

Chapter Eleven

STOKER CAME into Pitt's office and closed the door behind him.

'Sir, something's happened I think you should know about.' His expression was bleak, his eyes sharp and troubled.

'What is it?' Pitt asked immediately.

Stoker took a deep breath. 'There's been another very nasty rape of a young woman, sir, and I'm afraid this one is dead. Seventeen, her father says. Respectable, good family. Walking out regular with a young man in the Grenadiers.'

Pitt felt horror ripple through him, then an overwhelming pity for the father, but also a sense of relief he was ashamed of. This was not Special Branch business. He could leave the pain and the bitter discoveries to someone else.

'I'm very sorry to hear that,' he said quietly. 'But it's for the police to handle, Stoker, it's nothing to do with us.'

'I'm not sure about that, sir,' Stoker shook his head. 'Very violent, it was. Quite a lot of blood, and her neck was broken with the force of the blow.'

Stoker stood rigid, almost to attention, like a soldier.

'Way I see it, sir, young women don't usually say they were raped, unless they're beaten so badly and . . . and injured in a way you can't mistake it. Or else they're dead, like this poor girl.'

'It's still not ours,' Pitt said hoarsely. 'It's for the regular police. You're not going to tell me she's a foreign diplomat's daughter, are you?'

Stoker raised his chin a little.

'No, sir, just an importer and exporter of some sort. But her young man's a friend of Neville Forsbrook and his crowd, even met Miss Castelbranco once or twice, so her father says.' He waited, staring at Pitt.

'Are you saying there's a connection?' Pitt framed the words slowly, still trying to reject the idea.

'Don't know, sir.' Stoker attempted to smooth his face of anger and frustration, and failed. 'I doubt the newspapers will make one. Nobody else knows Miss Castelbranco was raped, and she was certainly alive until she went through that window herself. And, by the way, they've arrested someone for raping Mrs Quixwood, but it's a close thing as to whether he was in custody at the time of this one.'

Pitt was startled. 'Have they? That's Inspector Knox, isn't it?' He thought of Narraway, and wondered why he had not yet mentioned it.

'Yes, sir. A very good man, from what I've heard.'

'Well, who did they arrest?' Pitt said sharply.

'Alban Hythe,' Stoker said flatly, his voice expressionless. 'Young man. A banker, so they say. Married. Not what you'd expect. Seems they were lovers – at least that's what I hear from a friend I have in the police.'

Pitt said nothing. Perhaps that was why Narraway had not told him. He had not wanted to think Catherine Quixwood was in any way to blame, even remotely. Rape and suicide. Very different from this new case.

'What's her name?' he asked, meeting Stoker's eyes again. 'This new one, I mean.'

'Pamela O'Keefe, sir. It'll make a big splash in the newspapers, I should imagine. When it does, the Portuguese Ambassador's going to be very upset. I would be.' He stood still in front of the desk until Pitt should respond, his back stiff, his bony hands moving restlessly, not quite clenching.

Normally Pitt would have resented the pressure, even the suggestion of insolence, however, he knew it sprang from Stoker's own sense of helplessness in the face of what he felt was an outrage. He expected Pitt, as head of Special Branch, to do something about it.

'Be careful, Stoker,' Pitt warned. 'The Foreign Secretary personally has warned me that there's nothing we can do about Angeles Castelbranco. If we try to prosecute we would only make it worse for her family. We can't prove anything.'

Then suddenly his own anger overwhelmed him, the obscene injustice of it. 'Damn it, man! I was in the building when the poor girl went through the window. Forsbrook says she was hysterical, and so she was. The only question is, what made her so. Was she terrified of him, and for good reason? Was she blaming him for something that happened with her and someone else? Or was it all in her own fevered imagination?'

Stoker's eyes blazed and he stood so stiffly his shoulders were clenched and high, but he knew to keep silent.

Pitt's temper snapped, not with Stoker, but Stoker got the brunt of it simply because he was there.

'Do you think I wouldn't arrest the bastard if I could?' he shouted. 'No charge would stick to him and we'd end up looking ridiculous. Far more to the point, the poor girl is—' He stopped, appalled. 'God! I was going to say decently buried – but she isn't. She's just shoved into some hole in the ground, because the sanctimonious bloody Church has decided she might have taken her own life!'

He very seldom swore, and he heard his own voice with disgust. He was shaking with fury, much of it from the complete uselessness he felt. Every instinct in him was to attack, to punish Forsbrook until there was nothing left of him. And all he could do was stand by and watch.

And now Stoker, too, was expecting something of him he could not give. He was ashamed of it. He wondered for a brief instant if Narraway would have done better. Perhaps he would.

Stoker did not flinch. 'So are we going to let it go . . . sir?' he asked. His voice was so tight in his throat it was a pitch higher.

'When was Alban Hythe arrested?' Pitt said coldly.

'Last night, sir, or more accurately, late yesterday evening,' Stoker replied. 'Shortly after Pamela O'Keefe was raped and killed, if that's what you're asking. Too close to call.'

'Of course that's what I'm asking!' Pitt snapped. 'So could he be guilty of killing Pamela O'Keefe, regardless of any other crimes with Mrs Quixwood or Angeles Castelbranco?'

'No, sir, not likely,' Stoker said grimly. He took a breath. 'We've got two violent men raping respectable women. Or even maybe three. Or are you thinking that Angeles Castelbranco wasn't raped, and maybe killed herself over something else? Maybe the papers are right and she was with child, so her fiancé threw her over and she couldn't see any way out of it?'

'No, I'm not thinking that!' Pitt all but snarled. He knew he was being unfair, but the sense of outrage and futility suffocated him. 'Coincidences happen, but I don't believe in them until there's nothing else left.' He stared up at Stoker's blank face. 'Find out if there's any connection between Forsbrook and this poor girl, or any of his group of friends, for that matter. Maybe he was the leader of the bunch of cowards that went after Angeles, but he might not have been the one who raped her. We don't know for certain. It seemed to be him she was frightened of, witnesses say, but maybe they were all in it, as far as she was concerned.'

'A gang of them?' Stoker said with disgust, his hands curled into fists. 'Isn't that some special sort of crime?' There was a lift of hope in his voice.

'If he killed the O'Keefe girl we can hang him just as high as if he was responsible for Angeles' death as well,' Pitt replied. 'Go and find out. But, Stoker . . .'

Stoker was at the door and turned. 'Yes, sir,' he said with a blankness close to insolence.

Pitt understood, even respected it.

'Be careful!' he warned. 'I would very much rather the Foreign Secretary had no occasion even to think of us at the moment, let alone know anything. I've been told to leave it alone. It was an order. I need to be damn careful not to be seen disobeying. Your enquiries are for the purpose of making certain Mr Forsbrook is not mistakenly blamed for any of this. Do you understand?'

Stoker snapped to attention, his eyes brilliant as sunlight on ice. 'Absolutely, sir. We must protect our national honour from any suggestion that an upstanding young gentleman like Mr Forsbrook is slandered by some foreign ambassador, no matter how upset the poor man might be about his daughter's most unfortunate death in our capital city.' He took a breath and went on. 'And we must make certain there is no connection made in anyone's mind between that and this other poor girl's rape and murder, sir. Mrs Quixwood is quite another matter . . . no connection whatever. Regrettably London appears to be full of rapists and I suppose young ladies are not careful enough who they keep company with—'

'Stoker!' Pitt shouted.

'Yes, sir?' Stoker opened his eyes wide.

'You've made your point.'

Stoker lowered his voice. 'Yes, sir.' There was something close to a smile on his lips. 'I'll report to you as soon as I have anything, sir.' And without waiting to be dismissed, he turned on his heel and went out.

Pitt picked up the telephone to call Victor Narraway.

Two hours late Pitt and Narraway walked along the Embankment with the magnificent Palace of Westminster towering above them in the sun. Pitt had told Narraway of the new rape case very briefly on the telephone, keeping the details until they met. Narraway in turn had given him nothing beyond the bare fact of Alban Hythe's arrest. His own ambivalent emotions about it were there in his voice.

On the river to their left a pleasure boat passed with people crowding the decks, laughing and pointing, straw hats waving, bright with ribbons. Somewhere out of sight a barrel organ was playing a popular song. The sound of laughter drifted on the breeze.

'Stoker told me this morning,' Pitt said quietly. 'Apparently it happened yesterday evening. They can't be sure as to the exact time. Quite early.'

'Alban Hythe was already under arrest by nine,' Narraway replied. 'I know that beyond doubt. I was there when they took him. He'd been in the house for some time.'

Pitt looked across at Narraway's face, trying to read his emotions. As always, it was difficult, but he was getting to know him far better than he had when Narraway had been his superior. Even in the short time Pitt had been in charge of Special Branch he had carried the burden that Narraway had borne for years, and with that came a different kind of understanding. Perhaps he himself was harder to read than he had been before. He hoped so.

Now, in Narraway's features he saw uncertainty and unhappiness. In a way they had changed positions. Narraway was tasting the personal shock and pain, the dismay in the face of crime. Pitt was feeling the terrible loneliness and weight of responsibility he could not pass on to anyone else, could not even share.

'You don't think he's guilty of raping Catherine Quixwood, do you?' Pitt observed.

Narraway looked at him sharply. His eyes were nearly black in the sunlight, the pale streaks at his temples silver.

'I don't know,' he admitted, expression half concealed. 'I'm not used to this . . . this sort of crime. It's nothing like anarchy or treason. I don't know how the devil you dealt with it, with the people and their . . . lives.'

'One at a time,' Pitt replied drily. 'It's not worse than being the one who decides who gets charged, who doesn't, who's let go quietly, and who gets killed. It's just different. In the police you find the facts, then pass it all over to someone else to make the judgement.'

'*Touché*,' Narraway said quietly, glancing at Pitt and then away again. 'And no, I don't think I believe Alban Hythe raped Catherine Quixwood and drove her to suicide. But that may well be because I don't want to. I liked him. And I like his wife. I don't want to watch while all her hopes and dreams are laid bare and broken for the public to watch. And also I don't want to think Catherine Quixwood took a lover who did that to her. What a hell of a betrayal!'

'Liking people has very little to do with it,' Pitt pointed out. 'Even sympathising with them sometimes. More than once I've thought I could have done the same thing – had I been in the same situation.'

Narraway stared at him, incredulity in his eyes. As Pitt did not flinch, slowly it became the beginning of an understanding. 'You mean kill someone?'

'I don't mean rape them!' Pitt retorted a little waspishly. 'I've felt like killing those who beat and terrify women, children, the weak, the old; those who blackmail and extort and the law doesn't touch them.'

'Rapists?' Narraway asked.

'Yes, those also.'

'Pitt . . .' Narraway started.

Pitt smiled with a twisted humour. 'Only if it happened to my wife, or daughter. But I can understand it.'

Narraway bit his lip. 'So can I, and I have no wife or daughter. Do we need to watch Quixwood, once he knows it's Hythe? Or if Hythe gets off?'

'If he gets off, yes, very possibly,' Pitt admitted.

'And the Portuguese Ambassador?' Narraway added quietly.

Pitt shivered. 'I am watching. It is one of several things I am afraid of.'

Narraway looked at him closely. 'And the others?'

'That whoever is doing this will not stop,' Pitt replied.

'All the same man? It can't be, unless Hythe is innocent?' Narraway said it with something that could have been hope.

'Or we have two, or even three men of such violent and brutal disposition loose in London right now,' Pitt finished the thought.

Narraway did not answer.

Pitt had not seen Rafael Castelbranco for nearly a week. There had been no news to report that would ease any of his distress. However, Pitt felt compelled to inform him of the arrest of Alban Hythe, and that as far as he was aware, Catherine Quixwood's death had nothing to do with Angeles.

He made the appointment formally and presented himself at the Portuguese Embassy at four o'clock, as requested.

He was received in a large study with elegant furniture, a wooden floor with beautifully woven rugs, and portraits of past kings and queens of Portugal on the wall.

Castelbranco came forward to greet him. He was at least outwardly composed, still wearing black relieved only by a white shirt, with no jewellery, not even a pocket watch. His face was calm but his eyes looked hollow, and his skin brittle and drained of colour. He did not even pretend to smile, nor did he offer refreshment.

'Good afternoon, Commander Pitt,' he said in little more than a whisper, as if his throat were painful. 'Have you come to tell me that

179

you can do nothing to prosecute the man who drove my daughter to her death?' There was no bitterness in his voice, no accusation, just pain.

Pitt hesitated. He had been prepared to be less blunt and this took him by surprise, but to be evasive now would be insulting.

'I suppose, for the meantime, that is the truth,' he replied. 'But the reason I came today is to tell you that a man has been arrested for the rape, and thus causing the suicide, of another woman. It is not public news yet, but it will be at the latest by tomorrow morning.'

Castelbranco was startled. His body stiffened. His dark eyes met Pitt's with bewilderment. 'Another woman? And you can arrest him for raping her?'

Pitt was embarrassed and he knew it showed in his face. 'He appears to have had a relationship with her that can be proved,' he explained, feeling as if he were making excuses. 'They were seen together. There are letters, gifts between them.'

Castelbranco said nothing, his eyes unmoving, his mouth closed tightly.

'She let him into her house, after dark,' Pitt went on. 'When her husband was at a function in the course of his business, and she had dismissed the servants. The man raped her and beat her extremely badly. She was very seriously injured indeed, but it was actually an overdose of laudanum that directly caused her death, even though the rape was responsible.'

Castelbranco was stunned. He stepped back and sank into one of the chairs. He breathed in and out heavily, his fingers gripping the leather of the arms. For several moments he did not speak. When he did, it was with difficulty.

'Are you saying that this same . . . creature . . . raped my daughter, Mr Pitt?'

Pitt felt again as if he were making excuses, totally ineffectually.

'No, Ambassador, I'm not. Nor am I suggesting that your daughter had any relationship with the man who did. I'm telling you of this only because the case bears a superficial resemblance, and I don't want you to hear of it without some warning. Also, the man is only accused. He has not stood trial yet, and he has denied his guilt completely. Indeed it is possible he may be innocent.'

'You said there was a relationship between this man and the woman he raped? Letters, gifts, meetings?' Castelbranco accused.

'Yes, it seems so. And he cannot account for his time on the evening this poor woman was attacked.'

'She let him in? What kind of a woman was she?' Castelbranco glared at him, bewildered and hurt, desperately seeking escape from the thoughts that crowded in on him.

'According to what I have heard, a beautiful woman in her early forties, trapped in a lonely and sterile marriage,' Pitt replied.

'And so she took a lover who was depraved?' Castelbranco closed his eyes as if by not seeing Pitt he could deny the reality of what he had said. 'Her poor husband. He must be insane with grief. I hear my daughter spoken of as if she were a loose woman, without virtue, but at least I know it was not true.' The tears seeped between his eyelids and it took him some moments to master himself. 'What must he feel, poor man?'

'I can't imagine,' Pitt confessed. 'I've tried to. I have a wife and a daughter. And a son,' he added.

Castelbranco stared at him. 'And a son?' Clearly he saw no sense in the remark.

'I look at my son,' Pitt did not avert his eyes. 'He's nearly twelve. What will I do to make certain he never misuses any woman, no matter who she is, or how she uses him?'

'Do you imagine this man's father is thinking such a thing?' Castelbranco asked bitterly. 'What guilt could be greater than that?' He gave a slight shrug, painfully, as if his shoulders ached. 'Or perhaps he refuses to believe it? It takes great courage to accept the very worst you can imagine.'

'The courage would serve better to accept the possibility beforehand, and do what you can to prevent it,' Pitt answered him. 'I apologise for us all that we did not, and now that it has happened, we can offer you no justice, for whatever small satisfaction that would be.'

Castelbranco did not answer, but he inclined his head in acknowledgement.

Pitt weighed his words carefully. He still had not delivered the message that was his reason for coming. He must do so.

'If this man proves to be guilty of raping Mrs Quixwood – and that is by no means certain yet – but if he is, I would not blame Rawdon Quixwood if he were to find the opportunity to kill the man himself,' he admitted. 'But much as I dare say Inspector Knox, the policeman concerned, would regret it, he would still have to arrest him and charge him with murder. He would then be tried, and if found guilty, perhaps not hanged, but certainly spend many years in prison. It would magnify the tragedy immeasurably for his family. He has no children, but no doubt there are those who love him. Parents, or a brother or sister.'

'And if the law excuses this man who raped Mrs Quixwood, or you cannot find sufficient proof of his guilt?' Castelbranco asked. His voice was hoarse, barely audible, his eyes fixed on Pitt's. 'What if he murders him then? Or what if this man was found dead, how hard would Knox, or any of you, search to discover and prove who killed him?'

'You are hoping I would say that we would make only a token effort, and be delighted to fail,' Pitt said with considerable compassion. 'I would be tempted to, believe me. I dare say Knox would also. But then this man has a young wife who not only loves him, but believes in his innocence. Perhaps he has a father, or brothers who would look more diligently for whoever killed him? How long does it go on?'

Catelbranco looked at the floor, his eyes closed. 'I understand your message, Mr Pitt. I shall not murder my daughter's rapist, even if I should believe that I have found him. Who would then look after my wife? She needs, and deserves, more of me than that. She too has lost her only child.'

Pitt struggled for an answer, anything that would offer even a crumb of comfort, but everything that came to his mind was a lie, and Castelbranco would know it. He did not deserve that kind of condescension.

'I'm sorry,' he said instead.

Castelbranco did not answer.

Pitt arrived home a little early. He had received a brief report from Stoker. So far there was nothing whatever to suggest that Alban Hythe had ever met, or even heard of Angeles Castelbranco. He had not attended any of the same social events, or moved in the same circles. Added to which, any theatres, dinners or balls he enjoyed, he had gone to in company with his wife. The galleries and museums where he had met Catherine Quixwood were not places to which Angeles Castelbranco had ever been; but if she had, she would have been chaperoned by her mother.

Charlotte must have heard his footsteps because she greeted him in the hall, kissing him quickly and then pulling away.

'Is it true?' she said urgently. 'Have they arrested a man for the rape and murder of Catherine Quixwood? Is he the same man who raped Angeles? They won't have to charge him with both, will they? Or would it be better if they did, then at least people would know she was a victim, and not a loose woman? I heard that he and Catherine were lovers? Is that true? Then why would he rape Angeles?'

'Where would you like me to begin?' he said with a smile. The warmth of his own home, the smells of clean laundry, lavender and furniture wax on polished wood, all closed around him and he wanted to forget the violence and loss of other people's lives. He couldn't prevent it; he couldn't always solve it with answers or with justice. He needed to build a barrier around himself and, for a time, close it out beyond his awareness. But he looked at Charlotte's troubled face, the anxiety in her eyes, and knew that she would not allow him to. She was thinking of Isaura Castelbranco, seeing in her a woman too much like herself to ignore.

'Don't equivocate, Thomas!' she said sharply. 'You know perfectly well what I mean!'

'I know what you would like me to say,' he replied, his lips stiff, his tongue fumbling with the words. 'That yes, we have someone. That he's locked away and we'll prove him guilty. That one day everyone will know that Angles was innocent and her good name will be restored.'

'You think I want a comfortable lie?' she said incredulously. 'We've been married for fifteen years, Thomas, and that's what you think? Then how many times have you told me what you imagined I wanted rather than the truth? Sometimes? Often? Always?'

'What are you so frightened of?' he demanded furiously. 'You think someone's going to attack you? They're not.'

'Aren't they?' She looked at him with real anger and fear. 'And not Jemima? Why not? Isn't she pretty enough? Important enough? Or are you saying they only attack foreigners? Catherine Quixwood was as English as I am!' She drew in a deep breath and went on, 'You said he was her lover! So it wasn't some stranger who broke into the house, it was someone she knew and trusted. That could happen to any of us, especially someone young, who doesn't know the difference between real love and—'

'Charlotte!' He cut across her words sharply. 'I didn't actually say anything at all, I just asked which question you wanted answered first.'

She was hurt, the more so because he was right, and in the face of her fear it was irrelevant. 'I want all of them answered. Have you told the Castelbrancos?'

'Yes, I have. They would hear of it soon enough, but I wanted to warn Rafael not to do anything foolish.'

She paled, the anger in her eyes instantly replaced by horror.

He put his arm around her and gently pushed her towards the parlour. When they were inside he closed the door.

'They have arrested a very respectable young married man named Alban Hythe,' he told her, his voice calmer now. 'His wife is young and charming, and so far still believes in him totally.'

Charlotte's eyes widened, all fury turned to pity. 'Poor woman,' she whispered. 'I imagine she loves him – loves what she thought he was. She won't be able to bear thinking anything else . . . until she has to.' She shook her head and all the tiny muscles in her face tightened as she imagined the other woman's pain. 'I didn't think there would be anything worse than losing a child, but perhaps that would be. It has robbed her not only of the present and the future, but of all that she believed of the past as well.'

'We don't know that he's guilty,' Pitt said gently. He wanted to comfort her, but he would not dare say anything less than the truth. She would not forgive him for that, no matter how much she understood. It was part of the courage and the passion in her that he loved. It did not matter whether she was right or not; she was never a coward, and never without pity.

She stared at him now, ready to accuse him of equivocation again.

'Victor Narraway isn't at all sure that Hythe is guilty,' he said, watching her face.

She was startled. 'Victor isn't?' Without thinking she had used his given name. She pretended not to be, but she was perfectly aware that Narraway had been in love with her during the Irish adventure, and for some time before that. She also was quite certain that it would pass, and possibly even that it would leave him a better man for both the awakening, and the pain.

'No,' Pitt agreed. 'And Narraway has been doing some investigation of his own.' He made no comment on her use of his name, but he remembered that disturbing knowledge too.

'Was this Hythe man Catherine's lover?' she asked.

'He says not. She was lonely, intelligent, starved for someone with whom to share ideas, discovery, beauty.'

'And her husband is . . .' she chose her words delicately, '. . . a bore?'

'Perhaps insensitive,' he amended. 'Yes, from her point of view, very possibly a bore. Maybe he is too involved in business to realise that in order to be a complete person, one needs pleasure as well, laughter, things to share.'

'Lonely enough to take a lover?' she pressed.

'Enough to seek a friend,' he corrected. 'At least that is what Narraway thinks. He says Mrs Hythe is also warm and interesting, and quite individual.'

Charlotte smiled. 'For him to have noticed, she must be! So do they have the wrong man?'

'I don't know, but it seems quite possible.'

'And what about Neville Forsbrook?' she challenged. 'There is no doubt whatever that he is the one Angeles Castelbranco was terrified of.'

'Isn't there? You don't think it could have been one of the other young men with him? Think carefully, remember exactly what you saw.'

'Would that be his defence, if you charged him?' she said quickly.

'I imagine so.'

'Well, it was him. The others were only following his lead. She was

185

looking at him all the time she backed away.' There was absolute conviction in her voice and in the bright anger in her eyes. 'I'll swear to it, if I have to,' she added.

'You won't have to.' Suddenly he was weary of it, of the injustice and the futility. 'There's nothing with which to charge him.'

'So Hythe may be innocent, and yet he'll go to trial, whereas Forsbrook is guilty, and he'll walk away without anyone even mentioning his name? What's the matter with us?' Now there was fear in her face again: fear of the unreason, the lack of justice.

Pitt wanted desperately to give her an answer that would offer comfort, or at least hope. She was looking at him, wanting it not only for herself but for everyone, for her children, and there was nothing honest he could say. If he lied now and she found out, no matter how much she wanted to, she would not be able to believe him again, next time there was injustice, threat of violence or tragedy.

'We haven't tried Hythe yet,' he said quietly. 'We may find him not guilty, and clear his name.'

'Will it clear his name?' she asked. 'Or will people go on thinking it was him, and he just got away with it? Do you suppose people in general will really listen to the evidence?'

'We may get someone else for it,' he said, trying to force hope into his voice, and his eyes.

'And Forsbrook?' she went on. 'Will justice ever catch up with him? Or will people go on happy with the easy answer that Angeles was a foreigner, and no better than she should be? She wasn't raped at all, she was just with child, and couldn't stand the shame of it.' Then she saw his face, and blushed miserably. 'I'm sorry, Thomas. I know there's nothing you can do. I wish I hadn't said that.'

He smiled and kissed her gently. 'I'm still looking for proof.'

'Be careful,' she warned. 'It won't help anybody if the government throws you out.'

'I won't give them the excuse. I promise you that.' And even as he said it, he wondered if that would prove eventually to be untrue.

They ate dinner at the kitchen table with the late sun streaming in through the back windows. The smell of clean cotton emanated from the sheets on the airing rail, and there was fresh bread on the rack above the oven.

Daniel ate with relish, as usual, but Jemima pushed her food around her plate. Her face was miserable, eyes down.

'If you don't want that potato can I have it?' Daniel asked hopefully, looking at her plate.

'"May I",' Charlotte corrected him automatically.

Daniel was disappointed. 'You want it?' he said with surprise.

'No, thank you.' She stifled a smile. 'The word "like" is better than "want", in that way. "I would like it, please." But "can" refers to ability. If you are asking permission for something it is, "may I please".'

Wordlessly Jemima passed the potato over to her brother.

'Papa, what happened to Mrs Quixwood? Why did she kill herself?' she asked.

Charlotte drew in her breath, held it a second, staring at Pitt. Then she let it out in a sigh.

'Was she in love with someone she shouldn't have been?' Tears brimmed Jemima's eyes and her cheeks were pink.

'You don't kill yourself over that!' Daniel said with disgust. 'Well, I suppose girls might . . .'

'It's usually men who run out of control in that area, not women,' Charlotte said sharply. 'And we don't know what happened yet. Maybe we never will.'

'She was attacked in a very personal way,' Pitt replied, looking at Daniel. 'Parts of the body that are private. And then she was so badly beaten that there was blood all over the place. She drank some wine with medicine in it, possibly to dull the pain, and maybe she took too much, and that is what she died of.'

Daniel looked startled, and suddenly very sober.

Pitt ploughed on. 'When you are older you will develop certain appetites and desires towards women. It's a natural part of becoming a man. You will learn how to control them, and that you do not make love to a woman unless she is as willing as you are.'

'You do not make love to her unless you are married to her!' Charlotte corrected him firmly, with a quick glance at Jemima, then back to Pitt.

In spite of himself, Pitt smiled. 'We will have a long talk about that, a little later,' he told his son. 'And not at the dinner table.'

'If he really hurt her, and it was his fault, why is everybody angry with her?' Jemima asked.

'Because they're frightened,' Charlotte said before Pitt could frame an answer he thought suitable for his daughter, not really knowing how much she knew of the whole subject. He had left such discussions to Charlotte, as the subject with Daniel would be his responsibility.

Jemima blinked and a tear slid down her cheek. 'Why are they frightened?'

'Because rape can happen to any woman,' Charlotte said. 'Just like being struck by lightning . . . and about as often.'

'Hardly anyone gets struck by lightning,' Daniel pointed out. 'And if you don't go out and stand in the middle of a field in a thunderstorm, there's nothing to be afraid of.'

'Thank you,' Charlotte smiled at him. 'That was the point I was trying to make. But when it does happen to someone quite well known, and it's very tragic, then some people become afraid and they blame the person it happened to, because if it was their own fault, then everyone else is safe.'

'Was it her own fault?' Jemima did not seem comforted.

Charlotte looked at her steadily. 'We have no idea, and it would be cruel of us to assume it was until we know. But perhaps you and I should have a longer talk about it this evening, at a more suitable time. Now please eat the rest of your dinner, and let us discuss something pleasanter.'

But the conversation could not be avoided. Charlotte knew from Jemima's unhappy face that something was troubling her profoundly, something more than the usual day-to-day dreams and nightmares of being fourteen.

'Would it be my fault if – if I . . . really liked someone?' Jemima asked, her eyes lowered, too afraid to look up at her mother.

'What you feel is not your fault,' Charlotte picked her way through the minefield of emotions. 'But what you do about it is your responsibility. Perhaps in view of what everyone is talking about, it is a good time to discuss what is wise behaviour, what is becoming, and what is very likely to be misunderstood and taken as permission you really do not mean to give.'

'We've already talked about it, Mama.'

'Then why are you still unhappy and apparently confused?'

Jemima looked up and blinked, tears in her eyes again. 'What is rape? I mean exactly? Could it happen to me? Would I die? I mean, would I have to commit suicide? That's a terrible sin, isn't it?'

'If someone is so desperately unhappy that that is what they want to do, then I think I would forgive them,' Charlotte answered. 'And I think God has to be better than I am, and love people more, so I think He would forgive them too. There might be a price to pay, I don't know. There normally is for anything done less well than we could have done it, for acts of omission as well as comission. But it is not my place, thank heaven, to judge anyone else. And as far as Catherine Quixwood and Angeles Castelbranco are concerned, we don't know if either of them meant to die. I certainly don't believe Angeles did. I was there and I am sure she did not realise how close she was to the window, and she simply fell.'

'So she'll be all right? In heaven, I mean?' Jemima said earnestly.

'Certainly. It is the man who raped her who will not.'

'Everybody says "rape", but they don't say what he actually did to her.'

Charlotte knew that she must face the issue now, or make it even worse.

'We have talked about love and marriage before, and having children,' she said frankly. 'If you love someone, and he is gentle and funny and wise, as your father is, then the acts of intimacy are wonderful. You will treasure them always. But if you imagine that kind of act with someone you do not know or like, and he tears your clothes off you and forces you, hurting you until you bleed, then beating you . . .'

Jemima let out a gasp of horror and amazement.

'That is what is called rape,' Charlotte finished. 'It is terrible at the time – it must be – but that is not all. You may find that you are with

189

child, which will have consequences for the rest of your life, because the child is a person, and one you have brought into the world. You will love him, or her, but the child will also remind you of what happened.'

Jemima stared at her, blinking slowly, tears on her cheeks.

'And as you have already heard, people will tend to blame you,' Charlotte continued. 'They will say that somehow it was your own fault. You were dressed in such a way that he thought you were willing to take any man, or you invited him and only said "no" at the last moment. Or he may even say you were perfectly happy, you just say it is his fault now, so that you are not to blame for losing your virginity, and therefore your reputation. It would be very difficult indeed to make a good marriage, because men do not want a woman who has had that kind of experience.'

'I think I might kill myself too,' Jemima said slowly.

'There will be no need,' Charlotte told her steadily. 'It will not happen to you. You will not see young men alone until you are a very great deal older, by which time you will also be wiser and more able to make your own wishes known, unmistakably. No one ever treated me that way, nor will they treat you less than as the woman you choose to be.'

Jemima nodded. 'And Papa will catch the man who did that to Mrs Quixwood, and to Angeles, won't he?'

'Mrs Quixwood is not his case, and yes, he will do something about the man who raped Angeles, but it will not be easy, and it may take some time.'

Jemima smiled. 'We're lucky, aren't we, to have Papa to look after us?'

'Yes, we are. But you will still not see young men alone, no matter who they are.'

'But . . .' Jemima began.

Charlotte raised her eyebrows slightly.

'But with others? If Fanny Welsh is there too, it's all right?' Jemima insisted.

'I will take it under advisement, and let you know,' Charlotte replied.

Chapter Twelve

NARRAWAY HATED prisons, but it had quite often been necessary in the past for him to visit people awaiting trial, and sometimes even afterwards when they were convicted. However, seeing Alban Hythe was more personal, and therefore painful in a quite different way from the anger at betrayal and the need for information he was familiar with in the past.

Hythe looked ill. He was clearly exhausted and he seemed undecided whether even to try to appear calm. He greeted Narraway courteously, but with fear jumping in his eyes.

Narraway tried to dismiss the overwhelming pity from his mind. He needed clarity of thought if he were to be of any help. They sat opposite each other across a scarred wooden table. Narraway had had to use considerable influence even to gain access, and now to be left alone with Hythe, while the barrel-chested gaoler remaining outside the door.

'I haven't seen that brooch, and I never received love letters from Catherine!' Hythe said urgently. 'I've no idea where that one came from, but I never saw it before.' His voice shook a little. 'We were friends, that's all. Never more than that. Maris is the only woman I've loved, since we first met.'

'Did they show you the letter?' Narraway asked him.

'Yes, but that's the first time I ever saw it!' Hythe was barely in control, his hands twitched and there was a wild desperation in his eyes.

'Do you believe she wrote it?' Narraway pressed. 'They say it is her handwriting, but is it the kind of language she would use?'

'About love? I've no idea! We didn't speak of love. We only—' He stopped abruptly.

'What?' Narraway asked. 'What did you talk about? And this is no time to be modest or circumspect, even to protect her memory. You're fighting for your life.'

For a moment Hythe shivered uncontrollably. 'I know! I know!'

Narraway leaned forward. 'Then tell me, what did you talk about? Somebody did this to her. If it wasn't you, then who was it?'

'Don't you think I've racked my brains to remember anything she said that could help me to know?' Hythe was close to panic.

Narraway realised he had made a tactical error in frightening him with the worst outcome so soon. He moderated his voice. 'Have you any idea how often you met? Once a week? Twice a week? Her diaries suggest at least that.'

Hythe looked down at the scarred tabletop. His voice when he spoke was quiet. 'The first time we met by chance, at a dinner party. I forget where. It was a business matter, and rather tedious. Then a little while later I was at an art gallery, filling in time before meeting a client for luncheon. I saw Catherine and recognised her. It seemed quite natural that we should speak.'

'What did you discuss?' Narraway asked.

Hythe smiled for the first time, as if a pleasant memory had given him a few moments' respite from reality. 'Pre-Raphaelite paintings,' he answered. 'She wondered what the models were thinking about when they sat still so long while the artist drew them in such fanciful surroundings. We wondered where they had actually been – some studio or just an ordinary room – and if they even knew the legends and dreams in which they were set.

'Catherine was very funny. She could make one laugh so easily. Her imagination was . . . quite unlike anyone else's that I have ever known. She always had the right word to make one see the absurdity of things, but without unkindness. She liked eccentricity and she wasn't afraid of anything.' His face shadowed. 'Except loneliness, having no one with whom to share the miracles, or the sorrow of all that was beautiful and past.'

'Not Quixwood, clearly,' Narraway observed.

'A clever man, but with a pedestrian soul,' Hythe answered without hesitation. 'Her soul had wings, and she hated being made to spend her time with her feet in the dust.' He bent his head suddenly. 'I'm sorry, my judgement is unwarranted and cruel. She was so alive; I hate whoever did this to her. They have spoiled something that was lovely and destroyed a friend I cared about. She was . . . she was good.' He seemed to want to add more but not know how. It was in that moment that Narraway knew he was lying, in essence if not in word.

'Just a friend?' he asked sceptically.

'Yes!' Hythe jerked his head up. 'Just a friend. We talked, we looked at pictures painted from great imaginations, at pages from books written on papyrus from the very first poets and dreamers in the world. We saw carvings of grace made by artists who died before Christ was born. She escaped from her loneliness, and I from my world of facts and figures, interest on loans, duty on imported treasures and prices of land.'

His voice trembled.

'It wasn't love, it was friendship. Haven't you ever had friends, Lord Narraway? People you like enormously, who enrich your world, and without whom you would be poorer in a dozen ways, but you are not in love with them?'

Narraway instantly thought of Vespasia.

'Yes, I have,' he said honestly, feeling the warmth himself, for a moment.

'Then you can understand.' Hythe looked relieved. The ghost of a smile returned to his pale face.

Narraway felt a sudden stab of surprise, a question in his mind. What exactly did he feel for Vespasia? She was older than he by several years. He had been elevated to the House of Lords because of his skills, and as a sop perhaps to his pride for being dismissed from his position as head of Special Branch. She had been born into the aristocracy. They had become friends by circumstance. He had begun a little in awe of her, and he was quite aware that she had never been in awe of him – nor perhaps of anyone else either.

But she could be hurt. He had realised that only recently.

Her feelings were far deeper than he had imagined, and she was not invulnerable. Was she also, occasionally, as lonely as Catherine Quixwood? And was that really why he felt the savagery of Catherine's murder so painfully?

He forced it out of his thoughts. He was concerned with Alban Hythe: and whether he was guilty or not, and what it was that he still lied about, even though the shadow of the noose hung over him.

'Did you ever write to her?' he asked a little abruptly.

'No,' Hythe said urgently. 'We met by chance, or . . .'

'Or what?' Narraway demanded. 'For God's sake, man, they've charged you with rape, and the victim died. If they find you guilty they'll hang you!'

He thought Hythe was going to pass out. The last vestige of colour drained out of his face and for a moment his eyes lost focus.

Narraway jerked forward and grasped hold of his wrists and forced him upright.

'Fight!' he said between his teeth. 'Fight them! Damn it, give me something to use! If you weren't lovers then what the hell were you doing meeting a married woman in half the galleries around London? You have no room and no time to protect anyone else!'

Hythe sat upright against the hard back of the chair where Narraway had pushed him, breathing in and out slowly, trying to steady himself. Finally he lowered his eyes.

'We met by arrangement,' he said huskily. 'But it was nothing to do with love. I liked her very much. She was one of the funniest, wisest and bravest people I know, but I love Maris.'

Narraway bit back the angry, disbelieving answer that was on the edge of his tongue.

'So why were you meeting another woman with such elaborate care to make it appear by chance? And if you want to survive your trial, don't lie to me.'

'I promised her . . .' Hythe began, then tears of grief filled his eyes.

'She's dead!' Narraway said brutally. 'Three weeks after they find you guilty, so will you be! Perhaps less brutally than she, but not much.'

The silence in the room was thick, as if the air had turned solid, too heavy to breathe.

Had Narraway gone too far? Was he fatally clumsy and he had frightened Hythe into a mental collapse? His mind raced for something to do, anything to rescue the situation. He had been irretrievably stupid, lost his touch completely. No wonder they had retired him!

'Hythe!' he started, his voice choking.

Hythe opened his eyes. 'She wanted me to do something for her,' he began, gulping for air. 'Advice.'

Narraway felt the sweat break out on his body and relief flood through him. He drew a deep shuddering breath.

'What kind of advice? Financial?'

'Yes. She – she was concerned for her future,' Hythe said miserably. He was breaking his own professional code of honour to speak of it, and it was obvious how profoundly difficult that was for him.

And yet Narraway still felt there was evasion in it somehow. There was something incomplete. He should not have broken a confidence, but there was nothing immoral in a woman being afraid her husband was rash about money, even a husband usually skilled in such affairs.

'Yes?' he prompted. 'Go on.'

'Her husband was involved in investment,' Hythe said quietly. 'She was afraid that something he was doing was going to be disastrous, but he would not listen to her. She wanted to have her own information and not depend on what he told her. It was . . . detailed. It took me a long time to gain it and I gave it to her piece by piece, as I could. Each time it fell into place she would ask for something further. She believed that some investments that were worth a fortune might become useless, and others gain enormously.'

He was still lying, at least in part. Narraway knew it, but he could not understand why. Did Hythe still not understand his own danger?

'Was she trying to save her husband's finances?' he asked. 'Did she have money of her own, or expectations?'

Hythe stared back at him. 'I don't know. She didn't tell me why she needed to know, but I think it was more than that. I don't know. She would never tell me, but I had the increasingly powerful feeling that she was afraid of something calamitous happening. I asked her, but she refused to say.'

'Why?'

'I don't know. I didn't press her.'

'How many times did you meet altogether?'

'A dozen, maybe.' He lifted his shoulders in a gesture of helplessness. 'I liked her, but I never touched her in a familiar way, and I certainly did not rape her! Why on earth would I? We were friends, and both her husband and my wife were perfectly aware of it!'

'You are sure that Quixwood was aware of it?' Narraway pressed.

'Of course I am! We even mentioned an exhibition at the National Geographical Society, photographs of Patagonia. He told me how beautiful Catherine found it: great sweeping, wilderness country; all pale, wind-bleached colours, light and shadow. It was superb.'

'Did she speak to anyone else about the financial issues?

Hythe thought for several moments, then met Narraway's eyes.

'I don't think so. From what she said to me, I gathered I was the only person she trusted.'

'She came to you for financial information, but you said she was warm, amusing, a lovely woman.'

'She was!'

'And Quixwood was cold, without understanding of her?' Narraway insisted.

'Yes.'

'So she was lonely, maybe desperately lonely?'

Hythe swallowed painfully. 'Yes.' His voice was husky with emotion, guilt, and perhaps pity. 'But I did not take advantage of that. I had no wish to. I liked her, liked . . . cared . . . but I did not love her.' He added no oaths, no pleas, and his words were the more powerful for it.

'For heaven's sake, think, man!' Narraway leaned forward, a note of desperation in his voice. He heard it and forced himself to speak more levelly. 'Whoever it was that raped her, she let him in! Her husband was out, she had dismissed the servants for the night, and she let him in!' He swallowed hard. 'She trusted him. She wasn't afraid to be alone with him. She didn't send for the butler or the maid or even a footman. What do you conclude from that?'

'That she knew him,' Hythe said miserably. He shook his head a little. 'It doesn't sound like Catherine at all, not as I knew her.'

'Then as you knew her, how do you explain it?' Narraway demanded. 'What do you think happened?'

'Do you think I haven't tried to work it out?' Hythe said desperately. 'If she let the servants go then she wasn't expecting anyone. Letting them all retire like that makes it obvious, if she'd let someone in. Catherine was never careless like that. It would be . . . unnecessarily dangerous. What if a footman had come down to check a door, or the butler just went to check she didn't need anything, before he retired? Isn't that what actually happened?'

'More or less,' Narraway agreed. 'But she did let someone in; that is what actually happened as well.'

'Someone unexpected, it must have been,' Hythe argued.

'Why did she let him in?' Narraway persisted. 'Why would the woman you knew have done that?'

'Then it must have been someone she knew and had no fear of,' Hythe answered. 'Maybe they claimed to be hurt, or in some kind of trouble. She would assume that and try to help.' He stopped abruptly. He made no display of grief, but it was so deeply marked in his face that it was unmistakable.

With a jolt of loss, and then of fear, Narraway realised that at least in this he believed him. Hythe had not either raped Catherine or beaten her. Someone else had, but Hythe was going to face trial. The letter and the gift would damn him. And there was no one else to suspect.

Who was going to defend him in court, at the very least raise a reasonable doubt? That would not clear his name, but guilt would hang him, and finding the right person after that would matter little. Hythe would be dead, and Maris a widow and alone.

'Do you have a lawyer, a really first-class advocate?' Narraway asked.

Hythe looked as if he had been struck. Brutally he was returned to the present. 'Not yet. I – I don't know of anyone . . .' He tailed off, lost.

'I will find you someone,' Narraway promised rashly.

'I can't pay . . . very much,' Hythe began.

'I will persuade him to act for nothing,' Narraway replied, intending if necessary to pay for the barrister himself. Already he had the man in mind, and he would speak to him this afternoon.

He remained only a little longer, going over details of facts again so they were clear in his mind. Then he excused himself and went straight from the prison the short distance to the chambers of Peter Symington in Lincoln's Inn Fields. If any man would take on the case of defending Alban Hythe, with a chance of winning, it was he.

Narraway insisted on seeing Symington immediately, using the suggestion of more influence than he possessed to override the clerk's protests.

He found Symington standing in the middle of the well-carpeted floor, a leather-bound book in his hand. He had clearly been interrupted against his instructions. He was a handsome man in his early forties. Most remarkable about him were his thick, fair hair, curling beyond the barber's control, and the dazzling charm of his smile.

'My lord?' he said quietly, reproof in his voice.

Narraway did not apologise. 'A matter of urgency, can't wait,' he explained as the clerk closed the door behind him.

'You've been charged with something?' Symington said curiously.

Narraway was in no mood for levity. 'Inspector Knox has charged a man with the rape of Catherine Quixwood, and therefore morally, in the minds of the jury, with her murder. I would like you to defend him. I believe he's innocent.'

Symington blinked. 'You'd like me to defend him? Does he mean something to you, to the government, to Special Branch? Or is it just because you think he's innocent?' There was amusement in his voice, and curiosity. 'I presume he told you he is?' He put the book down on his desk, closed, as if it no longer interested him. 'Why me? Or am I the only one you think fool enough to take it?'

In spite of himself Narraway smiled. 'Actually, the last,' he admitted. 'But you are also the only one who would stick to it long enough to have a chance of winning. I really believe he's innocent, and that there is something large and very ugly behind it – maybe more than one thing. Certainly someone raped and beat the woman so badly she died as a result. She was a funny, brave and beautiful woman. She deserves justice – but even more importantly, whoever did it needs to be taken off the streets and put where they can never hurt anyone else.'

'Like a grave?' Symington raised his eyebrows.

'That would do nicely,' Narraway agreed. 'Will you take the case? I would like Hythe to believe it is without charge, because he doesn't have the means to meet it. I'll pay you myself, but he must never know. And if you doubt I am capable of lying about it, or anything else I judge necessary, then you are a fool.'

Symington's utterly charming smile beamed again. 'I'm not a fool, my lord. The case sounds like a challenge. I think I can clear my desk sufficiently to give it my very best attention. And I'll weigh the matter of my bill, and send you what I feel appropriate. I give you my word that Hythe will believe I do it for the love of justice.'

'Thank you,' Narraway said sincerely. 'Thank you very much.'

He hesitated, wondering if he were risking the frail thread of trust he had just established with Symington, and yet it was the only hint he had of any other answer than Hythe's guilt. But he also believed that at least in some sense Hythe was lying, or at the very best wilfully concealing something.

Symington was waiting for him to speak.

'Hythe admitted meeting Catherine Quixwood as often as her diaries suggested, but he said she arranged it. He said she wanted him to give her financial advice.'

'And you believed that?' Symington said with a twisted smile. 'Quixwood's a financier himself, and an extremely good one.'

'I know,' Narraway admitted. 'Hythe said she was afraid he was into something dubious, and over his head. She wanted to know more of it. If she was afraid for her future, if he were reckless, then that would be believable.'

'Do you believe it?' Symington asked. 'If he has any proof of it, why didn't he tell Knox?'

'I don't know,' Narraway admitted. 'He's lying about something. I just don't know what.'

'But you think he didn't kill her?' Symington looked puzzled and not angry.

'Yes,' Narraway answered, unable to explain himself. 'I think I do.'

'I'll try,' Symington promised.

'Thank you,' Narraway said again.

That evening Narraway went out rather later than was customary to call on a woman alone, particularly one with whom he had only the slightest acquaintance. He stood in the small parlour of Alban Hythe's house and told Maris what he had achieved.

Maris was so pale that her dark dress, more suitable for autumn than summer, drained the last trace of vitality from her face. However, she kept her composure and stood straight-backed, head high, in front of him. What effort it must have cost her he could only guess.

'And this Mr Symington will defend my husband, in spite of the evidence?' she asked. 'Why? He can't know that Alban is innocent. He's never even met him. And we can't pay the sort of money such a man as you describe would ask.' She struggled to keep control of her voice and very nearly failed. She stopped before she let herself down, at least in her own estimation.

'Then I did not describe him very well,' Narraway apologised. 'Symington cares far more about the case than the money.'

She studied Narraway's face for several moments, searching his eyes to judge whether he was lying to her, or at the least, prevaricating. Finally she came to the conclusion that he was not. It was the truth, as far as it went, and she did not know him well enough to see through his subtlety or his experience. No one did, except possibly Vespasia, and he had the suspicion that she saw through him rather more often than she allowed him to know.

Maris's answer was interrupted by a maid at the door to tell her that Mr Rawdon Quixwood had called and wished to speak with her.

Narraway was startled but, turning to look at the maid, he saw that her face was completely expressionless. Clearly she was not surprised.

Maris looked pleased.

'Thank you. Please ask him to come in,' she instructed.

The maid withdrew obediently and Maris turned to Narraway.

'He has been so kind. Even with all his own grief, he has found time to call on me and assure me of his help.' She lowered her eyes. 'I fear sometimes that he believes Alban guilty, but his gentleness towards me has been without exception.' She gave a small, very rueful smile. 'Perhaps he feels we are companions in misfortune, and I have not the heart to tell him it is not so, because it does seem that Catherine was more familiar with someone than she should have been. I would so much rather think that was not true, but I have no argument that stands up to reason.'

She had not time to add any more before Rawdon Quixwood came in. The hollowness was eased a little from his face, perhaps with the arrest at last of someone for the crime, even though the loss must still have been just as bitter.

'Maris, my dear . . .' he began, then suddenly realised Narraway was also in the room. He checked himself quickly, but his face was without shadow. 'Lord Narraway! How agreeable to see you. I wonder if we are on the same errand? I'm afraid I can offer little comfort. Perhaps you have better news?'

Narraway met Quixwood's eyes and found he could read nothing of what the man was thinking. The idea occurred to him that the effort of hiding his own pain might be the only way Quixwood could turn his mind from his grief.

Still, Narraway found himself reluctant to trust him, or to risk wounding him still more deeply with the possibility that they had not actually caught his wife's rapist, and, morally, her murderer.

'I am still searching,' he replied quietly. 'Without much profit so far, for all the information I can find. I hear contradicting stories of Mrs Quixwood.'

Quixwood gave a very slight shrug, with a graceful gesture. 'I dare say they are exercising the customary charity towards the dead who cannot defend themselves. I appreciate it. Women who are . . . assaulted . . . are often blamed almost as much as the men who assault them. The euphemisms and occasional silences are a kindness.'

201

'But not helpful,' Narraway pointed out. 'We need the truth if we are to obtain justice, for any of the people concerned.'

Maris gestured to both men to be seated. As soon as they were, Quixwood continued.

'Justice.' He turned the word over in his mind. 'I began wanting justice for Catherine as a starving man wants food. Now I am less certain that it is really what I wish. Silence might be more compassionate. After all, she can no longer speak for herself.'

Maris looked down at her hands folded in her lap, white-knuckled.

'Rawdon, you have been the essence of kindness to me,' she said gently. 'In spite of the fact that it is my husband the police have arrested for the terrible wrong done to your wife. But Alban is not guilty, and he needs justice also. Apart from that, do you not wish the real monster to be caught, before he goes on and does something similar to another woman?'

Quixwood's face reflected an inner conflict so profound, so intense, he could barely keep still. His hands in his lap were more tightly twisted than hers. In that moment Narraway knew beyond any doubt that Quixwood was certain that Alban Hythe was guilty, and he was here to do what he could to help Maris face that fact. It was a startling generosity. What did he know that Narraway and Maris did not?

Quixwood was still searching for words, his eyes on Maris' face, troubled and almost tender. 'I don't think it is likely,' he said at last. 'It is far better that you do not know the details, but I assure you, it was not some random maniac who will do such things to anyone. It was very personal. Please, think no more of it. You must concern yourself with your own wellbeing. If there is anything I can do to help, I will.' He gave a very slight smile, wry and self-deprecating. 'It would be a favour to me. It would give me someone to think of other than myself.'

A warmth of gratitude filled her face, and also a very genuine admiration. Narraway was sure that Quixwood had seen it, and it must indeed have given him some small comfort.

The following day Narraway called early at the club where Quixwood was still living. He had to wait until he rose and came into the dining room for breakfast. He joined him without asking permission, because he had no intention of accepting a refusal.

Quixwood looked startled, but he made no objection. He regarded Narraway with some curiosity.

Narraway smiled as he finished requesting poached kippers and brown toast from the steward. As soon as the man left, he answered Quixwood's unspoken question.

'I hear several different accounts of Catherine,' he said, watching Quixwood's eyes. 'I assume that you loved her, but you also knew her better than anyone else. Nothing need come out in court, still less in the newspapers, but I think it is time we discussed her without the glittering veil of compassion that usually shrouds the dead.'

Quixwood sighed, but there was no resistance in him. He leaned back a little and his dark eyes met Narraway's. 'Do you not think it was Alban Hythe who killed her?' he said anxiously. 'It will bring terrible grief to poor Maris if it is. She still believes in him.'

Narraway did not answer the question directly.

'If they were lovers, Catherine and Alban Hythe, why on earth would he suddenly turn on her like that?' he said instead. It was a reasonable question.

'Does it matter now?' Quixwood wrinkled his face as if he were deliberately looking at the idea, forcing himself to see it, and then beg for it to be ignored.

'If we are going to convict the man and hang him, it has to make sense,' Narraway said brutally.

Quixwood winced. 'Yes, of course you are right,' he conceded. He began to speak in a very low voice. His eyes were downcast, as if he were ashamed of being forced into such admissions.

'Catherine was a very emotional woman, and she was beautiful. You never saw her alive, or you'd understand. She hated going to the sort of functions where you and I might meet. And to tell you the truth, I didn't press her. It wasn't only out of kindness to her, but also because she was so charming, so very alive, that she attracted attention she was not able to understand for what it was, or to deal with.'

Narraway was puzzled, but he did not interrupt.

'She loved attention,' Quixwood continued, a warmth lighting his face for the first time since the night of Catherine's death. 'She responded to it like a flower to the sun. But she also bored easily. When someone did not live up to her expectations of their knowledge, or have the imaginative enthusiasm that she did, then she would drop their acquaintance. It could cause, at the very least, a degree of embarrassment.'

At last he looked up and met Narraway's eyes. 'I loved her, but I also learned not to take her sudden passions too seriously. She lived a good deal of her life in a world of her own creation: mercurial, entertaining, but quite unreal.' He shrugged his shoulders. 'I fear young Alban Hythe would have had no idea how changeable she was, how . . . fickle.'

He made a slight gesture of dismissal with his strong, lean hands. 'She would mean no cruelty, but she had no conception of how deeply an idealistic, rather naïve young man might fall in love with her, and – when she rejected him – feel utterly betrayed.'

He blinked and looked away. 'If they were lovers, or he thought she had implied they would be, and then without warning she felt he had not lived up to what she expected of him, he would have felt utterly cheated. He might have damaged irreparably a wife who was devoted to him in favour of a woman who was incapable of loyalty to anyone – who had built a castle in the air out of his dreams, and then destroyed it in front of him. Do you see?'

Narraway did see. It was a persuasive image, hideously believable. And yet he was not sure if he did believe it. Perhaps Catherine's lovely, brutalised body had cheated him also, even in her death?

'And then she took laudanum to end her own life?' he asked, his voice sounding harsher than he had meant it to.

'Perhaps she realised what she had done,' Quixwood said with a small, helpless gesture of his hands, barely a movement at all. 'She was passionate, but she was not strong. If she had been, she would have lived in the real world . . .' He left the rest and all its implications unsaid.

'Thank you,' Narraway answered quickly, just as the steward arrived with his poached kippers, and bacon, eggs, sausage and devilled kidneys for Quixwood. They both turned, with little joy, to their food, and harmless, matter-of-fact subjects of conversation as the dining room filled up.

After leaving the club, Narraway decided that he still did not know enough about Catherine Quixwood. The woman her husband had described was very different from the one that Alban Hythe had seen and believed he knew, and had liked so deeply. And both were different again from the one Narraway had seen in death.

Who would have known all of her, fitted the disparate pieces into a whole, however complex? No one wished to speak ill of the dead, and most particularly someone who had died so horribly.

And then, of course, there was the question of blaming her in some way, so the tragedy was unique to her and would visit no one else. Safety would always come before even compassion for the dead. The fear of violation was deep to the marrow of the bones.

Would there be any point in asking Knox for his help? Probably not. He had arrested Alban Hythe, which meant that he had formed a picture of Catherine he could not now afford to alter.

Perhaps the person who knows a woman the best is her lady's maid. But would Flaxley speak frankly? All her working life at the Quixwood house she had been loyal, as such people almost invariably were. To be otherwise, if it were known, would disqualify her from ever finding a further position. She was still the best person to try.

Narraway stepped into the street and hailed a cab, giving Quixwood's address.

Then the obvious way around it came to him like sudden daylight. If anyone could persuade a loyal servant to discuss the details of her mistress's character, it would be Vespasia.

He leaned forward and knocked on the front of the cab, asking the driver instead to take him to Vespasia's house.

'Really, Victor,' she said with slight surprise when he told her what he wished her to do. 'And what shall I give the poor woman as a reason why I consider her mistress's character to be any of my concern?'

They were sitting in her morning room, all cool colours and stark white frames to the windows. There was a bowl of early blooming white roses on the low table, and the sunlight through the glass was hot and bright. In spite of his reason for calling, Narraway found himself relaxing. It was extraordinarily comfortable here, as if the proportions and the grace of it were familiar from some half-hidden memory.

'I'm sorry,' he said. He found himself telling her not only what Alban Hythe had said of Catherine, then what Quixwood himself had said, but also his own impressions and the depth of feeling it aroused in him, the outrage and the loss far wider than one woman's destruction.

She watched him gravely all the time, without interrupting.

'I see,' she said when she was certain he had no more to add. 'It is not possible for both opinions to be entirely true, and perhaps neither of them is. It is a curious thing to see yourself as others do, and I imagine it is seldom comfortable.' She smiled very slightly. 'I am very glad that I shall not be present at my own funeral, even to hear the eulogies that make me sound quite unreal, or the dislike that I had not known people felt for me behind the mask of good manners.'

He was caught with a sudden icy coldness. He had never even imagined her dying. The thought was so painful it shocked him.

'My dear, don't look so tragic,' she said with a slight shake of her head. 'I quite see the necessity of someone speaking to her, and your argument that it should be I who do so is perfectly sensible. I shall make arrangements to do it.'

'Thank you,' he said a little awkwardly, afraid that she might understand what it was that had really shaken him so much.

Narraway dined with Vespasia the following evening. He chose to make it a formal affair – a dinner at the finest restaurant he knew. For his own pleasure, he wished to behave as if it were a celebration of something, rather than the pursuit of the last act of a tragedy.

She flattered him by dressing with all the glamour he had associated with her when they had first met. She wore heavy ivory silk with guipure lace at the neck and over the bodice, and as so often she ornamented it with ropes of pearls. The waiting staff knew him and treated him with respect, but he saw other diners, especially several gentlemen and senior Members of Parliament, look at him with distinct envy.

Vespasia conducted herself with the nonchalance he would have expected, but he did notice a slight flush of pleasure in her cheeks as well. He wanted to ask her if she had succeeded in learning anything, but it would be unbecoming to ask too soon. Additionally, it might give her the totally mistaken idea that that had been his sole motive in inviting her. Perhaps she would not then believe him even if he tried to explain that it was not.

They had reached the dessert (a most exquisite French apple tarte) before it was she who raised the subject.

'I spoke at some length to Catherine's maid,' she said, setting her fork down on her plate. 'At first she was naturally reluctant to say anything but the sort of respectful praise that loyalty would dictate. I'm afraid I took the liberty of saying that if we did not prosecute the right man, then whoever it was would escape detection and very probably commit a similar crime against someone else. I am not certain if that is true, but I am quite sure that Catherine herself would not wish such a thing.'

'I'm afraid it probably is true,' he replied gravely. 'What did she tell you? Is Quixwood right about Catherine?'

'No,' she said without hesitation. 'But of course I can't say whether he believes he is. It is quite clear that she did not find in him either the love or the friendship she wished for. His defence against that may have been to see her as the cause of the problem rather than he himself, or simply the fact that they were mismatched.'

'Are you sure the maid was not merely being loyal?' he pressed.

She smiled. 'Yes, Victor, I am quite sure. I have had lady's maids all my life. I can read between the lines of what they say, or decline to say.' Her eyes were bright with amusement, but there was no impatience in them, no condescension. He had the distinct feeling that she was pleased to have been asked for her help.

'Would you like Armagnac, perhaps?' he said impulsively.

'Champagne is sufficient for me,' she answered, smiling.

He hesitated.

She looked at the light, sparkling wine in her glass and raised her delicate eyebrows. 'Is this not champagne, then?' she asked.

For a moment he was not certain of the compliment. Then, meeting her eyes, he understood it and found himself colouring with pleasure, and even a little self-consciousness. He raised his glass to hers without answering.

In the morning Narraway went to find Knox again. He began at the police station and was told that there had been an unpleasant brawl down on the waterfront and Knox had been called to the scene.

Narraway obtained the precise location, thanked the man, and left to find a hansom to take him there. It was not a long journey but it took time weaving in and out of the traffic, dense at this time of day, the roads crowded with drays, wagons and men and women on foot busy with their early errands. He passed lightermen, stevedores, crane drivers, wagon masters and ferrymen, already busy. Gulls wheeled and dived, screaming as they fought over fish. Up and down the highway of the river Narraway saw strings of barges ride the tide, and on the land behind them men shouted at each other and the rumble of wheels jolted over the uneven cobbles.

He found Knox standing on the stone slipway where the fight had taken place, his jacket collar high round his ears, wind whipping his hair.

Fortunately in this crime no one was dead, although there was still blood on the stones from a knife wound.

'I know you didn't want Hythe to be guilty,' Knox remarked after he had greeted him. 'Neither did I. Sometimes I don't understand people at all. I'd 'ave sworn he hadn't it in him, but you can't argue with that letter.' He pushed his hands into his coat pockets. 'And don't tell me it isn't in her hand, because it is. First thing I did was have it checked by people who can spot a forgery. Although I don't know why anybody'd be bothered. It's not as if we had any other suspects.'

Narraway felt crushed by the logic of it. 'Then there's something about this case that we've missed,' he answered stubbornly, although he could think of nothing.

Knox looked at him with a frown, puzzled. 'Haven't you ever found a traitor or a dynamiter where you really didn't expect to, my lord? Didn't you ever discover that an anarchist, who wanted to bring the whole social order down around our ears, was actually quite a nice fellow if you met him down at the pub?'

'Yes, of course I have,' Narraway said irritably. 'But Hythe actually liked her, and he understood her a lot better than her husband did.'

Knox hunched his shoulders and pulled his coat more tightly around him, as if he were cold, although the wind off the river was mild.

Water slopped noisily on the stones as the wash from a string of barges reached them.

'My lord, we both know what was done to Mrs Quixwood. Think what you like about Hythe, but if he's the guilty party – and he is the one charged – there was never like nor understanding between him and Catherine Quixwood at the end.'

Narraway said nothing. He stood in the sun by the water. The rising tide would wash away the bloodstains at his feet, but, remembering the injuries Dr Brinsley had described, he thought nothing would ever rid his mind of the images, or the sick misery that filled him.

Chapter Thirteen

SEVERAL DAYS later, Charlotte was attending a luncheon at the very beautiful town house of her sister Emily, which she had inherited from her first marriage to Lord Ashworth. His early death had left her with a considerable fortune, and several very fine properties, held in trust for her son, who was heir to his father's title as well as the benefits that went with it.

Her very happy second marriage was to Jack Radley. Early in his career he had been a gentleman of fashion, and little else. Now he was a Member of Parliament, and had grown into a considerable responsibility.

Half a dozen ladies were sitting in the large garden room, which was open onto the paved terrace and the sloping lawn and flowers beyond. It was as beautiful a place in which to dine as any in London, and they were taking full advantage of the very pleasant weather. Pastel silks and muslins fluttered in the fitful breeze. Parasols carefully placed kept the sun's harsher light from fair skins.

'Everything seems to be in such a turmoil,' Marie Grosvenor said with a slight frown. 'People are talking about all kinds of wealth, and loss. I have friends who are saying they'll end up with unimaginable money, and others who are terrified they'll be ruined. Some say Dr Jameson's a true patriot, and others that he's an irresponsible madman. I really don't know what to believe.'

Charlotte glanced at Emily and saw her attention quicken. The presumably harmless conversation had suddenly taken a darker turn with talk of financial ruin. Was she going to struggle against the tide, or go with it? It was her duty as hostess to govern the mood of the party, but it would require a very strong will to alter its course. Not that Emily was without such a will, simply the desire to use it when not doing so might be far more entertaining.

'Will you attend the trial?' Arabella Scott asked, her fair eyebrows raised, interest sharp in her pale blue eyes. 'I'm thinking of it myself. Poor Dr Jameson. But heroes are so often vilified, do you not think?' She looked from one to the other of them, her gaze finally resting on Charlotte.

Everyone else turned to look at her also, clearly thinking she had some special knowledge. They had heard, at the very least, that Pitt had been in the police. Of course it was not an occupation for a gentleman, but there was a certain gruesome fascination in it, all the same. It was the sense of eavesdropping, or reading someone else's private diary. Many did it but no one admitted to it except to their closest friends, and their friends' friends.

Charlotte was annoyed. She had to guard her tongue in so many things that she was compensating for it by being less conciliatory in others. Right now she was ready for battle. She looked at Arabella with a smile.

'Oh, yes, I agree with you,' she replied, ignoring Emily's look of surprise. 'We are very hard on heroes, exactly as you say. And so often we praise the wrong people anyway, not even realising who has done what. We can accept the most superficial of explanations and attribute courage to people who are merely foolhardy, or even stupid and self-serving. Then we totally ignore those who set the good of others before their own profit. How wise you are to see it, and brave to point it out, if I may say so.'

Arabella looked completely nonplussed. The last thing she had intended to be was brave, as Charlotte well knew. In these circumstances it was the word used to mean rash and probably foolish.

Flora Jefferson blinked. 'Maybe I am not paying due attention, but I am not certain if you mean that Dr Jameson is a hero, or that he is not,' she said pointedly.

Emily drew in her breath, watching Charlotte.

'Neither am I,' Charlotte said charmingly. 'I hear one story, then I hear another. According to some people, Dr Jameson led an army of patriots to save Mr Rhodes' railway in the Pitsani Strip, which I believe borders on the Transvaal, which belongs to the Boers, and of course is said to be riddled with gold, and diamonds.'

'He did it to protect the Uitlanders,' Arabella explained with slightly condescending patience. 'They are being thoroughly exploited by the Boers.'

Flora and Sabine Munro nodded agreement.

Charlotte's smile became a little more fixed. She was not about to back down. 'And then I hear that this army of about five hundred well-armed men actually crossed over into the Transvaal and marched on Johannesburg,' she went on. 'And were met by the Boers, whose city it is, and thoroughly thrashed.' The moment she had said it, she wished she had used less emotive words, but it was too late.

'Heroes do not have to win in order to be heroes,' Arabella said with a flash of anger reddening her face.

'Of course not,' Charlotte cut across Emily before anyone else could attack, or defend her. 'It is hardly heroic to fight if you cannot lose. Any jackanapes can do that. It was unquestionably brave. The question I hear raised is as to whether it was wise or not. In fact, I suppose, as to whether it was right.'

'Right?' Arabella said indignantly.

'Morally right,' Charlotte elaborated patiently. 'We invaded Boer land.'

'For heaven's sake, do you want the Boers to rule South Africa?' Arabella said, aghast at the idea.

'Not at all,' Charlotte answered levelly. There was no backing out now. 'But the fact that I want a thing does not automatically make it right – or wrong.'

Marie Grosvenor now returned to the fray.

'It is a matter of loyalty,' she said stiffly. 'Loyalty is always right.' It was a statement and she expected no dissent.

'Is it?' Charlotte looked from one to the other of them all sitting in gorgeous silks, and delicate embroidered muslins in the dappled shade. 'So even if we are loyal to opposing sides, we can all be equally right?'

'Charlotte!' Emily said quietly.

213

'We are all equally right, then,' Charlotte ignored her. 'It is just that the Boers, being loyal to their own homes, and fighting for their own lands, were better at it than we were, so they beat us?'

'We were fighting for the Queen and Empire,' Arabella said stiffly. 'Are you not British, that you don't understand that?'

'I am British,' Charlotte kept her voice level. 'But I am not always right.'

'Indeed you are not!' Sabine agreed heatedly.

'Nor are any of us,' Charlotte added. 'Even Dr Jameson. We can all make mistakes, especially when we are frightened, or there is a great deal of money involved.'

'It has nothing to do with money!' Sabine was openly angry now. 'That is a dreadful thing to say.'

'Of course it has to do with money,' Flora put in. 'Those who invested in this raid stand to lose a fortune, if the verdict goes against Dr Jameson . . .'

'So you think he's guilty?' Marie accused.

'I think he could be found guilty,' Flora corrected. 'That is not always the same thing. Has he ever denied he led the raid?'

'Of course not!' Arabella snapped. 'He's no coward!'

'I wonder how much of it is his money?' Emily said, and the instant afterwards clearly regretted it. She scrambled to make amends. 'I suppose he risked everything?'

There was a moment's silence while each one of them weighed up what they thought, and what they judged wise to say. The shadow of immense financial gain and loss was suddenly far more real. All the beauty and pleasure around them, the safety itself might one day prove ephemeral.

'I don't know what will happen,' Charlotte said thoughtfully. 'Trials sometimes throw up evidence no one had foreseen, and make the verdict quite unexpected. I have heard that Mr Churchill said it may lead to war. Is that not so?' she looked at Emily.

Emily shot her a look like daggers. 'So I am told,' she conceded grudgingly. 'And Mr Chamberlain of the Colonial Office is caught in a most embarrassing situation because he can neither deny knowledge of the raid, nor admit to it.'

'I dare say the British South Africa Company will have to pay a great deal of compensation to the Transvaal,' Charlotte added, hoping she had her facts correct. 'It will depend, of course, on who has staked fortunes in that.' She had overheard it and did not really know, but it seemed a reasonable thought.

Flora and Sabine looked at each other, both now clearly anxious.

'A great deal?' Arabella said with an edge to her voice. 'What do you mean by that?'

It occurred to Charlotte that a great deal might be made and lost in such ventures, including the fortunes of those in this quiet London garden. She had meant to discomfort their unthinking arrogance, not seriously frighten them.

'There is gold in the Transvaal, and diamonds,' she replied. 'Where there are fortunes to be made, there are fortunes to be lost as well. The raid failed. It was a big gamble, and we have no idea yet what the end may be. Perhaps you are right and, to take the chance with such high stakes, Dr Jameson is a hero.'

There were several moments of silence. No one was comfortable. The peace and satisfaction of the party was shattered by a sudden and very chilling reality.

'There won't be war,' Sabine said dismissively, waving her hand with its heavy emerald ring. 'Mr Churchill is talking nonsense, as usual. He will say anything to draw attention to himself. All kinds of people have invested in Africa. They won't allow this to fail. If you knew a little more about real money, finance and investment, you wouldn't even say such a thing.'

Charlotte decided to let it go. 'Perhaps not,' she agreed. 'And undeniably, Mr Rhodes is usually very successful. No one needs to win every skirmish to win a war.'

'It's not a war,' Arabella said waspishly. 'It was an attempt to—' She realised she was not sure what she meant and stopped abruptly. 'Mr Churchill is a buffoon,' she finished, glaring at Charlotte.

At last Emily was stung to defend her own position. 'I cannot allow you to say that unchallenged,' she spoke quietly and with a smile, but there was a degree of steel in her voice. 'He is not always right – I know of no one who is – but at times he is remarkably perceptive, and a voice of warning that should be heeded. The Jameson Raid was a fiasco, and Mr Chamberlain has had to order Sir Hercules Robinson, the Governor-General of the Cape Colony, to repudiate it.'

'He wouldn't have if it had succeeded,' Marie pointed out.

'Of course not,' Emily made a slight gesture of conciliation.

'If . . .' Charlotte smiled also. 'If wishes were horses, then beggars would ride. Unfortunately they aren't. Perhaps that is what heroes are about, which is why one nation's heroes are another nation's enemies.'

'Well, I am British, and I shall honour our heroes,' Arabella fixed Charlotte with a stony glare. 'You must choose whatever you will.'

Charlotte kept her smile, although she felt it false. 'I shall wait until I know more about it. At the moment I confess my ignorance.'

'Considering the depth of it, that is an excellent decision,' Arabella snapped.

In spite of herself, Charlotte laughed, which was the last thing Arabella expected. She was thoroughly put out of her stride.

Emily stepped in quickly. 'Perhaps we should attend the trial and at least become informed in the affair?' she suggested.

'Half London will be there,' Marie said, nodding her head.

'I dare say the other half will be at the other miserable trial,' Flora remarked with a shudder. 'I think I prefer not even to know about that one. I should have nightmares.'

'I'm sure you have no need,' Marie said comfortingly. 'You are in no danger whatever.'

For a moment Charlotte was not certain what they were referring to.

'Another thing about which you know nothing?' Arabella enquired with a slight smirk. 'Catherine Quixwood was having an affair with a younger man, and he assaulted and then murdered her. All dreadfully sordid. No doubt they will hang him.'

Charlotte felt her fury return like a tidal wave, all but taking her breath away. Any consideration of Emily's party was swept away.

'No, I had no idea,' she said with cloying sweetness. 'But then I do not interest myself very much in other people's more . . . intimate lives.

As you so correctly say, it is all dreadfully sordid.' She enunciated each word with distaste. 'I merely know of her as a woman who had great charm. That was all I wished to know.'

Flora stifled a giggle. Charlotte realised with sudden perception that she also disliked Arabella, but she could not afford to let it be known. Now she remembered the sense of freedom she had felt at being no longer involved in Society. The loss of its glamour was far outweighed by the opposing gain of freedom.

Emily rushed into the thick silence to rescue what she could of her party.

'I feel so sorry for poor Rawdon Quixwood,' she said, looking from one to the other of them, except Charlotte, evading her eyes with care. 'He must be suffering appallingly. I can't even imagine it.'

'What a terrible thing,' Marie agreed. 'Is there anything more painful than total, devastating disillusion? Poor man. He must be distracted with grief.'

'Disillusion?' Charlotte heard her voice hard-edged with incredulity. 'His wife was raped and beaten half to death, then in her unbearable pain she dosed herself too heavily with laudanum, and died of that. I should imagine that is the cause of his devastating grief.'

'My dear Mrs . . . Pitt?' Arabella hesitated as if she were not certain as to exactly who Charlotte might be, 'decent women do not get raped. Perhaps you did not read in the newspapers that she let the man in herself? I ask you, what decent woman dismisses the servants for the night, then lets a younger man into the house herself, and entertains him alone, while her husband is out?'

Charlotte raised her eyebrows. 'Was he younger? You clearly read different articles of the newspapers than I do. Or perhaps different newspapers altogether.'

Arabella's face flared red. It was an insult even she could not ignore. Ladies with the slightest pretension to gentility did not read sensational newspapers. 'It is common knowledge!' she snapped.

'Very common,' Charlotte said under her breath. Only Flora, sitting closest to her, heard it. She effected a fit of sneezing to stifle her laughter. Sabine handed her a glass of water.

'Standards are slipping all over the place,' Marie remarked, perhaps to fill the silence. 'That poor Portuguese girl committed suicide as well. Heaven only knows why.'

Sabine looked at her in surprise. 'Well, everyone says she fell in love with Neville Forsbrook, and when he didn't want her, she completely lost her senses and threw herself out of the window. Far too highly strung, these younger girls. And to blame young Forsbrook is awful. Poor Pelham Forsbrook. Such a nice man. First he lost his wife, now this wretched scandal. Not that it's in the remotest way his fault, of course. Nobody imagines that.'

'First his wife?' Flora asked. 'She died too?'

'She died in an accident,' Emily put in.

'Nobody imagined she was having an affair,' Arabella added. 'It was a tragic accident in a coach.'

'An ordinary hansom, I believe,' Sabine corrected her. 'Late at night. The road was wet and something made the horse bolt. Poor cabby was killed as well. Dreadful.'

'Such a terrible thing to happen,' Charlotte said with as much sincerity as she could manage through her anger. She remembered Vespasia telling her of the tragedy. She had not known Eleanor Forsbrook, but she would not have wished her any harm. Her son's brutality would surely have caused her as much grief as it would to any other woman. 'Perhaps we should treasure our own safety with a little more gratitude.'

'I don't know what you mean,' Arabella said coldly.

Flora looked at her with a bright smile. 'I do. You are perfectly right, Mrs Pitt. We take our happiness and our safety far too much for granted. I am alive and well. It is a beautiful day and I am in a lovely garden, among friends. I shall enjoy it to the full.' She looked at Charlotte, meeting her eyes directly. 'Thank you for a most timely reminder. I'm so glad you came.'

There was another moment of startled silence, then Emily picked up a dish of tiny cakes and passed them round. She bit her lip to stop herself from smiling, and carefully looked away from Charlotte's eyes.

Pitt stood in his office facing Rafael Castelbranco. He had dreaded this moment since he had heard the date set for Alban Hythe's trial.

The Portuguese Ambassador was white-faced, except for the bruised shadows around his eyes and the hectic spots of colour high on his cheeks. If Pitt did not know his story and imagine his pain, he would have thought he was drunk.

'This man raped a married woman with whom he was having an affair. You arrested him and you are now bringing him to trial,' he said, his voice wavering, catching in his throat as if he could barely force the words out. 'If he is guilty, you will hang him, and her family will at least have justice. And yet you know who raped my child, and you can do nothing? Is this how your justice works?'

He made it sound absurd, outrageous, as if it were connived at deliberately. He was trembling with the savagery of his emotions.

'Rafael,' Pitt said gently, 'I do not know who raped Angeles. I had believed it was Neville Forsbrook, but the husband of Catherine Quixwood, the married woman who was raped, says that he was in the company of young Forsbrook at the time we believe the rape of Angeles to have happened. And I do not doubt that it did happen, but we have no proof. In Mrs Quixwood's case her beaten body was found on the floor of her own house. There was no place for doubt as to what happened, only as to who the man was.'

Castelbranco gulped. 'It was Forsbrook. She told us.'

Pitt knew better than to argue. Castelbranco believed his daughter. He had to: every loyalty in him demanded it. It was now about the only tribute he could pay her.

'If I could prove it I would charge him and bring him to trial,' Pitt said with absolute honesty. 'But if I charge him and can't bring it to trial then public sympathy will be with him. If I can rake up enough evidence to try him, and fail to convict – which needs evidence beyond a reasonable doubt – then I will have made all the details public and given him the opportunity to say whatever he pleases about Angeles, blacken her reputation with whatever he wants to invent. No one can prove innocence or purity for every minute of their lives, and you and I both know that. The fact that it is so will not protect her. An accused man has the right to defend himself.'

Castelbranco stared at him in horror, swaying a little on his feet.

'Rafael,' Pitt went on, his voice even lower, 'the jury will be composed entirely of men, as it is everywhere. Some of them may be fathers, some may not. Most of them will have seen women who were not their wives, whom they lusted after, particularly when they were young and unmarried. They will all, at times, have been tempted to behave badly, and I dare say most of them will have done so, to one degree or another. And most of them will have been accused in things they considered unfair. Forsbrook would be there, sober and sad-faced, swearing to his innocence, very English, very gentlemanly. He will say that she was beautiful and he complimented her. She misunderstood, her English not being fluent.'

Castelbranco blinked back tears as memory flooded his mind.

Pitt forced the pictures of Angeles out of his mind, and then – with even more difficulty – made himself forget Jemima: her passionate face so like Charlotte's; the trust in her eyes when she looked at him, the father who had protected her all her life.

'Angeles will not be there to tell them what truly happened,' he said. 'All I can offer you is the promise that I will not forget it, and if I can ever prove Forsbrook's guilt without crucifying Angeles in the process, then I will do it. But if I try, and fail, then even if I had all the proof in the world, afterwards, I could not try him a second time. The law does not allow anyone to be tried twice for the same offence. And he will know that as well as I do. Let the threat, at least, remain over his head.'

Castelbranco nodded very slightly, in an acknowledgement. Too stunned, too broken to speak, he turned and walked out of the door, leaving it open behind him, and Pitt alone in the room.

Chapter Fourteen

IT WAS a hot summer day at the Old Bailey, the central criminal court in London, when the trial began of Alban Hythe, charged with the rape of Catherine Quixwood.

The gallery was crowded. Without influence Narraway would not have been able to find a seat, except possibly at the very back. He had wanted to ask Vespasia if she would come. He would have valued her opinion, possibly even her advice. If he were honest with himself, most of all he would have liked her company. He knew this was going to be painful.

He had been willing to pay Peter Symington out of his own pocket, although it had not proved necessary because Symington was willing to defend Hythe for the interest and the fame of the case. Still, clever, inventive and individual as Symington was, not only the evidence but the mood of the court was overwhelmingly against Hythe. Perhaps it was to keep up his own courage and not to feel so bitterly alone that Narraway really wished Vespasia were with him.

He had considered asking her if she would come. His hand had hovered over the telephone, and then he had realised how often he had asked for her time recently, not for any social or pleasurable reason such as the opera or the theatre, but because he wanted to talk to her. She had always been willing, even gracious about accepting, but surely one day she would politely and gently refuse. She must have put up a warning hand to hundreds of men during her life, to tell them that they were asking too much, presuming on friendship a trifle too often.

Was he doing that?

He was not used to rejection, not when it actually mattered, and he realised with a shock like a stab of physical pain that it did matter. It would hurt him in a way and with a depth that he had not experienced for years – possibly not at all.

He had been attracted to women who had chosen someone else. It happened to almost everyone. It had stung his vanity more than his heart. He had felt embarrassment, certainly guilt, even self-doubt and despondency at times. But to be rebuffed by Vespasia, however softly or reluctantly, would wound him in a place he had considered invulnerable. He must not allow it to happen. The friendship was important enough to him that the loss of it was frightening.

He sat alone near the front of the gallery as the proceedings began. The jury was called and sworn in, and the charge was read.

Hythe stood in the dock, high above the well of the room. He looked so pale as to seem almost grey. He made no move, no sound, except to state his innocence in a voice so quiet that the judge had to ask him to repeat it.

Maris Hythe would be waiting outside, perhaps alone, in case she might be called to testify, and therefore must not be permitted to hear the previous evidence. Could there be a more exquisite torture of the mind?

The charge did not include murder, only the brutal rape and beating. In his opening statement Algernon Bower, QC for the prosecution, faced the jury and spoke with a soft but curiously penetrating voice. He was not a large man, barely of average height, but he had a presence that could not be ignored. His face was powerful with a dominant nose, keen eyes. He had a high forehead where the dark, straight hair was beginning to thin, although today, of course, he wore the lawyer's costume of white wig and black gown.

'We will prove to you, gentlemen,' he said levelly, removing almost all emotion from his tone, 'that the accused man was having a love affair with the dead woman, Catherine Quixwood, and that he visited her late on the evening of her death. She herself was the one who let him into her home. No servants saw him, but that is because she wanted it so. She herself had dismissed them.'

The jurors stared at him, sombre and unhappy. There was a distinct rustle of movement in the gallery.

Next to Narraway a large man pursed his lips in disapproval. His thoughts were almost as clear in his face as if he had spoken them aloud.

'We may never know exactly what happened,' Bower continued. He looked at the jurors as an actor regards his audience, weighing them. 'But we will prove beyond any doubt at all that there was a terrible quarrel, which became physically violent. You may surmise the cause of it to be that Mrs Quixwood had grown tired of Mr Hythe's attentions, or even that her conscience had at last asserted itself and she had decided to think again of her loyalty to her husband.' He held up a hand, although Symington, in his seat on the other side of the aisle, had made no move to interrupt him.

'We will prove to you, by medical and other evidence,' Bower went on, 'that this quarrel ended in the most brutal rape and beating of Mrs Quixwood, leaving her broken and bleeding on the floor. Later she crept on her hands and knees over to the sideboard where she poured an overdose of laudanum into her glass of Madeira wine and thus took her own life.'

There were head shakes in the jury box. A woman in the gallery let out a cry of horror.

Narraway winced. Despite the heat in the room he was cold, as if despair were settling inside him and filling his body. It was as well he had not asked Vespasia to be here, even had she been willing to come. This was, in a sense, the beginning of a public execution. She could be spared that.

Bower finished and Symington stood up. His face looked as it had in his office when Narraway had engaged him on the case: smooth, handsome, younger than he actually was. The light caught the pale wig, which concealed almost all his hair, but there was no sign whatever of his quick, wide smile or the totally irresponsible sense of humour that were ordinarily characteristic of him. Watching him now, Narraway had no idea if Symington really had a plan, even a believable idea how to defend Alban Hythe. He himself certainly had none.

Symington stood in front of the jury. He smiled at them charmingly, but the warmth was without lightness. One of them frowned at him, looking as if he disapproved that anyone should attempt to excuse Hythe, as though that were the same as excusing the rape itself. Two smiled back, maybe sorry for him because in their eyes he was already beaten.

'A dreadful crime.' Symington's smile vanished and it was as if the sun had gone in, changing him entirely. 'I'm sorry that you will have to listen while the police surgeon tells you, probably in detail, how poor Mrs Quixwood was raped and beaten, almost to death.' He shook his head fractionally. 'It will be a terrible experience for you. I have had to go through the details as part of my duty, and I admit it turned my stomach and all but made me weep in pity for her.'

Bower fidgeted. He neither liked nor trusted Symington, and as much was clear in his face.

Symington was still facing the jurors. 'And just as powerful as grief, it frightened me because it could happen to any woman, to those I love.' He lowered his gaze and met theirs individually. 'And to those you love – your wives, your daughters. Catherine Quixwood was a respectable married woman, behind locked doors in her own house on the evening of the crime. Who could be safer?'

He hesitated.

The jurors were clearly uncomfortable. Many of them looked away.

Symington spread his hands. 'It would be much more comfortable if it were in some way her own fault. If she brought this upon herself, then we are all right, because we won't do the things she did, will we!'

Suddenly his voice became stronger, darker in tone and yet also more intimate. 'But we are not here to think of ourselves, or even to thank God for our own comfort and safety. We are here to learn the truth about the tragedy and horror of other people's lives – to look at them honestly, to rise above our own fears and prejudices, should we have them. And we can all feel terror, not just of violence, but of loss, of disgrace, of public humiliation, of the impulse to lie rather than be stripped in front of the world.'

He shrugged very slightly, and the smile lit his face again. 'But we are chosen by our fellows, by fate, if you like, to be fair, to be honourable above our everyday selves, and to set our natural self-protection aside. I ask you to be merciful to the quirks and the weaknesses that we all have, and to be relentlessly just to the facts.'

The jurors looked puzzled. One middle-aged man blushed hotly.

'I will show you how else this terrible thing could have happened,' Symington said finally. 'And why Alban Hythe had no part in it at all. I will convince you of this until in good conscience you cannot return a verdict of guilty. You cannot see him hang.' He smiled agian, warmly, as if he liked them, and turned away, walking quite casually back to his place.

Narraway wondered how much of that was bluff. Watching him, listening, he could see no doubt in him at all.

Bower called his first witness: a very nervous man in a plain, dark suit, which did not fit him comfortably, as though he were unused to wearing it. Narraway recognised him only when he told the court that his occupation was as butler to Rawdon Quixwood.

'I'm sorry, Mr Luckett,' Bower started, 'but I must ask you to turn your mind back to the evening of April the 19th. Mr Quixwood was in the city at a function, I believe, at the Spanish Embassy, and Mrs Quixwood had allowed all the servants to retire early, leaving her alone in the withdrawing room. Is that correct?'

Luckett was clearly distressed and still having some difficulty composing himself. The judge looked at Symington to see if he objected to Bower putting so many words into the witness's mouth, but Symington sat in his place smiling and silent.

'Mr Luckett . . .' the judge prompted.

'Yes . . .' Luckett said jerkily. 'Yes, she often allowed us to retire if she knew she would need nothing.' He gulped. 'She was very considerate.'

'She did not even retain a footman to answer the door?' Bower said with surprise.

'No, sir,' Luckett replied, shifting his weight from one foot to the other.

'Did you yourself go to bed, Mr Luckett?'

'No, sir. We . . . some of the younger servants, girls, went upstairs. The housekeeper and I sat up with a pot of tea. The cook was doing something in the kitchen, I believe.' He was twisting his hands. He knew, as did the rest of the court, what was coming next.

In the gallery no one moved.

'Did Mrs Quixwood send for you?' Bower asked.

'No . . . no, sir.'

'But you did return to the front of the house? What time would that have been?'

'I . . . can't say, sir. I didn't look at the clock. It was late.'

'Why did you go back after Mrs Quixwood had expressly dismissed you?'

'I saw the lights still on, sir. It was a lot later than Mrs Quixwood usually retired. I thought she must have forgotten to turn them down. And . . . and I wished to check the front door a last time.'

'Would you tell us what you found, Mr Luckett?' Bower looked grave. He was an excellent prosecutor. It flickered through Narraway's mind that he would also have been a good undertaker. He had an expression made for disaster.

Luckett gulped. 'I – I went into the vestibule and I saw . . . I saw Mrs Quixwood lying on the floor. For an instant I thought she had slipped and fallen, perhaps fainted.' He was not looking at Bower but at some terrible memory within himself. 'She was sort of . . . sprawled out, on her side. There . . . her . . . her clothes were torn and there was blood on the floor. I bent to touch her and I could see that she was . . . dead.'

'What did you do then, Mr Luckett?' Bower said gently.

'I – I went back into the housekeeper's room and informed her of what I had found. We sent the footman for the police.'

'Thank you, Mr Luckett,' Bower said gravely. 'I regret the necessity to pursue this, but there is no alternative if we are to find the truth. Did you let anyone into the house that evening, before Mrs Quixwood's death? Did you hear the doorbell ring, or were you made aware in any way of anyone entering the premises?'

Luckett stared at him with the same expression of revulsion he might have worn had he discovered a caterpillar in his dinner.

'No, sir, I did not.'

'Then how did any visitor gain entrance?' Bower raised his eyebrows.

'I don't know, sir.'

'But you locked the door before retiring?' Bower would not allow him to evade the issue.

'Yes, sir.'

'So who unlocked the door and let in whoever attacked Mrs Quixwood?'

Still Luckett said nothing.

'You did place the bolts in their sockets, did you not?' Bower insisted.

'Yes, sir. Mr Quixwood expected to be very late from his function. When that happened he stayed at his club.' Luckett looked as if he were having teeth drawn.

'Just so,' Bower agreed. 'So who let in the man who raped Mrs Quixwood and beat her?'

'I don't know, sir.'

'Must she not have let him in herself?' Bower demanded.

'It would seem so,' Luckett said very quietly.

'Thank you.' Bower turned to Symington.

Symington rose to his feet. He walked over towards the high witness box, which was something like the prow of a ship, or a tower several feet above the floor of the courtroom. He smiled up at Luckett.

'It does seem rather as if she let him in herself, doesn't it?' he said ruefully. 'But my learned friend has run the whole question into one. Let me rephrase it. Was there anyone else in the house who could have answered the door and let someone in, for whatever purpose?'

'No, sir.' Luckett regarded him warily.

'So Mrs Quixwood opened the door. Is there any way to know whom she expected to be on the other side? A friend? Someone in trouble needing her counsel or help, perhaps? Even Mr Quixwood, returning from his function earlier than he had expected? Or someone with an urgent message?'

'Yes, sir, it could have been any of those,' Luckett agreed with relief.

'Had Mr Quixwood ever mislaid his key?'

'He did not carry a key, sir. It was his own house. He would expect one of us to answer the door. He had intended to spend the night at his club.'

'Quite my point.' Symington smiled dazzlingly. 'You have been butler to the household for several years, and a footman before that, I believe? You must have known Mrs Quixwood since her marriage?'

'Yes, sir.' There was warmth in Luckett's face, and a flood of grief.

'My learned friend said she must have let in the man who attacked her so terribly. Do you suppose she imagined he was there for that purpose?'

'Of course not!' Luckett was astonished.

'My thought exactly,' Symington agreed. 'She let him in believing him to be harmless, even a friend. Thank you, Mr Luckett.'

The judge looked at Bower, who declined to pursue the subject and instead called Inspector Knox.

Narraway realised he was sitting with his shoulders so tense his neck ached. At least Symington was putting up a fight, but he had been given no ammunition. Every avenue Narraway had followed regarding Catherine's enquiries for financial advice had proved useless. She had inherited no money of her own, and Quixwood himself kept his affairs from her. They were complicated and extremely successful. It was his profession.

Knox was sworn in and Bower began immediately asking him about the message he had received, and his arrival at the Quixwood house. Knox described what he had seen, being as brief as he could about the details. Apart from the fact that his voice trembled, he might have been speaking of a burglary, not what at that point had seemed to be a particularly dreadful murder.

'After you had sent for the police surgeon, what did you do then, Inspector Knox?' Bower asked.

'I sent my men to see if they could find how the attacker had gained entry, sir,' Knox replied. 'We found nothing out of order at that time, and in the daylight the following morning we ascertained that that was indeed so. He must have been let in through the front door.'

'Did you ever find evidence to contradict that?'

'No, sir.'

'But you looked?' Bower insisted.

'Yes, sir.'

'I shall call the police surgeon to give his own evidence,' Bower warned him. 'But from what he told you, what did you conclude had happened to cause Mrs Quixwood's death?'

Symington rose to his feet. 'My lord, Mr Bower has asked the witness a question, and at the same time directed him not to answer it. How can the poor man know what to say?' He looked apologetic, and slightly amused.

'Perhaps you should rephrase your question, Mr Bower,' the judge suggested. 'Or else have the police surgeon testify, and recall Inspector Knox after you have established how Mrs Quixwood met her death.'

There was a rustle of interest in the gallery. Two of the jurors nodded. But it was light without substance, and Narraway knew it. It would make no difference in the end.

Without any outward loss of composure Bower said he would recall Knox, and he sent for Dr Brinsley.

Narraway half listened as Brinsley described the appalling injuries sustained by Catherine Quixwood. He used no emotive adjectives, and somehow his calm voice and bleak, sad face made the brutality of it even more horrific. The packed court could not but be reminded of the intimate and intensely vulnerable humanity of all of them.

Narraway had heard it before, but it still appalled him. He had seen her body lying on the floor, but he had not then imagined the fearful damage done to her. Only when Knox had described it to him had it become real.

The court listened in silence. There was no sound in the gallery, no whisper or rustle of movement, only the occasional gasp. A little further along the row Narraway saw a woman reach out and take hold of her husband's hand, and his fingers close over hers tightly. Again he was glad he had not asked Vespasia to come, deeply as he would have liked her company, her courage to help him still believe in Alban Hythe's innocence and not allow revulsion to draw him away from the issue.

What could have possessed any man to do such things? Surely only gut-wrenching fear or insane hatred drove this kind of depravity?

Why had he gone there, whoever he was – Hythe or anyone else? If she had intended to break off the affair, why had she let him into the house without a servant within call? Had he never lost his temper before, never shown any inclination towards violence? Was that possible? Had she never had any other bruises, cuts, abrasions, from him before – nothing to show his nature?

Narraway fished in his pocket and found a pencil and paper. Hastily he wrote a note to Symington, then gave it to the usher to pass it to him.

'What was the cause of Mrs Quixwood's death, Dr Brinsley?' Bower asked finally.

'Her wounds were severe,' Brinsley replied. 'But she actually died of an overdose of laudanum, taken in Madeira wine.'

'Self-administered?' Bower asked.

'No idea,' Brinsley said tartly.

'Could it have been just a little more than the usual medicinal dose?' Bower persisted.

'It was several times the usual medicinal dose,' Brinsley answered him. 'No one could take it by accident.'

'You are saying it was suicide,' Bower stated.

Brinsley leaned forward over the railing of the witness stand, his face flushed. 'I am saying it was approximately four times the usual medicinal dose, Mr Bower. She appears to have drunk it voluntarily, but whether she put the laudanum in the wine herself, or it was added by someone else, I have no idea, and – so far as I know – neither have you.'

Bower's eyes flashed with temper but he did not retreat. 'Is it possible that in shame at her betrayal of her husband, and the pain and humiliation of being raped by her lover – which inevitably her husband would come to know of – she deliberately took her own life?'

Brinsley glared at him. 'I am not going to speculate, sir. I am a doctor, not a clairvoyant.'

'Have you known of women who have been raped to take their own lives?' Bower said between his teeth.

'Of course. People take their own lives for all sorts of reasons, and frequently we do not ever fully understand them,' Brinsley answered.

'Thank you, Doctor,' Bower responded with exaggerated patience. 'Your witness, Mr Symington.'

Symington rose and strolled over to the witness stand. He looked up at Brinsley and smiled.

'You must see many tragic and very distressing cases, Dr Brinsley.'

'I do,' Brinsley agreed.

'You have described poor Mrs Quixwood's wounds in some detail for Mr Bower. I won't ask you to go over them again. I think all of us are distressed enough. Just tell me one thing about them, if you please. Were they all sustained at that one awful attack?'

Bower stood up slowly. 'Is my learned friend suggesting some other attack that same evening, my lord? That is preposterous! There are no grounds whatsoever for such a suggestion. And even if there had been such a – a mythical attack, how would Dr Brinsley differentiate one wound from another?'

Symington looked at Bower as if he had taken leave of his wits.

'Good gracious,' he said incredulously. 'Such a thing never occurred to me. Surely if there had been two such attacks, she would hardly have let the second one into the house, would she? What on earth are you suggesting?'

'It was your suggestion, sir!' Bower all but spat the words.

'Not at all,' Symington shook his head. 'I was thinking that if her lover was prone to violence then there might have been old bruises, half-healed scars, abrasions, from earlier quarrels. A deep bruise can take some time to disappear altogether.'

'I saw no older injuries at all,' Brinsley replied, but now his face was keen with a spark of interest.

'Then would it be reasonable to assume, from the evidence, of course, that the attack was sudden, and would have been completely unexpected?' Symington pushed his hands into his pockets and leaned back a little to look up at the doctor in the stand.

'It would indeed,' Brinsley agreed. 'In fact if the same man had ever shown any violence towards her we would assume she would have been very careful to keep male servants well within earshot. Yes, we may safely conclude that it was unexpected.'

'Then one may assume also that she was not afraid of him?' Symington waved his hands in denial. 'Oh, I'm sorry. That was simply my own thought. Foolish of me. Of course she was not afraid of him, or she would not have let him in. Thank you, Dr Brinsley.'

Bower half stood, then changed his mind and sat again, his face hard-edged and angry.

The court adjourned for luncheon, a little late. When they resumed in the afternoon, they were tense and there was a buzz of heightened emotion when Rawdon Quixwood took the stand.

Narraway felt his own breath catch in his throat. The man looked ten years older: paler and withdrawn into himself. He climbed the steps up to the stand as if it cost him an effort. When he finally faced Bower he leaned very slightly against the railing to support himself. He seemed thinner. His clothes hung on him.

When Quixwood was sworn in, Bower approached him with both respect and grave compassion.

'Mr Quixwood, I regret having to call you to this ordeal at all, and I will make it as quick as I can so that you may be excused from this experience, which can only be a terrible suffering for you.'

Quixwood inclined his head in thanks.

'Are you acquainted with the accused, Mr Alban Hythe, sir?' Bower asked.

'Yes, I am. We have done business with each other on various occasions,' Quixwood answered.

'And do you know him socially also?'

'Much less so, but yes, we have attended the same functions from time to time.'

'Were you aware, sir, that your wife had met him on a number of occasions over a matter of months, at lectures, museums, galleries and so on, when neither you nor Mrs Hythe were present?'

'No, I was not.' Quixwood looked pained.

'Did you know that Mrs Quixwood attended such events quite frequently?'

'Yes, of course I did. She had many interests, and friends. These were natural and very pleasant places to meet.' He sounded a little annoyed, as if Bower were tainting Catherine's reputation gratuitously.

'Did she ever give you cause to be concerned that she was forming a romantic attachment to another man? Please think carefully. I regret asking such an ugly question, but circumstances force me to.' Bower looked genuinely distressed.

'I understand,' Quixwood said softly. 'If you please, let us get it over with. Allow me to answer the question you are leading towards too delicately.' He straightened his shoulders with an effort. 'Yes, looking back with hindsight, it is perfectly possible that my wife was having an affair with Alban Hythe. He is a charming and delightful man and has many interests Catherine shared – interests I myself had not time to indulge. She may have hungered for someone with whom to discuss them, and friendship may have led to more. It never occurred to me at the time. I trusted her absolutely. But she had the freedom to come and go as she wished. We – we did not have children, and I asked no social duties of her except the occasional dinner party.'

Narraway could feel a wave of sympathy for him emanating from the court. The jury was all but overcome by emotion.

Quixwood took a deep breath and let it out with a sigh. 'Perhaps I should have asked more of her; then she would not have . . .' He seemed unable to complete the thought aloud.

Bower did not press him.

'You were at a business function on the evening she was . . . attacked?' he asked.

'Yes,' Quixwood agreed. 'At the Spanish Embassy. I was in conversation with Lord Narraway when I was told . . . told that Catherine had been . . . attacked.'

There was a shudder of horror in the gallery, a sigh. Two or three women let out little moans of pity and grief.

'Quite so,' Bower nodded. 'I regret raising the question, but there is one more matter I need you to answer. Had you noticed any change in Mrs Quixwood's behaviour over the last few months before the incident? Was she absent-minded? Did she wear any very attractive new clothes? Did she seem to take more than the usual care over her appearance? Was she evasive about where she had been or whom she had met?'

Quixwood smiled bleakly and the pain in his face was evident.

'You are asking me if she was having a love affair. The answer is that I noticed nothing at the time. Perhaps I should have, but I deal in major finance, enormous sums of money, all of which belong to other people. It is a great responsibility. I paid her too little attention.' He blinked several times and took some time to regain control of his grief.

Sitting on the front row of the gallery, Narraway could feel the crowd's pity wash over him like a physical wave. Quixwood had said nothing against Hythe whatever, and yet at this moment the jury would have convicted him without even retiring to debate the issue. The anger and the pain in their faces testified to it more vividly than words. Symington would have to be more than a genius, he would need to be a magician to turn this tide.

Narraway sat with his hands clenched, nails digging into his palms. It was all so desperately believable he began to doubt Hythe himself. The affair seemed inevitable, given his nature and Catherine's. But what on earth had possessed him to rape her with such insane savagery? It was the only part of the whole miserable story that did not yet fit. Was it only a matter of time before that answer fell into place also?

'I have no further questions for this witness, my lord,' Bower said gravely. He looked at Symington with slightly raised eyebrows.

Symington stood up. For once there was no smile on his face. He thanked Bower and walked over towards the witness stand.

'I hate this,' he said candidly. 'Heaven only knows how you have suffered already. But I'm sure you want justice, and since you have answered all my learned friend's questions, I'm sure you will also answer the few of mine.'

'Of course,' Quixwood replied with something like a wince of pain.

Symington's face was full of compassion as he began.

'From the portraits of her, and all that I have learned, Mrs Quixwood was a beautiful woman, and gifted with both grace and intelligence. Many men must have admired her, and no doubt she was accustomed to behaving with charm, but not misleading anyone into imagining she would offer them more than a slight friendship. Would that be true, do you think?'

'Yes, yes that is true,' Quixwood agreed after only a moment's hesitation.

'In hindsight, what makes you believe that with Mr Hythe it was any different?' Symington asked innocently. 'And that she was not simply looking forward to events that interested her?'

'I . . .' Quixwood began, then stopped. He seemed confused. 'She was . . . it is very subtle, just a . . . a change in her spirits, a greater eagerness to attend certain lectures or recitals, more care with a gown, or a piece of jewellery.'

'With hindsight,' Symington repeated. 'Of course you were not aware of this at the time. You have already told my learned friend that you had no idea at all that she was romantically involved.'

Again Quixwood found it difficult to come up with an immediate answer.

'Perhaps I should have,' he said at last.

'Or perhaps she was not deceiving you at all,' Symington suggested. 'The terrible injuries that the police surgeon has described hardly fit in with the nature of a lover. They are more the acts of a madman.' Before he could be cautioned by the judge, or Bower could object, he smiled at Quixwood and went on. 'The police surgeon also said that he noticed no old injuries to Mrs Quixwood, old bruises or marks of any sort. Did you notice anything like that?'

Quixwood had only one possible answer, since he had not heard the surgeon himself, and if he had, then surely he would have said so before.

'No,' he said flatly. 'No, I didn't.' He seemed about to add something more, then changed his mind.

'Thank you,' Symington replied with an inclination of his head, almost a bow. 'I can't see that it is necessary to harrow you any longer with reliving this grief. I appreciate your patience and your honesty, Mr Quixwood. I have no more questions.'

Bower considered the matter for only a moment, then agreed that he also had no more to ask this witness. Quixwood was excused.

The court was adjourned for the day.

Narraway glanced up at the dock and saw Alban Hythe rise to his feet, looking back at the court only once before the gaolers led him away. His face was white, terrified and despairing, searching for even one person who believed in him.

Was Narraway such a person? He was glad Hythe had not met his eyes, or recognised him, because he was not certain that he was that person. He was sure beyond any doubt at all that he had no idea how to help him.

In the evening Narraway sat alone in his study and weighed in his mind everything he knew or believed about Catherine Quixwood and Alban Hythe. He had read Catherine's social diary. Apparently Catherine had kept no personal diary noting her emotions after particular meetings or events. She had also left no financial notes that anyone had found. Was it really credible, as Hythe claimed, that she had been seeing him in order to learn more about major investments her husband might have made, and if they were as safe or as profitable as he believed?

Did she actually know or understand enough of Quixwood's finances to fear that he would lose badly? There was no hint of economic study or skill in what Narraway had learned of her. Her education was what would be expected of a young woman of her social class. She was well read in literature, spoke a little French, knew English history and had the usual familiarity with the classics. She had added greatly to the last of these in her own private reading and attendance at various lectures. As far as he could see, none of them had concerned economics or investment strategy.

Her own private spending involved supervision of the kitchen expenses, and a dress allowance, which she had never exceeded. Quixwood himself saw to all other bills, and he was more than comfortably situated.

Was Hythe telling the truth, or building an elaborate, and frankly rather ridiculous excuse for having met Catherine so frequently where they could speak without being watched or overheard?

If he offered that to Symington, without highly credible evidence, no jury would believe it. Even though he would very much like to have, Narraway did not believe it himself.

What would such evidence be? Was it all paper investment, or real? Was it conceivable that the figures in Catherine's diary were not telephone numbers but amounts of money? Thousands of pounds? Had Quixwood sunk a lot of his fortune in something Catherine had feared was morally or ethically questionable? Or in something she feared to be against British interests? In the Transvaal? Or in diamonds or gold specifically? In some venture with Cecil Rhodes? In the Pitsani Strip, in railways, in building? If Catherine was worried, why on earth look for vague information from Alban Hythe? Why not simply tell Quixwood that she was afraid, and ask him for assurance that he was not taking risks with their safety?

Was there any point in learning as much he could about dubious investment Quixwood might have considered, this late in the issue? And what could any of it have to do with rape?

The answer was almost certainly nothing at all.

He went to bed tired and discouraged, and slept badly.

Chapter Fifteen

ON THE morning of the second day of Alban Hythe's trial, Knox sent a message to Pitt to meet him at the home of a Mr Frederick Townley, in Hunter Street, just off Brunswick Square. The footman had instructions to admit him as soon as he arrived.

It was a damp, hazy day, already warm at half-past nine, with a very fine drizzle falling. As Knox had been promised, a grim-faced footman opened the door so immediately after Pitt's pulling of the bell that he had to have been waiting for him. He was shown into the morning room where Knox and a very clearly distressed Frederick Townley were waiting.

Knox introduced Pitt, with his full title.

Townley was gaunt, middle-aged, with dark hair, receding at the brow. At the moment he was restless, fidgeting and unable to control his nerves.

'I've told you, Mr Knox, I was in error,' he said urgently looking at Knox, then at Pitt, then back again. 'I do not wish to make any such complaint. You may say anything you please. I withdraw the complaint. I have no idea in the world why you should think to involve Special Branch. It is completely absurd.' He turned to Pitt. 'I apologise to you, sir. This is just a domestic matter. In fact, it is no more than a misunderstanding.'

Pitt looked at the man's face and saw fear and grief, which at this moment were overridden by acute embarrassment.

'I'm sorry,' Townley regarded Pitt with discomfort. 'You have been disturbed unnecessarily. Now I must return to my family. I would like to hope you understand, but at this point it really makes no difference to me. Good day to you, gentlemen.'

'Mr Townley!' Knox said with asperity. 'I may not have the authority to require a statement from you, if you choose to let this matter go unreported, but Commander Pitt cannot ignore it if the safety of the realm is in question.'

Townley's jaw dropped in disbelief. 'Don't be absurd, man! How can my daughter's . . . misfortune, possibly concern the safety of the realm? I don't know what it is you want, but I am laying no complaint whatever. You have wasted this gentleman's time.' He gestured towards Pitt. 'Please excuse me.' Again he moved towards the door, lurching a little and regaining his balance with a hand on the jamb. 'My footman will be happy to see you out,' he added, as if he thought his meaning might have been unclear.

'If you do not speak the truth, Mr Townley, whether in the form of a complaint or not, then an innocent man may hang,' Knox said peremptorily.

Townley swung around and glared at him. 'Not because of anything I have said, sir!'

'Because of what you know, and have not said,' Knox retorted. 'Silence can lead to damation as much as speech, and still cost a man his life.'

'Or a woman her reputation!' Townley snapped back. 'I look after my own, sir, as does any decent man.'

'Have you a son also, Mr Townley?' Pitt said suddenly.

Townley stared at him with disbelief. 'And what is that to you, sir? None of this . . . this supposed affair has anything to do with him.'

'I have a son and a daughter also,' Pitt told him. 'They are children still, but my daughter is fast turning into a woman. It seems to me that she is more and more like her mother with every few months that pass.'

Townley tried to interrupt him, but Pitt overrode him.

'Because of an incident involving someone of whom she knew, my daughter has asked me, and her mother, very urgent and awkward questions about rape. She wishes to know what it is, and why people are so terribly upset about it. Who is to blame? We have tried to answer her both delicately and honestly, bearing in mind that she is only fourteen.'

'I wish you well, sir,' Townley succeeded in interrupting this time. His face was grey-white and he seemed to have trouble forming his words coherently. 'But that is of no concern to me.'

'And I look at my son,' Pitt went on, disregarding the interruption. 'He is nearly twelve, and has no idea what we are talking about. How do I explain it all to him, so that his behaviour towards women is never coarse or, worse still, violent? But perhaps more terrible than that, how do I protect him from being accused of something he did not do? What father, what mother, would see their son at the end of the hangman's rope, jeered at by the crowd, insulted and abused, for a hideous crime of which he was innocent, but could not prove it?'

Townley was trembling where he stood, his fists clenching and unclenching. 'Then you will understand, sir, why I make no complaint. You have answered your own question.' He took a shaky step closer to the hallway and his escape.

'Mr Townley!' Pitt said as if it were a command.

'You have my answer,' Townley said between his teeth.

'I am not asking that you lay a complaint,' Pitt said, quietly now. 'Only that, man to man, you tell me the truth. You can deny it afterwards. I will not ask you to sign anything, or to swear anything. I need to know, because the daughter of a foreign ambassador was also a victim recently. That is why Special Branch has been involved.'

Townley hesitated. 'I will not testify!' he said, his voice a little shrill.

'I'm not sure that I would, if it were my daughter,' Pitt admitted. 'I would do what I thought was best for her.'

'I will not allow you to speak to her,' Townley warned. 'Even if I would, her mother would not. Seeing the doctor . . . was bad enough.'

Pitt drew in his breath to say that he understood, and realised that he had no idea. Instead he simply asked what she had told them had happened, whether to her mother, the doctor or to Townley himself.

Townley closed his eyes and repeated in a flat hesitant voice. 'Alice is nearly seventeen. She was at a ball in the house of a friend. I will not tell you their names. There were naturally young gentlemen present also. She enjoys dancing and is particularly skilled. She was flattered when a young man in his late twenties asked her to dance, imagining he thought her older, more sophisticated, which she has a great desire to be. To – to get to the point . . .' he gulped. 'He spoke pleasantly to her, inviting her to see one of the galleries in the house where there were some remarkable paintings. Alice likes . . . art. She suspected nothing and went with him.'

Pitt felt himself clenching inside. He saw not Alice Townley but Jemima: happy, flattered, also suspecting nothing.

'He took her first to one gallery with some art as lovely as he had said it would be,' Townley continued. 'Then promised more works, even better, but that they were in another part of the house . . . a private part where they should not trespass, but he said they would touch nothing, merely look at the paintings.'

Pitt almost said it for him, to break the unbearable tension, and to save the man from having to say it himself. Then Knox moved a fraction, no more than shifting his weight from one foot to the other, but reminding him of his presence. Pitt let out his breath without speaking.

'He . . . violated her,' Townley said hoarsely. 'She had not the power to fight him off. He left her bleeding and bruised on the floor. She had hit her head, and was knocked senseless for a while. When she came to she climbed to her feet, and was staggering to the door when a different young man met her. He assumed that she had taken too much wine, and rather than tell him the truth that she . . . had lost her virginity, she said that was true, and she accounted for her bruises and the blood by saying she had fallen down some steps. That was the story she gave her hostess, and no one pressed her further.' Townley's chin lifted and he glared at Pitt, then at Knox. 'And that is the story I shall tell, if I am pressed. I will swear to it on oath, if I have to.'

'Did she say who the young man was who assaulted her?' Pitt asked.

'It will do you no good,' Townley said bluntly.

'Possibly not, but I wish to know,' Pitt insisted. 'It would be very much better if she tells me than if I have to investigate all the balls in London last night, and find out who attended which. People will inevitably ask why I need to know.'

'You are a brutal man,' Townley said icily, but his eyes filled with tears.

Pitt was silent for a moment. Would it really help to know? Yes, it would. Not just for Rafael Castelbranco, but for all other young women, he needed to get Neville Forsbrook off the streets, if he could just be certain it was he.

'Please?' he repeated.

Wordlessly Townley led them upstairs and across a wide landing to a door with a porcelain floral handle. He knocked, and when his wife answered, he told her that this was unavoidable. At his insistence, she allowed Pitt inside, but not Knox.

The girl propped up in the bed was white-faced, except for the tear stains on her cheeks, and the pink rims to her eyes. Her long honey-brown hair was loose around her shoulders. Her features were soft, but in a year or two would also reflect a considerable strength.

Pitt's step faltered as he walked across the carpet and stood near the bed, but not too close.

'My name is Thomas Pitt,' he said quietly. 'I have a daughter who will be your age soon. She looks quite a lot like you. I hope she will be as lovely. I understand you like paintings?'

She nodded.

'Yesterday evening you were shown some particularly beautiful ones, is that correct?'

Again she nodded.

'Do you prefer portraits or landscapes?'

'They were mostly portraits, and some animals, very out of proportion.' She almost smiled. 'Horses whose legs looked so thin I don't know how they could stand on them.'

Pitt shook his head. 'I've seen some like that. I don't like them very much. I like to see horses with movement in the lines rather than standing still. Who showed you these pictures?'

'He wasn't going to steal them,' she said quickly. 'At least I don't think. He has lots of money anyway . . . or his father does. He could just buy them.'

'Maybe he was thinking of offering to buy them,' he agreed. 'Who was he?'

'Do . . . do I have to tell you?'

'No, not if you really don't want to.' The minute the words were out he regretted it. Narraway wouldn't have been so weak.

'It was Neville Forsbrook,' she whispered.

He let his breath out in a sigh. 'Thank you, Alice. I appreciate knowing. Thank you for letting me visit you.'

'It's all right.' She gave him a tiny, uncertain smile.

He thanked Mrs Townley and walked outside onto the landing, Townley at his heels. The door closed with a faint click.

Townley stood on the landing by the window, surrounded by vases of carefully arranged flowers. His face was ravaged with fear and grief.

'Thank you,' he echoed. 'Now that is the end of it.'

Pitt nodded and followed Knox down the stairs.

Alice Townley's face haunted Pitt as he walked away from the house. It was as if he had met a ghost of Angeles Castelbranco, and what troubled him like an open wound was the fact that in his own mind he was certain that there would be other girls in the future, perhaps not lucky enough to escape with their lives. Perhaps Pamela O'Keefe had been one of them? They would probably never know.

He could not blame Townley for wanting to protect his daughter. Had it been Jemima, Pitt doubted he would try to prosecute. In fact, if he were honest, he knew he would not. Whatever Forsbrook went on to do, one protected one's own child first.

Alice Townley had been violated, but not seriously injured, certainly not beaten as Catherine had been. Pamela O'Keefe had been murdered, her neck broken. Why the difference? What injuries had Angeles Castelbranco sustained?

At least two different men? One Neville Forsbrook, the other perhaps Alban Hythe – perhaps not.

Had Pamela O'Keefe's death been an accident? Had he forced himself on her, and in the violence of her struggle he had lunged back at her and snapped her neck? Was he then terrified? Or exhilarated?

Was the difference in his perception of the woman, or in the way they reacted to him? Did he need their fear to excite him?

Pitt must check on the degree of violence, the bruises of self-defence, note all the differences and the similarities.

It was not difficult to find Brinsley, the surgeon who had examined Catherine Quixwood. He was in the police morgue performing a post mortem on another body, a man stabbed in a bar-room fight. Pitt waited half an hour until he was finished. He came out of the autopsy room cold, his hands still wet. He carried a faint odour of carbolic with him.

'Commander Pitt, Special Branch,' Pitt introduced himself.

'What can I do for you, Commander?' Brinsley asked. 'Tea? I'm tired and I'm cold and I've still a long evening ahead of me.'

'Thank you,' Pitt accepted. 'I'm looking into several rapes, to see if I can compare them to one that concerns me particularly. I need to know if they're related.'

Brinsley reached his office and put a kettle onto a small burner. It was only moments before it boiled and he made tea for them both in a round-bellied china pot.

'Look for similarities,' Brinsley said with a shrug. 'I assume you have no testimony, no description?'

'I have some, but if it is accurate, the man seems to be far more violent some times than others.'

'Interesting,' Brinsley said thoughtfully. 'Usually they escalate with time. Are you certain it's all one man?'

'No, I'm not. Can you describe the injuries to Catherine Quixwood?'

'They were very grave, but not fatal,' Brinsley replied. 'She was deeply bruised on her body, upper arms, more so still upon her thighs and there was tearing of her genital organs by forceful penetration.' His mouth twisted in a grimace. 'There was also a fairly deep bite on her left breast. The man's teeth had torn the skin and left distinct bruise marks which were more pronounced after her death.'

'Thank you,' Pitt said quietly. 'Was there anything about these injuries that would be distinct to the man who inflicted them?'

'From what you say he was a great deal more violent than the perpetrator of the other rape you describe, or else it was the same man more deeply sunk in his state of . . . depravity.'

'That crime happened before the two others,' Pitt said unhappily.

'Then it seems you have at least two rapists,' Brinsley shook his head. 'I'm sorry.'

'Thank you anyway.' Pitt turned to leave, his tea only half drunk. His throat felt too tight to swallow.

Brinsley took a breath.

Pitt turned back. 'Yes?'

'Was there anything particularly different about the victims? Or about the places of attack, or the circumstances?'

'Would that account for it?'

'I don't know. I suppose it's possible.' There was no lift in Brinsley's voice, no brightness in his face. 'But you should look.'

'Thank you,' Pitt said again.

He did not tell Charlotte what Brinsley had said when they sat alone in the parlour late into the evening. There was no need for her to hear the details Brinsley had told him. He could spare her that much. She sat in one of the big armchairs. Pitt was too restless to sit, and too angry. He had snapped at her, and he knew it, but the sense of helplessness burned inside him like acid, eating away at his belief in himself.

'He'll go on,' he said bitterly, staring out of the french windows at the familiar garden. This was where his children had grown up. They had played here with hoops, a skipping rope, built castles with piles of coloured bricks, ridden imaginary horses, used as make-believe swords the garden canes that now held up the delphiniums in bloom.

What good was he if he could not protect Jemima from such hideous violation of all her future promise? Or Daniel from turning into a monster? Would they ask of him one day – 'Papa, why did you let it happen?' Charlotte wouldn't accuse him, but it would be in her mind, it would have to be. Try as she wished, she would never again see him as the man she trusted in, the man he wanted to be.

And what was he doing? Advising Townley, advising Castelbranco to do nothing but to admit that the law, his law, was helpless to protect them or to find any justice. The legal system too would look the other way and pretend nothing had happened: timid, circumspect, afraid of making a fuss.

Neville Forsbrook, and anyone else like him, would go on without anybody standing in their way or calling them to account. He reached to pull the curtain closed and it stuck. He yanked it harder and it tore.

'Thomas . . .' Charlotte began.

'Don't tell me to sit down!' he shouted, yanking harder at the curtain and pulling the whole thing down off the wall to lie in a heap.

'I wasn't going to,' she replied, standing up herself and walking over to join him at the glass, completely ignoring the pile of velvet on the floor. 'You said you are sure Forsbrook will go on and rape other people.'

'I'd stop him if I could, Charlotte!' He felt his hands clench. He was behaving like a fool and he knew it. It was not her fault, but every word seemed like criticism, because he blamed himself. It was his responsibility to do better than this.

She took a deep breath and held it a moment or two. She was controlling her own temper, and he was sharply aware of it. There was no point in apologising because he knew he would do it again, probably within moments.

'I was going to say . . .' she was choosing her words carefully, still ignoring the curtain, '. . . I was going to say that if this pattern of violence stretches into the future, how do we know that it does not also stretch into the past?'

'I imagine it does,' he said slowly.

'Then might there not be something there that you could find, and prosecute, without mentioning Angeles, or this new poor girl?' she asked. 'Perhaps it was something less serious, but still enough to bring a charge?'

He let the idea take form slowly, testing every step of it. 'No one who did not accuse him then would be likely to do so now,' he pointed out. 'The disgrace would be the same, but the proof even harder to find.'

'But if you know the pattern of the past, then you can predict the future more accurately, maybe even prevent him next time?' She would not give up. 'One woman alone can't do anything to him, but several might? Or at least the fathers of several, if they know they are not alone?'

He turned to look at her. In the evening light the tiny lines of her face were invisible. To him she was more beautiful at forty than she had been in her twenties. The softness of youth was gone, and she was better in her maturity at governing her tongue. She still looked at life bravely and honestly with her steady eyes, but was better able to deal with it in a measured way.

'And do what?' he asked quietly, but he was not dismissing it. 'It still may not be possible in law. Pelham Forsbrook will defend him to the very last ditch. It is his own reputation, as well as his son's.'

'The victims won't accuse him because to do so would ruin them socially for the rest of their lives,' she began.

He almost interrupted her, then bit back the words.

'But surely the accusation from many people, all prepared to stand together, whether it was proved in law or not, would also ruin him?' she asked. 'Reputation doesn't require legal proof. If it did there'd be thousands of people still in Society who are not here now, because ill is believed of them, although never more than whispers. They do not fight because there is nothing said plainly enough for slander.'

He blinked. 'You mean spread a rumour?'

'No!' Now she was angry too. 'You don't need to do it! Just prove you could, so Pelham Forsbrook knows it is true, and you mean to stop his son, because he has to be stopped.'

He turned it over in his mind, carefully, uncertain.

'Thomas?' She put her hand on his arm. He felt the strength of her fingers as well as the warmth.

He waited.

'How would you feel if it were not Alice Townley, but Jemima?'

'The same as Townley, exactly,' he answered. 'I would see him in hell, if I could, but more than anything else I would want to protect my daughter.'

'And if it were me, instead of Catherine Quixwood?'

He clenched inside, cold to the bone. 'You wouldn't be letting a lover into your house at that time of night.'

'We don't know that she was,' Charlotte pointed out. 'We only assume it. She let in someone she trusted. It may not have been a lover. Say it was someone I trusted, perhaps come with information for you, or to ask for help?'

'I would want to kill him,' he said honestly. 'I might even do it.'

'Isn't it worth at least trying?' She smiled very slightly, pleased at his anger, as if it were a shield for her, at least in her mind.

'Yes,' he said with growing comprehension. 'A little unorthodox, but then the orthodox isn't working. But don't do anything yourself! Do you understand me?'

'Yes, of course I do,' she said obediently. 'If I were clumsy, it would warn him. Give me credit for a little sense, Thomas.'

He had several answers for that, but he forbore from giving them. Fifteen years of marriage had taught him at least something.

'I want to know anything that might be interesting,' he told Stoker the next morning. The door was closed and he had given orders that he was not to be interrupted. 'The man's a rapist. We can't charge him because it wouldn't result in a conviction. There's no proof. And it would do the victim even more harm than is already done. But he may have started years ago.' He explained Charlotte's reasoning, without mentioning her name.

Stoker looked a little puzzled. 'What am I looking for, sir?'

'I don't know,' Pitt admitted. 'Why does a young man have this kind of rage inside him? He barely knows the young women concerned. Who does he really hate? Could he help himself if he wanted to? Who else did he hurt in the past, who also dared not accuse him? Does his father know? Does he care? Has he ever disciplined him himself, or paid off anyone to keep their silence?'

'Pelham Forsbrook?' Stoker said in surprise. 'Why would he need to? He's one of the most influential bankers in London. His loans can make or break people. If he grants you a loan for business venture capital, you're made. If he puts around the word against you, then no one else'll back you either. Although whisper has it that he'll lose pretty badly with the British South Africa Company having to pay damages to the Boers after the Jameson Raid.'

Pitt was suddenly interested. 'Really? Has he partners in the venture, or is he all on his own?'

'No idea. Do you want me to find out?'

'Not unless if has anything to do with his son. Do you suppose he intends to ship him off to live there? Get him away from our jurisdiction?'

Stoker shrugged. 'If I had a son like that I'd want him where I could keep an eye on him, and definitely where I had enough influence to protect him.'

'Would you? Would you protect him?' Pitt thought for several moments. 'I'm not sure what I'd do if it were Daniel. Maybe I'd ship him off to Australia, and let him take what's coming to him if he didn't straighten himself out. I've no idea. I need to make damned sure it doesn't happen, then I won't ever have to find out. I like to think I'd have the strength to deal with it, but maybe in the end I'd see the child in him that I'd loved, and I wouldn't be able to. God knows.'

'I'll bring you all I get, sir. It'll take a day or two. I dare say the trial of the bastard who killed Mrs Quixwood will be close to an end by then.'

'Be discreet, Stoker!'

'Yes, sir. Believe me, I don't want to get caught at it.'

'Neither do I,' Pitt said with feeling. 'We can't afford it. Oh – Stoker?'

'Yes, sir?'

'Find out where young Forsbrook was the night before last. And if a girl called Alice Townley was at the same place. And for God's sake, be doubly discreet about that!'

'Yes, sir.'

Pitt followed a different path himself. If there were really something in the past with which they could trap Neville Forsbrook then the home in Bryanston Mews where he had grown up would be the place to find it.

He knew from experience in his police days that servants were almost always loyal, so instead of going to the Forsbrook house where failure was certain, he went to the servants of neighbours, beginning with enquiries that were completely fictitious.

He was very careful, to start with perhaps too much so. He had concocted an imaginary story, of which the Forsbrooks, father and son, could have been the heroes. He thought it necessary, in case any whisper of it should leak back to them, and thus to the Home Secretary. He was quite open about who he was. To be caught in an evasion could have been damning, and made him seem ridiculous, a pantomime character not to be taken seriously.

He had been to a dozen houses without learning anything more than a general impression that the Forsbrooks were feared but not liked. At last he found an elderly groom in Bryanston Mews who was busy brushing down horses when Pitt interrupted him.

The smells of leather polish, dung, hay and horse-sweat brought back a sudden and very sharp memory of childhood on the big estate where he had grown up. His father had been the gamekeeper and his mother had worked in the house, before tragedy struck them and his father was deported to Australia for a crime of which Pitt had never believed him guilty, and still did not. The injustice of it was what had driven him to join the police in the first place.

Reminder of that childhood bewilderment and pain made the present injustice burn the more intensely. He had tried everything he knew how to then, and been helpless. But he had been a country boy, educated alongside the son of the manor house, as companionship and competition for him, but still a nobody, dependent upon Sir Arthur Desmond's patronage even to survive. Now he was a man in his late forties, and head of Britain's Special Branch. He would not allow himself to be helpless this time.

He smiled at the groom. 'Good animal you have there,' he remarked, looking at the horse.

'Aye, sir, she is that,' the man agreed. 'Can I 'elp yer?'

'Unlikely,' Pitt said with a slight shrug. 'I grew up in the country. I miss the friendship of horses, the strength . . . the patience.' Memory flashed back again. 'I used to clean the harness for the groom sometimes. There's a satisfaction in working the leather, in making the brass shine.'

'There is that, sir,' the man agreed. He was thin and strong, a little bow-legged. His hair stuck out in wisps from under the cap he was wearing. 'But if I can say so, you don't look like a country boy, sir.' He regarded Pitt's well-cut city suit. For once there was very little stuffed in his pockets and his cravat was almost straight. The only detail familiar from the past was the fact that his hair was too long and curled in no particular shape.

'Ambition,' Pitt admitted. He found himself wanting to trust this man. He was tired of evasions that achieved nothing. 'My father was a game-keeper, accused of poaching, a serious crime back then. I always believed him innocent, still do, but it didn't save him. Injustice cuts deep.'

The man stopped working for a moment and stared at Pitt with sudden interest deeper than mere politeness. 'Ye're right about that, sir,' he said with feeling. 'Yer got summink as yer workin' on right now, then?'

'Yes.' Pitt knew well enough to stop far short of the truth this time. 'Looking for a bit of understanding of the past, to get the present right, if you know what I mean? See that blame doesn't fall where it shouldn't.'

The man nodded. 'So wot d'yer want to know?' The horse swung its head round and nudged him. He patted it and began to brush again. 'All right, girl,' he said with a smile. 'I ain't forgot yer.' He smiled at Pitt. 'Like women, 'orses are. Don't like yer to put yer mind to someone else when it's their turn.'

'I know,' Pitt agreed. 'But they don't ask much.'

'Ye're right,' the man said happily. 'Give yer their 'ole 'earts, they do. Don't yer, girl?' He patted her smooth neck without altering the pace of the brush. 'What d'yer want ter know, sir?'

Pitt gestured behind him towards the back of the Forsbrook house. 'Do you know Sir Pelham Forsbrook and his family?'

The man's face tightened so very slightly that had Pitt not been watching closely he would have missed it. 'Yeah, some,' he said. 'Knew Lady Forsbrook – Miss Eleanor, as she used to be.' His face softened with memory. 'Wild, she was, but so alive. Couldn't 'elp but like 'er in the end. Wot they call ironic, in't it?'

'Is it?' Pitt said curiously. 'I heard she died in an accident. Was it ironic?' He sensed something further, something unsaid, but which the man half-expected him to know.

The man concentrated on brushing the horse's gleaming flanks for several seconds before he replied.

Pitt waited.

'Accident, right enough,' the man resumed at last. ''Ad her cases with 'er, an all. Knew that from Appley as were the groom there then. Runnin' away, she were. Some said it were to go with the feller as she was 'avin' an affair with. Others said it were just that she couldn't take the beatin' no more. Dunno the truth of it, but beat black and blue that night she were. Face all swole up.'

Pitt held his breath, afraid even to acknowledge that he had heard.

'Accident, all right,' the man was almost talking to himself as memory filled his mind. 'In an 'ansom an' the 'orse got spooked by summink. Some said it were a dog went fer it. Dunno. Terrible thing. Poor driver got killed too.'

'How long ago was that?' Pitt asked, trying to keep his voice level, the razor-sharp interest at least half concealed.

'Four years, maybe?' the man turned back to the horse. 'There y'are, girl. That's yer lot for now. Got other things ter do but talk ter you all day. Spoiled rotten, you are, an' all.' He picked up his brushes and patted her gently with his free hand.

'Going to clean the harness?' Pitt asked.

'Gotter,' the man replied. 'Not as I mind, like. It's a good job.' He led the way to the tack room and Pitt followed.

'May I help?' Pitt asked, mostly to keep the man in conversation, but also because it would be a physical job with good memories attached, something with assured purpose. He found he wanted very much to do it.

The man looked Pitt up and down. 'Get yourself dirty, 'ands and cuffs all messed.'

Pitt answered by taking off his jacket and rolling up his sleeves.

A few minutes later they were both working hard. It took one or two fumbles before Pitt had the art back, but the rhythm of it returned quickly and with intense satisfaction.

'That must have been very hard for Sir Pelham,' he brought the subject back again.

'Took it bad,' the man agreed, nodding as he watched Pitt work.

'Strange one, that. Never know wot 'e's thinkin'. Mind, that's true of a lot o' the gentry. Never knew whether 'e loved 'er, or was just angry 'cos she were leavin'. Not as I s'pose she'd 'a got away very far, poor soul.'

'Unless there was somebody else?' Pitt made it at least half a question.

'If there were, she were so bleedin' careful no one ever knew of it.' The man looked sad, as if he had wished there had been. Eleanor Forsbrook had belonged to another world: one he served, and caught glimpses of in unguarded moments, but one whose inner life he could only imagine, but he had liked her. In a sense she was a prisoner of her circumstances also, but with less freedom than he, a neighbour's groom.

Pitt worked on the leather for a few more silent minutes before pursuing the thought.

'I suppose young Neville found it hard too. Was he close to his mother?' he asked casually. Pitt had been close to his own mother. They were survivors together after his father had been sent away. His education, equal with that of Sir Arthur Desmond's son, had separated them in mind, and in language, but the affection, although hardly ever put into words, had never been doubted. When she had died it had been the end of a part of his life.

Perhaps that had been at least in part why he had found it easy to love Charlotte. He had trusted women all his life. He had seen too closely their loyalty, sacrifice and stoicism for it not to be part of his belief. He expected obedience from his daughter, but no more than from his son, in fact possibly rather less. She had too much of her mother in her not to question just about everything. But then she loved him too, and trusted his love for her. That was in her eyes, her voice, even at her most rebellious, and currently confusing tantrums.

'Did it change him?' he asked aloud, referring again to Neville Forsbrook.

'No,' the man said, shaking his head. 'More's the pity. Always was a cruel little bastard. Sorry, sir. Shouldn't 'a said that.' There was not a shred of regret in his weathered face.

'Said what?' Pitt asked with a smile.

'That's right, sir. Thank you,' the man agreed, his eyes bright.

'Fancy a glass of cider, when this is done?' Pitt invited him.

The man surveyed the array of harness a little doubtfully.

'It'll take less time with two of us,' Pitt pointed out.

'In't yer got nothin' else ter do, important gent like yerself?'

'Probably, but it'll wait. Everybody has to have an hour or two off sometime. And a glass of cider and a sandwich. Cheese and pickle?'

'Done,' the man agreed instantly. 'You're a rum one, an' no mistake. Maybe we'll be all right after all!'

Pitt bent to the harness again to hide the pleasure he felt at the compliment, and the hope that he would live up to the trust.

Chapter Sixteen

IT WAS a quiet summer evening as Vespasia walked along the gravel path beside Victor Narraway, moving from dappled sunlight into the shade. They had met by design at the end of a busy and, for him, unsatisfactory day. He was troubled, and as so often lately, he sought her company.

'Do you believe it?' she asked him directly.

He sighed. 'I would like to, but frankly it is highly unlikely, and I know of nothing whatever to substantiate it. It makes no sense.'

She measured her words with care. 'What did he actually claim? That Catherine had asked for further information about various financial investments because she was concerned her husband might lose money? Or that the money might be invested in ventures of dubious morality?'

'Briefly, yes, the latter,' he agreed. 'But if Quixwood had money invested dubiously, why not simply ask him? She was his wife. Surely he would tell her? He would have to, if indeed he lost heavily. They would need to reduce their circumstances, possibly even sell the house and move to somewhere less expensive.' He matched his step more evenly with hers. 'It doesn't seem reasonable that she would need to know the details to the depth a banker such as Hythe could explain them to her.'

Vespasia could think of no counter for that. He was correct.

'But if he is telling the truth, then she did want exactly such details,' she argued.

'He is not telling the truth,' Narraway said patiently. 'If something is unbelievable, then do not believe it.' His smile was twisted, unhappy. With anyone else he might have been impatient.

'Alternately,' she continued, 'suppose that he is telling the truth. Then there must be some facts of which we are not aware. It does not make sense, therefore it is incomplete. Why would an otherwise sensible woman seek financial facts about her husband's affairs by secretly cultivating the company of another man in financial business?'

'Because he is younger, handsomer and a great deal more affectionate and interesting,' he answered sadly. 'The explanation is not difficult. It is as old as love and betrayal.'

'Or else she does not trust her husband to tell her the truth,' she offered. 'That also is a very old story.'

'If it were her money, and he invested it foolishly and dare not tell her,' he said. 'But she had no money of her own, as far as we can tell.'

'I know,' she replied. 'I took the precaution of finding out about that myself. It is his money. He is a man of remarkable financial acuity. He has multiplied his original inheritance from his grandfather by at least ten times.'

'Then she should trust him this time,' he pointed out.

'To be wise, certainly, even to be fortunate,' she responded. 'But not necessarily to be ethical.'

He was startled. He stopped and turned to face her, a new idea dawning on his mind. 'Hence the detailed information. What is she afraid he might be doing?'

'Ah.' She stopped also and met his eyes. 'That I don't know,' she admitted. 'I propose to attend the Jameson trial tomorrow, and see what more I can learn of the whole affair of British South Africa investment, including Dr Jameson's part in it, and his connections to Mr Cecil Rhodes, and who apparently has financed this fiasco.'

'You won't get in,' he warned. 'Three-quarters of London Society have been trying to obtain seats. They are harder to find than tickets for the opening night of a play.'

'Probably more dramatic,' Vespasia said drily. 'I have done favours for certain people in the past. I have called upon one or two in particular, and I believe I shall be fortunate.'

'I see.' Different emotions conflicted in his face. 'I hope you will tell me if you learn anything at all that would be of use. The situation for Alban Hythe has become desperate.'

She stared at him, and he coloured very slightly. She was about to make a fairly sharp retort when she realised he was in some way uncomfortable, but she did not know in what.

'Of course I shall tell you,' she said more gently. 'That is my purpose in going. If it were merely for the result of the trial, I should be perfectly content with reading it in the newspapers. I don't see how they can do anything other than find him guilty. Whether you approve of it or not, he is unquestionably guilty of a serious misjudgement.'

His smile was wry, and quite gentle. 'Of course he is guilty, my dear,' he replied. 'He failed. It wasn't even a glorious failure, it was an idiotic one.'

'Oh, Victor, how wise we have become. It isn't always very pleasant, is it!'

'I think politics, and military escapades in particular, already have fools enough,' he answered. After hesitating a moment or two longer he offered her his arm again so they might continue along under the trees.

Vespasia needed to draw on more than one favour in order to obtain a seat at the High Court of Judicature for the second day of the trial of Leander Starr Jameson. It was 21 June, the longest day of the year. She was also obliged to rise early and be at the court over an hour before the proceedings commenced, such was the interest in the issue, and the almost hectic support for Dr Jameson himself.

She accompanied the Hon. Hector Manning, a long-time friend who had held a position of some weight in the Foreign Office, and thus was able to obtain a place in the gallery himself. No one had the temerity to question the fact that he brought a lady with him. There were many among the crowd who recognised her. She smiled and nodded to a few of them.

She had dressed in muted colours: silvers and greys, and a charcoal silk so dark as to seem almost black in the shadow, as befitted the occasion. A man was fighting not only for his freedom, but what was probably of more value to him: his honour.

After they had taken their seats, Hector, still a very distinguished-looking man, leaned towards her and spoke quietly. 'Unless you have changed beyond recognition, you have some better reason for being here than mere curiosity. Were that all, you would never have forced yourself to ask a favour of me. As I recall our last meeting, some twenty years ago, you did not view me with particular pleasure.'

She did not wish to be reminded of it, but his question was fair and he deserved an answer.

'You are quite right,' she conceded, looking not at him but straight ahead of her as the seats filled rapidly. The slight buzz of conversation made their voices inconspicuous among the rest. On impulse she decided at least to be moderately frank. 'A friend of mine is concerned about some of the financial repercussions of this whole affair. I wish to learn far more of it than I know at the moment . . .'

He swivelled in his seat to stare at her with concern, even anxiety. 'I hope you do mean a friend, and not yourself? And even if it is merely a friend, please do not involve your own finances in any way at all, not yet.'

She saw the gentleness in his eyes and was a little abashed to recognise an affection she had once dismissed.

'I have no money whatever in Africa, nor shall I, I promise you,' she said with a slight smile. 'But I appreciate your warning.'

'I have no right to tell you not to rescue anyone . . .' he began, then drew in his breath and let it out in a sigh. 'But don't, please.'

Should she tell him the truth? It was unpleasantly deceitful to cause him completely unnecessary anxiety, and yet the rape of Catherine Quixwood seemed to be so far from the escapades of Leander Jameson that she could hardly expect Hector Manning to believe her. She could not offer him any explanation to make sense of it. That evasion would also seem a rebuff.

'It is a matter of proving someone innocent of a terrible act,' she said, choosing her words carefully. 'So far as I know, no one I am acquainted with needs financial assistance, I promise you.'

He relaxed fractionally. 'This whole venture was an appalling mess, you know. Is this friend of yours involved in it?'

'I don't know yet,' she said frankly. 'I am not being evasive, Hector. I really don't know. If I understand the raid better, it may answer a few very delicate questions.'

'You're not going to tell me, are you?' he concluded.

She smiled at him. 'Not unless I have to. It would be indiscreet.'

Before they could discuss it any further the court was called to order and the trial commenced.

Vespasia listened with total attention. She already had a certain amount of information with which to catch up. She had never personally met Dr Jameson, and studied him with interest while the totally predictable formalities were conducted.

He entered the courtroom and walked towards his chair, taking his seat with care to arrange his dark frock coat so as not to crease it.

Every single person in the room was watching him, a fact of which he could not have been unaware. There was a dull flush visible over his complexion, even darkened by sun as it was. If he recognised anyone, he gave no sign of it.

Vespasia remained watching him out of a growing interest. He was a physician by training, not a soldier, and looking at him now she wondered what course of events had led him to this situation. She could very easily imagine him listening with attention to the symptoms of an injury or illness, then gravely prescribing a treatment. He sat with his large head a little to one side, as if weighing some deep consideration. He had fine, dark eyes, half concealed by drooping lids, a prominent nose and a full-lipped mouth. His hair was receding a trifle, his moustache neatly trimmed. It seemed the face of a city man, a doctor, a professor or even a clergyman, not a soldier leading adventurers across an African border armed with Maxim guns and Lee Metford rifles.

As the witnesses testified one by one, Jameson seemed unconcerned, even uninterested.

'Does he not care?' Vespasia whispered to Hector Manning. 'Is he expecting a dramatic rescue of some sort?'

'Looking at him, one would think so,' Hector murmured back to her.

'By whom?' she asked. 'What am I not understanding? Mr Chamberlain? Lord Salisbury?'

'I doubt it,' he said so quietly she had to strain to hear him. 'Poor old Joe Chamberlain is in a hell of a mess himself with this, and it'll get worse before it's over. He'll be lucky if Salisbury doesn't ask for his resignation.'

As the evidence and arguments continued she recalled what she knew of the entire matter.

In November of the previous year, 1895, a piece of territory known as the Pitsani Strip, a part of Bechuanaland bordering on the Transvaal, had been ceded by the Colonial Office to the British South Africa Company. The reason given at the time had been for the safeguarding of a proposed railway to run through it. The Prime Minister of the Cape Colony, Cecil Rhodes, had been very keen indeed to bring the whole of South Africa into British dominion. To that end he was willing to encourage the disenfranchised outsiders of the Boer republics into the fold, and thus out of the dominion of the Boer Afrikaners.

This was the spark that lit the fiasco of what came to be known as the Jameson Raid. It was in effect a British South African Company private army of about five hundred men, armed to the teeth. Their purpose was to rouse the workers on the Pitsani Strip, and with them to march across the border into the Transvaal, and overthrow the Boer government there, and then annexe the territory, with its fortune in diamonds and gold.

They got within twenty miles of Johannesburg before the Boer forces overthrew and captured them, forcing them to surrender.

Sir Hercules Robinson, the Governor-General of the Cape Colony, had been ordered by Chamberlain to repudiate the actions of Jameson. The Company's charter was in jeopardy if he did not.

Jameson was shipped home to England for trial. There could be no other action taken if the Company were to survive. Even so, there would be massive reparations to pay to the Boers of the Transvaal. Fortunes would be lost.

Was Jameson a hero betrayed? Or an adventurer who had jeopardised British interests for his own foolhardy ends?

At the end of the day Vespasia was still uncertain. As she walked away from the courtroom with Hector Manning she felt an urgent need to ask him for much more information. She already knew that there was too little time left to wait for a verdict on Jameson. Alban Hythe was also on trial, and his jury might return far sooner. There was hardly any evidence for Peter Symington to use in a defence. She needed more knowledge of the financial side of the venture before she could form any judgement at all as to whether Catherine Quixwood had really asked Hythe for advice, and in such detail that it had required them to meet so many times.

She was walking beside Hector Manning, holding his arm when she glanced to her left and caught sight of Pelham Forsbrook. He looked very pale, and his long face was clenched in an expression of extreme tension. She was afraid he would see her and realise that she was staring at him, until the fixedness of his eyes and the way he moved through the crowd, bumping people without care, made her realise he was oblivious of anyone else.

'Pelham Forsbrook looks distressed,' she observed to Hector, as soon as they were on the steps and clear of being jostled. 'Could he be financially involved in this, do you suppose?'

'Almost certainly, poor devil,' Manning replied. 'He was pretty thick with Cecil Rhodes, and everybody knows Rhodes was behind this bloody silly adventure. Pardon my—'

'For heaven's sake, Hector, I've heard the word before,' Vespasia said impatiently. 'Jameson was Administrator General for Matabeleland, of course he was tied up with Rhodes. This idiotic escapade must have pulled troops out of Matabeleland and left it vulnerable.'

'Naturally,' he agreed, going down the steps, matching his pace to hers. 'That is almost certainly why the Matabele revolted in March. Don't know the casualties yet, but it'll be into the hundreds.'

'I can't imagine it will stop there,' she said quietly. 'What a tragedy. But I need to know if many people will have taken serious financial loss. Do you know?'

'There can be no question about it at all,' he answered. 'Only I don't know who, or how much.'

'To judge from his face, Pelham Forsbrook may be one of them.'

They reached the bottom of the steps and turned left along the footpath, now clear of the crowd. 'Do you suppose he thought the Raid would succeed? If it had, would there have been a profit? I mean one worth the risk?'

He smiled. 'Not as it turns out, but could there have been? Yes, of course. If they'd taken the Transvaal, with its diamonds and gold? Unimaginable wealth.'

'Do you know Rawdon Quixwood?' There was no time to be wasted in approaching the subject obliquely. She must have something to tell Narraway before it was too late.

'Slightly,' Hector replied. 'Poor devil's rather out of things at the moment. What a nightmare.' His face was creased with pity. 'Can't even imagine it. I hear the wretched man's being tried right now. I hope they hang him.' He said it with a sudden surge of feeling.

'Providing, of course, that he is guilty.' Vespasia could not help putting that in, even though it was irrelevant. It surprised her. She was usually able to hold back her own emotions more effectively.

He was startled. 'Do you doubt it?' he said, his eyes wide.

'I don't know.' She kept on walking, but slowly. She did not want to discuss the subject. She did not want Hector Manning to know the real purpose of her attendance at Jameson's trial. 'Probably they are perfectly right. I hope so, for poor Quixwood's sake. I don't really know what would be the most painful.'

'I don't know what you mean.' Hector sounded confused. 'Surely he must want the man convicted?'

'If he's guilty, of course,' she agreed. 'But if it was he, then it also seems as if he was having an affair with Catherine Quixwood. That can hardly be what anyone would want to have happen at all, let alone be made public news.'

'Yes, I see. Of course. Poor devil.' He too was walking very slowly now. 'He loses, whatever the verdict. God help him.'

'Did he lose money in this miserable Jameson business as well, do you suppose?' she asked as artlessly as she could.

He stopped completely now, looking at her with a mixture of puzzlement and concern. 'What makes you think so?' he asked, frowning.

'There is a suggestion that Catherine was very afraid that he had,' she answered truthfully, or at least without telling any direct untruth.

'Really? And you mean she was already looking for someone else, in case he did? What a—' He stopped himself in time before using language he would afterwards be ashamed of.

'No, I don't think so.' She tried not to sound too firm, or as if she might actually know anything. 'It seemed to be rather more a concern that she might be able to give him advice to prevent it.'

'Bit too late for that!' he dismissed it out of hand. 'Any good advice should have been before this trial and whatever judgement they reach!'

'Do you suppose Quixwood invested in Africa?' she pursued.

'Thought about it, then didn't, I heard. Could be nonsense, but Quixwood is pretty astute.'

'Are you sure?'

'Yes, actually, I am,' he said reluctantly. 'But that's confidential. He took a better look at it, and could see the pitfalls.'

'But he didn't tell Pelham Forsbrook,' she added.

'Not from the look on Forsbrook's face, no. But of course he could have told him, and Forsbrook just thought he knew better. Well, he'll pay for it now, poor devil.'

'Indeed,' Vespasia said quietly. 'Thank you so much, Hector. I have found it one of the most interesting afternoons I have spent in a long time. It is most kind of you, and a great pleasure to see you again.'

'Always,' he said graciously. He seemed about to add something more, then looked at her again, and knew it would be unwise. He smiled, and bowed, then handed her up into her carriage.

There was no time to waste. Vespasia went to Victor Narraway's flat, prepared to wait for him if it should prove necessary. His manservant showed her to the sitting room and brought her tea, which was all she wished. She had no more than half an hour to occupy herself before he arrived.

He was disconcerted to find that she had been obliged to wait for him, but there was no time to indulge such emotions.

'I have learned a great deal which may, perhaps, be relevant,' she said as soon as greetings were exchanged and the manservant had brought fresh hot water and a second cup so Narraway could join her.

He was puzzled. 'The Jameson trial? Did Quixwood invest unwisely? Or could Catherine reasonably have feared he did? How could we find proof?'

She smiled very slightly at his eagerness. He so badly wanted to believe Catherine innocent, and somehow show it to the court. Some of that might have been to save Alban Hythe, some even to save Quixwood's own terrible grief, although nothing would bring Catherine back. And if Hythe were not guilty, then someone else was, and it was still a man she herself had let into the house.

She wondered if Narraway had thought of that, or was it too far ahead?

'Several people will have invested unwisely,' she replied, measuring her words. Perhaps she had not learned as much as she had assumed, or led him to hope. 'The prospects looked good enough to tempt many people. Had the raid succeeded Jameson would have been instrumental in causing an uprising that could have led to us annexing the Transvaal, with its incalculable wealth. The Uitlanders would have given us the excuse. As it is, those who invested in the raid will not only have lost everything, but also cost the British South Africa Company and its investors a fortune in reparation to the Boers.'

'And that was what Catherine was afraid of?' he said, carefully controlling his excitement, but it flared up in his eyes. 'Perhaps the figures in her diary were not telephone numbers, but really were money! Did Quixwood invest? Do you know?'

'Apparently he considered it, then withdrew in time,' she answered. 'But Pelham Forsbrook did not. He has lost a great deal. Whether it will ruin him or not, I don't know. He certainly looked very grim at the trial today.'

Narraway considered for several moments before replying.

'But Quixwood withdrew?' he said at last. 'I think we need to know a lot more about the relationship between those two men. Is it the mere acquaintance we assumed it to be? Even in his bereavement, Quixwood has gone out of his way to show that Forsbrook's son could not have been guilty of raping Angeles Castelbranco. In the circumstances, that is the act of an extraordinary friend.'

'Thomas does not believe it is true,' she pointed out. 'Which leads one to wonder if it is a mistake, or a deliberate lie. And if it is a lie, why Quixwood would do such a thing. Does he believe Neville Forsbrook innocent anyway, or has he some other reason?'

Narraway frowned. 'I don't see how it could be connected to the Jameson Raid, or the trial. There seems to be something very important that we have missed. And now we have little time indeed in which to find it.'

'How much longer do you think the trial of Alban Hythe will continue?' she asked quietly. The sitting room was calm, elegant, a little masculine for her taste, but very comfortable. The summer evening outside was still light. She could see the trees against the sky beyond the windows, clouds of starlings sweeping around in circles, all moving with some infinitely subtle communication, as though with one mind.

There was no sound inside, not even the ticking of a clock.

'I don't know,' he admitted. 'Perhaps two more days, three at the very outside, but Symington could be stretching the judge's patience, and the public's credulity.'

She said nothing. There was no need to struggle for hopeful words. Neither their understanding nor their companionship required it.

Chapter Seventeen

STOKER CAME into Pitt's office and closed the door.

''Morning, sir,' he said as he walked over and sat down on the other side of the desk. Pitt would not have presumed to sit without permission when this had been Narraway's office, he thought wryly. Stoker was becoming comfortable. Possibly that was a good thing; on the other hand it might have been a mark of the changing times.

'What do you have on Neville Forsbrook?' Pitt asked him.

Stoker pursed his lips. 'Not sure it's a lot of use,' he said a little awkwardly. 'He's never crossed the law, or if he did then his father paid people off for him and they kept quiet. Couple of whispers . . .' He hesitated. 'Honestly, I think you might find that about a few young men whose fathers help them get away with it.'

'What, exactly?' Pitt pressed. 'If it's nothing out of the usual I don't care: bad gambling debts; or fights, unless someone was very badly hurt. Did he seriously damage anyone? Use a knife? Maim them or disfigure them?'

'No. Most of his trouble was with prostitutes,' Stoker replied with evident distaste. 'One or two brothels had to be paid off, and accepted it only on condition he didn't come back.'

'Go on,' Pitt said sharply.

'Well, I don't know if it's true,' Stoker said tentatively. 'But there's a word going round, very quietly indeed, that he beat a prostitute pretty badly, and her pimp returned the favour, but with a knife. Left a few marks Forsbrook'll carry for the rest of his life. At least that's how the story goes.'

'How much credit do you give it?' Pitt was interested, but he was well aware that people boasted for many reasons, perhaps to build up their reputations as bad men to cross. It was a part of their image, and their vanity.

'Difficult to check,' Stoker replied. 'Couldn't get a precise date, but close enough. Forsbrook took a holiday just after that, and no one saw him at any functions for a couple of months. Told everyone he took a trip to Europe, but I haven't been able to check that yet.'

'Where in Europe?'

'Somewhere unusual,' Stoker answered with a twisted smile. 'Nowhere on the Grand Tour, where you'd expect someone to see him. Sofia, or Kiev, or somewhere. Not going to run into any of your neighbours there.'

'You believe the story?'

Stoker chewed on his lip. 'Put it this way: if he raped those two girls – the Portuguese one, and then Alice Townley – it would fit the pattern that he tried it on a prostitute first, and got beaten himself for it. In fact so badly he had to get away from London until he was healed up.'

He shifted his weight. 'On the other hand, if he didn't rape either of them, then he could quite genuinely have taken a holiday in Sofia, or anywhere else. We might be able to prove he went to those places, and at that time, but there's no way we can prove he didn't – unless we can show he was somewhere different. And I'll give a week's pay if his father didn't cover the tracks so no one'll find them.'

'Interesting,' Pitt said thoughtfully.

'No use,' Stoker pointed out.

'Unless we can find the pimp who cut him and learn exactly where the scars are.'

Stoker grinned. 'Yeah? I can see Mr Forsbrook letting us take a good look at the more private parts of his body to verify that!'

Pitt pulled a sour face. 'But if it's true, it fits the pattern of rage and savagery extremely well. From what else you learned, do you believe it, Stoker?'

Stoker was suddenly grim and very steady. 'Yes, sir, actually I do. I talked to quite a lot of people. No one is willing to say much against him. His father's got a great deal of power in financial circles. He could put in a good word, or a bad one, and make somebody's future success, or lack of it.'

He chewed his lip uncertainly. 'There is a bit of a whisper that he took a pretty hard fall over this Jameson Raid affair. Put more money into it than he can afford to lose. Bit of bad advice, I should think. Reckoned on us ending up annexing the Transvaal. A few real fortunes be made there.'

'Bad advice?' Pitt questioned. 'From whom?'

'Well, you'd have to think you knew something before you risked your shirt on a raid like that, wouldn't you?' Stoker said reasonably. 'Inside information somewhere.'

'Yes,' Pitt agreed. 'Doesn't excuse Neville Forsbrook for anything, even if it's true.'

'I suppose I could try to trace some of Pelham Forsbrook's deal-ings,' Stoker offered. 'But a lot of it's confidential, and there's no way to judge why he backed one person and not another.'

'You're right,' Pitt agreed. 'It's a waste of time, and could make us a lot of enemies where we need friends. Just look for anything recent in young Forsbrook's life that seems odd.'

'There's nothing Portuguese,' Stoker said straight away. 'Him or his father, I looked at that already. A few interests in Africa, but then so has everyone else with money to invest.'

'The British South Africa Company?' Pitt asked, thinking again of the gold and diamonds in the Transvaal, and the Jameson Raid. 'And what about Neville Forsbrook? Is all his income direct from his father? Any inheritance from his mother?'

'Not much, and doesn't come into it until he marries,' Stoker said with a shrug. 'He's tried one or two things, a couple of years in the army, but he didn't take kindly to the discipline. Gave it up. Good leader, not such a good follower.'

'Thank you, Stoker. See what else you can find that'll tie into rape.'

'Yes, sir.'

'Let me know as soon as you can. Now I have to go and see the Home Secretary.'

'About this?' Stoker was concerned.

Pitt smiled bleakly. 'I don't know. He didn't inform me.'

★ ★ ★

Pitt stood on the carpet in front of the Home Secretary's desk, too angry, and too aware of his own guilt, to do anything but remain at attention.

'The situation in Africa is very delicate, Pitt,' the Home Secretary said irritably. 'You can hardly be unaware of the Jameson fiasco, and the massive reparations we are going to have to pay to Kruger and the Boers.' He said it with considerable bitterness, and Pitt could not help wondering if he too had suffered some personal reversal in it.

'Yes, sir, I am aware of it,' Pitt said grimly. 'And of Mr Churchill's warning that sooner or later if we are not very careful, it will bring about war with the Boers in Africa, which will include the Cape as well. In my own judgement he is probably correct. I am also aware that feeling is very divided here in England, and many regard Jameson as a hero. We are doing what we can to forestall any violent demonstrations either for him, or against him, but it is largely a police matter of public order.'

'I know it is not Special Branch's responsibility!' the Home Secretary snapped. 'Why the devil are you enquiring into the personal affairs of Pelham Forsbrook? I thought I made it clear to you that the very nasty scandal surrounding the Portuguese Ambassador and his family was to be left alone. What was it about my orders that you failed to understand?'

Explanations raced through Pitt's mind, none of them what the Home Secretary wanted to hear.

'For God's sake, Pitt!' the Home Secretary went on furiously. 'Even Castelbranco himself understands that there is no proof of anything, and irresponsible accusations will serve no one. What the devil were you thinking of? The poor girl is dead and nothing can bring her back. Let what is left of her reputation be preserved from further speculation, for her parents' sake, if nothing else.'

He prodded a finger into the air. 'You are not a policeman to hound the case to its bitter end, you are head of Her Majesty's Special Branch! Your concerns are the safety of this nation within its own borders, the catching of anarchists, traitors, enemies of the state and its people. Didn't Narraway make that clear to you, for heaven's sake?'

Pitt clenched his hands by his sides, where the Home Secretary could not see them, and let his breath out slowly.

'Yes, sir. Lord Narraway explained my responsibilities in some detail, and the width of my remit, in pursuit of those ends. I believe that an attack on the family of a friendly nation's ambassador falls very clearly within that realm. We cannot afford the reputation of being a country where foreign women are not safe from rapists. Still less can we appear to be indifferent to such atrocities, as if they were commonplace in London, and we thought nothing of it.'

'Don't be absurd!' the Home Secretary snapped, his face scarlet. 'And offensive. Nobody is dismissing the tragedy, but to say that it is rape is mischievous and irresponsible. There is only a hysterical girl's account, totally without proof, that anything at all took place. You cannot and must not slander a man's reputation with such a sugges- tion. Not to mention the wretched girl's. What on earth do you imagine people are saying about her? Have you thought of that?'

Pitt made an intense, almost painful effort to keep his self-control. His body ached. His mouth was dry. 'I have made no remarks at all to suggest that Miss Castelbranco was raped, or even assaulted, sir,' he said between his teeth. 'Her own Church has declined to give her proper rites of burial, on the assumption that she lost her virginity, became with child in an illicit affair, and then intentionally took her own life. I hardly think there is anything I can add to make that any more exquisitely painful than it is.' He was unable to stop his voice from shaking. He was angry enough to have faced down the Queen, never mind a mere Cabinet Minister.

The blood drained from the Home Secretary's face, leaving him grey. 'The matter is tragic indeed,' he said quietly. 'But it is not our fault—'

'It is our fault if we do nothing about it,' Pitt cut across him, quite aware of what he was doing. He was past caring for the niceties.

'Slandering Neville Forsbrook's name will not help,' the Home Secretary was growing angrier again as the exchange slipped out of his control. 'One injustice does not help another. And if you imagine that it will, then you are the wrong man to have replaced Narraway. I didn't like the man, but by God, he had better judgement than that!'

'Actually, sir, my enquiries about Neville Forsbrook's past behaviour had nothing whatever to do with the death of Angeles Castelbranco,' Pitt said very carefully, measuring every word. 'The Portuguese Ambassador will become aware of it only in the future, if it should prove relevant. Which is why I considered it prudent, as well as morally right, to enquire now.'

The Home Secretary glared at him. 'What the devil do you mean? Explain yourself,' he demanded.

'Another young woman was raped, and survived the assault, although internally injured,' Pitt replied, fixing his gaze on the Home Secretary's eyes. 'The family does not wish to make a complaint, for the girl's sake. She is only sixteen. It would ruin her socially, prevent her from making a fortunate marriage, and ensure that for the rest of her life this repulsive violation is all that is remembered of her. I begin to understand why girls who are the victims of such violence sometimes take their own lives, and why so few charges are brought, even when there is proof.'

The Home Secretary stared at him, aghast. 'And what has this to do with Forsbrook?' It was clear in his face that he knew what Pitt was going to say. He tensed, as if anticipating a physical blow.

'She named Neville Forsbrook,' Pitt continued. 'She described the circumstances, the time and the place. Naturally I had it looked into. She refused to tell me the house in which it happened, but it was very easy to find out. There were not so many balls held in London that night. Her attendance was not secret, nor was that of Forsbrook. The rooms, the paintings, the other details were simple to ascertain.'

The Home Secretary let out his breath slowly.

'I see. And what is it you imagine this will accomplish? Let alone what it may be to do with Special Branch?' he asked. 'Her Majesty's Government's relationship with Portugal is the Foreign Office's concern, not yours.'

Pitt raised his eyebrows. 'Is the Foreign Office equipped to find out if Neville Forsbrook raped Angeles Castelbranco and thus brought about her death? If so, I shall be delighted to hand over all the facts that I have so far obtained to whoever is conducting the investigation.'

'Don't be damned impertinent, sir!' the Home Secretary snapped. Then he leaned back in his chair and stared up at Pitt, still standing on the carpet in front of the desk, towering over him. 'Be careful! Pelham Forsbrook is a very powerful man indeed. If you malign his son and you cannot prove it, he'll have your job, and I can't save you. Not that I shall try.'

Pitt felt the cold seep through him as if he were sinking into icy water. 'I shall be very careful, sir,' he said in little more than a whisper. 'But the man has to be stopped. The next victim could be your daughter.'

'Granddaughter,' the Home Secretary corrected him bitterly. 'Again, be careful!'

'Yes, sir.'

Late in the afternoon Pitt went again to the Portuguese Embassy. He half hoped that Rafael Castelbranco would be busy and unable to see him. It would be a coward's way out, but today he would be glad of it.

No, that was a lie. He knew it as he walked along the hot, crowded pavements. It would be a temporary escape, that would be all. He would have to wait. He must still see Castelbranco and tell him the latest news, as he had promised he would. So far he had kept his word. Not that it had been any use.

Before another few days were out the verdict would come in on Alban Hythe. Pitt knew from Narraway that there was no reasonable hope of his escaping conviction. Narraway seemed to think he might well be innocent. Pitt was less sure. It was unarguable that he had met with Catherine Quixwood an inordinate number of occasions at times and in places where there was no reasonable excuse, other than a romantic tryst. What else might have happened that would run rampant in the imagination?

They would convict Alban Hythe, and then hang him.

Angeles Castelbranco had been sixteen, raped by a near stranger, and the man who had done that would walk free. What could he say to her father? That Rawdon Quixwood had said Forsbrook was with him at the time of Angeles' supposed rape? If it had happened at all, then she had named the wrong person? She did not know one well-bred young Englishman from another?

Luck was not on his side. When he reached the Embassy Rafael Castelbranco received him immediately. They faced each other in the quiet study where they were accustomed to talk. Pitt had considered what he was going to say, and knew perfectly well what it might cost him, but he had no doubt as to what it would cost him if he did not.

'You have news,' Castelbranco said softly. 'I can see it in your face. What has happened?' There was anxiety in his voice and his eyes looked Pitt up and down, searching for the answers. He was not thinking of himself but of what this breach of protocol might cost Pitt.

If anything could have stiffened Pitt's resolve, this would have been it. He had gained a profound regard for the Portuguese Ambassador over the last weeks, even a kind of affection. In many people grief shows more vividly their weaknesses; it shakes the fault lines in their character. In Castelbranco it had marked more profoundly his strengths. There was a gentleness in him, a fortitude that was rare. He spoke quietly. The grief in him was too deep and too total to surface as anger.

'It is good of you to come,' he said quietly. 'May I offer you some refreshment? I have whisky, if you wish it, but in view of the pleasantness of the weather, you might prefer something longer? I have been drinking a concoction my wife enjoys, a mixture of fruit juices.' He stood still, waiting for Pitt's answer.

'That sounds excellent,' Pitt agreed honestly. 'We'll keep the whisky for the autumn.'

Castelbranco took another glass from the cupboard and filled it from a jug on the sideboard, then they both sat down. It had become something of a habit. Pitt was feeling in one sense more and more at ease in the company of this quiet man, even though he was six or seven years older than himself, in a different service of his country, and raised in a different land and culture. In normal circumstances they would have enjoyed many of the same pursuits, discussions of similar interests, or learning from one another of subjects one loved and of which the other knew nothing.

Pitt had spoken of art, learned from his time in the Metropolitan

Police in his earliest years there. Castelbranco loved history, especially of the ancient Mediterranean. His father had been in the diplomatic service also, spending many years in Egypt, and some in Athens. Pitt had drawn on his memories of rural England, with its huge parklands, ancient trees, rolling fields gold in harvest time. Castelbranco had spoken of the Douro Valley and its vineyards, heavy with fruit in the sun. It had been brief, a respite from tragedy, a moment's sanity in the midst of pain.

On the way Pitt had been trying to reach a decision. Now in this calm room he no longer wavered. It was disobedience to the spirit of the Home Secretary's orders, but to obey would be a betrayal of this man Pitt had come to think of as a friend, and even more than that, shared the love of a father for his child, a need to defend that was common to all life.

Castelbranco was waiting for Pitt to speak. The silence would stretch comfortably only so long.

'They are almost certainly going to find Alban Hythe guilty in the next few days,' Pitt said at last. 'I'm not certain it is the correct verdict, but there is little to refute it. The man who was head of Special Branch before I was, and for whom I have an immense regard, believes he may be innocent.'

Castelbranco's face creased with an even deeper sense of tragedy.

'More injustice,' he said softly. 'The whole matter of violence towards our women stirs a hysteria in us we don't seem to manage very well. Terror and unreason rage through it all. Can you do anything to help?'

'I doubt it,' Pitt admitted. 'But I know Lord Narraway won't give up. The charge is that they were lovers who quarrelled, not that he attacked her at random.'

Castelbranco smiled bleakly. 'I am aware of your point, Mr Pitt. I do not imagine that this young man assaulted my daughter. She told me it was Neville Forsbrook. I do not doubt her.' There was a question in his eyes. It was not a challenge, but his gaze was direct and unwavering. 'I don't know why this man Quixwood should say that it could not be. Perhaps in his own grief his memory is disturbed. His loss is terrible, and the whole of London must know that his wife betrayed him. How can I wish to add to his pain?'

'You can't,' Pitt agreed. 'But I have made it my business to learn much more about Neville Forsbrook, and that is the reason I came this evening in particular. The Home Secretary has commanded me to cease my investigations in the matter. If I don't he will remove me from my command, in fact I imagine from the Service altogether.'

'Then you cannot!' Castelbranco said in alarm, leaning forward in his chair, his eyes wide. 'You have done all you can to find justice for my daughter, and been a good friend to me. What ill return I would offer you to ask more!'

'I can tell you at least what I know,' Pitt answered. 'I have discovered quite a lot about Forsbrook.' He repeated what Stoker had told him about the incident with the prostitute and the resulting violence from the pimp. He added Neville Forsbrook's prolonged absence from England, apparently in out-of-the-way places where there would be no trace of him, were it to be questioned. He also mentioned his father's repeated violence, and that his mother had fled, whether to an imaginary lover or a real one, but tragically been killed in a carriage accident.

'It explains much,' Castelbranco said quietly, staring into his empty glass. 'But it does not excuse it. The man is dangerous. Do you not think he will continue to hurt others?'

'Yes I do,' Pitt answered. 'I would very much like him to be prevented, but so far I have no idea how I can do that.' He fished in his pockets and brought out a folded piece of paper. On it was a name and address. He held it out to Castelbranco. 'This is a man I knew on and off when I was in the regular police. It would be necessary to pay him, but he is not greedy and he is extremely discreet. He can make enquiries for you, if you wish.'

Castelbranco took the paper and read it. 'Elmo Crask? Is that how you pronounce it?'

'Yes. He is unimpressive to look at. He appears harmless, untidy, as if easily fooled, but he cultivates that intentionally. He is very clever indeed and has a memory like an elephant. But consider before you approach him.' Even as he said it Pitt still wondered if he were doing the right thing. It was what he himself would want, but that did not make it wise. He had not told Charlotte what he intended because he thought she might well disagree.

Castelbranco was waiting, watching him.

'No matter how careful he is, it is possible that one way or another Pelham Forsbrook will come to hear of it. There may be no proof that you are behind it, but it would be the obvious conclusion.'

'What more can he do than he already has?' Castelbranco asked with a quiver in his voice.

'Oh, he can,' Pitt said miserably. 'He can start more rumours about your daughter, ask even crueller questions. Please don't take it for granted that he wouldn't. If he believes he is protecting his son's reputation he will be as determined as you are, and possibly far less scrupulous.'

'That would surely show his guilt,' Castelbranco pointed out. 'But I hear what you say, and I shall weigh it before I approach this . . .' he looked again at the piece of paper, '. . . Elmo Crask. As you say, it is not only a matter of the past, there is the future to consider as well, all the other young women he has yet to destroy, the other families who will be wounded for ever by loss.'

Pitt stood up and held out his hand. 'I'm sorry it is so little.'

'It is much,' Castelbranco answered, his voice suddenly husky. 'You have already gone far beyond the bounds of your office. I hope you do not suffer for it.' He held onto Pitt's hand firmly for several seconds before letting it go.

Pitt left, and went out into the warm summer night hoping desperately that he had made the right decision, that he had acted with wisdom, not merely out of emotion.

Pitt took a hansom cab and rode through the heavy traffic barely noticing it, his mind in turmoil. He wanted to be at home in the comfort he was familiar with, and put other people's grief out of his mind, at least for a few hours.

But home would not afford him that. He would look at all he had, the things that were precious to him beyond measure, the centre of all value and happiness in his life, his wife and children. He would see Jemima, so like her mother, and on the verge of becoming a woman. In ten years she would almost certainly be married, and possibly have children of her own.

And Daniel? How would Pitt make sure that he grew up honest and gentle, with the courage and passion of a man, but appreciating all that was beautiful in a woman, not just physically but the fire and courage and intelligence as well?

By the time he reached the quiet of Keppel Street, and his own house, he had no answers, only a greater clarity as to the questions.

Charlotte was happy to see him, as always. If she had concerns, she was wise enough to keep them until after supper when he was more willing to listen, and at the very least, not hungry.

Jemima was excited and full of energy, her eyes shining, her face flushed. He half listened as she told him in hectic detail about something to do with a musical performance. He had learned to listen with an appearance of understanding and nod at the right times. She did not expect him to understand. Charlotte understood, and that was sufficient.

Daniel rolled his eyes now and again, then when it was his turn to receive the attention he asked numerous questions about the geography of the Empire, and answered them himself. His knowledge was impressive and Pitt told him so, to his immense pleasure.

Pitt was standing in front of the french windows, which were wide open, the perfume of damp soil drifting into the room. The last of the light was on the tops of the neighbours' trees. Starlings circled in the air. Apart from a very slight breeze moving the leaves, and a dog barking on and off in the distance, there was hardly any sound.

'What is it?' Charlotte asked quietly, coming to stand beside him.

'What is what?' His mind had been wandering and he could not remember the last thing he had said to her.

'Thomas! I know you are worrying about something. I imagine it is to do with Angeles Castelbranco. Whatever it is, it's not treason and anarchy, it's personal. The other things you can forget, at least for the evening.' There was a degree of exasperation in her voice, but it was gentle.

'Questions to which I don't know the answers,' he replied. He did not mean to worry her by telling her that he had given so much information to Rafael Castelbranco, or that he had given him Elmo

Crask's name. It might not have been wise, and it was too late now to undo.

She linked her arm into his and stood close enough he could feel the warmth of her body. 'About Angeles?' she asked. 'You are not sure it was Neville Forsbrook, are you? It was. I saw him taunting her. If he didn't do it himself, at least he was there. It was in his face. He knew exactly what had happened to her.'

'In spite of the fact that Rawdon Quixwood swears he was somewhere else and couldn't have been involved?' He smiled very slightly, disengaging his arm from hers and then putting it around her and holding her even closer.

'Is that the question you're asking yourself?' she said. 'Why on earth would Rawdon Quixwood lie to protect Neville Forsbrook?'

'Yes,' he agreed. 'Assuming that he is lying. Although I don't see how he could be mistaken. The information was very specific, and so was he when he gave it.'

Charlotte weighed it in silence for several moments before she spoke.

'People lie for several reasons,' she said thoughtfully. 'To protect themselves, or someone they love; or, of course, someone they are being pressured to protect. Or they lie to achieve something, or to avoid something. Or, I suppose, to pay a debt to someone. Do people lie to protect an ideal? Or because the truth is something they can't afford to believe, for some reason? Something they just don't want to believe? Refuse to?' She watched him, waiting for the answer. 'Or are afraid of?' she added.

'Blackmail?' he answered. 'Debt? Then the question arises, is it Neville Forsbrook, or his father? What could Rawdon Quixwood possibly owe to either of them?'

'Maybe they knew something about Catherine that he wants to keep secret?' she suggested. 'After all, the poor woman can't protect herself now.'

'No one can protect her,' he said grimly. 'She was already dead when Quixwood stepped forward to swear Forsbrook was innocent regarding Angeles.'

'Then it would have to be something that mattered very much. And considering how Catherine died, Rawdon Quixwood would be the very last man in London to protect a rapist.'

'And yet I think he's lying,' Pitt answered. 'I just can't work out what the truth could be. Nothing I can imagine makes any sense.'

'Let's go through them one by one,' she suggested. 'What might Forsbrook have, either father or son, that Quixwood would want? Not money, I don't think. Vespasia said Quixwood got out of an African investment before the Jameson Raid, and she is all but certain that Forsbrook didn't. She said he looked like a ghost at the Jameson trial.'

'All right,' Pitt agreed. 'Not money. To protect someone? That's obvious – to protect Neville Forsbrook, but why? Forsbrook certainly had nothing to do with it. But Angeles and the other young girl, Alice Townley, specifically said they were raped by Neville Forsbrook, not by two people. Neither of them mentioned Quixwood. And he know ourselves that he had nothing to do with Catherine's death. He was with us. In fact, I was actually talking to him when the police came to tell him of her death. And he had been there all evening.'

'You're right,' she said, biting her lip. 'It's difficult. Fear? Who is afraid of what? And don't even bother to suggest an ideal. There's no possible ideal involved. And Quixwood and the Forsbrooks are not related, are they?'

'No,' he said, turning it over in his mind. 'Not by blood, or business alliance that we can see.'

'Then something else,' Charlotte suggested. 'If we start off assuming that Angeles and Alice Townley are telling the truth, then Quixwood is lying. He has to be. He must have done it for a reason. We have to find out what it is.'

'Indeed,' he said, putting his other arm around her and tightening his hold. 'But how?'

She laid her head on his shoulder. 'If it isn't the men, try the women,' she suggested. 'Neville Forsbrook's mother must have had some influence.'

'She's dead,' he reminded her, but as he said it the beginning of an idea stirred in his mind. 'I'll try that tomorrow.'

Chapter Eighteen

NARRAWAY HAD hardly started his breakfast when his manservant interrupted him to say that Commander Pitt had called to see him, and the matter was urgent.

Narraway glanced at the clock, which read just before half-past seven.

'It must be,' he replied a trifle waspishly, perhaps because he was touched with a moment of fear. Only an emergency could bring Pitt at this time of the morning. 'Ask him if he would like breakfast, and show him in,' he instructed.

A moment later Pitt came into the dining room dressed formally, and rather more neatly than usual. He looked excited more than alarmed.

Narraway waved at the opposite chair and Pitt sat down.

'Well?' Narraway asked.

'If we assume that Alban Hythe is telling the truth,' Pitt began without preamble, 'and that Angeles Castelbranco, and Alice Townley were also, then we are left with the conclusion that Rawdon Quixwood must either be lying, or mistaken about being with Neville Forsbrook at the time of Angeles' rape.' He leaned forward a little. 'Which raises the question as to why he would do such a thing. One would presume he would be the last man in England to defend a rapist.'

'So why would we presume it?' Narraway asked. With anyone else he would have been sarcastic, but he knew Pitt better than to assume he spoke without an answer in mind. 'What have we missed?'

Pitt gave a very slight, rueful gesture. 'I'm not certain. Some connection between Forsbrook, either father or son, and Quixwood. Or if not that, then possibly between the women.'

'What women? We found no connection between Catherine and either of the Forsbrooks,' Narraway pointed out. 'Vespasia says there appears to be a connection between Pelham Forsbrook and Quixwood, but it's tenuous. They both considered investing in the British South Africa Company. Forsbrook did pretty badly, Quixwood changed his mind in time and lost nothing. Quixwood does a lot of financial advising, so possibly he told Forsbrook to leave it alone, and he didn't. Quixwood doesn't seem the sort of man to feel he should lie to protect the rapist son of a man who didn't take his financial advice.' He wished there were some truth in the idea, but it would be absurd.

'Perhaps he didn't give him the advice?' Pitt suggested.

Narraway sipped his tea. 'Why wouldn't he?'

'We need to find that out,' Pitt answered. 'It might make sense of why Catherine Quixwood was so intent on learning about investment, and British South Africa Company. She knew Quixwood was misleading people – or perhaps only Forsbrook – and she needed more knowledge from Hythe in order to be certain. What if Hythe was telling the truth all along, and it wasn't a romantic affair at all?'

Narraway thought about it for a moment or two. The manservant came in bringing Pitt a full breakfast, including fresh tea.

'It could make sense,' Narraway finally answered when the manservant had gone. Pitt was eating hungrily. 'Except then we are left with a complete stranger raping Catherine. Is that coincidence, and someone we haven't even thought of?'

'I don't know,' Pitt admitted. 'But we don't have any other solution that makes sense either.'

'Except that it is exactly what it appears to be.' Narraway did not like the answer, but he could not deny it. 'Catherine was desperately lonely and she gave in to temptation to have an affair with a charming and intelligent man, who shared her interests.'

'But why did he start an affair?' Pitt pressed. 'He had nothing of value to gain, and everything to lose.'

Narraway felt the sadness fill him again. In his mind's eye he could see Catherine's body broken and bleeding, sprawled on the floor. He was startled how clearly he could remember her face.

'She was lovely,' he said simply. 'From what I could learn of her, she was interesting: full of life, ideas, intelligence, even passions of the mind. Perhaps his wife had become boring compared with her?'

'Then why did he rape and beat Catherine?' Pitt said. 'Forcing a woman is a crude and vicious thing to do, but to beat her half to death is the act of a man driven by demons within himself and completely out of control. Is there anything else in Hythe's life to draw a picture of him like that?'

'No,' Narraway said thoughtfully. 'Nothing at all. But do we always see it? If we do, why does sudden, terrible violence ever happen? Why don't we see it in others and prevent it?'

Pitt smiled reluctantly and swallowed his mouthful of bacon and egg. 'You can't arrest a man for what you think he could be capable of. And we know a lot more about Hythe now than we do about most people. We also know a lot more about Neville Forsbrook.'

'We don't know that he had ever even met Catherine Quixwood,' Narraway argued.

'No. But if he called on her, would she have let him in? Would she have any reason to have feared him?'

'No,' Narraway conceded. 'But would she have let the servants retire and sat up alone waiting for him? Are you suggesting she was having an affair with him? There's absolutely no evidence at all that they had ever met. He's a generation younger than she is. What on earth could they have in common? He has never shown any interest in art, exploration, history, or anything she cares about.'

'I don't think she was having an affair with him,' Pitt replied, pouring himself more tea. 'Or anyone else, for that matter.'

Narraway raised his eyebrows. 'What then? He simply called by because he wanted to rape someone, and he chose her? For God's sake, Pitt, that makes no sense at all.'

'Of course not,' Pitt answered impatiently. 'There's something important that we don't know. A connection between the Quixwoods and the Forsbrooks.'

Narraway felt the panic well up inside him. They were losing the case, and the trial of Hythe might not last beyond today – tomorrow if they were lucky. He had spoken with Symington, who had nothing new with which to fight, no weapons at all. He was going to face the final battle with no more than charm and imagination, which was too little against facts.

'It's too late to look for evidence now,' he said quietly. The taste of failure was bitter in his mouth. 'Whatever we find we couldn't hope to prove it in a day.'

Pitt's face was set hard with determination. 'I know we have no evidence,' he answered, for a moment ignoring his excellent breakfast. 'We'll have to suppose, raise possibilities and doubts.'

Narraway tried to calm his thoughts and compose some line of reasoning. 'Is this how you personally work, Pitt?' he said curiously. 'On the other hand, please don't answer that. I don't want to know.'

'Do you have a better idea, except giving in?' Pitt reached for the toast. He was smiling, but there was tension in the lines of his body, and his eyes were perfectly serious.

Narraway swallowed. 'What sort of a possibility do you have in mind?' he asked.

'The women,' Pitt repeated. 'Actually it was Charlotte who suggested it. Apart from the business connection between Forsbrook and Quixwood, what about Eleanor Forsbrook? We haven't thought about her very much.'

'She's been dead for several years,' Narraway said patiently. 'She can hardly have anything to do with this.'

'About three years, actually,' Pitt agreed.

'Then how can she be involved? None of it goes back that long, unless you think she's responsible for Neville being violent? Lots of young men lose their mothers. It doesn't turn them into rapists.'

'I'm not suggesting that. I've no idea why Neville became a rapist, except that he was violent in the incident with the prostitute, when the pimp apparently knifed him. But Eleanor was beaten by Pelham Forsbrook, apparently, and she was running away with a lover when she was killed in a traffic accident. Horse bolted.'

Narraway was confused. 'Three years ago?'

'Yes. But who was the lover?'

'I've no idea. What are you thinking? Quixwood?' Narraway said incredulously.

'Why not?' Pitt asked. 'It would explain the hatred between the two men. What if Quixwood deliberately advised Forsbrook to invest in the British South Africa Company, knowing he'd lose badly, and that is what Catherine suspected and was trying to guard against?'

'To save Forsbrook? Why?'

'Doesn't matter why. It could be she simply thought it was wrong. Or maybe that it would rebound on Quixwood, and perhaps on her also.'

'Can we prove anything?' Narraway's mind was racing now, grasping for possibilities, for hope.

'I don't know, but we can try. I'll look for the possibility that Quixwood could have been Eleanor Forsbrook's lover, and some evidence that Forsbrook beat her over it. Someone must have seen her body after the accident. If I can find the doctor and he's someone I know, or at least can impress, he might be able to swear some of her injuries happened before her death. Just make sure Symington can get them into evidence.'

'I'll go and see him again before court starts today. But one thing, Pitt: if Hythe's connection with Catherine was professional not personal, why doesn't he say so? Why would he hang in order to protect Quixwood?'

'He wouldn't,' Pitt admitted, biting his lip. 'There has to be another reason for that too.'

'You're supposing an awful lot of other reasons,' Narraway said unhappily.

'Yes,' Pitt said, taking the last mouthful of his breakfast. 'I am.'

'What has this to do with Angeles Castelbranco and her family?'

'I don't know, except that I still believe Neville Forsbrook raped her. I want him off the street, without him or his father ruining her name even further.'

'Would you like the moon as well?' Narraway asked, sounding more sarcastic than he meant to be because he realised how much he also cared.

Narraway arrived at court early and was waiting for Symington when he came in, who was also early in hope of preparing some kind of defence. Circumstances had left him almost nothing. When he arrived he was neat, immaculate as always, but his face showed lines of weariness, making him look older.

'I have no good news,' he said as he saw Narraway in the hallway, and led him into the room he was using and closed the door behind them.

'Neither have I,' Narraway responded. 'But I have some ideas.'

'A little late,' Symington replied wryly. 'I'll hear them anyway. Bower was good yesterday and I have nothing to come back with. Hythe himself is my only witness. He's calling Quixwood today, and I don't know whether to attack him or not. Sympathy is with him entirely and I don't know a damn thing to shake him.'

'I might do,' Narraway replied. Before Symington could argue, he summarised what he and Pitt had discussed over breakfast.

Symington listened patiently, but there was no spark of hope in his eyes.

'Conjecture,' he said when Narraway finished. 'It could even be true, but there are big holes in it. The biggest one to start with: if Hythe was only getting financial information for Catherine, why in the name of heaven doesn't he say so now?' He shook his head. 'They'll hang him if they find him guilty, and he knows that. Secondly, you found no evidence in Catherine's belongings that she was collecting financial evidence. If she made notes, what did she do with them? The diary is so brief and so careful it proves nothing. The figures might be money, or they might not. Nothing says so. And thirdly, if it wasn't Hythe who raped her, who was it? There are no other suspects. And we know Quixwood himself wasn't involved because he was with you at the time! Bower could call you to testify to that if he had to.'

'We know Quixwood didn't rape her,' Narraway agreed. He tried to make his voice hopeful, but the chances were razor thin, and he knew it. 'But we don't know who put the laudanum into the wine.'

'Bower's saying she did herself, and that seems the most reasonable supposition,' Symington answered. However, he stood a little straighter, shoulders more square, chin a little higher.

Narraway raised his eyebrows. 'Injured as she was, beaten and bleeding badly, she dragged herself all the way upstairs, got the laudanum from the bedroom cupboard, then came down again and put it in the Madeira, then drank it and collapsed on the floor again?' Deliberately he made it sound ridiculous. 'Where were the bloodstains on the stairs? On the landing carpet? Did Knox see them? I was there, and I didn't! I searched the house too. There was no blood whatever on anything in the bedroom, and that's where the laudanum was kept. I'll testify to that.'

'You realise what you're saying?' Symington frowned. 'If someone else put the laudanum into the Madeira, then either it was whoever raped her, which means they knew where it was, left her and went upstairs to get it, put it into the wine and then roused her and dosed her with it. Or else Quixwood put it there himself, which suggests very strongly that he knew what was going to happen, and that she took the wine with the laudanum in it without realising it was there. Frankly, neither of those sounds anywhere near as likely as she taking it herself in despair and great pain, even agony, after being raped and beaten.'

'Then where is the blood on the stairs, and in the bedroom?' Narraway asked. 'And why in heaven's name did she come down again at all, in the state she was?'

Symington nodded slowly. 'Agreed. Bower will say Hythe knew where her laudanum was and mixed it for her and gave it to her, so she would die, and could not testify against him.'

'He beat her nearly to death, and then stayed in the house, risking the servants finding him, so he could fetch and mix laudanum for her, and dose her with it?' Narraway edged his voice with disbelief. 'I thought Bower painted him as a raving madman who had completely lost his mind and savagely raped a woman he had been in love with, because she suddenly rejected him. Why not just break her neck?'

'Right,' Symington agreed again. 'That doesn't make sense either. Pitt has an excellent point: we are missing something. But I'm not sure that the jury will perceive that difference. If Hythe wasn't her lover and their whole friendship, and the secrecy of it, was to do with finding financial information about Quixwood's investment, or not, and his advice about it to Forsbrook, then why doesn't Hythe say so now to save himself?'

Narraway himself was puzzled. 'I don't know. Perhaps either Forsbrook or Quixwood have some power over him?'

'Such as what?' Symington frowned as if he were searching his mind desperately for any thread to hang on to and weave some defence.

Pitt had said Charlotte told him to think of the women. She had meant Eleanor and Catherine. But what about Maris Hythe?

'If he's found guilty and hanged, what will happen to Maris?' he said aloud, a new urgency in him, impelling him forward.

Slowly the light came into Symington's vivid blue eyes. 'Disgrace and probably destitution,' he said, letting his breath out slowly. 'Catherine kept no papers, or if she did, they've been destroyed. If he had papers it would prove nothing. He's keeping silent to protect Maris. Quixwood must have promised to look after her, perhaps even made some commitment she could prove, and he couldn't go back on.' He leaned forward, desperately urgent. 'Find it, Narraway! Get somebody onto it! Get this Pitt fellow – now! Today! Then maybe we have a chance.'

Narraway rose to his feet. 'Can you get a message to Lady Vespasia Cumming-Gould that I am pursuing evidence and will not be in court today? It is important.'

Symington smiled. 'The beautiful Lady Vespasia. I should be delighted to have an excuse to speak to her. Of course I shall tell her. Do you wish me to say where you have gone, and what you are pursuing?'

'By all means. Thank you.'

Vespasia was in a seat reserved for Narraway himself and had received the message from Symington that Narraway had gone on an urgent errand to find Pitt. Symington had expressed no emotion in words, but there was an excitement in him that had no explanation other than hope.

As she sat watching the proceedings begin she could see no reason for hope at all, unless there really was some powerful new evidence that had totally eluded them before. However, she clung to that belief with difficulty when Rawdon Quixwood took the stand as the prosecution's last witness.

Quixwood looked haggard as he climbed the steps and took the oath to tell the truth. His dark hair was thick and tidy but his eyes were hollow and there was no colour to his skin. He wore black, as was appropriate for a man still in mourning for his wife. Looking at him as he faced Bower, no one could forget that he was the living victim of this terrible crime.

In the dock, Alban Hythe appeared like a man already sentenced to death. Did Symington really have any hope? Or was he a superb actor: one whose charm, magnetism and ability to create a world in his own imagination, and then live in it, surpassed that of even the finest actors on the stage?

Bower, looking as dour as ever, strode out into the middle of the floor and stared solemnly up at Rawdon Quixwood.

'I regret this, sir.' He said it quietly, but his voice carried in the utter stillness of the courtroom. No one stirred in the gallery. There was not even a whisper of movement. 'Were there some other way, I would take it,' Bower continued. 'But I promise you we will obtain justice for your wife, and it will not be much longer now.'

'I know that, sir,' Quixwood answered sombrely. 'You do only what is necessary, and justice demands. Please ask whatever you wish, and I shall endeavour to keep my composure. I have no desire to embarrass the Court, or myself.'

There was a murmur of approval from the body of the court. Several of the jurors nodded.

Bower inclined his head gravely, milking every moment for sympathy.

Vespasia had expected it, but she was still impatient. 'Proceed with it, man,' she sighed under her breath.

As if he had heard her, Bower looked up at Quixwood.

'I have kept your testimony until last, Mr Quixwood, because I want to give you the opportunity to sum up for the jury exactly what happened, as you are aware of it, and the desperate, even emotionally fatal blow that this terrible crime has dealt you. Let me begin at the beginning, so far as you are aware of it.'

He glanced up towards the dock, briefly. The eyes of all the jurors followed him to where Alban Hythe sat motionless, then back again at the silent, wounded figure of Quixwood.

As theatre it was superb. Vespasia found herself clenching her teeth and wondering where on earth Narraway had got to and what he hoped to achieve now. Time was slipping away from them.

'Mr Quixwood, were you aware of the friendship your wife had found with the accused, Mr Alban Hythe?'

'She mentioned that she had met him,' Quixwood replied. 'And I think something about his being very pleasant. I can't remember any more than that.'

'In other words you had no idea that she was seeing him increasingly often, up to as much as two or three times in a week, towards the end of her life?' Bower went on.

Quixwood gripped the railing in front of him. 'No, of course not.'

'Would you have acted differently had you known?' Bower asked.

'Naturally. I would have required an explanation from her, and then forbidden her to continue. It was foolish . . . and . . .' he swallowed convulsively, '. . . ill-considered, at best. As it turned out, it seems to have been tragic. I had no idea she was so . . . so emotionally fragile. I had not seen it in her character.'

Bower nodded sagely. 'She had always been of good judgement until this . . . friendship?'

'Yes. Excellent. Catherine was a beautiful and gracious woman.'

'You were happy in your marriage?'

'Very. No one who knew Catherine would be surprised at it. Many men envied me my good fortune. And I held myself to be fortunate.' Quixwood stood quite still. Never once did his eyes stray up towards Hythe in the dock, or towards the jury.

'We have heard that you were attending a function at the Spanish Embassy when the police informed you of Mrs Quixwood's death,' Bower continued.

Symington rose to his feet. 'My lord, we have already established that Mr Quixwood was at the Spanish Embassy, and in conversation with Lord Narraway, and that he had been there all evening. It is not in dispute.'

'Just so,' Bower raised his head in acknowledgement before the judge could intervene. 'Mr Quixwood, I will not harrow you by asking you to describe for us your feelings as you travelled back home, or when you saw your wife's body broken and bleeding on the floor, hideously violated.'

Symington was scribbling notes to himself.

Bower continued, ignoring Symington. 'Please tell the jury, Mr Quixwood, briefly if it is easier for you, what you yourself did after that terrible night, in order to assist the investigation. As much as you can recall. I am sure the Court appreciates that it has been a nightmare for you, one in which your memory may be imperfect.'

Vespasia was aware of the skill of the question, the careful making room for error. It would be almost impossible now for Symington to trip him up. Was that on purpose because Bower feared errors? Or was it just a usual precaution he would have taken with anyone?

Quixwood hesitated, as if arranging his thoughts, then began. His voice was low and very clear, his eyes downcast. He looked like a man controlling terrible pain.

'That night, as I recall, I asked Lord Narraway to give me any help he could personally. He was very gracious, and seemed to me to care deeply, both for justice in general, and in this case in particular. I knew of him, of course, as head of Special Branch, until recently, but I found him in this instance a man of remarkable compassion. He seemed genuinely appalled at the savagery of the crime, and moved to do whatever he could to find out who was guilty. I'm not sure if I ever told him how much his support meant to me.'

There was a murmur of approval around the gallery and several of the jurors nodded and smiled.

Vespasia felt the bitterness of the irony cut deep.

'He spent a great deal of time at my home,' Quixwood went on thoughtfully. 'He read through Catherine's diaries, things I would find too painful to do, but which I was glad that he did. The items are all in evidence, so he has not had to testify. I believe Catherine's maid authenticated them.'

'Thank you, Mr Quixwood,' Bower said with a gracious gesture, an inclination of his head in respect.

Symington sat fidgeting. He knew that Bower was asking the questions only to put Quixwood on the stand and draw the jury's sympathy even more. There was no real evidence to give. But if Symington challenged him on it and won, then the trial would be virtually at an end. He must drag it out as long as he could, to give Pitt and Narraway a chance to find any new evidence at all, any kind of a defence for Hythe. Bower would be profoundly aware of that, as would Symington. Bower had all the cards to play and Symington was desperate.

Bower was smiling now. It was a gentle, friendly smile, one of compassion. 'Mr Quixwood, was your wife a beautiful woman?'

Quixwood blinked hard several times before replying. 'Yes, she was, in every way. Her face was uniquely lovely, full of life and wit and grace. She could be terribly funny, when she wanted to, and without unkindness. She loved beauty of every kind, and knowledge. She was interested in everything. You may think I say that now because I loved her, but ask anyone else who knew her and they will say the same.'

'Have you ever had instances before where another man craved her attention more than was appropriate?' Bower asked.

'Yes, but Catherine was well able to decline without ill feeling,' Quixwood answered. 'I suppose every truly lovely woman has to learn that art.'

'So you had no cause to fear for her?'

'Of course not! For God's sake . . .' His voice broke. 'She was in her own home with the doors locked and . . . and a full complement of servants!' Quixwood said in a sudden burst of anguish. 'What should I fear? I was out at a reception my business required I attend. What sane man would imagine such a . . . a . . .' He struggled to regain his control, and failed. He bowed his head and the tears ran unchecked down his cheeks.

For a moment Vespasia thought Pitt and Narraway had to be wrong, at least in the assumption that Quixwood could have had anything to do with the crime. Perhaps it was Pelham Forsbrook, in revenge for Quixwood having been Eleanor's lover – if that were true? Yes, surely that made more sense? She would say so to Symington, when she had the chance.

Bower thanked Quixwood and invited Symington to question the witness.

Symington rose to his feet, then seemed to hesitate. He looked at Quixwood, then at the jury. No one moved.

'Mr Symington?' the judge asked courteously.

Symington smiled, a charming, almost luminous smile that Vespasia knew he could not possibly mean. The only chance he could have would be to win some sympathy from the jury, some shred of doubt. He dared not alienate them now, and Bower knew it as well as he did.

'Thank you, my lord,' Symington said gracefully. He looked up at Quixwood. 'Mr Quixwood, I cannot imagine what you have lost in this whole, terrible tragedy. I do not believe that the accused was the man who did this thing, but I do not believe that putting you through any further agony will assist me in proving that. I offer you my sincerest regrets over the fearful death of a woman who seems by every account of her to have been beautiful in all respects.'

He sat down again to the amazement of the gallery, the jury and the judge. Even Bower looked momentarily wrong-footed.

Vespasia felt her heart sink. Pitt and Narraway could not possibly have found anything yet. Why on earth did Symington not think of something to give them time? Was the man a fool? Or did he know he was beaten, and could see no point in stretching out the pain?

Bower stood up again, victory flushing his cheeks, making his eyes bright.

'The prosecution rests, my lord.'

If Symington was caught by surprise he did not show it, but he was pale as he stood again and asked the judge for an adjournment so he might speak privately with his client before beginning the defence. Was he going to give up?

There was a buzz of excitement in the gallery, confusion in the jury box.

Perhaps hoping that they could have a speedy end, the judge granted an adjournment until the following morning.

Vespasia stood up slowly, a little stiff, and waited a few minutes while the crowd pushed and jostled its way out. She had no idea of purpose in lingering, simply that nowhere else could she sense any hope either. She had reached the main doors to the street when she heard her name called. She turned to find Symington at her elbow.

'Lady Vespasia,' he said with a slight relief to the anxiety in his face, 'may I speak with you, perhaps in half an hour or so? It is extremely pressing, or I wouldn't trouble you.'

'Pressing is a magnificent piece of understatement, Mr Symington,' she replied. 'If there is anything at all that I can do, I am entirely at your disposal.'

'I'm afraid I must ask you to wait because now is the only chance I have to see Hythe again before tomorrow, although I have very little idea what I can say to him that will help, except a final plea to tell me the truth. I have nothing with which to defend him.'

'Of course I will wait.' She gave the only answer possible. 'If you can show me where I may do so without being asked to leave?'

'I have the use of a room. Thank you.'

She followed where he directed her, but as soon as he had gone, leaving her alone in the small room, she rose to her feet again and paced the floor. Her mind went over and over the facts she knew, seeking for any escape whatever.

The minutes ticked by. She heard voices and footsteps outside, but no one disturbed her.

They were going to lose tomorrow. It seemed inevitable. And Narraway was so convinced that Hythe was not guilty. Perhaps after all he was capable of deeper emotion than she had considered, but he would never be a sentimental man, following wishes where his reason denied. The violence against Catherine Quixwood had appalled him. He had never known her in life, yet in her terrible death she had touched something in him deeper than anger or pity at a crime.

Assuming both Catherine and Hythe were innocent of any romantic or physical liaison and it was, as Pitt and Narraway had conjectured, a matter of his finding information for her regarding investment in the fiasco of the Jameson Raid, then why did Hythe not say so now? If he were the man he claimed to be, what could possibly be worse than the fate of conviction and hanging for a shocking crime?

What love or honour would make Vespasia face such a hideous death, had she the courage? Was Alban Hythe so brave and selfless a man?

And if he was, then for what? Surely in the last it could only be 'for whom'? It had to be Maris, whom he loved, and who had been loyal to him throughout. To save her from what? Destitution. He was prepared to remain silent about the truth to protect her. That could only mean that the truth would ruin someone else, but if he were silent then that person would care for Maris.

That in turn must be Quixwood, or conceivably Pelham Forsbrook. Except that Forsbrook had lost heavily from the Jameson Raid. Quixwood had not.

Would Hythe trust Quixwood? Not without something that committed him and he could not escape it even after Hythe was dead. What could that be? Who had preserved it, in some place where no one could destroy it?

Vespasia was still pondering what that might be, with whom, and if Maris Hythe were even aware of it, when Symington returned. The courage and grace he had shown in the courtroom had vanished. He looked totally beaten.

She did not ask if he had succeeded; the answer was apparent.

'I don't know what else to do,' he said, dropping into the chair and indicating with a weary gesture that she should sit opposite him.

She remained standing, unable to relax and he was too exhausted to stand again.

'Mr Symington, a reason for Mr Hythe's refusal to defend himself has occurred to me,' she said gravely. 'He believes he cannot be saved, which in the circumstances is a reasonable assumption. However, if he is as noble a man as his wife believes, then he will not fight a hopeless battle for his own life or honour when to give in silently might preserve some comfort and protection for her.'

Symington looked up, frowning. 'If he is hanged, as he well might be, then her life will be wretched, and unless she has family, which she says she does not, then it will probably also be destitute. I hated doing so, but I told him that. It is past time for comforting lies.'

'What if Quixwood has promised to look after her, even given Hythe some written commitment that cannot be broken?' she suggested. 'On condition, of course, that Hythe does not reveal the financial information that he obtained for Catherine?'

Incredulity in Symington's eyes changed slowly to a dawning understanding. He looked up at her with amazement.

'You realise what that means?' he asked, his energy returning. 'A whole new motive for killing Catherine Quixwood! Not because she was raped at all, but because she had discovered financial information that Quixwood could not afford to have made public.' He stood up, his face eager. 'Both Catherine and Hythe had to be silenced, and her death and his accusation of rape accomplished both. He will go to the gallows in silence to protect his wife. God Almighty! It's diabolical. But how the devil do we prove it?'

'I don't know,' she admitted. 'But for the sake of a man's life, we must spend all the time we have left in trying. I intend to go to Thomas Pitt's home and wait for his return. He and Lord Narraway will solve this, if it can be done. I shall report to you as soon as there is anything to tell.'

'No you won't,' he insisted. 'I shall come with you. We have no time to waste in relaying messages to one another. Come.'

Chapter Nineteen

CHARLOTTE WAS completely unprepared when Vespasia arrived with Peter Symington immediately behind her. Vespasia looked magnificent, dressed in an exquisitely cut costume of dark blue-grey with flawless white silk at the neck and pearls on her ears. If the intent had been sombreness appropriate for a trial she had just missed it. The vitality and determination in her face accepted neither tragedy nor defeat. Symington was clearly weary and bruised from battle, but the warmth of his smile robbed Charlotte of complaint.

'I apologise, my dear,' Vespasia said as a stammering Minnie Maude held the parlour door open for her. 'But the situation is desperate. May I introduce Mr Symington. He has undertaken the defence of Alban Hythe, for what I fear will be scant reward, and we are on the brink of defeat. We are beaten on every side and unless we can think of something tonight, tomorrow will deal us the *coup de grâce*. Although there will be little of grace about it. I do not like Mr Bower, who represents the prosecution. There is a self-righteousness in the man, and a lack of imagination.'

'How do you do, Mrs Pitt?' Symington said quietly. 'I am aware that we are intruding, and I apologise.'

'If you can help, then you are welcome,' Charlotte said sincerely. 'Have you come straight from court? It's early, isn't it?'

'Yes,' he replied. 'The judge allowed me time, I assume, to prepare myself for a strategic surrender. But we are not quite at the last ditch. Lady Vespasia hopes that Commander Pitt might yet be of assistance, and almost certainly Lord Narraway.'

Charlotte's mind raced. She had no idea where either Pitt or Narraway might be. What should she do if they did not return until late? It was only just after three in the afternoon.

'Have you eaten?' she said practically. No one's mind was at its best when lacking nourishment.

'Yes, we have had luncheon, thank you,' Vespasia said, still standing. 'But perhaps Minnie Maude would be kind enough to make us tea. I remember in the past most profound conversations across the kitchen table. Might that be possible again?'

Charlotte did not bother to consult Symington. His easy smile and a certain grace in the way he stood suggested he would agree.

'Of course,' she said quickly. 'Minnie Maude will make us tea, and perhaps cake. Neither hunger nor discomfort must mar our thoughts. I shall use the telephone to see if Mr Stoker can help us to get a message to Thomas. I imagine Lord Narraway's manservant might be able to find him, if it is possible.'

'Excellent,' Vespasia nodded. She turned to lead Symington to the kitchen, followed by a startled and uncomfortable Minnie Maude.

Around the kitchen table, with plenty of tea and some very good home-made cake, Charlotte was brought up to date with the day's happenings in the courtroom.

'What we lack is any kind of proof,' Vespasia said unhappily.

Symington ate the last of his cake. 'I would settle for a witness or two and a good deal of suggestions,' he said. 'You can scare people into admitting all kinds of things, if you get the balance exactly right. I would like to prove Hythe innocent, but at this point I'd be grateful simply for reasonable doubt.'

'What evidence could there be?' Charlotte asked. 'Who could have witnessed anything that would help?'

Vespasia thought for several moments. 'Let us consider what we know for certain,' she said. 'In the order of their happening, as far as is possible.' She looked at Charlotte. 'What does Thomas know?'

'That Neville Forsbrook beat a prostitute very badly, six or seven years ago, when he was about twenty,' Charlotte replied. 'And the woman's pimp beat Neville equally badly, in return. Apparently he scarred him with a knife, although we aren't likely to prove that, unless we find someone who has seen far more of him than we are likely to.' She pulled a slight face at the thought.

'And your husband knows this for certain?' Symington asked. 'Or he believes it?'

'He knows,' Charlotte answered. 'He has spoken to witnesses.' She did not mention Elmo Crask at this point, bearing in mind the Home Secretary's prohibitions.

'He is still certain that Neville raped Angeles Castelbranco, and so am I,' she went on. 'Although at the moment there is nothing that we can do about it. Any attempt would only hurt his family more than it would hurt Neville anyway.'

Symington looked puzzled. 'Is this a Special Branch case, Mrs Pitt?' His voice implied that he doubted it.

'There is no case,' she told him. 'It's just a tragedy we saw, and we care about very much. Would I like to see Neville Forsbrook punished? Yes, I would. But not at the cost of slandering Angeles' name any more.'

'I heard about it,' Symington said thoughtfully, and there was a sudden sharp pain in his face. 'It is one of those where the woman cannot win. And I gather she was only a child.'

'Yes.' Charlotte kept her composure with difficulty. 'About two years older than my own daughter. But we are here now to try to save Alban Hythe from being hanged for a crime he did not commit, not convict Neville Forsbrook for one that he did.'

'They both involve rape,' Symington thought aloud, his eyes unfocused, staring at the far wall. 'Certainly that's the part of the Quixwood case that makes the least sense. If Hythe and Catherine were lovers, when did it turn to the sort of savagery involved in the rape? And why there, in her own house? I can find no mention of his ever having visited her there before – and, for that matter – no evidence that he was there that night.'

He looked from Charlotte to Vespasia and back again. 'Is there any? No one has suggested it to me, but then Forsbrook as a suspect never crossed my mind.'

'No,' Charlotte said miserably. 'There is no reason even to ask him where he was. Although I know for myself that he was at the party at the Spanish Embassy earlier in the evening, because I was there also. But I did not see him after about ten o'clock.'

'Interesting,' Symington said as much to himself as to anyone else.

'Hythe claims to have been walking and thinking, but no one can swear to it. He passed neighbours but didn't speak to anyone.'

'Can there be proof that he found any of the financial information for Catherine regarding investment in the British South Africa Company?' Charlotte asked, trying another angle of approach.

'No,' Symington answered. 'Most of his access to it was probably illegal anyway, and even if we could prove it, there is nothing to say he obtained it for her. She seems to have kept no record of it, which is peculiar.'

'Then why did she want it?' Vespasia asked. 'Surely she meant to take some action?' She turned to Symington. 'What would that be? Was she trying to stop Quixwood, or protect him? Why did she care if he ruined Pelham Forsbrook? For that matter, why would Quixwood want to ruin Forsbrook?'

Symington opened his eyes wide. 'Did he? Do we know that?'

'We need to know if Quixwood advised Forsbrook to invest, and then failed to warn him of the possible failure and consequent cost of the Jameson Raid,' Vespasia answered. 'And we have no time for that.'

Symington turned to Charlotte. 'Could Commander Pitt help us? Is there any way he could obtain, if not information on the major investors, then at least word-of-mouth reports? It would do, at a pinch. Quixwood won't know that I'm guessing.'

Charlotte stood up. 'I'll telephone Mr Stoker again,' she replied. 'It is worth trying, at least.'

She was back five minutes later. 'I spoke to Mr Stoker. I have no idea whether it will help or not. He will come here this evening with whatever he can find.'

Vespasia returned to her original question, having borrowed a piece of notepaper and a pencil from Minnie Maude.

'First we know Neville Forsbrook attacked a prostitute and was in turn beaten by the pimp,' she said, looking at what she had written. 'He left England to recuperate somewhere where he would be highly

302

unlikely to meet anyone he knew. We may presume he was rescued in this by his father, who therefore knows his nature, and was either unwilling or unable to curb him in it on any permanent basis.'

'Then about three years ago Eleanor Forsbrook ran away from home,' Charlotte added. 'We don't know whether it was with a lover or not, nor do we know who he may have been. Possibly she was beaten beforehand, but we have no evidence yet.'

'No evidence yet? Then how do you know this?' Symington asked her.

'My husband found out, from a man who works nearby, in Bryanston Mews,' she answered. 'Thomas said he was intending to find the doctor who examined her body after the accident to see if any of the injuries were inflicted before that.'

Vespasia wrote it down. 'And the next thing?'

'I suppose Forsbrook and Quixwood both invested in Africa, only Quixwood withdrew his money again immediately and did not tell Forsbrook.'

'Proof?' Symington asked.

Charlotte shook her head. 'Not yet, but it makes sense of it. Then we have the Jameson Raid, at the very end of last year, which has just now come to trial, and since Jameson is clearly guilty, the British South Africa Company will have to pay a fortune in damages to the Boers in the Transvaal. Some investors are going to be very badly damaged.'

'Which, according to our suppositions, was of great concern to Catherine Quixwood,' Vespasia remarked.

Symington sat up straighter. 'Why, I wonder? Protecting Forsbrook? Afraid for her husband, in case he had not taken his own money out? Or afraid that Quixwood was deliberately setting Forsbrook up for a bad fall? Again, why?'

Charlotte was struggling to make sense of it. 'Could she have been a friend of Eleanor Forsbrook's? Or of Pelham Forsbrook?' she asked. 'I can't imagine she was of Neville.'

'Has anyone investigated to find out?' Symington asked.

'Victor will have,' Vespasia said with certainty. 'He has learned enough about Catherine to have an informed opinion.'

'Then who required her dead?' Symington asked, looking from one to the other of them. 'The answer seems to be her husband. But we know beyond any doubt at all that he was at the Spanish Embassy, speaking with Lord Narraway, at the time of Catherine's death.'

'Another question,' Charlotte said, 'is why did Rawdon Quixwood come forward and say that he was with Neville Forsbrook at the time Angeles was raped, if it is not true?'

Symington looked at her. 'Are you sure it is not true? I mean really sure that you are not assuming it because it makes sense of other things we don't understand? And to be honest, because you don't like him, and you believe he's guilty?'

She hesitated a moment. 'Do I know it? No. I couldn't prove it. I know he raped Alice Townley . . .'

He was confused. 'Who is Alice Townley?'

'I'm sorry,' she said. 'Another young girl. Her father refused to bring any charges, but Thomas went to see her, and she swore to him that it was unquestionably Neville Forsbrook who raped her. Her account was very similar to that which Angeles Castelbranco gave her mother, but with a lot of details filled in. And before you ask, no, they didn't know each other.'

Symington clenched his teeth and breathed in and out slowly several times. 'Then I think we may believe them,' he said at last. 'Let us take it that Neville Forsbrook raped Angeles, and this Alice Townley. Quixwood lied to protect him. The question is why did he do so?'

'Because he does not wish Neville Forsbrook to be charged with rape,' Vespasia answered.

'Why not, if he is guilty?' Charlotte said quickly. Then another wilder thought came to her. 'Is it even imaginable that Neville Forsbrook raped Catherine Quixwood too?' she said in little more than a whisper.

Symington stared at her. 'Why in God's name would her husband protect him from another charge of rape? Wouldn't that be the perfect answer? He could be convicted, without the shame and humiliation of a trial making the wretched details of Catherine's death public? It's what I would want, if it were my wife.'

'Unless you wished someone else convicted of it,' Vespasia pointed out.

'Her lover?' Symington said, his eyes wide. 'But we are supposing that Hythe was not her lover. Or have you changed your mind about that?'

'Not at all,' Vespasia denied quickly. 'He wants Hythe convicted because he had information that Quixwood was deliberately bringing about Forsbrook's financial ruin.'

'It's a bit late to do anything about that now,' Symington observed.

'But it wasn't when Catherine began,' Vespasia pointed out. 'And if it were known that Quixwood deliberately gave a client disastrous advice in order to ruin him, that would be the end of his own financial career. If Catherine really knew something, he had to keep her silent, and Hythe as well.'

Symington thought for a few moments, then looked up again. 'Quixwood could claim that he advised Forsbrook to sell, and Forsbrook didn't take the advice. No one could prove otherwise. Quixwood might even have a letter to that effect. I would, if I were doing such a thing. I would say that I begged Forsbrook not to invest, and he was greedy and ignored me. That's quite believable. London is full of people who think Jameson is a hero.'

'We need proof of something.' Vespasia passed the empty cups to Minnie Maude and thanked her. 'Without proof, or at least witnesses, we are merely slandering a man who already has the total sympathy and support of the court, not to mention the jury.'

Charlotte rose from the table and went into the scullery to consult with Minnie Maude as to what they might serve for dinner, with at least three prospective guests. Vespasia and Symington returned to the parlour.

Jemima and Daniel came home from school and were greeted, and then politely but firmly dismissed to their own rooms, with promises that Minnie Maude would bring them their supper.

A full hour later Narraway arrived, and within a few minutes Pitt came in also, in answer to Stoker's summons. Stoker himself was a step behind. They all looked weary and defeated, though each tried in his own way not to show it.

Pitt looked at Symington after no more than a glance at Charlotte, a meeting of the eyes, and then away again for an instant to Vespasia, as an acknowledgement.

'It went badly,' he concluded.

Symington made a slight gesture with his hands. 'We've still got tomorrow,' he replied. 'I have no way of stretching it any further than that, because although we have lots of ideas – we might even have the answer – we have no proof. We haven't even a witness to call that we can tie up in contradiction, or to raise doubts.'

'Ideas?' Narraway said with a flicker of hope. He was standing near Vespasia while Minnie Maude waited by the doorway to know if she should add more to the supper.

Charlotte nodded to her and she disappeared in a flurry to meet the challenge. Charlotte stopped even trying to think what else there was in the larder, and returned her attention to the things that mattered.

'Do we know anything now?' she asked Pitt, trying not to invest her voice with too much hope.

'I spoke to the surgeon who examined Mrs Forsbrook's body after the accident,' he replied. 'He said there were old bruises, even a frac-tured rib that had healed, but it doesn't prove anything.'

'It seems it could be true that he beat her,' she said quickly.

'Or not,' he replied ruefully. 'It could have been an earlier accident: riding, or even falling downstairs.'

'Maybe.' She would not give up. 'What if Quixwood deliberately advised Forsbrook to invest in the British South Africa Company, specifically the Jameson Raid, knowing it would fail, thus causing his ruin?' she suggested.

'Why?' Pitt asked reasonably.

'We don't know,' she answered. 'What if it were something to do with Eleanor and whoever her lover was? Catherine seems to have been very involved. The whole crime centres on her, after all. If Hythe is telling the truth, then he was looking for proof of that for her—'

'Again,' Pitt interrupted, 'why? Would she care if Forsbrook were ruined?'

Symington blinked and frowned. 'Maybe that was the affair? Pelham Forsbrook and Catherine, not Hythe at all.'

Everyone turned to stare at him.

'Then who raped her?' Narraway asked.

'Pelham Forsbrook, maybe?' Charlotte replied, seizing the idea. 'He beat Eleanor. He's a violent man. She was running away when she was killed . . . wasn't she?' She looked to Pitt.

'Yes,' he agreed quickly. He turned to Narraway. 'Was Pelham still at the Spanish Embassy when Catherine was raped?'

Narraway thought for a moment. 'I saw Neville leave quite a while before. I think Pelham went at the same time. It would just have been possible. He would have known Quixwood was still there, and likely to remain at least another hour or more.'

'How do we suggest that?' Symington asked, returning to the practical. 'I've tried everything I can, and I can't persuade Hythe to admit that he was doing financial investigation for Catherine, even though it might offer the only defence he has.'

Vespasia spoke for the first time in several minutes. 'Realistically, Mr Symington, what chance has that defence of succeeding, even in raising a doubt?'

He sighed. 'Very little,' he confessed.

'Then if Hythe's greatest concern is to keep someone safe, so they can provide care for his wife, dare he take the chance of trying what we are suggesting? If Quixwood has made some commitment he cannot break, as long as Hythe remains silent as to Quixwood's deliberate misleading of Forsbrook's financial affairs, in his place I wouldn't, would you?'

'Not if I loved my wife enough,' Symington said. 'In fact if I were almost certain of dying anyway, I would go with dignity, and keep silent to save her, I hope.'

Now Pitt was frowning. 'Are we saying that Quixwood would look after Maris Hythe to keep Alban silent about his financial deceit, and he would do it to save Forsbrook, the man he hates enough to ruin, and who raped his wife, and killed her, morally if not physically? You can't convince me of that, let alone a jury. And I would like to believe you.'

'And there is another question to be answered,' Vespasia continued. 'Why did Quixwood lie to defend Neville Forsbrook over raping Angeles Castelbranco? What was his purpose in that? We are still presuming he lied, aren't we?'

'Yes,' Pitt said instantly. 'And rape Alice Townley as well, and very possibly several other girls: one we know of, others we may not. And there's the incident of the prostitute, and the pimp who beat him and knifed him.'

'Have we two rapists, father and son?' Narraway asked, frowning. 'That might explain where Neville learned his behaviour, from his father's violence and disregard for women, and why his father protected him when he beat the prostitute, and for all we know, raped her too. But what can we even suggest in court, let alone prove?'

'Find something to prove that Hythe was getting financial information for Catherine,' Symington answered. 'I'll find a way to force him into admitting that was what he was doing for her, if I have anything I can hang it on.'

There were several moments of frantic and miserable silence while each one of them struggled for a way to find anything at all. Finally it was Narraway who spoke, looking at Pitt.

'The Jameson Raid could provoke war with the Boers in Africa, which would be a very serious thing for Britain,' he said, measuring his words. 'Even if we win, it will cost lives, and at this distance be highly expensive. It could reasonably be within the remit of Special Branch, because the Boers will fight hard, and any country at war seeks to disturb the domestic life of its enemy. You can make an excuse to look into the cost of the Jameson Raid, and who was affected by it. You don't have to give reasons.'

Pitt stared at him, understanding beginning to take a hazy shape in his mind.

'You have to start somewhere,' Narraway went on. 'Begin with exactly what losses or gains Forsbrook and Quixwood made. You don't need to prove it, only justify what Hythe was looking for to give Catherine, and show a cause for enmity between Forsbrook and Quixwood.' He turned to Symington, who was now sitting upright, his eyes wide, his face with a smile dawning on it.

'Will that serve?' Narraway asked, although the answer was now obvious.

'Yes,' Symington said firmly. 'Yes, it will! It could just be enough.'

'Good,' Narraway nodded, then turned back to Pitt. 'You'll need a little help. It might take us most of the night. Then first thing in the morning we'll get proof, or at least affirmation, and get it to you in court by noon. Will that be soon enough?' he asked Symington.

'Don't worry,' Symington assured them. 'I'll create enough of a display to keep it going until then. Thank you.' He stood up. 'Thank you very much. I'll go home and plan.'

'Wouldn't you like supper first?' Charlotte invited him. 'You need to eat, and to sleep, in order to fight your best.'

He grinned at her, a wide, charming expression full of warmth, and sat down again. 'How wise you are,' he accepted. 'Of course I would.'

The trial of Alban Hythe resumed in the morning. Vespasia was again in attendance, this time aching with the double tensions of hope and dread. She watched Symington and was impressed with his air of confidence. Had she not known his anxiety from the previous evening, she would have assumed he had the perfect defence in his hands as he called Alban Hythe to the witness stand and listened to him take the oath.

Then after a glance at Bower, he walked with grace into the centre of the floor and looked up at Hythe's ashen face.

'You are an expert in banking and investment affairs, are you not, Mr Hythe?' he began gravely. 'Indeed, I hear you have remarkable skills for one so young. Modesty notwithstanding, is that not a fair assessment of your ability?'

'I have some skill, yes,' Hythe replied. He looked puzzled.

Bower rose to his feet. 'My lord, the prosecution will agree that Mr Hythe has high intelligence, an excellent education and is outstandingly good at his profession. There is no need for Mr Symington to call evidence to that effect.'

Symington's expression tightened so slightly maybe no one other than Vespasia noticed, and she did so because she had spoken with him the evening before and knew his purpose.

Symington inclined his head towards Bower. 'Thank you. I had not intended to call anyone, but you save me the anxiety of wondering if perhaps I should have.'

A flicker of annoyance crossed Bower's face. 'I fail to see the purpose of your observation.'

'Patience, sir, patience,' Symington smiled. 'You have had several days to make your points. I am sure you have no quarrel with allowing me one day?' Before Bower could answer he turned again to Hythe. 'Are you acquainted with Mr Rawdon Quixwood?'

'Yes, slightly,' Hythe answered. His voice was husky, as though his throat were dry.

'Socially, or professionally?' Symington asked.

'Mostly professionally.'

'You advised him on investments?' Symington raised his eyebrows as if he were interested.

Hythe tried to smile and failed. 'No. That would be superfluous. Mr Quixwood has great financial expertise himself. I doubt I could add anything to his knowledge.'

'He is excellent also?' Symington asked.

Bower started to rise again.

Symington turned sharply, his face showing a flicker of temper. 'Sir,' he said irritably. 'I afforded you the courtesy of letting you speak without unnecessary interruptions. Unless you are at your wits' end to keep your case together, please don't keep wasting everyone's time with pointless objections. His Lordship is perfectly capable of stopping me, should I wander all over the place without reaching a point. You do not have to keep leaping up and down like a jack-in-the-box.'

There was a titter of laughter around the gallery and one of the jurors indulged in a fit of coughing, handkerchief up to obscure his face.

'Proceed, Mr Symington,' the judge directed.

'Thank you, my lord.' Symington turned again to Alban Hythe, who stood rigid, his hands on the witness box rail as if he needed its support. 'So you did not advise Mr Quixwood as to his investments, say, for example, in the British South Africa Company?'

Bower sighed and put his head in his hands.

'No, sir,' Hythe replied, his body suddenly more tense, his voice sharper.

'Would you have advised him to invest, for example, before the news came of the raid led by Dr Leander Starr Jameson, into the Transvaal?'

The judge leaned forward. 'Is this relevant to the crime for which Mr Hythe is on trial, Mr Symington?'

'Yes, my lord, it is,' Symington assured him.

'Then please get to the point!' the judge said testily.

'Did you advise Sir Pelham Forsbrook to invest?' Symington asked, looking up at Hythe.

Hythe was, if anything, even paler. 'No, sir, I did not. I did not advise anyone to invest in the British South Africa Company, either within a year before the Jameson Raid, or since.'

'Is Sir Pelham Forsbrook one of your clients?' Symington asked.

'No, sir.'

'Are you quite sure?'

'Of course I am!'

Before Bower could stand up Symington raised his hand as if to silence him. 'Let us leave that subject for a while,' he said to Hythe. 'Was Mrs Catherine Quixwood a client of yours?'

'I have no knowledge that she had money to invest,' Hythe said, trying to look as if the question surprised him.

Bower turned one way then the other, appealing for sympathy and some respite.

'Mr Symington,' the judge said sharply, 'I understand Mr Bower's impatience. You do appear to be wasting the Court's time. The charge is rape, sir, not bad advice on investment.'

'Yes, my lord,' Symington said meekly. 'Mr Hythe, were you socially acquainted with Mrs Catherine Quixwood?'

'Yes, sir,' Hythe said almost inaudibly.

'How did you meet?'

Vespasia watched with unnecessary anxiety as Symington drew out the growing friendship of Hythe and Catherine Quixwood. It seemed to be moving so slowly she dreaded that any moment Bower would object again and the judge would sustain him, and demand that Symington move on. She knew he was delaying until the luncheon adjournment in the desperate hope that Pitt and Narraway would come with something he could use. She knew that even if they did, the hope was still slender. It seemed more and more remote as the morning wore on. There was no sympathy for Hythe in the gallery, and nothing but loathing in the faces of the jurors.

Symington must have been as aware of it as Vespasia. He ploughed on, raising the pace. She could see no despair in his face, but his body was stiff as he turned, his left hand clenched by his side.

'Mr Hythe,' he continued, 'all these encounters with Mrs Quixwood, which you admit to, took place in public. What about in private? Did you meet her in a park, for instance, or in the countryside? Or at a hotel?'

'No!' Hythe said hotly. 'Of course I didn't!'

'No wish to?' Symington asked, his eyes wide.

Hythe drew in his breath, stared desperately around at the walls above the heads of the gallery. The question seemed to trap him.

For the first time Vespasia believed him totally: that his interest in Catherine Quixwood was no more than friendship.

'Mr Hythe?' the judge prompted. 'Please answer your counsel's question.'

Hythe stared at him. 'What?'

'Did you not wish to meet Mrs Quixwood in a more private place?' the judge repeated.

'No . . . I did not,' Hythe whispered.

The judge looked surprised, and disbelieving.

'Was that in case your wife should find out?' Symington asked Hythe.

Again Hythe was at a loss to answer.

Vespasia watched and felt a desperate pity for him. She believed that he had liked Catherine, but no more than that. It was Maris he loved, and he was trying now to protect her future. Symington was forcing him into a corner where he had either to admit that he had been seeking financial information for Catherine, to prevent Quixwood deceiving Forsbrook, or that it had been a love affair after all. He could not afford either answer.

Vespasia found that she was sitting with her hands clenched, nails digging into her palms. Her shoulders were stiff, even her neck was rigid, as if waiting for a physical blow to fall. She kept glancing to see what time it was. Where was Narraway? Wasn't he aware of the urgency?

'Mr Hythe?' Symington spoke just before the judge did.

'Yes . . .' Hythe said. His face was pinched with pain.

'Was your wife, then, unaware of your frequent meetings with Mrs Quixwood?' Symington continued.

'No . . . yes . . .' Hythe was trembling. He could barely speak coherently.

'Which is it?' Symington was ruthless. 'She knew, or she did not know?'

Hythe straightened himself up. 'She knew of some,' he said between his teeth. He regarded Symington with loathing.

'You were afraid she would suspect an affair?' Symington went on.

Hythe had committed himself to a path. 'Yes.'

'And be jealous?' Symington added.

Hythe refused to answer.

'Is she a jealous woman?' Symington said clearly. 'Has she had cause to be in the past?'

'No!' Now Hythe was angry. The colour burned up his face and his eyes blazed. 'I have never—' He stopped abruptly.

'Never deceived her?' Symington said incredulously. 'Or were you going to say you have never allowed her to know of your affairs before?'

'I have had no affairs!' Hythe said furiously.

'Catherine was the first?' Symington asked.

Bower looked confused, unhappy because he did not understand what Symington was trying to do. Finally he rose to his feet.

'My lord, if my learned friend is attempting to cause a mistrial, or to give grounds for appeal because of his inadequate defence, I ask that—'

Symington swung round on him, glancing briefly at the clock, then launched into a denial.

'Not at all!' he said witheringly. 'I am trying to show the Court that there is someone with more motive to kill Catherine Quixwood, out of jealousy, than any cause Alban Hythe might have had to kill a woman with whom he was, as my learned friend for the prosecution has demonstrated, having a romantic affair! Albeit, one in which the two parties never met in private.'

'That's preposterous!' Bower said, the colour scarlet up his cheeks.

'Mrs Hythe may well have been jealous, and it seems she had more than just cause, but Mr Symington surely cannot be suggesting she raped Mrs Quixwood and beat her almost to death? That is farcical, and an insult to the intelligence, not to say the humanity, of this Court.'

Symington steadied himself with an effort. 'My lord, may I ask for an early adjournment in order to consult with my client?'

'I think you had better do so, Mr Symington, and get your defence into some sort of order,' the judge agreed. 'I will not have the trial made into a mockery for the lack of skill or sincerity on your part. Do you understand me? If your client decides to plead guilty it will make little difference to the outcome, but it may be a more graceful and dignified way to shorten his ordeal. The court is adjourned until two o'clock.'

It was half-past eleven.

Vespasia waited an agonising half-hour, watching the minute hand creep arthritically around the face of the clock in the hall. At five past midday she saw Pitt's tousled head an inch or two above the crowd, and with no thought for dignity at all, she pushed her way towards him.

'Thomas!' she said breathlessly as she reached him and clasped his arm to prevent herself from being buffeted by those eager to pass. 'Thomas, what have you found? The situation is desperate.'

He put his arm around her to protect her from the jostling of several large men forcing their way through, a thing he would never do in normal circumstances.

'I have papers,' he replied. 'If the judge asks to see them they may stand up to scrutiny, or they may not. But they will at least give Symington something to use to persuade Hythe he knows the truth . . . if that is the truth, and we are right as to what he and Catherine were doing.'

'Thank God!' she said, not blasphemously but with the utmost gratitude. 'Where is Victor?'

'I don't know,' Pitt admitted. 'He may arrive with more later. I thought you might not last much longer.'

'No longer,' she said. 'This is our last stand. We had better find Mr Symington.'

The trial resumed at exactly two o'clock. Symington rose to continue the examination of his client. He moved with a new vitality as he walked across the open space, papers in his hand, and looked up at Hythe.

'Circumstances have placed you in a most unfortunate position, Mr Hythe,' he began smoothly. 'You have an expertise that was sorely needed by a charming woman, with a conscience regarding financial honesty. I can call witnesses to testify to all that I will say, but let us begin by allowing you to testify to it first, and then if my learned friend, Mr Bower, disagrees, we can proceed from there.'

He looked up at Hythe, a wide, charming, sunny smile. 'Catherine Quixwood knew of your financial reputation and sought you out, is that correct? I believe from what I have heard of her, and read in her diary, that she was quite frank with you. Is that so?'

Hythe hesitated.

'Do not oblige me to repeat the question, Mr Hythe,' Symington asked gently. 'You know the answer, and so do I.'

Hythe gulped. 'Yes.'

'Thank you. She sought you out and cultivated your acquaintance. She was a few years older than you, a beautiful woman of a slightly higher social rank, and she was troubled by a matter in which she very urgently wished for advice?' He held up the papers in his hand, still smiling. 'Do not make me pull your teeth one by one, Mr Hythe.'

'Yes,' Hythe admitted again, his eyes on the papers as Symington lowered them. Everyone in the court could see that they were covered on one side with writing.

Symington looked at the judge. 'My lord, I shall put them into evidence, and give them to Mr Bower, if it is necessary. But since they are financial papers of some very private nature, I would prefer not to do that, as long as my client co-operates, and at last we can get to the truth. Other, innocent people may suffer.'

Bower stood up.

The judge held out his hand. 'Mr Symington, I am not going to allow you to dazzle the court with any of your parlour tricks. Show me what it is you have.'

Symington passed them to him without a murmur.

The judge read them, his face darkening. He passed them back and Symington took them again.

'Where did you get these?' he demanded grimly. 'And if you do not tell me the truth, Mr Symington, you are likely to find your legal career at an end. Do you understand me, sir?'

'Yes, my lord. I have obtained them from Her Majesty's Special Branch, in the interests of justice.'

The judge rolled his eyes, but held out one hand to require Bower to take his seat again.

'Very well. Do you intend to call Commander Pitt of Special Branch to testify?'

'Not unless absolutely necessary, my lord.'

'Then get on with it. I warn you, one toe over the line, and I will stop you!'

'Yes, my lord. Thank you.' Symington turned again to Hythe.

From the front row of the gallery Vespasia could see that Symington's hands were shaking. Hythe looked grey-faced. The jurors stared at Symington as if mesmerised. There was absolute silence in the gallery, not a movement, not a breath.

Symington began again.

'Did Catherine Quixwood tell you why she wished for this information, Mr Hythe? I have her diaries, so please don't prevaricate.'

Hythe looked as if he were about to faint. He had to struggle for several moments with the decision.

Bower had a slight sneer on his face.

'It is not a pleasant thing to hang, Mr Hythe!' Symington said with a hard edge to his voice. 'Not pleasant either for those who love you! I ask you again, why did Catherine Quixwood wish for this information? If you don't answer, I can do it for you, and I will.'

This time Bower did rise. 'My lord, Mr Symington is bullying his own witness, possibly asking to condemn himself out of his own mouth.'

The judge looked at Symington, his contempt clear.

Symington turned to Hythe.

Vespasia knew this was his last chance. The court was against him. He was losing the few precious shreds of sympathy he had won before.

Hythe drew in a deep breath. 'She believed that her husband had advised someone very badly on investments in Africa,' he said with a catch in his voice. 'She wanted to prove either that it was true, or that it was not. If . . . if it were true, she thought he might repay some of the terrible loss.'

'Voluntarily, or that he could be compelled to?' Symington asked.

Hythe gulped again. 'That the damage to his reputation as a financial adviser would oblige him to – to keep the matter private,' he said hoarsely.

Symington nodded. 'And that was the reason she sought you out, and saw you increasingly frequently, and with a degree of privacy, at places your conversations would not be overheard, and where her husband would not know of it?'

'That is what she said,' Hythe agreed.

'And have you any evidence that that is the truth?' Symington pressed.

'She was very knowledgeable in the matter,' Hythe answered. 'You have the papers in your hand. You know exactly what she wanted, and that it all makes sense. If you look at the dates you will see it is cumulative. After understanding one piece she then asked for more, based upon that knowledge. She was . . . she was most intelligent.'

'Was she aware of the plans for this Jameson Raid before it took place?' Symington asked with interest.

There was a rustle of movement in the gallery. Several jurors looked startled, one leaned forward, his face tense.

'She was aware that something of that nature would happen, yes.'

'But not that it would fail?' Symington continued. 'Or did she know that too?'

'She believed it would,' Hythe answered.

Symington looked surprised. 'Really? Very perceptive indeed. Do you know why she believed that?'

Hythe hesitated again.

'Mr Hythe!' Symington said sharply. 'What did she know?'

Hythe jerked up his head. 'She observed the behaviour of other people,' he said so quietly even the judge was obliged lean forward to hear him.

'What other people?' Symington asked. 'Did she have access to plans?'

'No,' Hythe said instantly. 'She was aware that some people were investing, and of who was not. She deduced that they knew something.' He looked exasperated. 'The Raid cost a fortune, Mr Symington. People invested in it: for men, guns, munitions, other equipment. She had some idea of it. She watched and listened. She was a very intelligent woman and she cared deeply. And she was brave.'

'Indeed,' Symington said with sudden emotions thickening his voice. 'And I believe she was also beautiful. Altogether a remarkable woman, and her violation and death is a tragedy that must not go unpunished.' He hesitated a moment before going on.

One of the jurors had tears on his face. Another pulled out a large white handkerchief and mopped himself as if he were too hot.

Even Bower sat still without looking as if he were about to object.

Symington cleared his throat and went on. 'So Catherine Quixwood had gathered a good deal of financial information regarding the Jameson Raid, and various people who had made or lost money that had been invested in guns, munitions and other speculations in Africa?' he asked Hythe.

'Yes,' Hythe said simply.

'Could this have been damaging to anyone, financially or in reputation, had she made it public?' Symington was careful to avoid naming anybody.

Hythe stared at him. 'Yes, of course it would.'

'Very damaging?' Symington pressed.

'Yes.'

'Financial reputations depend upon trust, discretion, word of mouth, is that correct?'

'Yes.'

'Is it then possible, Mr Hythe, indeed probable, that there is someone named in these papers,' Symington held them up, 'who would be ruined if she were to have made them public – had she lived?'

'Yes.' Hythe's voice was barely able to be heard, even in the silent courtroom.

At last Bower rose to his feet. 'My lord, this is all supposition. If this were truly the case, why on earth would the accused not have said so in the first place?'

The judge looked at Symington.

Symington smiled. He turned back to Hythe. 'Mr Hythe, you have a young and lovely wife to whom you are devoted. If you are found guilty and hanged, she will be alone and defenceless, disgraced, penniless, will she not? Are you afraid for her? Are you specifically afraid that if you name the man Catherine Quixwood could have ruined, and whom her evidence could still ruin, that he will take out his vengeance on your widow?'

There was a gasp of horror around the gallery. Several of the jurors stiffened and looked appalled. Even the judge's face was grim.

Hythe stood frozen.

Symington was not yet finished. 'Mr Hythe, is that why I have been obliged to force this information from you, with the help of Special Branch, and financial papers that should have been confidential? Are you willing to be found guilty of a crime you did not commit, against a woman for whom you had the greatest admiration, because if you do not then your own beloved wife will be the next victim, when she is alone, destitute and you are no longer here to care for her?'

It was a rhetorical question. He did not need or expect an answer.

It was as if no one in the room dared breathe.

He turned to the judge.

'My lord, I have no way of forcing Mr Hythe to reply, nor in any honourable way could I wish to. I hope were I in his situation I would have the courage and the depth of loyalty and honour to die even such a hideous death as judicial hanging, to save someone I loved.' His face was devoid of all his confidence and easy charm; and there was nothing in it but awe, as if he had seen something overwhelmingly beautiful, and it had robbed him of pretence.

Vespasia, watching him, hoped with an intensity that surprised her that that was true. And then with pain almost physical, she longed to love with that depth again herself. She dreaded sinking into a graceful and passionless old age. It would be far better to die all at once than inch by inch, knowing the heart of you was gone.

She forced the thought from her mind. This moment belonged to Alban Hythe. It was his life they must save. Where was Victor? Why had he not found something, or at least come here?

Someone in the gallery sobbed.

It was Bower's turn. He walked forward into the centre of the floor. For a moment he appeared confused. For the first time in the entire trial, the public tide was against him. If he criticised Hythe now he would seem boorish, a man close to brutality.

'Mr Hythe,' he began slowly, 'my learned friend has suggested, but not proved, that you were seeking information for Mrs Quixwood so that she could expose certain financial advice that was . . . shall we say, dishonest. You have been, for whatever reason of your own, desperately reluctant to co-operate with him.' He cleared his throat awkwardly. 'Did you come by this information honestly? Mr Symington has said that his copies were provided by Special Branch. How, then, were you able to obtain them?'

Hythe looked wretched. 'I don't know what papers Mr Symington has, sir,' he replied, his voice hoarse. 'I had bank papers from several different sources, which put together, produced the conclusions you mention.'

'I see. And you are suggesting that one of the men implicated in these dealings raped Mrs Quixwood? If he feared her information so much, why on earth did he rape her, but leave her alive to testify against him? That appears unbelievably stupid, doesn't it?'

'I have no idea,' Hythe admitted.

Symington stood up. 'My lord, Mr Bower is sabotaging his own case. Surely that is precisely what he is accusing Mr Hythe of doing: raping Mrs Quixwood, for no reason at all, and then leaving her alive to testify against him?'

The ghost of a smile lit the judge's face for an instant, then vanished again. 'Mr Bower, Mr Symington seems to have made a distinct point.

If no one else would do such a thing, then why do you wish us to suppose that Mr Hythe would?'

'Because he was having an affair with Mrs Quixwood, my lord,' Bower said between his teeth. 'And she refused him. It was not a natural thing to do, but men in the throes of passion and rejection do not always behave naturally. The suggestion that she was raped to silence her evidence would be presuming a totally cold and rational crime.'

'Mr Symington?' the judge enquired. 'What do you say to that?'

Symington hid his chagrin well, but Vespasia saw it, and knew that at least one or two of the jurors would also.

'Mr Hythe was not having an affair with Mrs Quixwood, my lord,' Symington said. 'There is no evidence at all to suggest that he was. They met always in public places and no witness whatever has been called to testify to any behaviour that would not be perfectly in keeping with simple friendship. If there were any, I'm sure Mr Bower would have produced it with pleasure.'

At that moment there was a slight stir in the gallery. Vespasia half turned in her seat to see Victor Narraway walk down the centre aisle and stop at Symington's table. He handed him a folded piece of paper, then moved back again to find a seat wherever anyone would make room for him.

Bower ignored the interruption and looked back again at Hythe.

'Mr Hythe, do you seriously expect the Court, the jury of sensible men of business and professions themselves, to believe that some man, like themselves, invested money unfortunately in an African venture that went wrong – possibly about which they were badly advised – that such a man as you invent knew that this outwardly respectable, pretty young married woman had unearthed evidence that would be embarrassing to them? Then instead of stealing the evidence, or seeking to keep it confidential in the normal way, he went to her home and raped and beat her, but left her living? And all this was in order to hide their embarrassment at an unfortunate business venture? One in which, I might add, they are hardly alone? Sir, you strain credulity to the point of madness!'

Vespasia felt the wave of despair wash over her until she was drowning in it. Only minutes ago they had been winning – now, suddenly it was all over.

Bower made an elaborate gesture of invitation to Symington, who was already on his feet.

Symington had no papers in his hands this time. He walked over to the stand and looked up at Hythe.

'That does sound rather absurd, doesn't it?' he said with his charming smile back again. 'Some stranger choosing such a course would have been an idiot. How could it possibly have succeeded? Why rape? That is an act of hate, of contempt, of overwhelming rage against women, but hardly one designed to rescue a financial reputation in trouble.'

He looked at the jury. 'But, gentlemen, that is what my learned friend suggested to you, not what I suggest. Imagine instead, if you will, an old hatred, centred on two men and one beautiful and wilful woman, the wife of one of these men, and the mistress of the other. It is a story of high passion and hatred, the oldest jealousy in the world. It is woven out of the very fabric of human nature. Is this believable?'

'My lord!' Bower protested eagerly.

The judge held up his hand to silence him. 'Mr Symington, I presume you have some evidence for this? We are not off on another fairy story, are we?'

'No, my lord. I will call Lord Narraway to the stand to testify, if necessary. I am hoping to save the Court's time by asking Mr Hythe himself. I am sure if we can reach a conclusion this afternoon, the Court would be better served.'

'Get on with it, then,' the judge directed. 'Is Lord Narraway in court, should you require him? I presume we are speaking of Victor Narraway, who used to be head of Special Branch, until recently? I do not know him by sight.'

'Yes, my lord, we are. And he is present in court. It was he who just passed me the information I now wish to offer.'

'Proceed. You will get your turn, Mr Bower.'

Symington thanked him and looked again at Hythe.

'To continue our story, Mr Hythe. This beautiful woman was

violently beaten by her jealous husband, justifiably jealous. She attempted to run away with her lover, but met with a tragic accident instead, and was killed. The lover never forgave the husband for beating her, and to his mind, causing her death. He planned a long and bitter revenge.'

He glanced at the jury, then back at Hythe. There was not a sound in the room.

'But he was unaware that his own wife had learned of the affair,' he continued. 'And the circumstances of it, and she also learned of his revenge. She was an intelligent woman, observant, and she knew his nature. She was afraid of his rage succeeding, with all the destruction it would cause. She sought to prevent it.'

Someone in the gallery coughed and the sound was like an explosion.

'But he realised what she was doing and needed to stop her,' he went on. 'Revelation of how he used his professional knowledge and power would ruin his reputation, and his career, even if it were too late to stop the plan from succeeding.'

Hythe was ashen, but he seemed beyond the ability to speak.

Symington gave him little chance.

'It so happens that the husband of the woman now dead was a violent man, as we know. What was known by far fewer people, and not by the woman herself, is that his son is also an even more violent man, a man already guilty of several rapes, exactly within this pattern of brutality. Are you following me, Mr Hythe? No matter, I am almost at the end. One husband who needs to protect his revenge from exposure by his wife, pays his enemy's son to rape this same wife, violently and terribly. He himself leaves her favourite wine laced with a deadly dose of laudanum, certain that in her extremity she will drink it.'

No one stirred.

Symington continued.

'He also manages to place a love letter of his own from his wife to make it seem that the man who provided her with evidence of his revenge will be blamed for her rape. Thus in one terrible night he has destroyed his enemy's son, the wife who would have exposed

323

his revenge, and the man who provided her with the information. And he has done one more thing to protect himself. He has befriended the wife of this man he has blamed, and promised to look after her when the unfortunate man is hanged. No doubt he has also said that he will see her destroyed if this man does not take the blame, silently and bravely, without speaking a word of the truth.

'Do I have your attention now, Mr Hythe?'

Hythe was hanging onto the railing of the witness stand, but even so his knees crumpled and he all but collapsed.

Symington turned to the jury. 'Gentlemen, was ever greater evil planned and all but succeeded in fulfilling its dreadful purpose? But you know now what is going on. You can prevent it. You can find justice for Catherine Quixwood. You can save the life of the young man who tried to help her prevent ruin and exploitation. You can save the wife he loves so much he will die to protect her. Leave it to others to find and punish the rapist. Already action is taking place to bring that about.'

He turned a little with a gesture to include them all.

'The manipulators of money and investment will be punished. The wife who took a lover and was beaten for it is dead. Her husband has lost his fortune. We are almost at the end, gentlemen. Life and death, love and hate, greed and innocence are all in your hands. I beg you, act with the same mercy and forbearance we shall all need when we stand before the bar of judgement ourselves.'

Symington bowed to the jury and returned to his seat.

It was Bower's turn to address the jury. He spoke little of fact, mostly of the brutality of the crime, repeating the worst details, his face twisted with rage and pity. He dismissed Symington's theories as a magic trick, a wealth of nothing, designed to mislead them. There was no substance, he insisted, only a desperate and self-seeking lawyer's castles in the air.

When the jury retired Vespasia was joined almost immediately by Narraway.

'Victor! What did you find?' she asked urgently.

'Catherine went to Brynaston Mews,' he answered. 'She knew that Quixwood was Eleanor Forsbrook's lover. A lot of what Symington said was guesswork, but it's the only thing that makes sense.'

'Then Neville Forsbrook raped Catherine? Or are you saying it was Pelham himself, in revenge for Quixwood having seduced Eleanor?' she asked, still puzzled.

'I think it was Neville. Just as it was he who raped both Angeles Castelbranco and Alice Townley, and possibly others.'

'And the laudanum?' she persisted.

'Quixwood put it there, knowing she would drink it. If she hadn't he could always have given it to her when he got home. It wouldn't have been as safe for him, but it would still have worked.'

'What are we going to do about it?' she asked.

He smiled. 'Trust we are going to get a verdict for Alban Hythe. Then we will consider breaking Quixwood's word protecting Neville Forsbrook. I still want to see that young man pay for both rapes . . . and in a moral sense for murder – at least of Angeles. She was sixteen!' His voice caught. She could see in his eyes an understanding of horror that he had never even imagined. There was a vulnerability, a knowledge of helplessness that scoured deep into places untouched before.

The jury returned after two long hours, every minute of which dragged by at leaden pace.

The courtroom was packed. There were even people standing in the aisle and at the back.

The proceedings were enacted at the majestic pace of the law. No one stirred. No one coughed.

The foreman of the jury answered in a calm, level voice.

'We find the prisoner, Alban Hythe, guilty as charged, my lord.'

In the dock Hythe bent forward, utterly beaten.

Maris Hythe looked as if she were about to faint.

Vespasia was stunned. She had truly hoped, and the tide of despair that washed over her momentarily robbed her of thought. It was seconds, even a full minute before she could think of what to do next.

She took a long, slow breath and turned to Narraway. 'This is not right,' she said quietly. 'We have only three weeks. We must find something very quickly.'

Chapter Twenty

PITT REFUSED to accept defeat. It was intolerable. He was now certain beyond any doubt at all that Alban Hythe had not either raped or killed Catherine Quixwood, and yet he had sat in court and watched the judge put on a black cap and sentence him to death. As always three Sundays were allowed, a period of grace – hardly much in which to mount an appeal, even if they could find new evidence.

They needed more time. The only way to get that would be to have the Home Secretary grant a reprieve, and there were no grounds for it. Pitt had remained at his office, wanting to be alone, at least from those closest to him. Their pain distracted his mind, and he needed to be absolutely undivided in his concentration. He had no emotional strength to spare for comfort.

He paced back and forth across his office floor, shoulders hunched, muscles knotted. He went over it in his mind again and again, but there was nothing on which to appeal. Symington, crushed and miserable, had already said as much.

He was convinced that the answer they had found, and in part concocted out of fragments of evidence, was the truth. The unimaginative, pedestrian-minded jury had not believed them. Why not? What had they missed, done wrongly? Had it all rested on Bower's stirring of rage and fear in them so passionate they could not think? Did they simply not believe that Catherine could have been as intelligent or as brave as they had shown her? Did they need so intensely to punish someone that they could not wait for the right man?

Had they not followed the evidence? Surely Symington had stirred their pity and their anger with Hythe's willingness to sacrifice his own life to save Maris? Were they so gullible as to be taken in by Quixwood's feigned grief?

He pulled himself up abruptly. The reason didn't matter now. He needed a reprieve from the Home Secretary, a stay of execution long enough to find grounds for an appeal. They must not allow it to be over. Proof of Hythe's innocence after he was dead was no use at all – and also once the execution had taken place it would be twice as hard to convince anyone that they had made an irretrievable mistake, judicially murdered a totally innocent man. Who is willing to face such a truth and carry that burden for the rest of their lives? Who is able to accept that the judicial system on which they rely is appallingly flawed? If it is, then no one is safe.

What argument did he have to take to the Home Secretary? It was there in the shadows at the back of his mind, knowledge crowding the darkness. That was the power of his position.

He snatched his hat off the rack at the door, jammed it on his head, and went out into the passageway.

In the street he hailed a hansom and gave the driver the Home Secretary's private address. He hated doing this, but there was no other way to save Alban Hythe's life.

He sat in the cab, rattling over the cobbles, oblivious of the traffic.

Much interesting and highly confidential information came his way. As head of Special Branch there were potentially dangerous secrets that he knew about many people in power. He had to guard their vulnerability to blackmail, or any other kind of inappropriate pressures. The Home Secretary was a decent man, if a little pompous at times. Pitt did not personally like him. Their backgrounds, experience and cultural values were different. There was no natural sympathy between them, as there had been between Pitt and many of the men he had worked for in the past. They had been well bred, in many cases ex-military or naval, like Narraway, but not politicians, not used to keeping the favour of others by always seeking the art of the possible coupled with the confidence of the majority.

As a young man the Home Secretary had studied at Oxford and been an outstanding scholar, a man well-liked by his friends. One friend in particular had been charming, ambitious but a trifle equivocal in some of his moral choices. He was not averse to cheating when he needed to pass an exam that was beyond his ability.

He had begged the Home Secretary to cover for him, necessitating a lie. In loyalty to his friend he had done so. He had learned afterwards, painfully, that he had been used, made a complete fool of. He had paid for it bitterly in regret and had never done such a thing again.

The friend had fared well, progressing financially. That exam success had laid the foundation of his career. He had climbed higher in his chosen field, still using people at every step. The Home Secretary had never betrayed him, nor had he ever spoken with him again, except as was necessary not to raise public suspicion. As far as Pitt was aware, very few other people had even known of the incident, and most of those were long dead.

Unwillingly without question, but the Home Secretary could be persuaded to grant a stay of execution to Alban Hythe. Pitt could make his alternative far too painful for him to refuse. Pitt had the upper hand.

It was an abuse of power, exactly like rape. If he did this, at what point would he not use power, if he possessed it? A little more pressure, a little force, a little twisting of the fear. What was the difference in essence?

There had to be another way.

He leaned forward and rapped on the partition to attract the driver's attention. 'Changed my mind,' he said. He gave the man Townley's address instead.

'Yes, sir,' the driver agreed wearily, adding something else less courteous under his breath.

Pitt leaned back in the seat, sweat running on his skin, and yet cold enough to shiver. Was it so easy to misuse power, and to let it misuse you?

Townley's footman permitted him in only because he insisted.

'I'm sorry,' Pitt said to the man. 'Time is short and I am fighting for a man's life, otherwise I would not disturb you at this hour of the evening. I need to speak to Mr Townley and very possibly the rest of his family. Please inform him so.'

Townley came out of the sitting room to where Pitt was waiting in the hall. His face was grim and anger lay as close to the surface as good manners and a level of fear would allow it. He did not bother with a greeting.

Pitt was uncomfortable, wretchedly aware of how close he had come to exercising the power he possessed in a way he would ever after regret.

'I'm sorry to disturb you, Mr Townley,' he said quietly. 'I need your help—'

'I cannot give it to you, sir,' Townley interrupted him. 'I know who you are, and I have a good idea of what it is you wish of me. My answer is the same. I don't know what can have made you imagine it could be different.'

'The conviction of Alban Hythe today of a crime he did not commit,' Pitt said simply. 'In three weeks they will hang him, then any evidence that proves his innocence will be of little use to him, or to his young widow. I shall pursue it, eventually I will prove our terrible mistake, and in so doing shake everyone's faith in our system of justice and I dare say ruin a few men's careers in the process. Then I may also catch the man who is actually responsible, but not before he will have raped other young women and, unless they are very fortunate, ruined their lives as well – perhaps even taken them. I am sure you understand why I would very much prefer to correct it while I still can, rather than try to mitigate the disaster afterwards.'

'I cannot help you,' Townley repeated. 'Neville Forsbrook violated my daughter and there is nothing I can do about it, except protect her from public ruin. Now will you please leave my house, and allow my family to have what little peace we may.'

Pitt clenched his fists by his sides, trying to control his voice.

'Will you come and watch the hanging?' he asked levelly, even though he was trembling. 'Will you try to confront his wife afterwards? She is not so very much older than your daughter. How will you comfort her in the years to come, when she wakens in the night knowing that it was possible she could—'

'Get out of my house before I strike you, sir!' Townsley said between his teeth. 'I don't care a jot who you are, or what office you claim to hold.'

The sitting-room door opened and Mrs Townley came out, her face stiff, eyes wide.

Townley swung around. 'Mary! Go back to the withdrawing room. Commander Pitt is leaving.'

Mrs Townley looked past her husband, her eyes meeting Pitt's.

'I don't think he is, Robert,' she said quietly. 'I think he will remain here until we tell him what we know, because we are standing in the path of justice, and I do not choose to do that.'

'Mary . . .' Townley began. 'For heaven's sake, think of Alice!'

'I am doing,' she said with gathering confidence. 'I think she would rather speak to Mr Pitt and gain some kind of justice than believe that her experience has so damaged her that she would see a man die wrongly rather than tell him the truth.'

'You have no right to make that decision for her, Mary,' Townley said quietly, struggling to be as gentle as he wished.

'Neither have you, my dear,' she pointed out. She turned to Pitt. 'If you will be good enough to wait, sir, I shall ask my daughter whether she will tell you anything further, or not.'

'Thank you, ma'am,' he said, the sudden release of tension rippling through him like an easing warmth.

Five minutes later Pitt was in the withdrawing room facing Alice Townley, who was pale, clearly very apprehensive, but waiting with her hands folded in her lap, knuckles white.

'I am sorry to ask you again,' Pitt began, sitting opposite her. 'But events have not gone at all as I would have liked them to. Mr Alban Hythe has been convicted of raping and beating Mrs Quixwood and causing her to take her own life.' He did not shrink from using the the appropriate words. 'I believe he is not guilty, and I have only three weeks in which to prove it—'

'Mama told me,' Alice interrupted. 'Do you think Mr Forsbrook did it? He wasn't anything like so – violent with me. Not to hitting me, or anything like making me want to kill myself. Although . . . although I did feel pretty dreadful.' She moved her right hand off her lap, lifted it, then let it fall again. 'It was revolting. He did things I didn't know people did.' She blushed scarlet. 'It wasn't anything like love.'

'Violence isn't,' Pitt said gently. 'Can you tell me again exactly what he did?'

She looked at the floor.

'Perhaps you would prefer to tell your mother, and she could tell me?' he suggested.

She nodded, not raising her eyes.

Pitt stood up and left the room, Townley, still angry, on his heels.

They waited in silence in the morning room, chilly, fire unlit at this time of the year. After just over a quarter of an hour Mary Townley came in.

Pitt rose to his feet as a matter of courtesy.

'I think it would be a good idea if you were to go and sit with her,' Mrs Townley said to her husband. 'I'm sure she would find your presence comforting. She doesn't want to feel that you disapprove of her decision, as if she has defied you. She is doing what she believes is right, and brave, Robert.'

'Of course . . . of course.' He stood up and left without even glancing at Pitt.

Mary Townley sat down, inviting Pitt to do the same. She was very pale and clearly found the matter embarrassing. Hesitantly, in a voice so carefully controlled as to be almost expressionless, she told him exactly what had happened, in Alice's words, including that Forsbrook had bitten her painfully hard on the left breast.

That was it, the connection with Catherine Quixwood, and with Pamela O'Keefe, perhaps with Angeles Castelbranco too, although they would never know that now, unless Isaura knew and would testify to it. It might also prove to the Church that Angeles was a victim, not a sinner. Pitt would not rest until he had done that.

He addressed the present. 'Thank you, Mrs Townley. Please tell Alice that her courage may have saved a man's life. Did you see the marks yourself?'

'Yes.' She touched her own left breast lightly.

'If it should be necessary, would you swear to that? I ask because Mrs Quixwood was bitten in exactly the same place, and so was another girl who was killed. I think now perhaps he killed her accidentally, when he lost his temper and was more violent with her than he meant. She might have fought with him, as Mrs Quixwood did. That seems to enrage him beyond control.'

'Are you going to see that he is put in prison?' she asked with fear in her voice.

'At the least,' he replied. 'At the very least.' He was making a rash promise and he knew it, but in this quiet, modest home it seemed the only possible answer. To have said less would be to belittle the people in it, and the countless others like them; his own family, for that matter.

He thanked her again and went out into the silent street. Now it was time to go to the Home Secretary, and ask, respectfully, for a reprieve.

Narraway sat at the dining room table at Pitt's house, the following day. Charlotte and Pitt were there, and Vespasia, and also Stoker, who was looking slightly uncomfortable. The Home Secretary had granted a temporary stay of execution, but that was all it was. Symington was working on an appeal. He had refused to accept any payment from Narraway, although he had been offered it. He had said that victory itself would be enough reward. He would be at Narraway's service any future time he might be needed.

Now the five of them sat around the table over a plain but excellent luncheon, for which Minnie Maude had been duly praised.

Of course, since Neville Forsbrook was still free there was no easing of the Castelbrancos' grief or knowledge of injustice, except that they now had hope of the grace of the Church. Most gravely, they were all certain that until he was stopped, Forsbrook would rape, and perhaps kill again.

'We can't let it go,' Charlotte insisted as the dessert was been served and the last of the main dishes removed. 'They may arrest him in a month or two, or he may even hear of it and leave the country again.' She looked at Narraway. 'Are you sure Quixwood himself killed Catherine?' Her face was troubled, bitterly aware of the unfinished nature of the case.

'I am,' Pitt answered gravely. They all knew he was thinking of the solution Symington had put forward in court.

'Is that the truth?' Charlotte looked from Pitt to Narraway. 'Is that what happened? It was all started by Eleanor Forsbrook having an affair with Rawdon Quixwood? He blamed Pelham Forsbrook for her getting killed? Do we know that was true? I mean *know* it, not *deduce* it? Is there really anything to anchor it to reality? Possible doubt is a wonderful tool to free Alban Hythe, and heaven knows we must do that, but will it convict anyone else?'

She looked at Narraway. 'Is Rawdon Quixwood as terrible as Symington said? Did he deliberately create this whole appalling tragedy, and protect Neville Forsbrook, knowing what he'd done?'

'Yes,' Narraway said with some embarrassment. 'I've never made such a serious complete misjudgement of anyone in my life.'

Charlotte smiled at him. 'We might respect you, but we wouldn't like you very much if you had withheld your compassion until he had proved himself innocent or guilty. You can't go through life always guarding against the most awful thing you can think of. You'd be miserable, and worse than that, you'd push away from you every possible good thing there is.'

Narraway looked down at his plate. 'It was not a slight error. I was rather seriously wrong.'

'It was a magnificent one,' Charlotte agreed, glancing at Vespasia, and seeing her smile. 'I hate half-heartedness,' she added.

Narraway smiled in spite of himself.

It was Pitt who brought them back to the business in hand.

'The affair between Eleanor and Quixwood is fact. We have witnesses to that now. And the surgeon who examined her body after the accident said many of the bruises pre-dated her death, so Pelham did beat her. Narraway found other facts today. Elmo Crask also added to the story about Neville Forsbrook and the prostitute he beat. Biting seems to be a weakness of his. That story is also provable, and is even uglier than we first assumed. Neville Forsbrook is a very violent young man with an uncontrollable, and increasing disposition to rape women. Sooner or later he is going to kill someone else, if he hasn't already. Pamela O'Keefe seems to have been his victim too.'

'What are we going to do?' Vespasia asked, looking from one to the other of them, including Stoker, who had been silent much of the time.

'I've been thinking,' Pitt said to no one in particular. 'We know of Eleanor's affair and can prove it beyond reasonable doubt. We know that Quixwood advised Forsbrook to invest in the British South Africa Company, with almost certain knowledge of the Jameson Raid, and that it would fail, and reparations be enormous. It was worth the risk because for him the worst that could happen would only be that it succeeded, and Forsbrook would make money. He could always try something else in the future.'

'Did he know of Neville Forsbrook's rapes?' Narraway asked.

Stoker came to attention. 'Yes, sir. He was friendly with Sir Pelham Forsbrook at the time, and he helped settle the business with the prostitute and get Neville out of the country. Still can't find out exactly where he went, but he started out in Lisbon, then seems to have gone on by sea.'

Narraway was surprised. 'Lisbon? Not Paris?'

'Apparently not. Paris might have been the first place anyone would have looked for him. It was a pretty nasty business,' Stoker replied. 'And Quixwood had connections in Lisbon.'

Narraway nodded slightly. 'Interesting. So unquestionably Quixwood knew of Neville Forsbrook's nature, and the savagery of it. Isn't there a way we can hang Quixwood?' he asked, looking up at Pitt.

'Only if we can prove he poisoned his wife intentionally,' Pitt replied. 'I'd rather hang Forsbrook for raping her.'

'Why?' Stoker demanded. 'Quixwood murdered her.'

'Because Forsbrook has to be stopped,' Pitt answered. 'I suppose I want him not just for Catherine, but for Angeles Castelbranco too, and Alice Townley.'

'You can't get him for Angeles,' Charlotte said miserably. 'Quixwood swears he was with him and it would have been impossible. If he's guilty, why would he do that?' She hesitated only an instant, then understanding flooded her face. 'Oh, of course. They're both protecting themselves by protecting each other!'

'That's it!' Pitt sat upright with a jolt.

'I know that,' Narraway was weary.

'No!' Pitt said urgently, turning slightly to face him. 'That's the way to catch them! It's dangerous, very, but it might work.' He went on without being prompted, leaning forward a little, his voice urgent. 'Quixwood doesn't really need Neville any more. But what if we could persuade Neville of that, and tell him Quixwood was preparing to give him up, now that Hythe's conviction isn't certain any more, and we are still desperately looking for someone else, in order to prove his innocence! If we had Neville for Angeles' rape, and knew he'd also raped Catherine, we wouldn't be looking for anyone further. Neville could protest all he wanted that Quixwood put him up to it, it would do him no good. There's no proof, and he'll know that.'

Narraway was staring at him. 'And what? Neville would go after Quixwood to silence him?'

'Wouldn't you?' Pitt said. 'Persuade Neville that Quixwood now needs to protect himself, and he can only do it by giving up Neville.'

'Dangerous,' Narraway warned, but the light was back in his face and there was a keen edge to his voice. 'Very dangerous.' He did not look at either Charlotte or Vespasia, or even at Stoker. 'How would we do it? If you tell him yourself he'll instantly suspect a trap.'

Pitt's mind was leaping forward. 'Crask,' he answered. 'Elmo Crask. Neville would believe him. He's been nosing around the whole affair for days. He found us a lot of the early information about Quixwood and Eleanor. Can you think of a better way, or any other way at all, for that matter?'

'No, I can't,' Narraway admitted. 'But we must plan this very carefully indeed. We can't afford to have Neville succeed in killing Quixwood.'

'Or the other way around,' Pitt said with a twist of his mouth. 'If Quixwood killed Neville he could legally, and morally, claim self-defence, and still walk away, and there'd be nothing we could do to touch him.'

'His reputation would hardly be untouched, after the evidence in court yesterday,' Vespasia pointed out.

'He was never named,' Narraway said, his face tight with anger. 'And anyone who did so could be sued for libel, and I imagine Quixwood would win. He'll still have the vast weight of public sympathy. We know he's one of the most evil men alive, but we can't prove a thing.'

'If we do this right we'll get both of them,' Pitt answered.

'If we do this right we'll be damned lucky!' Narraway retorted. 'But let's try.'

'Are you sure?' Vespasia said cautiously. 'If we lose it would be a disaster.'

'Of course it would,' he agreed. 'If we don't try it's a disaster for certain – but it's one of cowardice because we gave up rather than take a risk.'

Vespasia smiled very, very slightly. 'I thought you would say that.'

The next evening Pitt and Narraway were together in Bryanston Square, waiting until Neville Forsbrook should appear. Stoker was in the Mews, just in case he left the house that way. Elmo Crask had already been and gone. Three men should be sufficient to follow Forsbrook, particularly since they trusted he had no idea that they suspected anything. Both Narraway and Pitt would have preferred there to be more men, but they dared not trust anyone else, nor morally involve them in something which was, at the very best, questionable.

They were in a hansom cab, slumped down so as to be all but invisible from the street. The cab driver was from Special Branch, but he had no idea of the purpose they were pursuing. He sat as if waiting for someone who was visiting the house nearest them.

Crask had been gone from Forsbrook's house for nearly half an hour. It seemed like far longer.

Pitt was wondering if Neville could have gone out of the back into the Mews to take his father's carriage and Stoker had missed him, or been unable to get any message to them at the front of the house. He was about to suggest going to look when the front door opened and Neville Forsbrook came out onto the step, hesitated a moment, then walked down to the pavement.

Narraway sat up instantly. 'Get Stoker,' he ordered. 'I'll meet you just beyond the corner.'

Pitt was out on the road in a moment and going rapidly in the opposite direction from Neville, keeping the hansom between them for as long as possible so he would not be seen if Forsbrook glanced behind him.

As soon as Pitt reached the corner he crossed the street and started to run along the distance of George Street to Bryanston Mews.

Stoker was looking back and forth and saw him immediately. They had to return to Upper George Street again. A glance told them that the hansom now faced the other way, and Neville Forsbrook was no longer in sight. They raced along the pavement and scrambled into the cab as it lurched forward and the horse broke into a trot.

They caught up with Neville on Great Cumberland Place just as he hailed a cab and got into it. They had already assumed that he was going to Quixwood's house in Lyall Street, and so were not surprised when he crossed Oxford Street and went on south on Park Lane. They expected to turn right on Piccadilly and then along Grosvenor Place, and then finally right again on any of the possible turnings towards Eaton Square.

The light was fading and the traffic was growing heavier. They needed to follow him more closely. There were carriages and goods wagons in among the lighter, faster hansoms. Pitt found himself leaning forwards. It was completely pointless, but it was instinctive, as if he could urge the horse himself.

They reached Piccadilly and there was a jam as two four-wheelers all but collided. In a matter of seconds everyone had stopped, but twenty yards ahead of them Forsbrook's cab was clear and racing towards Hyde Park Corner. Surely it would turn down Grosvenor Place, but what if it did not?

Pitt clenched his hands and fidgeted with impatience. How long would it take for Forsbrook to face Quixwood and attack him, kill him, if that was what he intended? What if the whole tragedy played itself out before they got there? It would be a disaster, and they would be to blame. No, he would, not Narraway. Narraway was a civilian. The responsibility was entirely Pitt's.

What could he do? It was too far to run . . . wasn't it? He glanced sideways at the street, considering it. Perhaps he should go on foot, and Narraway follow him? If he caught up, then he would pick him up there?

He tried to suggest it just as the carriages ahead unlocked and they lurched forward, picking up speed, weaving in and out dangerously. He broke out in a sweat of relief. He did not deserve the rescue, he thought. This was a totally irresponsible idea. But it was too late to back out now.

It was another full ten minutes before they pulled up outside Quixwood's house off Eaton Square. There was no hansom outside, and nothing on the street except one Brougham coming towards them with a man and woman in it, their outlines visible but without colour in the fast-fading light.

Narraway swore and leaped out onto the pavement. Pitt was only a step behind him. It was the middle of summer and the air was still warm. His clothes stuck to his body with sweat.

Narraway tugged on the bell pull. Then, seconds later, he yanked it again.

Silence. Another cab rattled along the street.

The door opened and a footman stood there patiently, his face expressionless.

'Yes, sir. May I help you?'

'Lord Narraway. I need to see Mr Quixwood immediately,' he said.

'I'm sorry, sir, that won't be possible,' the footman replied calmly.

'I'm not asking you,' Narraway snapped. 'I'm telling you. This is business of state.'

'My lord, Mr Quixwood is not at home,' the footman said. 'He left about four minutes ago.'

'Alone?' Narraway demanded.

'No, sir, there was a Mr Forsbrook with him—'

'Where did they go?' Narraway cut across him. 'Now, man! Quickly!'

The footman was trembling. He was the same man who had been there the night Catherine Quixwood had been killed.

Narraway controlled himself with an effort and spoken again more gently. 'I need to find them both, immediately. Mr Quixwood's life is in danger.'

The footman gulped. 'He said to tell you, my lord, that he had gone to the house of Lady Vespasia Cumming-Gould. He said you would know where that was.'

Narraway stood motionless, as if an icy wind had frozen him.

'And Forsbrook?' Pitt said, dreading the answer.

'With him, sir.'

Narraway whirled around, leaving Pitt to follow him down the steps and into the hansom again, shouting Vespasia's address at the driver. They were barely seated when the cab lurched forward. It threw them hard backwards and then swung them against the sides as it swept around the corner and picked up a crazy speed.

Neither of them spoke as they hurtled along the now lamplit streets. The horse's feet were loud on the stones; the wheels rattled. One moment they were almost at a gallop, the next veering around a corner and skidding to straighten up before pitching forward again.

Pitt's mind created all sorts of pictures of what might be happening, and what situation they would meet with. More than once he even wondered if the footman had lied to them, on Quixwood's orders, and they had not gone to Vespasia's house at all. Or what if they were actually at Pitt's own house, and it was Charlotte, or even Daniel and Jemima who were hostage? Might Neville Forsbrook this moment be raping Jemima? The thought was unbearable.

Instinctively he leaned forward and shouted at the driver, but his voice was lost in the hiss and clatter of their progress.

Or what if Forsbrook had murdered Quixwood and left him in his own house, and was escaping to who knows where? Maybe the same place as after he had beaten the prostitute, and he was on his way there even now?

They slewed to a stop outside Vespasia's house. Pitt all but fell onto the pavement. Here again there was no other vehicle in sight, but now it was dark. It must be an hour or so short of midnight.

Narraway was beside him as they moved silently up to the front door. Here there was no manservant to let them in. What if no one answered? The maids might even be locked in the kitchen. That is what Pitt would do, were he in Quixwood or Forsbrook's place.

Who was the master, anyway? Was Forsbrook Quixwood's hostage, or the other way around? Or were they allies?

Or was this a fool's errand and they were not here at all?

Pitt could feel hysteria welling up inside him, total panic as he imagined losing everything he loved in one terrible night.

Narraway shot out a hand and gripped his arm, his fingers like a vice. 'Back,' he whispered. 'Garden door.'

Without a word Pitt turned and led the way. There was a brief, highly undignified scramble over the wall and down again, then tiptoeing through the garden, probably treading on all kinds of flowers.

The light streamed across the grass from the french doors of the sitting room. The curtains were at least half open, but there seemed to be no one in the room, then Pitt saw a shadow move beyond the curtains, and then another. He froze. He looked at Narraway and observed that he too had seen.

Might it simply be Vespasia and her maid? He motioned Narraway to stand well to the side, and he himself moved out of clear sight of the windows. Feeling his way he moved a step at a time until he was outside the glass and about a yard away from it. Inch by inch he leaned forward.

Inside, Vespasia was standing motionless in front of Neville Forsbrook, her face pale. On one side of her, between her and the door, Rawdon Quixwood was standing facing them. He had a revolver in his hand, held steady. It was pointing downward, but any second he could lift it and shoot Vespasia and, when she fell, Forsbrook.

Pitt stepped back slowly and motioned to Narraway. When they were a couple of yards from the window he spoke.

'Quixwood has a gun. Forsbrook appears unarmed. They have Vespasia. They're talking, but I can't hear what they're saying through the glass.'

'He's playing for time until we get here,' Narraway said softly. 'Then he'll shoot Forsbrook, and claim it's self-defence, which I dare say it will be, by then.'

'Why here?' Pitt asked. 'Why not do it at his own house?'

'Because he needs an impartial witness,' Narraway answered bitterly. 'And I dare say one or both of us will be accidental deaths as well, probably blamed on Forsbrook.'

'He'd never get away with that,' Pitt agreed. 'Vespasia would . . .' Then he stopped, realizing that Vespasia would be part of the tragedy as well. His brain seemed to be unable to think.

'I'll go in from the kitchen,' Narraway whispered. 'Give me time, and then you come in from this way. He can't get us both at once.'

'What about Forsbrook?'

'To hell with him,' Narraway hissed back. 'We've got to get Vespasia out of there. I'm going around to the back way.'

Pitt grasped his arm, holding him with all his power, but Narraway was stronger than he had expected. 'Stop it!' Pitt said savagely. 'If you pull us off balance we'll alert them and we'll both be shot as burglars. I'll go round to the kitchen. I know my way, and I know how to break in without making a noise. Wait for me, then come in this way!'

Narraway drew in breath to argue.

'Do as you're damn well told!' Pitt said under his breath. 'I'm head of Special Branch, you're a civilian. Stay here!' And without waiting for further argument he let go of Narraway and crept through the flowerbed towards the back of the house.

He found a scullery window and, after fishing in his pockets, came up with a piece of sticky paper and a small, very neat glass cutter. He put the paper on the window near where the catch was and quickly, carefully, cut out a circle, holding onto an edge of the paper. He removed the glass soundlessly and reached in his hand.

A few moments later he had the window open and was inside. It was dark and he had to move very carefully. If he tripped over anything, upset a pile of boxes or bumped into stacked vegetables, he would alarm the entire house.

Step by step he went through the kitchen and into the hall. Outside the sitting-room door he stopped. He could hear the voices inside.

'You think Pitt will come?' Forsbrook said huskily, his voice high-pitched with fear. 'He won't. Why should he?'

'Because he's following you, you fool!' Quixwood snapped. 'He told you I'd betray you so you'd come and attack me.'

'You could betray me,' Forsbrook said more loudly, his voice wavering now. 'They'll let Hythe go and come after you. They know you poisoned the wine. Why would you do that if you didn't know she would be raped? They wanted it all out!' Panic was mounting in him, he was close to losing control.

'That's what they want you to think, you fool!' Quixwood said, his voice scalding with contempt. 'Get a grip on yourself. They'll come here. I told the footman to tell Narraway where I'd gone.'

'Why should he care what happens to me?' Forsbrook demanded.

He was nearly shouting now. 'Pitt would see me hanged for that Portuguese girl. He knows it was me, he just can't prove it.'

'No, he can't,' Quixwood agreed. 'Or any of the others.'

'They don't know about the others!' Forsbrook yelled. 'And you can't prove it! If you tell them I raped Catherine I'll tell them you paid me to.'

'No you won't,' Quixwood said levelly.

'If you shoot, you'll hit Lady Vespasia.' Forsbrook's voice was almost falsetto, panic tearing through him. 'How are you going to explain that? The bullet'll go on into me. You won't be able to say that was my fault!' Now he was crowing, high and shrill, sudden victory in sight.

Pitt chose that instant to open the door, pushing it hard and following straight in behind it.

Quixwood had moved a yard or two from where he had been when Pitt had seen him through the window. He was closer to Vespasia. He heard Pitt and swung around to face him, the gun in his hand. He smiled.

'At last! But slow, Commander. There's your rapist. Or perhaps I should say "my rapist". He's the one who raped and beat poor Catherine. But I dare say you know that? I admit, I didn't expect you to work it out.'

Forsbrook started to speak, then changed his mind. He held Vespasia tight and hard in front of him. 'No, I didn't,' he answered. 'Quixwood's mad. He kidnapped me and now he's trying to kill me. I don't know who murdered his wife. She must have had some other lover, if it really wasn't Hythe.'

'Yes, you did.' Vespasia spoke for the first time. 'And Angeles Castelbranco as well. Quixwood lied to protect you, probably the price for raping Catherine for him.'

Quixwood raised the revolver. His dark face was twisted with passion. Hate and pain were all but tearing him apart. Perhaps he was remembering Eleanor, and how she had been beaten.

Narraway crashed through the french doors and charged Forsbrook just as the gun went off. Vespasia fell sideways onto her hands and knees. Neville Forsbrook pitched after her, his chest blossoming scarlet blood.

Quixwood reacted instantly. With his other hand out, he dived towards Vespasia and yanked her to her feet, wrenching her shoulder and tearing her gown. He still had the gun in the other hand. His eyes were wild. He backed towards the door, swivelling his glance from Pitt to Narraway and back again, pulling Vespasia with him.

Forsbrook lay motionless on the floor, the blood spreading wider and wider around him. There was no movement of his chest, no breath.

The door was half open where Pitt had pushed it. Quixwood groped for it with one hand, still holding the gun in the other, with his arm around Vespasia.

Narraway seized his one, single moment. He snatched up the paper knife from the desk and charged at Quixwood. He did not go for his gun arm, or for his heart, or even his throat.

Quixwood hurled Vespasia from him and raised the gun, but he was too slow. The paper knife pierced him through the eye into his brain, and he buckled and collapsed to the floor, Narraway on top of him. The gun roared uselessly, the bullet crashing into the ceiling, an inch past Narraway's head.

Vespasia climbed to her knees and stared at Narraway. Her face was ashen, her hair half undone. Her eyes were wide with terror and her whole body shuddered.

'Victor, you idiot!' she said, sobbing to get her breath. 'You could have been killed!'

Narraway sat up very slowly, leaving the paper knife where it was, embedded in Quixwood's head. He swivelled around and looked at the tears on Vespasia's face.

'It was worth it,' he said with a slow, beautiful smile. 'Are you all right, my dear?'

Pitt said nothing. He also was too full of exquisite relief even to look for words. He watched Vespasia move over to Narraway and very gently put her arms around him.

'I am very well indeed,' she told him.